Horror-struck at the scene, she gazed upon the wild group before her without power of utterance.

MAY GRAYSON;

OR,

LOVE AND TREACHERY.

A ROMANCE.

BY THE AUTHOR OF "A LEGEND OF OLD ST. PAUL'S," "KATHLEEN,"
"THE TOWER OF LONDON," "HEBREW MAIDEN," ETC.

" Where rose the mountains, there to him were friends ;
Where rolled the ocean, thereon was his home ;
Where a blue sky, and glowing clime extends,
He had the passion and the power to roam !
The desert, forest, cavern, breaker's foam,
Were unto him companionship : they spake
A mutual language, clearer than the tome
Of his land's tongue, which he would oft forsake
For Nature's pages glassed by sunbeams on the lake.''
CHILDE HAROLD.

LONDON :

PUBLISHED BY E. LLOYD, AT THE OFFICE OF " THE PENNY
SUNDAY TIMES," 231, SHOREDITCH.

———

1842.

PREFACE.

At the conclusion of every work it falls, pleasingly enough, to our lot to thank our numerous readers for the liberal patronage they award us. On the present occasion we have every reason to congratulate ourselves upon a continuance of the favours we prize so highly, and the Public may feel assured that no exertions on our part shall be wanting to deserve them in future.

Our readers are, of course, aware that a new Copyright Act has just been passed to satisfy a few greedy authors and publishers, at the expense of those whose means or inclination do not extend to the extravagant prices charged for works which in many instances are below mediocrity. A species of monopoly has thus been formed amongst " the great ones of the land," and it now remains to be seen whether the humbler classes of society shall not secure for themselves the advantage of cheap reading, combining utility and amusement.

To this end the publisher of this and similar works issuing from his press, has devoted much of his attention, and he is gratified in being able to announce that he has succeeded in engaging gentlemen of well-known literary talent to produce for him a series of works, which, though sent forth to the public in a cheap form, will be found equal to the best of the high-priced publications, and certainly, in most instances, far superior to the trash that finds its way into the circulating libraries under the auspices of high-sounding names. Thus, in spite of the Copyright Act, the humbler classes will not be deprived of the rational enjoyment that is at all times to be found in works of merit.

" Save me !" she exclaimed wildly, but ere she could escape from the room
he had seized the hapless girl, who, overcome with terror, sank in his arms.

MAY GRAYSON;

OR,

LOVE AND TREACHERY.

CHAPTER I.

" Two fierce and warlike spirits
That uncontrolled burst forth and like a storm
Scatter destruction."   HENGIST.

IT was a calm, tranquil night, about fifty years since, that two young men quitted the festivities of a ball-room to settle a quarrel that had suddenly sprung up between them.   The place of meeting was a bluff headland rising abruptly from the sea, and favoured by the light of the full moon which shone brightly above them, they commenced a contest in which each sought to prove his superiority over the other.   But both of them were admirable swordsmen, and with such skill did they handle their weapons, that after some time they, as if by mutal consent, lowered their sword's points for breathing time.

" My lord," said the one whose appearance denoted him to be the inferior, " this quarrel has been provoked by yourself, but I am willing to let it drop now and for ever on condition that you promise to renounce your libertine views towards my sister."

But the other, whose dress and deportment shewed him to be a man of

No. 1

rank—smiled, at first, scornfully upon his more lowly antagonist, and, then, holding forth his hand, as if in friendship, said, with affected unconcern :—

"Why, John, dost thou thus wish to force a quarrel on me?—Have we not been as brothers together, and shall a mere idle suspicion break those bonds which have hitherto united us?"

"Let our friendship end here and for ever!" cried the other, fiercely; "thou hast smiled upon me only to deceive me, and now thou wouldst wrong my sister, even at the moment when thou dost most profess thine esteem for myself."

"I tell thee again, John, thy sister has nothing to fear from me."

"How, my Lord Dalmeny!—have you not this night taken her from her partner in the dance, and do I not well know that when thy heart is once fixed upon a maiden, no guile is left untried until thou hast brought her to dishonour?"

"Upon my life, John Ruthven, you wrong me."

"Say'st thou so?"

"I do."

"Wouldst thou prove thy sincerity?"

"Most assuredly would I."

"Then never speak to her again, my lord, and I will once more hold out to you the right hand of friendship."

"Really," laughed the young nobleman, "you would exact more than I can promise to perform. Your sister happens to possess a captivating face; hitherto she has not told me that my attentions are disagreeable, and, to speak the truth, I do not feel inclined to banish myself from her society merely at the bidding of a hot-headed young fellow like yourself."

"Then," replied Ruthven, "we must fulfil the errand for which we just now left the ball-room. Aye, you smile contemptuously upon me, but I may yet prove that the lowly born is fully equal to his more courtly-bred antagonist."

"Granted, John," answered Lord Dalmeny; "I have never yet disputed either your skill in the management of a sword, or your courage, when called upon to defend yourself. I, however, have no quarrel with you at present, and, therefore, I do not feel inclined to raise my arm against the life of my foster-brother, merely because he has taken a foolish whim into his head."

"In plain words, then, you will not fight?"

"In plain words, I will not. On the contrary, I would wish our quarrel to end here, and that we may return to the ball-room, which we both so unceremoniously left."

"I will not hear you, my lord," cried Ruthven, with increasing anger;— "either you must promise to pay no more attention to my unsuspecting sister, or our swords must bring this affair to a close. Choose which it shall be, for the tide is now near its height, and ere it turns, this affair must be decided."

"What!" exclaimed the other, haughtily, "have you forgotten that you are the son of my own vassal?—or does your own vanity lead you to suppose that there is no difference between the high-born Lord Dalmeny and the peasant, John Ruthven—or, Red Ruthven, as he of late thinks fit to call himself?"

"My lord," replied the young man, in a tone of contempt, "I have yet to learn that a man of title and wealth is to trample upon those he may choose to conceive beneath him."

"And yet you may live to see that there always will be such a difference," answered the nobleman.

" Not always," exclaimed Ruthven, " for society is already undergoing a change, and the time will come when all paltry distinctions between men will be forgotten."

" I understand you ; the base churl, whose blood boasts no pure beginning, is to rank with those whose ancestors have fought and bled in the cause of their country ?"

" Your lordship," exclaimed the other, " associates me with the base churls as you are pleased to term them. However, let that pass—for I am better satisfied to be what I am, than to change places with Lord Dalmeny, the profligate and libertine."

" Sirrah!—would you insult me ?"

" Aye, if the honest truth would do so."

" Beware, lest you provoke your own punishment !"

" I am no coward, Lord Dalmeny," exclaimed Ruthven, with increasing vehemence, " and as a proof of it, I came hither to meet you sword to sword. My own life I care not for, and willingly shall it be sacrificed in the defence of a sister whose honour—dear to me as my own—is threatened by a monster like yourself."

" You are insolent."

" Perhaps so ; and, yet, it is in. a cause that would provoke the wrath of any man that cares for the honour of his family."

" You wish, then, to try your prowess with me ?" exclaimed the nobleman, whose temper began to fail beneath the repeated sallies of his antagonist ; " forgetful of your own inferiority in the use of weapons, you would madly seek to involve yourself in the affray, where the chances will be so much against you."

" I care not for that," answered the young man, resolutely ; " my sister's danger has aroused me to take measures for her safety, and never will l leave this spot till I have proved that, though my skill in the use of weapons may be inferior to your own, my courage is not to be daunted by the boastings of a puny lordling."

" You are resolved, then, to prosecute this quarrel to the utmost ?"

" I am; nay, more—though yonder tide is now near its fall, it shall not ebb, ere one of us has proved himself the victor in the affair between us."

" By Heavens ! young sir, you shall have your will !" exclaimed Lord Dalmeny, unable any longer to control his fury. " Too long already have I endured your insults with patience, and now, since it is your will, our swords shall decide which of us shall have to answer for the other's death."

" Hold! while I make one proposition," exclaimed Lord Dalmeny, stepping back, and dropping the point of his sword. " It appears that our quarrel is not likely to be settled till one of us has fallen mortally wounded, and I would suggest that the survivor, whoever it may be, shall precipitate the body of his vanquished opponent over the Mermaid's Rock yonder. It will prevent an awkward discovery taking place, and save a world of trouble to him who is fortunate enough to prove the victor to the coming conflict."

" Agreed !" cried John, and then advancing towards his antagonist, he commenced a furious assault, which the other seemed well prepared to meet. At first the contest seemed to be maintained pretty equally between them ; but, at length, the superior coolness of his lordship obtained a considerable advantage over his opponent, and there is little doubt that the contest would have terminated in the death of John Ruthven, had not a female, at that moment, rushed between them, imploring them, in accents that betrayed a disordered intellect, to forbear their bloody purpose.

" Oh, do not—do not slay each other," she cried, in piteous tones ; " ye would commit murder in your headlong rage, and scorn even the decrees of Heaven, that has declared man shall not destroy the life of a fellow-creature."

"What dost thou here, May Grayson?" demanded Ruthven, angrily; "dost thou not see we are engaged, and that this is no place for a woman to intrude herself?"

"I came to prevent murder."

"And had nearly lost thine own life in the rash attempt," exclaimed our hero; "my own sword was within an inch of thy breast, and grieved should I have been, had the death of a poor demented creature like thyself laid at my door."

"And had it been so," she replied, "there would have been no witness of the deed, save thine antagonist, and yonder bonny moon, that rides and smiles so calmly above us. Look, John, how calmly she looks on whilst blood was about to be spilt, and, yet, there is One above all that would have seen and punished him who slew his friend."

"Psha!" thou art mad, wench!" exclaimed Ruthven, pettishly; "this is no business of thine, and, therefore, I command thee to go home and leave us to settle the dispute that is between us."

"And what care I for home, now that all peace is fled for ever?" she demanded. "I came forth to gaze upon the calm blue waters, and to watch for the ship that is, one day, to bring home my own true love. But, some say he is dead, and others, that he is married to some rich heiress, flaunting in gold and finery; yet, I will not believe them, for he swore that never would he love another woman than myself, and, upon the faith of his vows, I became——"

"Aye, aye, my poor girl," interrupted John, "I know your sad history well enough. The villain deceived, and you fell beneath his specious promises."

"Yet still I love him," sighed the heart-broken May.

"Then, more's the pity," exclaimed Ruthven, "for he is a villain, and deserves not thy remembrance."

"Oh, but I think not that," she cried—"for nightly do I dream of him, and then all seems bright and fair, as in happier times, when I was pure and innocent. Nay, it was but yesterday that I fell asleep beneath yonder rock, and methought he stood before me smiling, and gentle as he used to be. In that moment I forgot all the past; a bright and happy future seemed to open before me, and I could have died happy in the arms that, methought, encircled my waist."

"And, on awaking," observed Ruthven, "all the bitterness of the past rushed upon you with tenfold violence?"

"A change came upon my dream," she continued, mournfully, "and I saw him dressed as a bridegroom, with a fair damsel on his arm; and they took their way towards the church, whilst crowds followed them—some rejoicing in his happiness, and others cursing the inconstancy that had made him cast off his old love for a new one. 'That's Lord Dalmeny and his fair young bride,' said an aged man. 'Alas!' thought I, "then am I completely forgotten!' And I ran to pass them on the road, and when I had got before them, I turned around and, instead of seeing a fair young maiden, I beheld nothing but a fleshless skeleton! Oh, it was a horrible sight; and, with a loud scream, I sank fainting on the ground at the feet of this hideous spectre!"

"And yet, May, this was nothing but a dream."

"Aye, and a horrible one; but, somehow, I do not despair for all that—for it has given me fresh hope, and, in spite of all that I saw, depend on it the day is not far off that will see me the bride of Lord Dalmeny."

"How!—do you still think so, after he has thus basely deserted you?" asked Ruthven.

"I do—I do," she replied with sudden gaiety, and then pointing towards the sea, she continued—"do you not see yonder sail there, sparkling in the moonlight? It is my lover's ship that comes riding over the bounding waters, and if you stay here but a short time longer, you will behold him at my feet, loving me as he ever did, and promising to make me his bonny wife. Then shall Scotland's bells ring from one end of the country to the other, and I shall be happy—aye, happy—happy."

"Go home, May, I entreat you," cried Ruthven, earnestly; "this is no place for you, and the night air begins to grow cool and damp."

"And what matters it if it does?" she asked, "it will the better serve to cool my burning brain, and prepare me for the happy meeting that is to take place. Besides, I came out to gather fresh flowers, for I would weave a garland fitting for our nuptials, and heart's ease shall be there, and roses, because they betoken love, and lilies, because they are the emblems of innocence."

"Leave thine errand till to-morrow, sweet May," exclaimed Ruthven, taking her hand, and endeavouring to conduct her from the spot; but the poor crazed girl resisted him, and breaking away, clapped her hands and laughed wildly at the ease with which she had effected her escape. Then, becoming more serious, she said, with some solemnity :—

"You ask me to come to-morrow to gather flowers for my garland; but it will be too late, for the footsteps of ruthless man will, by that time, have trodden all down, and the place that looks so fair to-night, will then be changed into a cheerless and gloomy desert. Such has been my fate, sir, and the thought of it had made me almost mad."

"Leave us, woman!" exclaimed Lord Dalmeny, whose patience was now nearly exhausted; "leave us, I say, for we have business to settle that needs not thy presence."

"Aye, ye would fight and slay each other," she replied; "ye would send me hence that ye may commit murder, without having a witness to say a word against you. But I will not go home, young sir; I came hither to watch from yon cliff the return of the bonny ship that brings home my own true love, and he would be angry were he to set foot upon the shore, and no May Grayson there to greet him on his return."

"Come, May," said Ruthven, coaxingly, "be a good girl, and do as we have told you."

"And why do ye wish me gone?"

"Because we have business—private business, May, that we would confer together upon."

"Ah! ye would deceive me with honied words—would ye?" she exclaimed; "ye think I am mad, and know not what brought you at this hour to the Mermaid's Cliff. But I know all; it is each other's blood ye crave after, and a woman is the cause of the strife that is between ye."

"I tell you, May, you are mistaken in our motives," answered John; "we wish you to leave us; but our errand here is not of the matter you seem to imagine."

"You would deceive me," she cried; "but crazy though my poor brain is, I am not to be cheated by fair words; did I not come upon ye just now, when both your swords were drawn, and when one, who had obtained the mastery over the other, was about to shed the blood of his rival; this, my eyes beheld, and yet you would tell me that you meet here only as friends."

"And what is it to thee, girl, if we choose to risk our own lives in a private quarrel?" demanded Lord Dalmeny, in no good humour at her perversenesss in remaining near them. "May not a difference exist between us, but you must interfere to prevent the execution of our plans?"

"Ah!" she cried, "you confess it, then, at last!"

"He confesses nothing, May Grayson," exclaimed Ruthven, interposing. "In truth, we both desire your absence, and, unless you leave, we must go elsewhere to finish the affair we have on hand."

"Go where you will I'll follow you."

"You will, May?"

"Aye, truly will I," she replied; "both of ye thirst for blood, and I will be a peace-maker if ye will but let me persuade ye to shake hands and be friends. Come, come, make it up, and when ye have sworn eternal friendship for each other, then will I take my departure, and no more trouble you with my presence."

"Try and prevail on her to leave us, John," whispered Lord Dalmeny; "say what thou wilt to her; tell any falsehoods, but only get rid of her."

"Nay," answered May, who had overheard these words, in spite of the low tone in which they were uttered; "it is in vain that you ask him to tell falsehoods, for he is a youth that loves honour rather than deceit; I have known him since we were children together, and never has he deceived woman as a villain once deceived me."

"Humph!" exclaimed Lord Dalmeny, "just now you told us that you were anxiously looking for the very person of whom you now complain."

"And I told you the truth," she replied; "I came here to look for the ship that bears him to his native land; and why do I look so anxiously for him, think you?—why, but that he may fulfil his vows, and make me the happy girl I was ere the accursed hour that we met?"

"And, think you, he will ever wed one who so easily yielded up her honour to him?" asked his lordship.

"If he does not," answered May, with startling energy, "he is a blacker villain, even, than people say he is."

"Perhaps, he cares not for what people say," exclaimed Lord Dalmeny, mortified by the words he had been compelled to hear.

"It be as you say;" whispered Ruthven in his ear, "but, if he cares not for the thoughts of his fellow-men, there may be one found who will not hesitate to adopt sterner means to bring him to repentance."

"Mean you that for a threat, sirrah?"

"Aye," answered the other, "if you are pleased to take it as one.—You, however, know full well that I am not used to use big words without meaning them, and it will be your own fault if you do not bring me to an account, seeing that I am always to be found whenever your lordship thinks fit to demand satisfaction."

"We have, it appears, more on hand than we know how to accomplish," answered the other, coldly; "we are interrupted as you see, but I am now willing that you shall name any time or place, that may be convenient, to bring this quarrel of ours to a termination."

"Wait a little longer, and this poor crazy victim of yours will have left us," exclaimed Ruthven. "See, she already turns away from us, and——"

"Dear gentlemen, will you promise me to fight no more?" cried May Grayson, suddenly turning back, as she was preparing to leave them;— "will you promise me this, for I am weary of watching here for my lover's ship, and would go down upon the beach yonder, to pick up the shells that have been left there by the waves, as play-things for the idle or the crazy?"

"Go, May, as soon as you like," said Ruthven; "here you are not wanted, for I have to settle that with this youth, that needs not the presence of a third person. Leave us, I say, or we must seek some other place where we shall be more secure from interruption."

"Would that I could see his ship sailing homewards, on the dark blue waters," she exclaimed, without seeming to heed the words that were last addressed to her; "but alas! I fear he'll never, never come, and that I shall live on to have the finger of scorn pointed at me, and to hear people say, 'there goes the wanton, upon whom Heaven has showered its anger for her previous sins.' This is what I dread, and the thought of it has well nigh driven me mad."

"Some people have said that it has quite done so," observed Lord Dalmeny, unmoved by the sight of the sad wreck his own crimes had caused; "depart from us, woman, and hide thyself from the world, for thy sins have made thee a mark for the scorn and detestation of thy fellow-creatures."

"Hush, my lord!" whispered Ruthven; "this, from your lips, is but adding to the crimes you have already committed. Gaze upon those pallid cheeks, and lack-lustre eyes, and then ask your own heart whether you are not a black and cankerous villain, to have made her what she is! Look at her, Lord Dalmeny, and then resist, if you can, the duty you owe her!"

"Duty, sirrah?"

"Aye—do you not owe her reparation?" asked the other earnestly, "is it nothing, think you, to wreck the happiness of a too-confiding female, and then to leave her at the mercy of a cold and heartless world?"

"Hush, John!" exclaimed the young nobleman; "at present, it seems that she does not recognise me; hold thy peace, man, and I promise, if I survive the conflict we shall soon be engaged in, to think of thy words, and, perhaps, I may yet make the reparation you speak of."

"Methinks your justice will have come but tardily," answered John. with a sneer: "first, you drive the poor creature mad with the thought of her shame and degradation; and then you talk of the possibility of making her your wife, when her intellects are gone and broken up, I fear, for ever."

"Psha! you moralize, and forget the wide difference that exists between her station and mine."

"Perhaps I do," answered John. "and so did your lordship when you wooed and won the confidence of a young and unsuspecting maiden. She believed your vows and protestations of honour, and, in an evil moment, became the prey of a fiend that had long been watching for her destruction."

"John!" exclaimed the nobleman, "beware how you urge me further, for my blood begins to rush madly to my brain, and I may be tempted to smite thee dead at my feet!"

"Not whilst I have a sword to protect myself," answered the other. with cool indifference. "From your merciful consideration, I know that I have nothing to expect, and, therefore, do I stand before you, fully prepared for any act of perfidy you may feel disposed to commit."

"Not yet!—not yet!" cried May Grayson, again turning impatiently from the cliff, where she had been anxiously gazing across the still advancing tide; "alas! alas! I have looked till my eyes ache, and not a sail is there to be seen, to give me even a single moment of hope that my lover is returning to make me his bride."

"Then look no longer, poor girl!" said John, tenderly. "Try to forget him, and, perhaps, some day he will come home when least you expect him."

"Do you think so?"

"Nay, I would not have you feel too confident, my girl," replied John; "he you expect has deceived others, and, therefore, may, in turn, deceive you."

"Psha!" whispered Lord Dalmeny, "why do you keep her here with this idle talk?—Tell her a vessel has just arrived off our coast, and I warrant she will soon leave us to hasten down to the beach."

"I leave your lordship to tell her your own falsehood," replied the other, haughtily; "at present, I would avoid the guilt of adding one deceit to another, and, therefore, I refuse the honour you would confer on me."

"Hah!—am I to be for ever sneered at by a peasant churl?" exclaimed the young nobleman.

"You must," answered our hero; "you have thrown yourself in my power; have made yourself a thing to be despised, and now come the bitter fruits of your own baseness."

"Slave!—you are insolent!"

"My lord—*you* are a villain!"

"By Heavens, John, this can be endured no longer!" exclaimed Lord Dalmeny, bursting into a torrent of rage. "Too long already have I endured your impertinence, but your last words have excited a fury that will bear no bounds, and either your life or mine shall this night be sacrificed."

"I am content to abide my chance, Lord Dalmeny," answered our hero, contemptuously. "I am ready to begin whenever you think fit, though between ourselves, it would be as well to get rid of this poor mad creature, ere we commence a conflict that, I suppose, will end only in the death of either you or myself."

"That shall soon be done," exclaimed Lord Dalmeny, and advancing near to May Grayson, he said:—"The ship you have been so anxiously looking for has just rounded yonder point; her passengers will shortly be landed in Dornoch Bay, where you will meet your lover, if you make all due haste."

With a cry of joy, May rushed from their presence, and, quickly descending the cliffs, left the two young men to re-engage in the conflict, which had been so suddenly interrupted by the arrival of the crazy victim of man's duplicity.

CHAPTER II.

"Thy destiny is written,
And the page of Fate too surely doth denote
A life of danger, and a death of shame."—THE SYBIL.

BOTH the young men gazed upon the form of May Grayson, as she sped like a timid fawn from their presence; and it was not until she had been out of sight some few seconds, that Lord Dalmeny turned round, and again confronted his antagonist.

"I have been thinking, John," he said, "that there is little cause why you and I should fall out with each other just now. That I am a wild fellow, when a petticoat is in the way, cannot be denied, and, yet, for the life of me, I cannot understand why you should call me to an account

for my actions, even though they may not exactly tally with your own views."

"Your lordship then, it appears, would persuade me that there is no cause of quarrel between us?"

"I am sure there is none, John."

"What!" exclaimed the other, indignantly, "did I not myself see you, scarce an hour since, paying attentions to my sister, that I know are dangerous?"

"Say rather, you believe them to be so," answered Lord Dalmeny. "The truth is, John, I have, somehow or other, obtained no very enviable notoriety in these parts, and if I do but look smilingly upon a pretty woman it is immediately imagined that I have a design upon her virtue."

"Your actions, my lord," replied John Ruthven "prove that few females may suffer civilities from you, without injury to their character."

"You do not, surely, doubt your sister's virtue?"

"I know her to be all that is excellent," replied our hero; "she has hitherto sustained a good name, and it is because I would not see her reputation blasted that I have this night called you out of your own ball-room, either to meet me as a deadly foe, or to give me an assurance, upon your honour, that you meditate no treachery against her."

"John!" ejaculated Lord Dalmeny, "and what, think you, would be the use of my making any promise of the kind? Love is not to be controlled like any other passion, and, even though I might pledge my honour in this affair, it is not at all unlikely that I should break my word in the event of my seeing that she was not quite as particular as her brother."

No. 2

"My lord!" exclaimed John, "you do but exasperate me the more by these allusions of yours. At present, the mind of my sister is as pure as the snow that lies on yonder mountain's summit, and rather than see her fall a victim to the arts of a shameless libertine, I would cast away my life in her defence. You smile at me, Lord Dalmeny, but, even were you my own brother, I would aim my sword's point to your heart, rather than see you triumph over a young and unsuspecting female."

"Upon my word, young man," cried his lordship, deridingly; "you have grown marvellously romantic since you left your native shores to become a wanderer upon the pathless ocean. You left us as reckless a dog as any in the neighbourhood, and, on your return, I find that you have grown a moralist, and a sworn protector of female virtue."

"Do you remember in what relationship the girl stands to me, whose peace you thus cruelly seek to destroy?"

"Aye, marry I do—she is your sister, and, truth to tell, one of the fairest damsels within many miles of this place."

"Her beauty," observed John, "is likely to be a curse to her, since it has attracted the notice of your lordship. However, we do but waste time in idle parley; we came hither to see who is the superior swordsman, and, by heavens, I will never quit the spot, until either you or I have been made to bite the dust."

"Do not be over rash, young man," exclaimed Lord Dalmeny, unmoved by what had fallen from his antagonist. "Remember, we are both nearly of an age; both can boast of being tolerably good swordsmen, and both of us have courage enough—if we once begin—to carry this affair to a fatal termination. Pause, then, and reflect whether it will not be better to sheath our weapons in peace, and return to the ball-room at my castle, where our abrupt disappearance has, no doubt, occasioned no little consternation."

"Shall we return as cowards?" asked Ruthven bitterly.

"Nay, I, for one, call it not cowardice," answered his lordship; "the truth is, we have ever been as brothers, though your own station in life was far inferior to my own; from the period of boyhood you were at all times a welcome visitor at the castle of Dalmeny, and, as years rolled on we forgot that we were not born equal, and our friendship became proverbial throughout the whole country."

"It was so," answered John, "and if the tie that bound us together is severed, the act that separates us is your own."

"By what means have I made you my enemy?"

"Can you ask me such a question," cried John, "when you so well know that the steps I have taken were provoked by your unsought-for attentions to my sister?"

"Psha! I merely danced with her at the ball."

"And yet, that," answered John, "was sufficient to call forth the observations, and ill-natured remarks, of all who beheld your attentions to her. I heard people whispering among themselves that my sister was doomed to become the next victim of your seductive artifices, and, stung to madness by the thought, I resolved immediately to call you out."

"Humph! and now that I have obeyed your call, you will, as a matter of course, accept my assurance, that I meditate no harm against the sister of my earliest friend?"

"You mistake me, my lord," answered our hero; "your word has been forfeited ere now, and I will listen to no protestations that you can make to me on this subject."

"By heavens, John!" exclaimed Lord Dalmeny, "there is no other man living that dare say as much to my face."

"Perhaps not, my lord, and seeing that I expect neither favour nor consideration, I now call upon you to fulfil the design that led to our hasty departure from your castle."

"And if I refuse to cross swords with my friend, I suppose he will at once write me down a coward?"

"Lord Dalmeny," exclaimed the other, "I know well enough from former experience that your bravery is, at least, equal to my own. So much I can give you credit for, and, therefore, am I the more surprised that you now refuse to give me the satisfaction I have demanded."

"It is because I have no wish to take the life of one who I have regarded as a friend," replied the young nobleman. "I would avoid a conflict that might terminate in your death, and, as the only alternative, I propose that we should part on this spot, never to meet again."

"And what security," asked John, scornfully, "would that afford me of my sister's safety from your fiendish arts?"

"Surely, my word will be sufficient to satisfy you?"

"It will not, my lord," replied the other; "the poor girl who has just now left us, affords a melancholy proof of the little faith that is to be placed in your promises."

"You are insolent," exclaimed the peer, "and presume too much upon our former friendship."

"I, at least, speak the truth," answered our hero, "and it is my will that you hear me out:—I was going to observe, that I well remember the time when May Grayson was one of the bonniest and most happy of the lasses amongst all our acquaintances. But then she was pure and innocent, and she was exultant in conscious innocence—at once, the pride and boast of the whole neighbourhood. Such was May Grayson when I left my native land, to visit far off foreign lands; and what do I find her on my return home?—A woman despoiled of her virtue by a heartless libertine; a mere wreck of what she was—the scorn of those who once loved her, and driven mad by the villany and falsehood of him in whose word she was weak enough to confide."

"Well," exclaimed Lord Dalmeny, concealing the anger with which he had listened to these words, "and, even granting that all this is true, what, I would ask, is it to John Ruthven?"

"Much, my lord," answered the young man, "for it has made foes of those who were once friends. I despise you for your perfidy, and when I see that you are bestowing your hateful attentions upon a sister, whom I love, it at once arouses me to a sense of her danger, and I take the only means that offer to save her from dishonour."

"And if you fall," observed his lordship, "will she not more than ever be thrown in my power?"

"It may be so," answered the other, "and yet, heartless as you are, I can scarcely think you would seek to destroy the happiness of her whose brother you had sent to an untimely grave."

"It is because I wish to avoid shedding your blood that I am thus unwilling to draw my sword against you," replied Lord Dalmeny. "I have no desire to exhibit my prowess upon one whom I have formerly esteemed as a friend, and, therefore, do I tell you again that I will not fight until I have received sufficient provocation to make me forget the many happy hours we have spent together."

"Have I not called you COWARD?"

"You did so, John, and, stung with your words, I drew my sword, and we fought. Nay, since you remind me of the indignity you cast upon me, I will tell you that, had it not been for the timely arrival of May

Grayson, you would not have been now alive to taunt me with the insulting words used against me."

"'Tis false !" exclaimed John, vehemently ; " my chances were fully as good as your own, and had it not been for the interference of May, I should now have had it in my power to say that my sister was no longer in danger from the villain that would bring her to shame and infamy."

"John !" cried the other, " you urge me beyond the powers of endurance ; that I can bear much from you, our present interview is sufficient to testify ; but, by heavens, I cannot longer hear thee make use of expressions intended to brand me with dishonour."

" Dishonour !" exclaimed John, with contempt ; " what honour has Lord Dalmeny to boast of, I would ask?—Has he not proved himself the scourge of all that is good and virtuous, and shall he now affect anger because one, whom he regards as an inferior, has the honour to tell him in plain terms that he is a libertine and a villain ?"

"This is more than I can endure !" cried his lordship, drawing his sword, and throwing himself into a threatening attitude ; " Heaven is my witness that I sought not this quarrel, but since it has been forced upon me, never will I sheath my sword again until its point has been dyed in the heart's blood of the man who has excited my fury."

Upon this, their weapons clashed, and each, resolving to defend himself to the last, determined to sell his life dearly, should fortune give the event of the combat against him.   At last, however, the better feelings of Lord Dalmeny began to revive, and trusting to his own superior management of the weapon he fought with, he tried only to disarm his antagonist, and thus compel him to desist from the strife.   But this was no easy task, for John was an excellent swordsman, and, in spite of all the efforts that were made to deprive him of his weapon, he still continued the fight, occasionally gaining the advantage, and never being altogether at the mercy of his antagonist.

Leaving the scene of strife, we must now conduct the reader to a splendid ball in the castle of Dalmeny, where music was resounding, whilst the dancers kept up the gaiety which had been prepared to do honour to the young lord's recent arrival from foreign travel.   Nor was the absence of himself and John noticed by those, whose whole thoughts were occupied with the pleasures in which they were engaged ; and, even the Lady Margaret Dalmeny, the stately grandmother of his lordship, seated as she was, beneath a rich canopy, at the further end of the apartment, was unaware of the disagreement that had taken place between these two young men, and their subsequent departure from the scene of festivity.   Not so, however, was it with the Lady Agnes Drummond, the fair and beauteous cousin of Lord Dalmeny, who had watched them out when they so fiercely left the ball room, and whose fears were naturally excited, lest mischief should ensue from a collision between two such ardent spirits.   She would have followed them, but was engaged in the next dance, and never did time seem to pass so slowly as during that interval, which, to every one else in the room was fraught with joy and happiness.   At last, the music ceased, and her partner was leading her to her seat, when abruptly withdrawing her arm from his, she wildly rushed from the room, glided down a flight of steps, and taking her way through the garden, was about to leave it by one of the gates, when she was met by a groom, who she found it was impossible to avoid without being seen.   Of him, therefore, she asked a few questions respecting the absence of his young master, and learning from the man that both Lord Dalmeny and Ruthven had directed their way towards the Mermaid's Cliff, she hurried onwards, determined to satisfy herself whether her fears were well founded or otherwise. But in her agitation she missed the path, which at all other times was so well known to her, and, after pursuing her way for some time, she was at length mortified and disappointed at finding herself on the sea shore. But this was no time for hesitation, and perceiving by the moonlight that the Mermaid's Cliff was at no very great distance from her along the coast, she rallied her flagging spirits, and ascending the rocks that rose before her, she was in a short time startled by hearing the clashing of swords, as of two persons engaged in mortal combat. Urged onwards by these fearful sounds, the affrighted maiden increased her speed, and presently afterwards coming in sight of the combatants, she uttered a piercing scream, and rushed madly between them, unmindful of the extreme peril she thus brought upon herself.

Happily she escaped the danger, for the combatants instantly ceased their deadly strife, and both of them gazing upon her with silent wonder, seemed uncertain whether the figure they looked upon was an earthly or spiritual being. Agnes saw her advantage, and, addressing them in a tone of extreme agitation, she exclaimed :—

"How is this, my lord ?—Have you left the ball-room only that you might shed the blood of a fellow creature, or haply lose your own life, in a mad quarrel that should not have been settled until both of you had reflected for, at least, one night on the consequences that might have resulted ? Shame on ye both, I say, for thus risking the life which it was rather your duty to preserve by every means in your power."

"Nay, my gentle cousin, do not cast the blame on me," cried Lord Dalmeny. "That I have been engaged in a conflict with this youth you have yourself been a witness. Yet the quarrel was none of my seeking, nor would I have drawn my sword had I not been urged to do so by his insulting words."

"John !" exclaimed the Lady Agnes, "I guessed, ere I came hither, that this affair was your own creating; I know your fiery spirit, and that vengeance burns within you like an all-devouring element. Yet, beware how you give way to your passions, for, though no prophet, I can but too well foresee that, unless a curb is put upon your actions, you will become at once the scourge and terror of mankind. Aye, you start ; but, rely on it, I speak only the truth, as the future, I fear, will but too plainly demonstrate."

"What means your ladyship?" demanded John, moved by the earnestwith which she had spoken.

"I mean," she replied, "that your temper is fierce, and your nature cruel and vindictive. All who are above you are looked upon with scorn and detestation ; you hate the control that one class exercises over another, and should an opportunity ever arrive, you will side with the multitude to bring about that equality of rank that you think is so essential to the happiness of mankind. The sea is your element, and you will seek command upon it either in the service of your country, or, being disappointed in that, you will become the leader of——"

"Nay, do not pause in your prediction," cried Ruthven, with a forced laugh ; "proceed with it, I entreat you ; you were saying that, being disappointed in obtaining a post of honour in the service of my country, I should become the leader of——"

"A band of pirates !" exclaimed the Lady Agnes, with a shudder that she could not control.

"Hah! that is a bold prophecy, truly," cried John, evidently mortified at the words she had given utterance to; "I, however, thank you for your candour, though I trust the fulfilment is never destined to take place."

"It will," she replied; "your fierce nature but too surely tells me so. With less rancour in your heart, you might have been the pride and glory of your land; as it is, you will prove to be the bitterest curse!"

"Really, my fair cousin," laughed Lord Delmeny, "it must be confessed, your prediction is not very complimentary to John; he, however, I dare say, will not mind it, seeing that, after all, you know nothing more of his future destiny than I do myself."

"Let us say no more about it, then," replied Lady Agnes, "for I came hither rather to heal, than open the wounds that have been produced by discord. You have abruptly quitted the ball-room to seek each other's lives, and having thus ventured to follow you to this wild spot, I would now learn from your own lips whether any further danger is to be apprehended from either of your fiery spirits?"

"I have told you already," answered Lord Dalmeny, "that the quarrel was not sought by myself, and, therefore, I am content to let it drop for ever, provided John will promise not to urge me to a fresh outbreak of passion."

"You hear him, sir?" cried Lady Agnes, addressing herself to our hero; "he is willing to abandon this quarrel at my solicitation; may I rely upon your forbearance, also, in this respect?"

"You may," answered Ruthven, with as much courtesy as he could assume; "Lord Dalmeny shall be safe for the present—how long he remains so must depend entirely upon his own conduct."

"Not a word about your sister, John," whispered his lordship; "Lady Agnes happens, unfortunately, to be most confounded jealous, and if she had the slightest suspicion of the trifling affair that caused our quarrel, just now, there would be an end of all my hopes of obtaining her hand, and, consequently, away would go an alliance upon which my grandmother has set her heart and soul for these dozen years past."

"Come," said Lady Agnes Drummond, by whom these words were not heard, "let us return to the castle, for the guests will be wondering at our absence, and I should be sorry that this hot-headed affair should be known to those who would laugh at you for a couple of fools, who were willing to throw away your lives in a mad broil, without knowing why or wherefore."

"I would rather not go back," answered John, sullenly; "at least, if I do so, it will only be to take my sister home, for it is already late, and——"

"Nonsense, John," exclaimed Lord Dalmeny; "your sister, I'll warrant you, is happy enough where she is if you only let her alone. Besides your sudden departure would only give rise to a thousand wild surmises, and as her ladyship says, there is no occasion for all the world to know that we could not pass this evening together without falling out."

"I see how it is," said the maiden, regarding them, by turn, with a glance of suspicion, "you are not yet reconciled, and, though I may have succeeded in appeasing you for the present, it will only give you both an opportunity to brood over certain wrongs that one is supposed to have inflicted upon the other, and, by and by, you will renew your combat, with a determination of seeking each other's lives."

"Pardon me, cousin Agnes," cried his lordship, "but I have given my word, and you shall find that, in this instance, at least, I will honourably fulfil my promise."

"And will you," she asked, addressing herself to John; "will you also keep the promise you have just now made?"

"Most religiously."

"I take your word, sir, and rest perfectly satisfied that I shall not have to regret my confidence. At all events, the trouble I have been at to find you to-night, has not been thrown away, and it will be a pleasant reflection hereafter, to know that I have been the means of saving, at least, one life, by my present visit to the Mermaid's Cliff."

" It was, indeed, a hazardous experiment to throw yourself between two armed and angry men," observed John ; "your own safety was perilled, and I feel but too happy in knowing that no harm has resulted from the generous motive that tempted you to follow us hither."

"The act was not so very particular either," answered her ladyship, "seeing that it was prompted solely by my desire to prevent bloodshed.— Happily, I have succeeded, and now, John, knowing as I do, that you are not without your own fair share of goodness, let me prevail upon you, henceforward, to avoid all occasions that may lead to quarrels with your friends. You heard my predictions just now, but it is only fair to add, that by governing your passions, it may still be possible to live and die respected by your fellow-creatures."

" I am what you see me, Lady Agnes," replied the young man, proudly, " and, whatever my fate may be, I shall take no means to avert it. The world and I are at variance upon certain points, for I see that the high-born trample upon their more humble fellow-creatures, and my blood boils with indignation at the tyranny of one class of men over another."

"And why should you trouble your head about the matter ?" asked Lord Dalmeny ; "it is, after all, the nature of man to rise as high as he can above his fellows, and having once obtained a superiority, he, of course, tries to maintain his position. Such has ever been the case, and it is not you, or any other human being, that will ever effect the change you desire."

" I may, at least try, my lord."

" Aye, and by so doing, ruin yourself for ever."

"Perhaps so," answered John Ruthven, following them as they now took their way towards the castle of Dalmeny ; "I may, probably fall in my efforts to elevate man from his present state of degradation ; but even if I do, it will be some consolation in my last moments to know that I have awakened millions to a sense of the wrongs they have too long endured."

"But, in my opinion, the wrongs you speak of are imaginary," observed the young nobleman.

"Or, at any rate," interposed Lady Agnes, "they have been greatly exaggerated by your own over-wrought fancy."

"That cannot be," answered John, moodily. "for I have seen tyranny prevail over the great mass of human beings, and I have asked myself why it should be that the few could so easily trample upon the multitude."

" And what was the answer ?" asked the maiden.

" That it only required the presence of one man among them, of strong nerve and resolute bearing, to give confidence to the oppressed. Let such a person stand forward, and the day would not be far distant when tyrants would be made to tremble at the rising tempest !"

" I see your meaning," cried Lady Agnes ; " you imagine yourself to be the man that is destined to carry out this great resolution, and are only waiting an opportunity to carry the design into effect ?"

" It would be dangerous, perhaps, were I to give utterance to my thoughts on that point," answered John, cautiously. " What I am destined for will soon be made manifest ; but, till the time arrives, I must remain silent."

" This is but a gloomy subject, John, for a lady's ears," exclaimed Lord Dalmeny, anxious to change the subject ; " so I pr'ythee let us hasten onwards, for the sounds of music from the castle are now plainly to be heard, and, to confess the truth, I would rather be dancing in the old hall, with Lady Agnes for my partner, than listen to the grumblings of a man who is discontented with everything he hears and sees without being able to give a good reason for it."

"Be it as you wish," answered John. "but remember, the subject, however disagreeable it may be to yourself, was none of my own introducing."

"And, above all things," added her ladyship, "do not let his lordship's good grandmamma, the Lady Margaret Dalmeny, hear you speaking against the aristocracy. She is a stickler for things as they are, and being a kind friend of yours, I should be sorry that you lost her esteem, through giving expression to an inadvertent word."

"Were all the high-born dames of the land like the Lady Margaret, their sons would not be brought up to despise those whom chance has placed beneath them," answered John. "She has been almost as a mother to me, and though sometimes she may have reproved my folly, it has never been either with anger or bitterness."

"Really, John," exclaimed Lord Dalmeny, "you speak so flatteringly of the lady, that I feel more than half inclined to forget the insults you just now passed upon me."

"I neither ask nor desire your forgiveness," answered our hero, sullenly ; "nor will I take your hand again in friendship, until you have——"

Here they entered the castle, and following his two companions, John once more entered the ball-room, where he had left his sister unconscious of the quarrel in which he was engaged, on her account, with Lord Dalmeny.

CHAPTER III.

"All people shun him for his wickedness—
The good despise—and e'en the reprobate
Will scarcely hold him company."—ALONZO.

THE castle of Dalmeny, though still a place of some consequence in the neighbourhood, had sadly fallen from the grandeur and magnificence that had once rendered it one of the most remarkable among the fortresses of Scotland. War had, in some degree, brought about this change, but the dissipation of its successive owners had, perhaps, more than anything else, served to cripple the resources of the family and reduced it from a state of affluence to a degree of comparative poverty. Over and over again, in earlier times, the castle had sustained the sieges of enemies, defying all attempts to take, and proving a secure stronghold to its noble owners.—— Then came a turn of fortune, and the proud family of Dalmeny began to behold the gradual decay of an illustrious line that had formerly been the pride and boast of their country.

The father of the present lord had been a man hated and feared by all who chanced to live within the circuit of his domains. Cruel and vindictive, he made enemies in every direction, and as it was known that he almost constantly secluded himself within one of the turrets of the castle, it was, at length, currently reported that his time was passed in the study of necromancy, and that he had it in his power to raise the spirit of Evil whenever he chose. Other things, too, served to add to the universal detestation in which he was held ; he had been one of the fiercest among the persecutors of the Cameronians, a class of religionists who were ever

willing to fight for conscience sake, and who hated, from their very souls, all who differed from them in their peculiar opinions. On one occasion, it appears, a party of them were engaged in a fierce skirmish with a troop of men from the castle, headed by Lord Dalmeny ; and with such blind fury was the battle fought by the Cameronians, that two only of their party escaped, whilst their foes left the field without losing even so much as a single man. Lord Dalmeny himself had performed prodigies of va- lour on this occasion ; his sword had struck down no less than eight of the religious enthusiasts, and though he was attacked on all sides with the greatest fury, yet, it so happened that he quitted the scene of sanguinary strife without having received even one wound. This circumstance, added to others, served to convince people more than ever that he was leagued with the fiend of darkness, and if anything were required to confirm this wild rumour, it was the singular manner of his death, which took place not long afterwards. Lord Dalmeny had retired to his chamber, in the turret, as usual, near about the hour of midnight ; no notice, however, was taken of a matter of such common occurrence, and all within the castle retired to rest, leaving his lordship to the enjoyment of his midnight stu- dies. About two hours afterwards, however, the inmates of the castle were aroused by a terrific report, that seemed to shake the ancient build- ing to its very foundations. In an instant, all rushed from their beds ;— lights were procured, and, in a body, the trembling servants, followed by Lady Margaret, proceeded to the much-dreaded turret. There a terrible sight presented itself—Lord Dalmeny lay stretched upon the floor, a black and hideous corpse ; the furniture was all in disorder, and several wide rents in the wall, served to assure them that the work of destruction had been produced by supernatural causes. It appeared strange to them,
No. 3

too, that no wound appeared on the black and disfigured body of his lordship, and as no cup, or other vessel, was found that might have contained
poison, it was generally believed that he had died by the hand of that
fiend, whom he had so often called from the infernal world. On the other
hand, however, the Cameronians declared that it was a judgment of
Heaven upon him for his persecutions of themselves, and loud were their
preachings throughout the land, denouncing a similar doom to all those
who should be wicked enough to follow in his footsteps.

The present Lord Dalmeny was an infant at the time of his father's
death, and had been placed under the care of the mother of John Ruthven,
or Red Ruthven, as he is now more generally called. Here commenced
the intimacy between the two, and for the first few years of their lives they
regarded each other in the light of brothers. But, at length, the young
Lord Dalmeny began to assume a tone of authority over his more humbly-
born companion, which the other, who possessed a spirit of independence
fully equal to his own, was little likely to brook with patience. Frequent
quarrels ensued thereon, and on some occasions they even came to blows,
for John would not quietly hear himself and his mother branded with the
names of paupers—a favourite expression of his youthful lordship—and
the consequence was, that many a sturdy fight took place between them,
which generally terminated in favour of John, who was not only a stout,
well-made youth, but had also courage enough to take his own part, even,
though his antagonist boasted a longer and a prouder pedigree. Still
these outbreaks were generally healed by the kindly interposition of John's
mother, and, perhaps, in an hour after the fight was over, they would be
as good friends again as possible.

At length, on one occasion, when the young plebeian had been taunted
with more than usual sarcasm upon the obscurity of his birth, his spirit
was roused almost to a state of madness, by the stinging reproaches that
were hurled at him by his lordly antagonist. John had endured these
insults as long as he could, without appearing to care much about them ;
but, at length, when galling epithets were applied to his parents, he could
no longer restrain himself, and, rushing towards his lordship, he struck
him a blow in the face that quickly laid the young peer insensible at his
feet. The uproar occasioned by this, soon brought John's mother to the
spot : restoratives were immediately applied, the blood was stopped, and
plaster applied to the wounds that had been produced by his own provoking conduct. Stung with the reflection that all this mischief had been
done by one so far beneath him in rank, Lord Dalmeny forgot the many
kindnesses he had received beneath the roof where he then was, and
rushing furiously from the house, he sought the nearest magistrate, laid
his complaint against John, and ere he left to return home, he had the
gratification to know that a warrant had been made out for the apprehension of his youthful assailant, who would have to lay in gaol for some
months, unless bail could be procured for his appearance at the sessions.——
This, in fact, was the origin of the extraordinary career afterwards pursued by the notorious John Ruthven. He was apprehended on a charge of
having assaulted Lord Dalmeny, and as nobody thought proper to be answerable for his subsequent appearance, he was at once transferred to gaol,
where he was to remain in confinement till the period of his trial arrived.
But the spirit of the youth could ill brook confinement in a felon's prison ;
a plot to escape was soon devised and executed, and ere John had been con-
signed to the gaol many hours, he contrived to remove the bars of the
window, and once again he breathed the air of freedom. Still, however,
he was conscious that his native land no longer was capable of affording
him a shelter, and directing his steps towards the nearest sea-port town,

he engaged himself to the captain of a ship that was just about to sail, and in a short time afterwards, bade farewell to his native shores. From this time, nothing was heard of him for some years, nor did he return again till within a short time previous to the commencement of our narrative, when the swarthiness of his complexion, and the general hardiness of his appearance, told that he had travelled much in sunny lands, and that his new habits of life were exactly such as suited him. His first inquiry, after hastening to greet his mother and sister, was respecting his former associate, Lord Dalmeny; he learnt, however, that he had been abroad some time on his travels, but that letters had lately been received from him at the castle, announcing his immediate return, and his determination to fix his future residence at the ancient castle of his ancestors. John felt somewhat rejoiced at this, for his anger against his lordship had worn away with time, and he longed to see him once more to recount the scenes in which he had been engaged, and in return to hear from Lord Dalmeny the adventures that had occurred to him during his long absence from home.

A few days after this a foreign vessel arrived in the bay, and no sooner did our hero hear of it, than, hurrying down to the place, he waited impatiently on the strand till the passengers had been landed from the ship, which was lying at anchor about a quarter of a mile off. Two or three boats full arrived, but still no Lord Dalmeny was to be seen among those that were put on shore. At length, however, the last boat was seen to leave the vessel, and as she came nearer, the quick eyes of our hero recognized the well-known form of the young man he sought. His heart palpitated with delight, his impatience grew more and more intense every moment, and when at last the keel was heard grating upon the sands, he rushed through the water, and catching hold of the hand of his early friend, called upon him by name.

"Why, John! is it you that are the first to come and greet me on my arrival on the shores of Old Scotland?" exclaimed the young nobleman, with surprise; "by St. Andrew, I began to think you were dead, for though I have often written home, inquiring what had become of you, the only answer I could get was that you had never been heard of since you escaped from the——"

"Hush! we are overheard, my lord," interrupted John; "leap ashore and you shall soon know where I have been, and what adventures have befallen me."

In another instant the two young men stood side by side on the beach, and when the directions had been given to some of the by-standers for the conveyance of his luggage to the castle, they set forward, arm-in-arm, as if they had never had a quarrel in the whole course of their lives. During their progress, they each related as briefly as possible the chief incidents of their travels, leaving, till another opportunity, the minor details that were necessary to fill up the pictures. At the castle gate the two friends separated; John to return home, and Lord Dalmeny to receive the welcome of those who had so long and anxiously looked for his arrival. By Lady Agnes he was received with all the ardour of a young and loving heart, and by Lady Margaret Dalmeny with the rapture with which a parent gazes upon a loved and only child—the treasure of a long-widowed heart. She embraced her grandson with rapture, sobbing upon his bosom in the fulness of her joy, and imploring him never to leave his home again until she was laid in the dark and silent tomb!

A few days after his return, however, served to prove to the whole neighbourhood that foreign travels had not improved his morals. He was, in fact, a confirmed libertine, and so glaring was his misconduct, that few prudent mothers would permit their daughters to leave home without being accompanied by some one who was able to protect them against the impertinence of the youthful nobleman. Still the joy at the castle for his return was undiminished, and as Lady Margaret Dalmeny wished to give her neighbours a favourable opinion of her grandson, a ball was announced to take place on a certain evening, to which all persons were invited, without regard being paid either to rank or station. This ball was the one alluded to at the commencement of our narrative.

It was the morning of this eventful day that a circumstance occurred which was not likely to add to the popularity of the nobleman in whose honour the fete was to be given. He had ridden out on horseback, and being overtaken by a sudden tempest, applied for shelter at the nearest cottage he could find. He was, however, known, and it was not without some hesitation that the good dame who came to the door would give him admittance. Yet, in the end, she was prevailed on to let him in, but not before she had desired her daughter to leave the room, and not return to it till she was assured of the guest's departure. This was gall and wormwood to Lord Dalmeny, who had heard much talk of the beauty of the fair Jessy; but disguising his mortification he entered the house, after having tied his horse to a tree, and having satisfied himself as to which was the room in which the maiden had been concealed, he began talking to the elder female upon a variety of indifferent subjects. The good dame answered him cautiously, and was determined to be upon her guard; but presently afterwards she was called out of the cottage by one of her sons, who required her immediate assistance at some little distance from the place. This was exactly the opportunity desired by the libertine nobleman, and having assured himself that the mother had taken her departure, he opened the door of the chamber that had attracted his notice, and immediately beheld the fair creature of whom he had heard so flattering a report.

"Be not alarmed, my dear girl," he said, advancing, and taking the hand of the abashed maiden. "I am here as your friend—your lover, if you please, and, therefore, I pray you shrink not from me as if my touch were pollution."

"I have been told," replied Jessy, struggling to disengage her hand, "that no modest maiden should ever suffer you to approach her. Indeed my mother bid me hide myself in this room, lest you should see, and afterwards tear me from her arms."

"Psha! your mother has taken up a prejudice that has been raised against me by my enemies," answered Lord Dalmeny: "I am aware that there are persons who say I am everything that is bad, but you, I hope, will not believe all the tales that are told of one whose only fault is an affection for your sex."

"If I have heard right, my lord," answered Jessy, "you are already engaged to a lady of high rank and virtue."

"That is but an idle rumour, believe me," replied Lord Dalmeny;— "my heart is not yet engaged, unless, indeed, your beauty should tempt me to throw off my bachelor habits and turn Benedict."

"Your flattery, my lord, is unheeded," cried the maiden; "I am poor and lowly born, and, therefore, am not a fitting mate for the lord of yonder castle."

"You are mistaken," he exclaimed; "nobles have ere now married girls of lower degree than yourself, and I see no reason why the fair Jessy should not aspire to become the much-envied Lady Dalmeny."

"My lord, I am not to be deceived by flattery," cried the maiden, resolutely. "As a stranger you have entered our house in quest of shelter from the storm; you have been received with hospitality, and I charge you not to abuse it by endeavouring to destroy the happiness of a whole family."

"I tell you again you are mistaken," answered his lordship; "I am not the villain you take me for, and if you will but accompany me to my castle I will introduce you to those who will assure you of your safety."

"Think you, my lord, that I will ever consent to leave my house upon the hollow promises of one who has ever proved himself the base betrayer of our sex?—No, Lord Dalmeny, I have learnt your character, and weak indeed should I be to trust myself with one who glories in the misery he has brought upon his wretched victims."

"Explain yourself, Jessy;—what know you of me that would reflect dishonour on my name?"

"That you are the heartless destroyer of women!" she replied, boldly. "Nay, interrupt me not, for I have been asked a question and will answer it. One of your victims, ere you left England, now lies cold and stark in yonder church-yard;—she yielded, was forsaken, and broken-hearted, found an early grave. Another, poor May Grayson, also put her faith in you, and the consequences are such as ought to deter others from following her sad example: she is now a wretched maniac, wandering about from place to place in quest of the faithless libertine who deceived her; and long will she wander, for never will Lord Dalmeny fulfil those promises that made her yield to him."

"Jessy, you wrong me," exclaimed Lord Dalmeny, passionately; "these rumours are without foundation, and yet you believe me the guilty wretch you have described."

"I have spoken nothing more than I know to be the truth," answered the maiden; "all the neighbours are aware of the crimes you have committed, and shun you as they would some fierce beast of prey. You are hated and feared, and, therefore, do I entreat you to leave me ere those come to my assistance who may make you rue this day when you intruded yourself in our humble cot."

"I shall not leave you," replied Lord Dalmeny, "until you have either promised to accompany me, or, at least, given me permission to see you again."

"Leave me, Lord Dalmeny," exclaimed Jessy, resolutely;—"leave me, I say, ere I call upon Heaven to strike you with the lightnings that are now flashing so awfully above us!—You seek to dishonour those who have given you shelter from the howling tempest, and take care that your crime is not punished when least you expect it."

"Would you have me quit the place ere the storm has subsided?" asked his lordship.

"I would," she replied, eagerly;—"the rain has given over, and it is time you were gone."

"But the lightning still continues to flash almost incessantly," exclaimed the young man.

"It matters not," cried Jessy; "my brother, I see, is now returning home, and should he discover the perfidy you would have been guilty of, it is not your high blood that would save you from his vengeance!"

"In that case," observed Lord Dalmeny, "there is no time to lose;—I have entreated you, Jessy, to listen to me with compassion; you have turned a deaf ear to my entreaties, and now but one alternative remains."

"What mean you, my lord?" cried the terrified maiden.

"That you must hence with me!" he exclaimed, hoarsely; "you have thought proper to spurn me, and it is now for me to prove that I am not to be thwarted.—Come, girl, you must away with me!"

As he gave utterance to these latter words, he threw his arms round her waist, and bore her, screaming, from the room. Darting from the house, he perceived that she had fainted away with terror; but in despite of this he made his way towards his horse, which he had fastened to a tree, intending to bear her off before anybody could come to her assistance. But there was a Power at hand that he little thought of; for just when he had arrived within a few feet of the tree, a terrific flash of lightning darted from a cloud overhead, and at the same instant the oak, which just before had been flourishing in all its pride, was riven into thousands of splinters. The same stroke, too, killed the noble steed which Lord Dalmeny was about to mount; and then laying his still insensible burden gently on the ground, he stood for a few moments gazing upon the ruin and destruction which a single instant had caused. From this reverie, however, he was aroused by approaching footsteps, and fearing to meet the reproaches of those whom he would have robbed of their dearest treasure, he hastily took his departure, muttering curses upon the chance that had so unexpectedly frustrated the evil design he had meditated.

Jessy was soon removed from the place where she had been left by the heartless libertine, and being conveyed to the cottage, the care and attention of her mother soon restored her once again to a recollection of all that had passed. She then recounted the conversation that had passed during her interview with Lord Dalmeny;—explaining the motives that induced him to compel her to accompany him, and earnestly imploring them, as they loved her, to take prompt means to prevent his evil designs against her from being carried into effect. But Jessy need not have given utterance to this request, for her brother had already vowed to have revenge for the insult offered to her, and the good dame herself had resolved never again to trust her out of her sight.

The story, with the awful incident that had occurred during the thunder-storm, was soon spread abroad; and when the company assembled at the ball, which was given in honour of the young lord's return, people whispered among themselves the terrible story, declaring that it was a visitation from Heaven to warn the libertine that his evil deeds did not pass unobserved.

CHAPTER IV.

"Let repentance
Reach thy proud heart ere it is too late—
Repent!—or tremble at thy doom!"—THE KNIGHT'S REVENGE.

THE event related in the last chapter occurred on the morning of that day when Lord Dalmeny and John Ruthven met at the Mermaid's Rock, and on the same evening the tenants and neighbours had been invited to a grand feast and ball which was given in honour of the young lord's return to the land of his birth. During his absence from home people had almost forgotten the wild extravagances that had marked his youthful career, and as hopes were entertained that he had reformed, few persons refused the invitation to greet him joyfully on his arrival. There was none, however, among the assembled guests, who had not heard of his narrow escape from the thunderbolt and the attempt he had made to carry off Jessy, but though the affair was whispered among themselves, the report was not suffered to reach the ears of the lord's mother, who, seated at the upper end of the ball-room, after the feast was over, enjoyed the exciting scene, and almost forgot the misfortunes that had nearly brought ruin on her ancient house.

John and his sister Effie were there among the numerous guests, but the former wore a gloomy and melancholy countenance, for Lord Dalmeny had been paying more attention to Effie than was agreeable to the brother, and he sat apart from the company, watching with anxious eyes the movements of the young libertine. Whilst he was thus moodily occupied Dame Brander approached, and laying her hand upon his shoulder, said, "How is this, Johnny Ruthven?—why are you so gloomy when all around is gaiety and joy?"

"I scarcely know, good dame," replied our hero, affecting a tone of indifference, "and yet I have strange thoughts and misgivings that weigh like lead upon my heart."

"I see—you like not these follies and excesses;—you have travelled much of late, John, and have returned a more steady man than you went forth from us."

"I wish it was so," answered the young man.

"What!—are you still the same reckless youth that you were before you left your mother's house to sail over the wide waste of water?"

"I am but little changed, I believe, dame," replied John. "It is true I may love my mother and my sister more than I did: long absence has made them dear to me; and now when I see Lord Dalmeny paying such marked attentions to Effie, I fear lest she may become the next victim of his libertine arts."

"Aye, aye," cried the old woman, "I saw your eyes were wandering in that direction; and, to speak truth, my own fears were roused by seeing the wolf crouched so near the lamb."

"Think you then," asked John, "that he would dare betray the sister of the man he calls his friend?"

"Lord Dalmeny cares little for friendship," answered the dame. "He seeks to make conquests among female hearts—nay, has succeeded in but too many instances, and what, therefore, is to prevent his making love to the innocent Effie, John?"

"A brother's vengeance!" exclaimed the young man fiercely.

"But he is a duellist—a skilful one, too, if report belies him not, and it would be madly seeking your own destruction to meet the like of him."

"And yet, in such a cause," answered John, "he would find in me an antagonist willingly courting death rather than live to be the witness of a sister's shame. But, perhaps, I have judged his motives too severely; Lord Dalmeny has little honour when women are concerned, yet I cannot believe he will be villain enough to seek the ruin of his foster brother's only sister."

"Do not trust him," whispered the old dame, drawing nearer to John; —"do not trust him, I say, for his plans are already formed, and Effie may fall into his snares whilst you are weakly trusting in his honour. I have made bold to speak thus plainly to you, John, because I see danger lurking in the maiden's path. Speak to her, man;—tell her not to listen to his honied words, but to remember how many have fallen under his seductive arts, and thus avoid a fate that will bring grief and heaviness of heart upon the remainder of her days. Ah! that angry frown tells me my words of caution have not been spoken in vain;—you will rouse yourself as a brother ought to do, when the sister of his heart's dearest affections is in peril, and Effie, John, may be saved from the evil practices of the spoiler."

"You speak confidently, good dame, of his designs against my sister; —what proof have you that his motives are treacherous?"

" From former conduct," answered Dame Brander; "have you forgotten the fate of Alice Roberts, who died when she found that he had betrayed her with false promises? or of poor Bertha, the pride of our hamlet, who was driven forth from house and home when her parents discovered that she had listened to the artful words of the fell destroyer? But why need I mention instances when the heartless deeds of Lord Dalmeny are known to every one?"

"It would indeed be vain to proceed further," exclaimed John; "yet, now I think of it, there is one whose cruel destiny I lament most bitterly. Poor May Grayson, whom I left a blithe, bonny girl, has been deceived by this libertine lord, and now wanders through the neighbourhood a wretched maniac!"

"Aye, she is indeed to be pitied," answered the old dame, "because she was virtuous enough to resist his arts until she was made to believe that she was his true and lawful wife."

"The villain!" muttered John.

"Ah! villain you may well call him," resumed Dame Brander; "for even her virtue was no protection when once he had made up his mind to effect his purpose. Many a time did he waylay her on her return home from the town, but May knew that he sought to betray her, and with scorn she bade him never to seek another interview. And what think you he did then?—Would you believe it, John?—he swore that his intentions were honourable;—that he would marry her, and proudly acknowledge her to the world as Lady Dalmeny. Well, all this dazzled and blinded her to his real pretensions; she consented to elope with him from her widowed mother's house, and ——"

"He basely broke his pledge!" interrupted John.

"He pretended to marry her," resumed the old woman, "and for some days she believed herself to be the happiest of wives. At length, however, the fatal truth was revealed;—the ceremony that united them had been performed by a hired villain who personated the priest; and when Lord Dalmeny himself confessed his cruel artifice, she awoke in horror from the dream she had been indulging in. From that moment poor May Grayson became a maniac."

"No wonder," exclaimed John, "that Heaven—as this morning happened—has aimed its lightnings at his guilty head!"

"Is he not a villain?" cried Dame Brander; "or can you wonder that I warned you to keep a strict guard over your sister, lest she should become the next victim of his hellish arts?—But see!—the dance is over and he leads her in triumph to a seat at the upper end of the hall."

John had listened eagerly to the words of the old woman, but never had he for an instant taken his eyes from the young lord, whose actions he so anxiously watched. Acting upon the impulse of the moment, he was about to approach the object of his suspicions, but ere he could do so Lord Dalmeny passed through an open door and left the festive scene. Determined, however, not to be thwarted, John quickly followed, and having overtaken him, exclaimed, with some agitation,—

"My lord, your freedom of behaviour towards my sister this night, fills me with uneasiness. The world gives you the character of being a libertine, and, therefore, I have made bold to tell you thus abruptly, that from this time forward your attentions will be considered injurious to her character."

"Why, John!" laughed his lordship, "you have turned moralist, it seems, all of a sudden."

"As the guardian of my sister's honour, it is necessary that I act with promptitude and decision," answered our hero. "I know your friendship

for myself will not restrain you from an act of perfidy towards a too-confiding girl, and, therefore, I warn you never again to speak to her."

"And what if the gentle Effie is less harsh in her opinion of me than her brother appears to be?"

"Effie knows you not as I do," answered John, "or she would shun the snare that has been laid for her. *She* believes you to be honourable, but *I* know you to be a villain!"

"Hah!—these are harsh words!"

"They are, my lord, but not more so than your conduct merits."

"Again!—am I to be insulted beneath my own roof?"

"If your lordship likes not my words, there is a ready way to resent them," answered John, haughtily.

"Humph! you expect, then, that I will stoop so low from my own rank as to meet you in single combat?"

"That, my lord," answered John, firmly, "will depend upon the conduct you mean to pursue. Consent never to see my sister again, and I will be satisfied."

"Truly this is a most moderate request of yours, sirrah!" exclaimed Lord Dalmeny, scornfully. "You ask me to turn coldly from your sister because, forsooth, some foolish notion or other has found its way into your head. But let it suffice that I am not to be dictated to in an affair like this. Your sister has a better opinion of my honour than you seem to have, and until she tells me my attentions are troublesome, I shall continue to cultivate an intimacy that I must confess affords me no little pleasure."

"It it in vain, my lord," answered John, "that you affect to carry this off so haughtily. I again declare you to be a villain, and if that term offends you there is a lonely spot near the Mermaid's Rock where we **may** settle our disputes without fear of interruption."

No. 4

"The place is suitable enough, no doubt," was the indifferent reply of his lordship, "and the only question is whether I should so far condescend as to meet a man who is in every respect so much my inferior."

"Your lordship may consider me beneath you," answered John, haughtily, "and yet, heap whatever reproaches you may upon me, you cannot say that I am the deliberate persecutor of women."

"Really, John," exclaimed the young nobleman, "you have grown quite a moralizer since it came into that wise head of yours to run away from your country."

"I was a mere boy when I ran away, as you call it," replied John; "nor should I have done so even then, had it not been that I knew how little favour I had to expect from you after the rupture that had taken place between us. I was aware that a degrading imprisonment would be the punishment inflicted upon me for daring to raise my hand against an insolent peer, and preferring a life of liberty to one of confinement, I submitted for a time to voluntary banishment."

"And during your absence," exclaimed Lord Dalmeny, tauntingly, "you have, if report speaks truly, been the associate of pirates."

"I am not bound to account to your lordship for the manner in which my time has been passed," answered John, whose lip quivered with rage at the insinuation that had been thrown out. "I have dwelt chiefly upon the broad ocean, roaming hither and thither at my will, and never shrinking, as your lordship does at this moment, from drawing my sword whenever there was occasion to assert my own honour."

"You believe, then," exclaimed Lord Dalmeny, "that I have refused your challenge through fear?"

"I do."

"In that case I will prove that you have judged me wrongfully," cried his lordship; "you have challenged me, John, and I will no longer shield myself under a privilege that I might have urged consistently. Turn thy steps, therefore, towards the Mermaid's Rock, and I will follow you there immediately."

"Why not go with me now?"

"Because I will give no ground for suspicion among my friends. We were seen to leave the room almost at the same moment, and should we be absent much longer, some officious fool or other would be coming to interrupt us. So away to the place you have named, John, and doubt not I will follow in the course of a few minutes."

Thus satisfied, our hero took his departure for the Mermaid's Rock, and at the same time Lord Dalmeny returned to the ball-room, joined in the next dance, and having quieted all suspicion by the ease and carelessness of his manners, again left the scene of festivity, for the purpose of keeping his appointment with John. What passed between them on that occasion has been already described in the foregoing pages, and the reader is by this time aware of the interruptions they experienced in the course of their encounter.

The night was wearing away fast when the young men returned to the Hall; the dancers began to flag in their exertions, and some of the elderly folks intimated that it was time they should separate and return to their homes. But the Lady Margaret Dalmeny was unwilling to let them separate until she had introduced the young lord to his tenantry and neighbours, and hoping to remove the unfavourable impression that she knew had been formed against him, she bade the visitors approach, and when all were gathered before her, she said, in a voice trembling with emotion—

"It is now many years, my friends, since first I entered this venerable mansion. I was then a bride—now I am an old woman, standing upon the verge of the grave : then I was young, wealthy, and envied—now years have crept upon me, the wealth of our family has been wasted, and few persons are, perhaps, less envied than she who now addresses you. Sorrow and grief have been my portion ; my husband perished in battle—my sons have gone to the tomb before their mother—and all that remains to sustain the honour of a once noble house now stands by my side. I speak to you, friends, of my Lord Dalmeny ; love him as you have respected me—look up to him as one far less criminal than his enemies would make you believe, and receive him among you as 'a man more sinned against than sinning.' Do this, my friends, and you will render happy the last hours of her who has, perhaps, but a brief space longer to live."

As she concluded, the old lady rose from her seat, and taking the arm of Lady Agnes, slowly left the hall. Upon many, her words had made a deep impression, and some even resolved to think better of the young lord until he gave them further cause to believe the thousand rumours that had been raised against him. But there were many Cameronians in the room who remembered the persecutions they and their fathers had endured under the lords of Dalmeny, and these men, stern as they were in their hate, were not to be appeased by the conciliating words of the Lady Margaret. They, however, remained silent whilst she was present, but no sooner had the doors closed upon her, than these men broke forth into muttered expressions of their wrath.

"She speaks of the misfortunes that have fallen upon her house," said one old man, "and who can wonder at it after the persecutions with which they have hunted down our faithful flock ? Have they not ever been the foes of the faithful, and shall Heaven spare them when its own good hour of retribution arrives ?"

"See," said another, "what a curse to the land the young Lord Dalmeny is likely to prove; his thoughts are given to women and loose pleasures, and who can doubt but that he will be the last of a line that has ever been a scourge to God's most faithful servants ?"

"Nay, be not too hard on the young man," exclaimed a third ; "he has been wild enough, no doubt, but he may yet turn from his wickedness and become a shining example to all those who have lost their way in the darkness of error."

"But what say you to the ruin and shame he has brought upon many an honest, well-meaning girl ?" demanded another.

"I say," replied an ancient dame, who had been eating and drinking so plentifully at the Hall, that she felt bound, out of gratitude, to say something in favour of the young man ; "I say that more than half the blame of their dishonour belongs to the wenches themselves. They must needs dress in all the fashion and trumpery of the day, apeing the manners of their betters, and at the same time learning some of the vices that such things always bring with them. Therefore I say it is the fault of the wenches themselves, and we have no right to find fault with his lordship for making free, when so many liberties are given. He is but mortal man, you know, and I, for one, am ready to give him credit for more good qualities than any of you seem inclined to allow him."

"Aye, aye, you are right enough there, my good dame," exclaimed Jonas Cargill, a jolly, happy-looking fellow, who had already been drinking pretty freely, but who thought it necessary to pour out another cup of wine to do honour to the toast he was about to propose. "The young Lord Dalmeny," he continued, "is a man after my own heart ; he can drink his liquor without flinching or hanging fire, and as for his loving the girls (bless their little hearts), why, so do I, and where's the harm of that, since they were made to be loved ?   So now, friends, fill your glasses, and drink with me in a bumper, the health of Lord Dalmeny."

This was a proposition so congenial to most of the persons present, that few were found to dissent from it ; there were some, however, who appeared not to relish the suggestion that had been thrown out, and great was the ire of Jonas Cargill when he found that there were dissentients in the company.   Indeed, to such a pitch had his wrath arisen, that he laid his huge hand upon the throat of the nearest Cameronian, and would have compelled obedience to his command by violence, had not Lord Dalmeny hastened forward to rescue the old man from his grasp.

"Shame on you, Jonas !" he exclaimed, angrily, "for seeking to make a broil where all has hitherto been harmony and peace.   The old man has reason, perhaps, for what he does, and we who like freedom ourselves should be the last to force our own opinions upon another."

"Well," cried Jonas, "if your lordship wishes it, there's an end of the affair ; and yet, to my thinking, it is hardly to be borne that a man should come and partake the hospitality of your table and yet refuse to utter a good wish in favour of the owner of the house."

"I will not drink the toast," said the old man, as he saw Lord Dalmeny retiring to the further end of the hall.   "What matters it that we have been entertained at his board ?   Have we not been brought together to try whether our good opinions are to be purchased by his viands and strong drinks, and shall we sell our consciences for the sake of meeting favour from the descendant of our persecutors ?"

"We will not !" murmured several of the sect to which he belonged, and who were equally uncompromising with himself.

"He belongs to an evil race," continued the first speaker, "and, therefore, it would be sinful were we to hold further communication with him. Did not his ancestors persecute us even to the very dust, and shall we now hold out the wand of peace when our hearts hold him in utter hatred ?   I, for one, denounce him as a son of Belial, and bid him beware of the wrath that ere long must fall upon him !"

"Did the young lord himself ever harm you ?" demanded Jonas.

"I care not whether he has or not," answered the Cameronian.   "All I wish to remember is, that our people have been hunted from their homes to the mountains and the caves like wild beasts.   Soldiers have been sent out by the enemies of the Covenant, to destroy us with fire and sword ; our hold places have been levelled with the dust, our altars desecrated, and ourselves compelled to worship with no roof above us except the blue vault of Heaven.   The persecutions we have endured are not yet forgotten ; they live in our memories as if engraven there on brass, and woe unto the Cameronian who forgives the enemies that have driven him and his people to such direful extremities !"

"Why, thou canting hypocrite !" exclaimed Jonas, "if I were only in this young lord's place but for a single day, I would prove that I had inherited the enmity of my ancestors by giving thee all up to the fury of my people.   I would teach thee what it is to flout a lord in his own castle."

"Friend," answered the Cameronian, meekly, "we have been used to persecution, and can endure more of it if it should be the will of Heaven to punish us for our offences.   Thou believest thyself privileged to trample on thy weaker brethren, and we, well knowing that it would be vain to resist the unrighteous, do yield with all humility.   But a time will yet come," he added, with more energy—"a time will come, I say, when the lowly shall be exalted, and the proud man be brought down, even with the very dust that he trampleth beneath his feet."

"If I thought that was a threat, sirrah," exclaimed Jonas, "I would so clip thy tongue that thou shouldst never swagger more about what thou hast endured, or what thou wilt do if ever thou and thy sleek-haired brethren had the power."

"I addressed myself not to thee, man of sin!" retorted the Cameronian, unmoved by the violence that began to manifest itself in the language of his antagonist. "I speak rather to the young Lord Dalmeny, who has sinned grievously, and, therefore, must endure much torment."

"And why should you trouble your head about me, my friend?" asked the young nobleman, who had approached during the latter part of the conversation; "I never harmed thee that I know of, neither—to speak the truth—was I aware before that there was such a person in existence."

"Thou mayst know more of me, though, ere long," answered the other.

"I may so," replied Lord Dalmeny, laughing; "and yet, allow me to add, I am by no means desirous of extending my acquaintance in such a quarter."

"But it may happen that thou canst not help it."

"At any rate, I shall not seek to do so," answered his lordship. "We have met to-day through the courtesy of the Lady Margaret Dalmeny, who was unwilling to exclude any one from the fête she thought proper to give on what she is pleased to call my happy return to England, and as this house is not usually open to Cameronians, it is probable that this will be our last and only meeting in this world."

"Wilt thou still continue to pursue the footsteps of thy forefathers?" demanded the old man—"wilt thou, I say, hunt us out from our secret places in the wilderness as thine ancestors have done before thee?"

"That will depend upon thine own conduct," replied Lord Dalmeny; "thy people have arrayed themselves against all who subscribe not to their doctrines; they have even taken up arms for the maintenance of their cause, and we who differ from thee have been compelled to resort to violence. What we have done has been from no hatred either to the Cameronians or their peculiar views, but merely to repress what we conceive to be open and direct rebellion."

"We fight for the Covenant."

"And we for the laws."

"And, between ourselves," interposed Jonas Cargill, "I have a shrewd notion that the laws will prove an awkward customer for this Covenant you speak of. And so now, old gentleman, the sooner you leave this house with your friends, the better it will be for all parties."

"Leave us, old man," exclaimed Lord Dalmeny; "go whilst there is yet peace between us, for should a quarrel arise, I know not where it would end, seeing there are many of both parties assembled here."

"Ere I go," answered the sturdy Cameronian, "let me exhort thee to repentance. Remember, thou hast sins out of number to atone for, and the day of thy death may not be far off. Ask mercy where alone thou canst hope to find it, and perhaps the gate of Heaven may yet be open to thee—repent, I say unto thee—repent—repent!"

With these words the old man stalked solemnly out of the hall, and was quickly afterwards followed by the remainder of the Cameronians. It was in vain that Lord Dalmeny endeavoured to laugh the affair off as a matter that gave him very little concern. It was evident to every one that he felt uneasy at the words that had been addressed to him, and when he perceived the impression that went so strong against him, he took off his richly-plumed and jewelled cap, and addressed himself to the company—

" My friends," he said, "let not the words of that madman give you any uneasiness on my account. That I might have lived a careless, reckless life all of you have, no doubt, heard. That, however, belongs to the past, and the future shall prove that every bad beginning must not necessarily have a bad ending. I have much to do to repair the dilapidations into which the affairs of my family have fallen; this will occupy much of my time, and when matters have once more been put straight, I shall begin to think of taking unto myself a wife, and then my course will run more smoothly than it has hitherto done. So you see I begin to think seriously of the future, and, therefore, I must crave of you all to bear as lightly as you can upon the past. And now, friends, as you are about to separate, I invite you all here to-morrow night, when an entertainment will be provided that I hope will afford satisfaction, and at the same time convince you that I am sincere in my desire for reformation."

Upon this, all retired to their homes, leaving Lord Dalmeny to his own reflections on the many and singular events of the day.

CHAPTER V.

" But a tempest will rise with a mighty sound,
    And the highest stone shall be hurled to the ground.
    When this comes to pass let the owner fear,
    For the fall of Dalmeny will then be near.'—ANCIENT LEGEND.

ON the morrow came many visitors to the Castle of Dalmeny, for the young lord was known to be a hospitable host, and it would have been almost an insult to have been absent after he had so freely invited them to be partakers of his entertainment. At the hour appointed, therfore, the guests began to arrive, who, upon being ushered into the great hall, disco-vered that the upper end of it had been slightly raised, and that, by means of drapery, it was converted into a sort of stage, such as are used for dra-matic performances. This was looked upon rather unfavourably by some of those who were rather strict in their religious notions, but their fears were silenced by the less austere, who seeing no harm in relaxing a little bit now and then, men who could see no great evil in amusement, so long as no vice was mixed with it, and who were willing to give Lord Dal-meny credit for good intentions in the present instance, till the result of the entertainment he had prepared might prove that they were mistaken in him.

Thus silenced, the conversation took a different turn, and Lord Dal-meny and his follies were almost forgotten, when the curtain was drawn up, and there were discovered a number of persons seated, representing so many elders of the kirk, and in the midst of whom, elevated on a higher seat, was another personage of grave and venerable appearance, who might be taken for the preacher. The whole, indeed, was intended to represent a field meeting of the Cameronians assembled together to pass a heavy cen-sure upon an erring member of their society. A little on one side, indeed, might be seen an elderly man standing upon a stool of repentance; his eyes cast down towards the earth, and his whole demeanour expressing the shame he felt at the situation in which he was placed. So far the affair was well enough acted, though it must be confessed there were many among the spectators of this scene who looked upon it as a sinful mockery, and one that was likely enough to call down the anger of Heaven upon all who had lent it their countenance and support. But there was not much time for expressing their opinions upon the matter, for almost as soon as the curtain drew up, the supposed preacher thus addressed himself to the imaginary culprit :—

"Jeremiah Hewitson, you have been guilty of many crimes and misdemeanours against the strict rules and regulations that have been laid down by those who would lead a godly and a holy life. You are old enough to see the error of your ways, and yet hath your heart yearned towards the vain and giddy of the other sex, some of whom you have despoiled of their innocence, whereby great shame hath fallen upon the land. As an erring son of the covenant, it is fitting you should receive admonition from the elders, and, therefore, have we condemned you to take your place on the stool of repentance, hoping that the admonishing we shall give you, and the disgraceful situation in which you have put yourself, will work in your favour, so that you may confess the heinousness of your faults, and leave this place under a promise to sin no more."

"And suppose," asked the culprit, "I should not feel inclined to make any such promise?"

"In that case," replied the preacher, "it will be my painful duty to hurl upon you the thunders of the wrath to come! But I will think better of you, Jeremiah Hewitson, than to believe you are so lost a sinner."

"Of what do my sins consist?" demanded Jeremiah.

"In many things, but chiefly, as I have before said, in your libertine love of women."

"And is that any fault of mine?" asked the culprit; "am I to blame if my heart takes fire at the sight of a pretty female? Are they not formed for love, and where is the man that can stand coldly looking on when the laughing eye of some fair damsel warms his bosom and excites his admiration? I, for one, never tried to wrestle with myself, nor do I believe that even you who come here to reprove me, would be proof against the fascinations of the gentler sex."

"That is a question," replied the preacher, "that cannot be entertained at present; we are here to reprove the sinfulness of an erring brother, and the business we are engaged in must not be disturbed by this lightness of speech. If evil is engrafted in you, then is my labour thrown away; but if you have power to wrestle with the fiend of pollution, I call upon you to renounce your wickedness, and by your example to become a shining light to those who, like yourself, are prone to sin."

"If I have committed a fault," replied the culprit, "the punishment will be my own; but as I do not yet see that I have done harm, I must beg of you to point out more clearly in what way I have offended."

"Your example has proved most pernicious," answered the preacher; "look, for instance, at the Lord Dalmeny, has he not already made himself the terror of the whole neighbourhood?—do not the maidens shun him as they would a pestilence, and do not mothers dread his approach, well knowing that he comes only to destroy?"

"Am I to answer for the crimes of Lord Dalmeny?" demanded the other; "because he sins am I to be called to account for it, as if it was impossible a great man can commit folly without having an example placed before his eyes? Methinks his lordship would think it no great honour were he to hear you lay all his faults to a weakness of which he would be ashamed."

"Lord Dalmeny is one of the great ones of the land," exclaimed the preacher; "yet he must beware, for the time may not be far distant when he will have to answer for the evil deeds he has committed."

"If you have cause of complaint against the nobleman," cried Jeremiah

Hewitson, " why not summon him before you as you have me ?   The stool of repentance would suit him as well as it does me ; and far better, perhaps, seeing that he ought to set us all a good example in morality."

The preacher was about to reply to this, but scarcely had he commenced, when a great bustle took place in the lower part of the hall, and immediately an old man was seen forcing his way through the crowd, who, leaping upon the stage, was at once recognized as David Cornie, the minister. To all who knew him, it was evident that the worthy pastor was incensed at the mockery that had been going on, and if any doubt had remained upon the matter, it would have been removed when the usually docile David laid his hands upon the man who was playing the part of the accused, to whom he administered so sound a shaking, that his stage attire fell off, and discovered the well-known form of Lord Dalmeny himself.   Hereupon some of the audience set up a loud laugh of delight, whilst others, who belonged to a graver class, turned up their hands and eyes, groaning for the profligacy of the young nobleman.   As for David Cornie, the poor man seemed utterly confounded at the awkward predicament in which he had placed himself, but probably thinking it would be better to carry the affair off with a high hand, he said with great severity :—

" How is this, my lord ? Is it the noble owner of this domain who has been a chief actor in a scene intended to bring the usages of our religion into contempt ?"

" Your eyes have not deceived you, worthy sir," answered Lord Dalmeny, who could not restrain his laughter at the singular termination of his dramatic entertainment.   " It is, indeed, the owner of Dalmeny Castle, that you have treated so unceremoniously, and he takes this opportunity to thank you for the friendly zeal that prompted you to give him so hearty a shaking by way of admonishing him of the heinous crime he had committed in seeking to entertain a few of his friends."

David was about to reply to this, but ere he could do so, a storm that had been threatening, burst over the castle with startling violence. The lightning now became incessant, and the pealing thunder roared awfully above, each crash being prolonged and echoed among the rocks and cliffs that surrounded the ancient edifice on every side.   To the superstitious, it appeared as if the venerable pastor had come upon the wings of the tempest; the seats were torn up and scattered about ; the stage and its trappings were quickly demolished, and further mischief would perhaps have been done, had not the minister interposed to arrest the progress of their wrath.

" Stay," he exclaimed ; " and do not vent your anger in a way that will be useless.   I am here to rebuke the sinner in the midst of his wickedness, and let no man seek to take upon himself that which belongs to the duty of his pastor.   And you, my lord," he continued, addressing himself to the young nobleman, " what excuse have you to make for exhibiting this entertainment which was produced for no other purpose than to bring contempt upon our holy religion ?"

" I have no excuse to offer," replied Lord Dalmeny ; " and even if I had, they would not be made to a man who has no right to question my actions. What I have done was for my own pleasure, and it is now my turn to ask what excuse *you* can offer for thus interrupting us ?"

" It is my duty to do so," answered the pastor ; " I have the ministry to perform in this parish, and I should be lacking in zeal were I to suffer these abominations to take place without endeavouring to prevent them. You have my answer, Lord Dalmeny, and let it suffice you, that I have done no more than a servant should do for his lord and master."

" You have exceeded your duty, sir," exclaimed the nobleman, haughtily ;

"this is my castle; I invited friends to meet me, and I have yet to learn by what right you thrust yourself into my presence to denounce an entertainment merely because you think it dangerous to your religion."

"It is not in this affair only that I have to complain of you," answered David Cornie; "your conduct has already rendered you a terror in the neighbourhood; innocent maidens have fallen through your unworthy artifices, and if these crimes are suffered to go on without rebuke, who but myself will have to answer before high Heaven for the consequences?"

"And what," demanded his lordship, "has a meddling priest to do with my actions? Can I not be lord and master here, or must I stoop and cringe like a whipped schoolboy before the pedagogue who has corrected him with the scourge?"

"My right to interfere," replied the priest, "consists in the duty I owe those over whom I have been placed as a shepherd. The people constitute my flock, and if a wolf breaks in among them, it is my part to preserve them from his attacks. Such is my answer, Lord Dalmeny, and my only desire is that you know your duty as well as I know mine."

"Am I not to be safe in my own castle?"

"Aye, for if you confine yourself to those limits, the danger cannot be very great."

"But suppose it is true that I have loved a few of the fair maidens in this neighbourhood; is it not a privilege given to me by my station in life, and shall I permit my pleasures to be interfered with because they happen not to meet the approbation of an over-zealous priest?"

"I have never interfered, my lord, till now," replied the minister; "at length, however, the complaints of mothers lamenting the fall of their daughters, have roused me to make an effort in their behalf. I came hither to remonstrate with you, when the scene of mummery that was just now

No. 5

going on met my view, and feeling that an insult was intended to the holy religion of which I am a minister, I took means to suppress the wickedness even at the hazard of your displeasure."

"The eagle can feel nothing but contempt for the worthless sparrow," replied his lordship, haughtily.

"Your sneers are without the desired effect," answered the minister, calmly. "I expected nothing else from your lordship, and therefore can endure them without anger. I came to warn you that the vengeance of Heaven will fall upon you, unless my words should bring you to repentance, and the voice of Heaven is even now sounding in your ears as if to second the efforts I would make to bring you to repentance."

"I have witnessed many a tempest as violent as this is," answered Lord Dalmeny, "and yet it has had no more effect upen me than your words are likely to have."

"I would at least entreat you," exclaimed the pastor, "to spare the innocent maidens, and not to draw them into the same gulf of ruin that awaits yourself."

"You may spare yourself the trouble of interceding in their behalf," answered Lord Dalmeny; "the wenches are not so unhappy as you would make them appear, nor is there one that would come before my face and reproach me as you have dared to do."

Scarcely had Lord Dalmeny done speaking, when a buzz was heard spreading itself through the hall, and a female making her way through the throng, stepped over the broken benches that lay scattered about, and placed herself upon the stool of repentance that, in mockery, had a short time previously been occupied by the youthful lord of the castle. It was May Grayson, one of the victims of the licentious nobleman, and the wildness of her eye betrayed the utter wreck that had shattered and disturbed her mind. The pastor immediately perceived the heart-broken girl, and pointing her out to the libertine, he said :—

"You see, my lord, you were mistaken, for yonder stands one who affords a sad proof of the heartlessness with which you pursue your pleasures. It is May Grayson, once the happiest of our village lasses, but what she is I leave it for your lordship to answer."

"This is some trick to annoy me!" exclaimed his lordship furiously; "the wench has been brought hither to throw a damp upon the evening's entertainment."

"She has not been brought here by me," answered David Cornie, "nor do I believe any one else has had a hand in her appearance here at this moment."

"May," exclaimed Lord Dalmeny, sharply, "why are you here? Why do you come unbidden where your presence was not desired?"

"I heard that the minister had come," she replied mildly, "and knowing that he hates vice and depravity, I come to hear what he would say to your lordship. Nor am I without sin myself, so I have taken my place upon the stool of repentance, and as there are many present to here me rated and scolded for my weakness in listening to the words of a seducer, I thought the public shame might scare other girls from falling, as I have done, through too much confidence."

"Can you hear her unmoved, my lord?" demanded David Cornie; "despair has overturned her reason, and who has she to thank for all this but the man who deceived her with false words, and then left her to become the prey of horror and remorse?"

"Let her repent, then," exclaimed the young libertine; "let her repent, I say, and her sins are not so great but they will find forgiveness."

"I do—I do repent!" cried May Grayson in a tone of touching sorrow;

" day and night—day and night do I bitterly repent the faith I placed in one whose falsehood has made me what I am. But oh, you know not how heavily the curse of sin hangs upon my soul;—it weighs me down, and the only consolation I can look forward to is to be found in the dark, cold grave."

"Do you hear her, my lord?" demanded the pastor, "and if you are not deaf to her words, do they not pierce your heart like poisoned arrows?"

"Why am I to be thus questioned?" exclaimed Lord Dalmeny. "Is it not enough that I am to be troubled with the presence of that woman, but that you also must seek to make me a mark of scorn to my assembled tenantry and friends?"

As he uttered these words, his lordship turned angrily away, and pacing up and down, he listened with a feeling of dread that he had never experienced before to the howling tempest which had lately increased to a state of fearful violence. At that moment, too, he recollected an ancient prediction that had been related to him in his childhood, and which foretold the future fall of his once powerful family. The legend ran to the following effect :—

> " The house of Dalmeny was founded in shame,
> Bloodshed and crime have defiled its high name;
> But a tempest will rise with a m·ghty sound,
> And the highest stone shall be hurled to the ground;
> When this comes to pass let the owner fear,
> For the fall of Dalmeny will then be near."

The highest stone alluded to in the above doggrel was a huge piece of granite, upon which the credulous believed they could trace a number of cabalistic characters. Various stories were current upon the subject, but the one which obtained most credit was as follows :—

The founder of the family of Dalmeny was a warrior more remarkable for his prowess in battle than for any good qualities in private life. On one occasion, it is said, he was engaged in single combat with a rival baron, and was in some danger of falling beneath the sword of his adversary, when the stone of which we have been speaking, was hurled down by some unseen power, and the enemy of Lord Dalmeny was crushed to death. Upon recovering himself, the survivor discovered a huge raven, sitting upon the stone, and as the bird seemed to be tame, he captured and took it home to his castle. In a few days afterwards, he dispatched some of his followers, who, with some difficulty, removed the ponderous stone, and raised it to the highest point on the central tower. Upon this pinnacle, it was said, the raven continued to roost for two or three centuries, but upon some crime being committed by a descendant of the first lord the bird quitted the place and never was seen again. A stone representative, was, however, erected in its stead, but this, in turn, disappeared most miraculously, giving rise to many strange rumours and reports. But the stone which had served as a pedestal, still remained in its former position, and it was this that the legend, previously quoted, related to.

It was the thought of this tradition that disturbed the young Lord Dalmeny on the night in question, and though seldom given to superstitious fears, he could not help feeling a dread, lest the hour foretold as that which would bring destruction on his house was at hand. With a quailing heart, he paced feversh up and down, now looking at the vivid lightnings as they shot across the windows, and now muttering to himself :—

"This surely is the tempest that shall remove from my castle the highest stone, and thus bring about the fulfilment of the fatal prophecy! I feel that the hand of destiny is upon me, and that not man only, but Heaven also stretches forth its right arm to crush and ruin me!"

Whilst thus speaking, a flash of lightning more intensely vivid than any that had preceded it, burst from the clouds, and almost before the glare had passed away, it was followed by a peal of thunder, so loud and violent, that the ancient castle seemed to rock even to its very foundations. At the same instant too, a noise was heard as if some heavy substance had fallen, and at once conjecturing that the prophecy had been accomplished, he rushed out of the hall, and passing through the corridor, hastened to the base of the tower. There he beheld the fulfilment of his worst fears — the raven-stone was lying half embedded in the court-yard, and thus it appeared to the bewildered Lord Dalmeny that the fatal hour of his downfall had at length arrived. Distracted by these fears, he would have rushed from the place, but at that instant he was arrested by the voice of Ronald, one of his attendants.

"And so it seems, my lord," he said, "that the prophecy has come to pass, after all! Here lies the raven-stone, and we shall now see whether the other part of it comes true or not."

"What other part?" demanded Dalmeny gloomily.

"Why those lines that say the fall of the Dalmeny family will be near when the raven-stone takes its flight from the place where it has stood so many centuries. For my own part, I never gave much heed to the doggrel, but sure enough some of it has spoken truly, and I only pray Heaven that the rest may not follow."

"This is the mere effect of accident," exclaimed Lord Dalmeny; "the lightning naturally struck the highest part of the building, and, therefore, the prophecy you speak of has nothing at all to do with it."

"Aye, but what a flash it was," answered Ronald; "I chanced to be looking up towards the raven-stone at the very moment it was struck. The whole tower seemed to be wrapped in flames, in the midst of which I fancied I could see all sorts of grim demons dancing, and making a sport of the ruin that was made. Oh! my lord,—my heart sank within me at the sight, and I should have run away, but I saw you rush to the place, and then I followed, to hear what you think of an event that I must needs confess fills me with alarm."

"There is no occasion for alarm," answered Lord Dalmeny; "the removal of this stone is the effect of accident, and with the assistance of a few stout fellows, it may be replaced in its former situation."

"That will not be so easily done as your lordship thinks," exclaimed Ronald, "the stone has been shattered in its fall, and no skill will ever serve to place it again on the top of the tower, where it has withstood so many tempests."

"The attempt must be made, at any rate," answered Lord Dalmeny, "or the superstitious fears of the people will be excited, and the matter will become the subject of conversation throughout the neighbourhood. Do you, therefore, make light of it, and tell them that, as an accident, it cannot be accounted any part of the prophecy relating to the downfall of my family."

"I'll do your lordship's bidding, certainly," replied the man; "but people are not to be so easily deceived when once they have taken a notion into their head."

Disconcerted at the events that had taken place, Lord Dalmeny moved away, and passing round the castle, gazed upon every part, which was now illumined by the moonlight, to see whether any further mischief had been done. All, however, remained perfect, except that part to which the legend belonged, and marvelling at the apparent fulfilment of the prophecy, he returned to the place from whence the had set out. Ronald was still there in nearly the same position that he had left him. Again the young lord gazed upon the raven-stone, and stooping down to touch it, he started back with alarm, exclaiming :—

"What means this, Ronald?—the stone is as soft as a piece of clay, and thus is taken from me the hope I had of replacing it on the summit of the tower!"

"Aye, aye, my lord," answered Ronald, "there's no disguising the truth of the matter; this is the devil's own doings, and say as you will, one part of the prophecy at last has been fulfilled. The highest stone has been hurled from your castle, and may Heaven preserve you from the remainder of the prediction!"

Lord Dalmeny heard not these words, for his thoughts were occupied in the destiny that seemed to await him, and turning aside, he once more returned to the hall, where he found all his assembled guests kneeling upon the floor, whilst David Cornie, the pastor, was offering up a thanksgiving to Heaven, for the mercy that had been extended to them. The young lord stood a silent spectator of this scene, until the minister rising from his knees, laid hold of such part of the scenery as yet remained in its place, and hurling it to the ground, said :—

"Thus perish the vain gaudes that man has erected for the gratification of his senses. They were put up for show and ostentation, but the voice of Heaven hath been heard in its terrible wrath, and it is time that man should think of the wrath to come!"

"Away from beneath my roof, thou contemner of other men's deeds!" exclaimed Lord Dalmeny, rushing forward, and confronting the pastor; "thou hast come here to excite my guests against their lord, and it is time that I should drive thee from my castle, as a pest that is no longer to be endured with patience."

"Thou art over wrathful, my lord."

"I have suffered thine insolence too long," interrupted Lord Dalmeny, "and it is now my will that thou shouldst instantly quit my roof. Out, I say, or forgetting thy sacred profession, I lay my hand upon thy throat, and thrust thee forth as I would a dog!"

"Thou forgettest the great mercy that has been shown to thee," answered the minister, coldly ;—"the highest stone of thy castle has been levelled with the dust by the mighty power of Heaven, and yet thou— sinner that thou art, hast escaped the vengeance thou hast merited."

"How much longer am I to endure this insolence?" cried Lord Dalmeny, whose rage had been excited to the highest pitch.

"Till I have convinced thee of the evil of thy ways," answered David Cornie ; "when thou dost assure me that thou art penitent, I will leave thee, in the hopes that my words have not been uttered in vain."

"They are uttered to one who heeds them not," answered Lord Dalmeny, angrily.

"Then thou art lost, and but a brief space of time is allowed thee in this world."

"Priest! I will hear no more of this!" exclaimed the young nobleman, incensed at the pertinacity of his assailant; and he was preparing to rush upon the pastor, when one of the spectators springing with a single bound between them, said :—

"My lord! my lord! check this unseemly wrath, I beseech you. Remember the sacred character of the man you would commit violence upon, and let not your hands commit an act which, in cooler moments, you would most bitterly repent. You are both wrong for thus embroiling yourselves, yet I cannot stand passively by and see a minister of the gospel placed in jeopardy of his life."

"Leave us to ourselves, John," exclaimed Lord Dalmeny, angrily ;— "leave us to ourselves, I say, and I will teach this meddling priest henceforth the duty he owes his superiors. We are both of us far above you in station, sirrah, yet have you dared to interpose between us, as if we could not settle a quarrel without the insolent intrusion of one who has no authority to urge in his behalf."

"I sought but to prevent violence, my lord," answered John Ruthven, " and I shall still remain firm to my purpose, even at the risk of offending the man who is ever taunting me with the difference of our station in life."

" Peasant slave, I will hear no more!" cried Lord Dalmeny; " begone, I say, and let me never more behold the countenance of one who can claim no higher parentage than that of being the son of my father's menial."

"Yet the son of your father's menial will ere long rise to eminence, whilst you, my lord, are hurled from the high place you at present maintain," answered John. " This is no idle boast, my Lord Dalmeny, for the day is not far distant when I shall be as much above you as you happen at this moment to be above me. My name is yet to be made, but I have a heart to accomplish great deeds, and ere I die, John Ruthven shall be counted among the great men of his time."

Lord Dalmeny's rage now grew to the highest pitch, and turning all his vengeance from the pastor to his humble dependant, he would have sprang upon him like an enfuriated tiger upon his prey, had it not been for the arrival of the Lady Margaret Dalmeny, who at that moment entered the hall, and whose venerable appearance cowed even the haughty spirit of her grandson.

"How is this?" she exclaimed, with terror;—" why do I behold this anger, when I had hoped that you had all met together in peace? Speak, David Cornie, for from you at least I expect to hear the truth of this disgraceful outrage."

" My lady," answered the pastor, " the fault rests upon your grandson; he has made a mockery of the religion I am commissioned to teach, and impelled by the duty I owe to my sacred calling, I boldly put myself forward to stop the mummery I could no longer endure with patience. This drew forth the anger of my Lord Dalmeny, and he would have struck me to the floor of his own hall, had it not been for the interference of this young man."

" You have done wrong, sir, in interfering without just cause," cried her ladyship, whose partiality for her grandson blinded her to his faults. " Lord Dalmeny invited friends to meet him; the entertainment he had prepared for them was by no means an uncommon one, and, therefore, though I cannot uphold him for his violence towards a minister of the gospel, yet must I say the mischief was entirely of your own seeking."

" Do you forget my duty, Lady Margaret ——

" You seem to have forgotten it in your own zeal, for what you conceive to be the interest of your religion," interrupted the lady. " But it is ever thus, priests interfere where they have no business, and thus have they brought upon themselves and the church the odium of people who would otherwise have been well disposed towards it. I have been upon my knees at prayer during the whole continuance of the terrible tempest that has but just passed away, and I must needs say that had you been occupied in a like manner, it would have been more creditable to yourself, and the tumult that has taken place would never have occurred."

" Your ladyship," exclaimed the pastor, " is angry with me?"

" I was," replied Lady Margaret, " but my anger is now lulled, even as is the storm, that but a brief time since shook these ancient walls to their foundation. We are now friends, David Cornie, and as I have much to say. come with me to my closet, where we will confer together on weighty matters, in which I have much need of thy counsel and advice."

Upon this the pastor followed her ladyship from the hall, and as they disappeared, Ronald, who had been watching his opportunity, stepped forward, and whispered a few words in the ear of his master. The words seemed to afford the young nobleman some satisfaction, for he smiled exultingly, and turning to John, held out his hand.

"It is time," he said, "that the foolish quarrel between us should cease; I will acknowlege it was wrong to taunt you in the manner I did, but if you are not of a more unforgiving disposition than I imagine, you will take my hand, and think no more of the past."

Satisfied with this apology, John took the hand of his lordship, and warmly pressed it.

"It must be confessed," he said, "that I did feel your taunts most severely, yet has my anger disappeared even more suddenly than it was excited. We are now friends again, my lord, and it will be your own fault if ever we disagree again."

"That's well said, John," exclaimed Lord Dalmeny; "and now I have a secret to intrust you with. Ronald tells me one of the fair maidens of this neighbourhood has consented to favour me with a private interview. I must away instantly, and as the company must not be suffered to depart at present, for fear we should be disturbed, I must beg of you to remain here as my substitute; ply them well with wine and ale, and I'll warrant you they will not think of stirring for the next two hours."

"Lady Margaret," observed Ronald, "has given orders for every one to depart without further delay. It seems she fears another disturbance may take place, and acting upon the advice of the pastor, she has directed the hall to be cleared, and the doors to be closed immediately."

"Well, her ladyship must be humoured, I suppose," replied the young man, after a moment's reflection; "let the guests depart, but see that David Cornie is delayed here as long as possible, for he is a terrible marplot in love affairs, and should he chance to hear of my interview with this maiden, I might chance to be called in reality to take my place on the stool of repentance."

"I will do my best to detain him," answered Ronald; "but he is now closeted with your lady mother, and I'm almost afraid there will be a small chance of my getting within ear-shot of him."

"My lord," exclaimed John, "there is one question I would ask of you."

"Let me know what it is," returned the other, "and if there is no great reason against it, I will answer the question."

"By your own acknowledgment, you are going to meet a female who is to give you an interview unknown to her friends?"

"I am indeed."

"May I ask the name of the maiden?"

"Why, that is rather an awkward question, John; but since you seem anxious upon the subject, I will so far relieve your fears as to declare that it is no one in whom you feel the least interest."

"It is not my sister Effie?"

"Certainly not."

"That," exclaimed John, "is some relief to me; and yet there are many other lasses in this neighbourhood who I should be sorry to see become the victims of your licentious love."

"Now you are going to moralize, John," cried Lord Dalmeny. "Hang it, man! let it suffice you to look after your own affairs; and since I tell you that your sister is safe, let me enjoy my triumph in peace, and I will give you my word never to interfere with your pleasures as long as I live."

"My pleasures and your's, my lord," answered John Ruthven, "are so different, that there is little fear of our ever clashing. You love women—I the busier scenes of life. You are for domestic joys—I would plough my way across stormy oceans, and win fame and honour in battle and strife."

"Well," answered Lord Dalmeny, "every man, say I, to his own humours. Not, however, that I altogether dislike the sort of life that you appear to have chalked out for yourself; there is something exhilarating in the idea of winning a fair name, and should England ever need my services, I shall not be backward in giving my trifling aid towards her support. I can fight when there is need for it, but hang me if I feel inclined to draw my sword unless it should appear that my country is likely to get the worst of it in a conflict with her enemies."

"And which service would your lordship choose—the army or the navy?"

"The navy, by all means."

"In that case, we may meet upon the bosom of the element I love so well."

"Perhaps so," replied Lord Dalmeny, observing with some surprise the peculiar tones in which these words were uttered. Affecting, however, not to have noticed them, he continued, with his usual gaiety—"You seem rather thoughtful to-night, John, and as I am in no humour to keep a pretty girl waiting, I shall bid you farewell, and hasten to keep my appointment with my bonnie Agnes Foster."

As he said this, the young lord bounded merrily from the hall on his errand of love.

CHAPTER VI.

" Mark the fierce lustre of his rolling eye,
The short, quick step—the pale and haggard cheek—
Do not those looks betoken him a villain?"—OLD PLAY.

ALMOST immediately after the departure of Lord Dalmeny from the castle, John Ruthven left the place which was now fast clearing of the numerous guests who had lately thronged it, and pausing for a few moments, uncertain what course to pursue, he at length directed his steps slowly towards home.

The cottage inhabited by the widow Ruthven was situated in a retired glen at no great distance from the castle, and so strictly did she seclude herself from her neighbours, that few ever cared to visit her in her lonely retreat. Her daughter Effie was, indeed, almost the only person she ever had to converse with, for her son, John Ruthven (or Red Ruthven, as he was afterwards called), spent the greater part of his time at sea, whither his own inclination had led him some years since.

It was on the evening of the day to which our story belongs, that the widow Ruthven was seated by her own snug fire-side; her thoughts wandering to the past, and occasionally endeavouring to penetrate the misty future. She would gladly have known what would be the fate of her children, but this was a revelation that it was in vain to seek, and rousing from the uneasy reverie into which she had fallen, she turned her gaze upon her daughter Effie, who was knitting at no great distance from her. The maiden observed her uneasiness, and at length dropping the work into her lap, she anxiously asked what was the matter with her mother.

"Nothing, dear Effie," replied the widow, with hesitation; "nothing ails

me, child; but I should be glad to hear your brother's footsteps, for he has been long absent, and I fear lest some accident may have befallen him."

"I have been thinking of the same thing," answered Effie, with a sigh. "I like not his being so frequently with Lord Dalmeny, for there is a fiend-like nature within the bosom of that young lord that I fear will some day burst forth to the destruction of my brother."

"Nay, you think too harshly of Lord Dalmeny," exclaimed the dame; "remember, child, he is the descendant of a noble family, whom our ancestors have followed for many generations. The present lord, it is true, has the character of being a heartless libertine; but he is yet young, and, therefore, I hope it is possible he will reform, and become all that his best friends could wish."

"But my brother is in danger from him," cried Effie.

"John Ruthven need not fear him," answered the widow, "for he has a bold spirit, and can protect himself if there should be need for it."

"My brother possesses far more nobility of soul than does he who boasts of being his superior," exclaimed Effie. "He is brave, and is ever foremost in the moment of peril, whilst Lord Dalmeny keeps aloof, as if fearful of venturing his life, even for the performance of a noble deed."

"Would that my son had less of the daring spirit you speak of," said the widow, "for I fear he will have few opportunities of making his way at a time when patronage and friendship are required to bring men forward. Lord Dalmeny might serve him, but a jealousy exists that will prevent his ever doing a kindness for the man who has so often proved his own superiority."

"Nor does John Ruthven need his kindness," answered Effie; "hitherto he has passed through life with tolerable credit to himself, and I fear not that he will be able to do so for the future. After his long absence from us

No. 6

he has returned with a more stern and manly look; his temper is more easily excited than it used to be, and for that reason I fear lest some danger should happen through his renewed intimacy with Lord Dalmeny."

"There can be little fear of danger happening to him," answered Dame Ruthven, "seeing that your brother is not likely to remain long in England."

"Alas!" replied the maiden, "we shall soon have to part with him again; he talks of leaving us, mother, and will not heed my prayers, though I have begged of him, with tears in my eyes, never to go abroad again."

"Thou art a simple wench for thy pains, Effie," exclaimed the widow; "Europe itself has bounds too narrow for the roving propensities of your brother, nor will aught content him less than a free range over the wide world. I have marked his aspiring disposition, child, and something tells me he is doomed to become a great man. His very looks give proof of his determination to overcome all obstacles, and we shall both of us yet live to bless the day when he left the shores of his native country to seek a field in which he might find an opportunity to raise himself to distinction."

"These," sighed Effie, "are the words of a fond mother excited in behalf of her only son. I, however, see things in a different light, for I fear lest the very spirit you speak of should lead him into perils that we little dream of."

"And who that follows the course he has chosen can ever hope to arrive at distinction without peril?" demanded the widow. "But there is a hope that sustains me, girl, and in spite of the dangers he may be exposed to, I yet anticipate the day when he will prove an honour not only to his family but to his country."

"My brother loves not his country," answered the maiden.

"Aye, so he says, girl," exclaimed Dame Ruthven; "but depend on it he will be as ready, when called upon, as any one to exert himself in its behalf. He possesses the spirit of his father, who nobly made an effort to rescue a number of drowning persons, and himself perished in the attempt."

"I have heard you speak of that sad event," cried Effie, "though I was too young at the time to be aware of the dreadful loss we had sustained."

"You were an infant when your father perished after having saved ten souls from a watery grave. The last effort proved fatal to him; one person only remained to be rescued; my husband again put out his boat, though every one warned him of his danger, and never shall I forget the agony that tore my soul when I saw his frail vessel turned over, and he who I loved sent, without time to breath a single prayer, into the presence of his Maker. They tell me I went mad, and I believe it was so, Effie; but Heaven spared me for the sake of my helpless children, and resigning myself to the loss I had endured, I endeavoured to rear my children by the labour of my hands. It was a hard struggle to keep poverty away from my door, but I succeeded without asking charity; nay, when Lady Margaret Dalmeny sent money to assist me, I returned it to her hands with a proud answer, that it was the duty of a mother to work for her children, and since Heaven had been pleased to give me health I would be under obligations to no one, even for a single farthing."

"I have heard people speak of the pride with which you refused their aid," answered Effie; "they speak of it to your praise, and many there are who wonder that you never married again, seeing that you were still young when left a widow, and that few could lay claim to more beauty."

"Had I loved your father less I should have taken another husband," replied the widow; "as it was, however, I have ever cherished his memory, and even now I often weep at the cruel destiny that separated us at so early a period of our lives."

"You must have been very young when you married?"

"Scarcely your age, girl," answered her mother; "I was under eighteen at the time, Effie, and yet you are still single, and if you are as particular as you have hitherto been, there is little chance that I shall live to see you a wife."

"There is time enough yet, dear mother."

"There may be, girl; but why not at once accept the offer that was made not long since by young Andrew Mac Ivor, who has a snug farm of his own, and, I should think, can well enough afford to keep a wife by this time."

"Andrew Mac Ivor will never be husband of mine," answered Effie; "he is too fond of his money, and people do say that he almost starves himself for the sake of hoarding up his gold."

"Well, then, what say you to Duncan Lawrie?"

"I like him no better than the other," replied the maiden; "he is a self-sufficient, swaggering fellow, with hardly more wit than he was born with, and, therefore, no fitting match for a girl who professes to be an admirer of common sense."

"Methinks you are somewhat hard to please, wench; yet will I ask one other question—do you not think Alexander Gowrie a good match for a poor wench like yourself?"

"Alexander Gowrie is an exciseman, and, therefore, too fond of interfering in other people's affairs," returned Effie. "Besides, nobody likes him, and I should not wish to have a husband that all the world looks on with coldness and contempt."

"Ah, girl!" exclaimed the widow, "it is easy enough to see how all this will end; one lover is too fond of his gold to care anything about his wife; another is a self-sufficient, swaggering fellow; and the third, happening to be an exciseman, is too fond of interfering in other people's affairs. Thus all have their faults, and the end of it will be that you will never get a husband at all."

"Perhaps not, mother, and perhaps it may so happen that I shall thus avoid the greatest curse that could possibly have fallen to my lot."

"And perhaps, on the other hand," answered the widow, "you may have thrown away a chance of happiness. But, however, as you seem to scorn all these humble suitors, Effie, what should you say, supposing a lord were to offer to share his title and fortune with you?"

"I know of no lord who would stoop so low as to ask a peasant's daughter to become his wife," replied the maiden.

"And yet there is one I know of who does not regard thee with a feeling far short of love. Ah! thy cheek grows red at that, and I am not far short of the truth; so confess to me, Effie, is there not a hope in thy bosom that thou mayest one day rise from thy present lowly state to become the rich and honoured lady of a wide domain?"

"I know to whom you allude, mother," answered Effie; "but sooner would I die by the most horrid tortures that man's ingenuity could invent, than ever give my hand to the proud lord you have hinted at, and who I so much despise. Lord Dalmeny is a libertine, and as such I would avoid him even as I would a venomous serpent."

"Yet Lord Dalmeny is not without his good qualities," exclaimed the widow. "When I was struggling against poverty he sought by every stratagem he could devise to assist me through my difficulties. I was, however, too proud to accept his proffered aid, yet I cannot forget that he would have been the friend of the widow and the fatherless if it had not been for my own obstinacy in rejecting it."

"You were his foster-mother," answered Effie, "and it would have been strange, indeed, if he had not felt some share of gratitude for the care you had bestowed in rearing him through the first years of his youth."

"You are determined, I see, to give him credit for no good qualities," cried Dame Ruthven; "prejudice has entered your heart, and, therefore, it would be vain were I to offer further testimony in behalf of this young lord. Yet do not forget, girl, that thy forefathers have ever been the followers of his ancestors, and that they served them with that zeal that I should be glad to see imitated were an opportunity ever to arrive."

"My brother will do as he pleases," returned Effie; "but for my own part, I shall ever avoid the presence of Lord Dalmeny as I would that of a demon that was watching to seize upon his unsuspecting prey."

Her mother was about to reply to this, but at the moment her ear caught the sound of approaching footsteps.

"Hush!" she said, "I hear some one coming."

"I know the step well," answered Effie, with alarm. "Lord Dalmeny has found his way to our cottage!"

The maiden was right in her surmise, for the door of the cottage was opened, and the young nobleman presented himself to their view.

"You are welcome, my lord," said Dame Ruthven; "we were just speaking of you when we heard you approaching."

"Indeed!" exclaimed Lord Dalmeny; "and may I ask what you were saying of one so little deserving of your thoughts?"

"I was observing," returned Effie, "that it was a pity your lordship had made yourself the terror of the neighbourhood."

"And am I so, gentle maiden?"

"So they tell me," she replied, "and I leave it to your lordship to say with what justice they do so. For my own part, I keep myself at as great a distance from you as I can, lest our being seen together should raise scandal against my name."

"Upon my word," cried the nobleman, "you are tolerably plain with me, and yet I feel disposed to ask how it was that you were a visitor at the ball I gave to my tenantry if it is so dangerous to be seen in my company?"

"I was over persuaded, my lord," replied the maiden; "my mother was fearful of giving offence to the Lady Margaret Dalmeny, and my brother said that as he was to be present there could be little fear of my meeting with insult."

"The girl speaks boldly, my lord," interrupted Dame Ruthwen; "but I trust you will not feel offended at her words."

"Not in the least," he replied; "I like to hear the truth even though it may be somewhat unpleasant. So speak out, Effie, and I promise you, you shall have free licence to say just whatever you please about me."

"If by so doing I could shame you from sinning any more, I would gladly take the opportunity," answered the maiden; "that, however, appears to be hopeless, and therefore I may as well spare myself the trouble."

"Girl! you are too bold," cried the widow, angrily. "My lord, you will pardon her rude speech, and believe me the girl means not half the foolish things she utters."

"'Tis the privilege of beauty to reprove the follies of mankind," exclaimed his lordship; "Effie knows well enough that I cannot be angry with her, and therefore she takes the opportunity of saying severe things in the hope that I am not yet quite irreclaimable."

"Indeed, my lord, I have no hope of the kind," replied Effie; "experience has taught me that sin is not to be so easily whipped out of you, and therefore I should be a sad economist of my time, were I to waste it in a fruitless endeavour."

"Again, Effie!" exclaimed Lord Dalmeny, smiling; "have you not yet got rid of your ill-humour towards one who has ever held out the palm of peace? By St. Andrew, I believed thee to be all gentleness and humility, but I find, to my cost, that thou hast more than a fair share of woman's spirit in thee."

"It is thine own conduct, my lord, that hath brought it forth," replied the maiden, indignantly; "I have watched thy progress with shame, and have seen happy maidens, who were once companions of my own, brought to infamy and ruin. Thou hast planted a mark upon their brow, their friends have forsaken them, as no longer worthy their esteem, and what has then become of them thou neither knowest nor carest. Some have died of broken hearts;—some have wandered away ashamed to remain longer in the scene of their innocent childhood—some have gone mad with despair. This, my lord, is but a faint picture of the misery you have caused, and yet you are still plotting further mischief, as if enough had not been already committed."

"By Heavens, Effie, you are too hard upon me," cried the young nobleman, quaking with conscious guilt before the spirited girl who had spoken thus freely. "I have been thoughtless, it must be admitted, but something is to be allowed for my youth, especially when I have given you my word, that the wild excesses you speak of will not be repeated."

"You hear, Effie," interposed the widow Ruthven; "his lordship has promised to reform, and surely it is now time that we should cease to reproach him for follies that are past."

"Can he restore those to life who have died heart-broken in the prime of youth?" demanded Effie;—"can he restore peace to the families that he has reduced to despair and misery?—or can he bring back the mind of those who have gone mad at the thought of the shame he has brought upon them? If he can do that, his repentance may be acceptable; if not, it is vain and useless."

"Is it nothing then," asked Lord Dalmeny; "to amend a rather free life, and thus offer all the reparation that may be in my power?"

"If the repentance you speak of were sincere, I should be one of the first to hail it with gladness," answered the maiden.

"You hear her, my lord," said Dame Ruthven; "she is anxious only for your reformation, and you will hear no more of the bitter words she has this night given utterance to."

"I repeat it," exclaimed the nobleman; "my regret for all that has passed, is most sincere."

"And yet," cried Effie, with scorn; "it is not many hours since your hand was raised against the life of my brother, because he ventured to step forward in defence of his sister's honour!"

"How!" exclaimed Dame Ruthven, with indignant surprise; "is it true, my lord, that you have sought to slay my son?"

"The truth is," answered Lord Dalmeny, "that I love John Ruthven as dearly as myself; words, however, certainly did arise between us;—we met at the Mermaid's Cliff, and a few passes were exchanged. But our difference has been made up, and we are now better friends than ever we were. I have his forgiveness for an injury that he supposed I meditated towards his sister, and surely I shall not find less favour here than I have experienced from the man who so lately stood before me as a foe."

"Leave us, my lord, I command you!" cried Effie, summoning all her energy; "leave us, I say, for this calmness is but assumed to deceive me into a belief of your sincerity. Your longer stay here will but add insult to insult, for never will I pardon the man, who not only commits crimes at which humanity shudders, but who exults in the infamy that should make his name execrated."

But Lord Dalmeny was not thus to be defeated in the object that had brought him thither, and taking the hand of Effie, he would again have urged her to think more kindly of him. The maiden, however, shrunk from him with horror that she sought not to conceal, and commanded him to advance no nearer to her.

"I will not hear you, my lord," she cried; "too long already have you contaminated this house with your presence, and either you or I must leave it this instant."

"My child! my child!" cried the mother, distractedly; "what means this wildness?—what deep wrong hast thou received from Lord Dalmeny, that thou dost thus loathe and execrate him?"

"I have been insulted, mother;—deeply, foully insulted, and yet the man who has done me this wrong, dares to enter your doors as if in mockery and derision."

"What insult has he offered thee, my child?" cried the widow Ruthven, almost breathless with agitation.

"She calls it an insult that I have confessed that she has won from me my affections," answered Lord Dalmeny. "But the truth is, she has been set on to scorn me thus, and I can pretty well guess who I have to thank for the scorn with which she treats me."

"Your suspicions point towards my brother?"

"They do."

"In that case it is time I should undeceive you, my lord," answered Effie, proudly; "I am, myself, no mean judge of your actions; I have seen the perfidy with which you have treated others; and knowing, as I do, the baseness of your heart, I should be worse than an idiot were I to believe the vows and protestations that you have poured into my ears. I see through the thin veil with which you would conceal your real motives, but be assured, my Lord Dalmeny, that I am not only aware of the irreparable injury you seek to inflict upon me, but that I am also resolved to publish your infamy to the world, in order that others may be put upon their guard against your treachery."

"Nay, daughter," cried Dame Ruthven; "you wrong the noble Lord Dalmeny; he may have been thoughtless and imprudent, but take my word for it, he would not seek to inflict an injury even upon his most inveterate enemy."

"You know him not as I do, mother," answered the maiden; "or you would not have suffered him to remain thus long beneath your roof. I have already told you that it is not long since he drew his sword against my brother's life, and he would have murdered him, had it not been that his antagonist was as well skilled in the use of the weapon as himself."

"Are you certain that your charge is well founded, Effie?" demanded the dame.

"As certain as that I now stand before you," she replied. "I was myself an unseen spectator of the fight that took place between them, and knowing, as I did, that my brother was standing up in defence of my honour, I vowed to Heaven that I would avenge his death, should he chance to fall beneath the sword of his proud antagonist. Aye, my lord, you look incredulous," she continued; "but I was armed, and had your foe fell, his death should have been revenged by your own."

"You have heard her words, my lord," cried the widow, looking sternly upon the pale countenance of the disconcerted nobleman ; " you have heard her, I say, and I would now learn from your own lips, whether you have indeed sought to take the life of my son ?"

" We certainly did fight," he replied ; " but I was compelled to defend myself, or be branded with the name of coward."

" And did you not reflect that you were thus placing in peril the life of one who has been as a brother to you ?"

" In such situations a man is deprived of his usual coolness," answered Lord Dalmeny ; " I confess I ought not to have stooped so low as to fight with one of my own dependants, but my own life was threatened, and therefore I had no alternative but to adopt the course I did."

" And had he fallen, what honour would you have gained by it ?" cried Dame Ruthven ; " would the world have esteemed you a brave man because you had steeped your sword in the blood of a fellow creature, or could you ever afterwards have dared to look in the face of her that you had deprived of a son ?"

" I tell you again, the quarrel was none of my seeking," answered the young nobleman. " John Ruthven is of a hot, fiery temperament; he accused me of having evil designs against the honour of his sister ; I re-pelled his charge with indignation, but he would believe no denial that I made. In the end I was forced to accept his challenge; we met, as Effie has described, and happy I am that nothing fatal resulted from our duel. There is a difference in our stations of life, that ought to have prompted me to treat his challenge with the scorn it merited, but somehow, my own warmth overcame my usual prudence, and I got involved in a difficulty that seems likely enough to lose me your esteem."

" You speak of the difference in rank that exists between yourself and my brother," exclaimed Effie; " and yet I'll answer for it, he possesses more true nobility than can be boasted of by my Lord Dalmeny. True, the birth of one may be more exalted than the other, but John Ruthven is no ignoble enemy, nor has your honour suffered by the meeting you were so *kind* as to give him. His honour is, at least, equal to your own, for never have I known him to be guilty of a falsehood, though hundreds are now living who have had bitter cause to repent the moment when they placed confidence in the deceitful words of your lordship. You have proved your-self unworthy of the high station you fill, my Lord Dalmeny, and, humble as I am, I loathe, execrate and despise you from the bottom of my soul."

Hitherto his lordship had contrived to wear a tolerable appearance of calmness, but the bitter words that were poured into his ear at length roused him to a state of anger that he could not controul. Starting from his seat, he paced impatiently up and down the room, and ever and anon he muttered forth the angry words that could no longer be suppressed. Whilst he was thus occupied, the widow Ruthven reached down from over the fire-place a richly-mounted dagger, the handle of which was orna-mented with armorial bearings, whilst the whole was scattered over with jewels of considerable price. Lord Dalmeny was too much occupied with his own thoughts to take much heed of this, nor was he conscious where he then was, until the old woman presented herself before him, and hold-ing up the dagger up to his view, said :—

" Lord Dalmeny, you perceive this relic, which has been in our family upwards of four hundred years. It was given to a forefather of mine by an ancestor of yours, for a service he did him in the hour of need."

" And what, I pray you, was the occasion of this magnificent present being given ?"

" Ere I give an answer," cried the widow, " I must hear from your

lordship whether there are any means by which you can satisfy yourself
that the weapon ever belonged to any part of your family ?"

"The arms," replied his lordship, gazing upon the dagger for a moment,
" would lead me to infer that the instrument once belonged to some of the
Dalmenys. It is, however, singular that I should find you in possession
of it, and therefore do I demand an explanation that seems absolutely necessary."

"It has belonged to us," answered Dame Ruthven, " ever since the days
of the great William Wallace. An ancestor of yours fought under him at
the battle of Stirling, and in the midst of the fierce conflict that raged, he
would have fallen beneath the sword of an enemy, had it not been for a
worthy progenitor of mine who had followed him to the field, who, fearless
of the consequences to himself, rushed between the combatants, and thus
saved the life of Robert, Lord Dalmeny."

"For which service," observed the young nobleman, " I have no doubt
his preserver was amply rewarded."

"Lord Dalmeny," resumed the widow, " had not the means at that moment of bestowing money upon his preserver, but taking this dagger from
the place where it was suspended, he gave it to the man that had saved
his life, swearing at the same time before High Heaven, that whenever this
instrument was produced in his presence, the bearer of it should be at liberty to claim any boon he might think proper. This pledge he made not
only for himself, but for his descendants, and never, down to this day,
have any of the Lords of Dalmeny ventured to refuse to fulfil the pledge
given by him whose life had been saved through the self-devotion of a
faithful follower."

"I see your motive for producing it now," observed the nobleman ;
" you have a favour to ask of me, and be assured I will not fail to execute
the singular pledge given by my noble ancestor. You are in poverty, and
require money ;—name the sum you want, and it shall be yours."

"Your gold I despise, my lord," answered Dame Ruthven ; "I would
ask a favour far more precious to me than that, though it will be less costly
to yourself."

"You want the rent of your cottage lowered ?—let it be so ;—nay, you
and your heirs shall live in it rent free, and never shall they be disturbed
in their possession of it. You see, dame, I am easily prevailed upon to
serve you, though your daughter has insulted me without provocation."

"Mine is no mercenary request, my lord," answered the old woman ;
" all I ask of you is that you will enter into no quarrel with my son.
Draw not your sword rashly against him, because he happens to fear lest
you entertain dishonourable designs against his sister. Promise me this,
Lord Dalmeny, and it shall be the last and only boon I will ever crave of
you."

"Were I to give the required pledge, exclaimed Lord Dalmeny, " I feel
assured that it would soon be broken. Your son has taken a mortal dislike to me for something that I know not of, and as he himself may provoke me to forget the promise, were I rash enough to give it, I think it better to wait till you have exacted a pledge from him never to say aught that
may serve to raise my anger."

"My lord !—my lord !" exclaimed Dame Ruthven, impatiently, " you
well know that it is impossible to obtain such a promise from my son ;—
he suspects evil designs against his sister, and even the most sacred oath
would be broken, were he to discover that you persisted in basely seeking
to destroy the peace and happiness of one he loves so dearly."

"Then why ask me to give a promise that must be broken if he should
provoke me to it ?" demanded the other.

"Because," replied the dame, "it would act as a restraint upon you in your unhappy attachment to my daughter. I have faith enough in you to believe that you would not willingly break a solemn promise that had been made, and, in order to remove all chance of your doing so, you would resolve never again to meet Effie Ruthven. Thus his jealousy of your intentions must be removed, and you might pass the remainder of your lives as friends, instead of as enemies."

"And why should I be bound by promises, whilst he is free to say and do as he pleases?" demanded Lord Dalmeny, haughtily. "Ruthven is of a proud and restless spirit; he hates all who happen to be placed in a situation superior to his own. More than once he has endeavoured to pick a quarrel with me, and there is but too much reason to suppose that he will one day or other tempt me beyond the bounds of prudence. I do not seek to injure the churl, but, should he urge me too far, the consequences must rest upon his own head."

"You will not give the promise, then," cried Dame Ruthven, "even though you now gaze upon this relic, which was bestowed upon us by an ancestor who was not too proud to acknowledge that he owed his life to one from whom my son is descended?"

"I cannot," answered Lord Dalmeny; "ask any boon of me but that and I will not refuse it. Demand gold, and, even if it should amount to half my possessions, it shall be freely yours, rather than yield to a demand that would ever afterwards make me the slave of a low-born peasant."

"Your gold, my lord, I despise!" cried the widow, earnestly; "I ask safety for my son, and your words imply that his life will be sought on the first occasion that offers."

"Aye, but he must seek the quarrel that will endanger himself," replied Lord Dalmeny.

No. 7

"Will you pledge yourself, then, to give him no cause for provocation?" demanded Dame Ruthven.

"I will make no terms such as you have proposed," answered Lord Dalmeny, impatiently.

"Then the curse of him who bestowed upon us this dagger as a sacred pledge, will cling to thee!" cried the widow.

"Nay, for that matter, I am already cursed enough," replied the young nobleman, in a tone of the utmost indifference.

"But with this one upon thee," cried Dame Ruthven, unwilling to yield the point whilst there was a chance of gaining; "with this one upon thee, Lord Dalmeny, thou wilt live hated by thy fellow-men, and deserted even by Heaven."

"Well," exclaimed the other, "let thy son behave with becoming courtesy to me, and thou wilt have no cause to fear violence from me. Let him act as a vassal should do towards his lord, and my hand shall never be raised against him."

"I cannot restrain my son," answered the widow, "if he should see cause to suspect thine intentions towards his sister. All I have to urge is that thou see'st before thee the token of a sacred pledge given by an ancestor of thine, and I demand thy fulfilment of it, as thou wouldst obtain honour and esteem amongst thy fellow-creatures, and the approbation of that Being, who I fear thou dost not worship in thy heart."

"I will hear thee no more, woman!" cried Lord Dalmeny, furiously. "Too long already have I endured thine insolent words, and it is now time that I tell thee my determination. I will be restrained by no vows that have been made by my ancestor; but, acting entirely upon circumstances, I shall not fail to hurl my vengeance upon thy son, should he give me cause to punish his temerity!"

"Then may the curse of Heaven light upon thee!" cried the widow, vehemently. "May'st thou become the mark for the world's scorn and detestation;—may thy worldly wealth be taken from thee till thou dost come to be a beggar in the land, and, dying in dishonour, may thy hideous corse lay unblessed upon the earth to become food for hungry hounds!—May——"

' Hold, woman!" exclaimed Lord Dalmeny, wrathfully; "thou hast already given sufficient vent to thine accursed malice, and it is now time that I teach thee what humility I expect from those who are my born vassals. Thou shalt no longer have a home to cover thee, for thy house, and all thou dost possess, shall be given to the devouring flames, and mine shall be thee hand to inflict upon thee thy well-merited punishment!"

Saying this, he seized a lighted torch, that was burning near the chimney, and was rushing towards some straw and heather that was heaped up in a corner, for the purpose of setting light to the pile, when Dame Ruthven, foreseeing his intention, sprang before him, and drawing the dagger which she still held in her hand, stood resolutely determined to prevent the fatal mischief he intended.

"Move but another step, my lord!" she cried, frantically, "and it shall be the last you will ever make in this world! Back, I say, and throw away that burning torch, or the weapon I now grasp shall find a sheath in thy black and guilty heart!"

"Woman!" exclaimed Lord Dalmeny, quailing before her fixed and resolute gaze; "what is it thou dost mean?—would thou slay thy lord beneath thine own roof?"

"Aye, for thou hast threatened to burn it to to the ground," answered Dame Ruthven, resolutely. This cottage has been my home from the moment when I entered it as a bride; within its walls my children were born, and it is as dear to me almost as they are themselves. Here I have seen much joy, though more of sorrow, and rather would I perish amidst the flames you would kindle around me, than tamely suffer injustice even from the proud and vindictive Lord Dalmeny."

Awed by her words, the haughty peer cast the burning brand upon the hearth, and muttering his curses upon those who had so firmly resisted the object for which he had entered the house, he rushed forth to cool his burning brow in the fresh midnight air. For a moment or two he paused to gaze upon the cottage he had just quitted, and then turning fiercely away, left the place angry and disappointed.

CHAPTER VII.

" What mystery is this ?
Is he then leagued with these deliberate villains ;—
These traffickers in crime ?"

THE PIRATE'S BRIDE.

EFFIE and her mother remained lost in thought at the fearful adventure that had just befallen them ;—they had now seen Lord Dalmeny in his worst colours, the malice of his heart had shone forth, and they dreaded the consequences of the quarrel that had happened between them. But their fears were chiefly for Ruthven, upon whom they expected the full wrath of the peer would fall; they knew him to be proud, cruel, and vindictive, and fearing his violence, gave free scope to the terrors that filled their hearts.

When the morning's light dawned, Effie left the cottage and proceeded to the Mermaid's Rock, from whence she could obtain a wide view over the broadly expanding ocean, and from which she could discern many an object that was rendered dear to her from the association connected with it. But chiefly were her eyes directed towards a range of caverns that lay extended along the cliffs, all of which it was said, were resorted to by smugglers, who there found a secure refuge from those whose business it was to interfere with their illegal traffic. Here she knew her brother had often gone in his boyish days, when his love of danger and enterprize led him to mix with men whose way of life had rendered them outcasts from all respectable society. It was not that she suspected he had anything to do with the smugglers now, but John had not returned home since he had interposed to prevent violence in the Castle of Dalmeny ; and wondering what had become of him, she had gone to that spot expecting that he had strolled to the sea side, from whence he might obtain a view of the ocean, on whose dark bosom he so loved to dwell. But no living object was to be seen, and she was just about to turn away, when a distant boat caught her sight and at once rivetted her attention. The little vessel rounded a point, and then shot across to an opposite promontory that jutted out into the bay, near the place where were situated the range of caverns of which we have spoken. As they passed, she recognised the well known form of her brother among the boats' crew, and, inspired by fear and curiosity, she watched them until they drove ashore, when two of the men, one of whom was John, leaped on land, and the boat again left the place, and was rowed behind ahead at some distance from the place. Wondering what all this meant, yet resisting the desire to become a spy upon her brother's actions, she turned away from the place with a sigh, and bent her steps towards the cottage, where she had left her mother. As she laid her hands upon the latch, however, she heard a low, moaning voice, as of some one pouring forth her griefs, and gently entering the room, she beheld the widow Ruthven upon her knees, praying to Heaven for pardon, and uttering aloud the terrible thoughts that agitated her bosom. Effie would have left the place with the same silence that she had entered it, but the words fell upon her ears ere she could hurry away, and their fearful impost compelled her to remain even against her will.

"Great Heaven, forgive my sins, for I am penitent, and the remembrance of them bows my once proud spirit even to the very dust. I have been false to my marriage vows, yet thou knowest how I struggled to overcome the tempter; how I resisted him; and how cunningly he urged his suit. Thou knowest also, how I felt from being a virtuous wife to become the paramour of a heartless libertine. Nor is my penitence unknown to thee, for with tears and groans and lamentations I have sought to make my peace with thee, though down to this time, I have witnessed no manifestation that the heavy curse inflicted by thy wrath, has ever been removed from me. Are not my children living reproaches for crimes long since past? Does not the sight of them raise in my heart a perpetual, a consuming fire? and is not what I have already endured sufficient to save me from the flames and punishment of another world, when death shall remove me from this? Then what thoughts, what agonies, drive me to despair, till I have been almost driven to throw myself from the cliffs into the roaring surge beneath! Visions haunt me by night, and conscience—ever busy and untiring conscience goads me by day! If this be the punishment of sin, have I not already endured enough to satisfy thy wrath for broken vows and the chastity that has been sacrificed on the altar of lust? If I am to endure more, grant me pastime to suffer without repining, for I know that I have deserved all, and am ready to bow with meekness and resignation to thy wil!!"

Horrified at the words she had heard, Effie fled precipitately from the cottage lest her mother should have the additional sting of knowing that her confession had been overheard by one of her own children. She fled scarcely knowing whither, but at length the roaring of the sea roused her, and raising her eyes from the ground, she perceived that she had unconsciously wandered to the neighbourhood of the caverns whose basis were washed by the ocean. Then again she turned her eyes towards the spot where her brother and his companion had landed from the boat, and she saw that they were standing talking to each other;—she would have left the place rather than appear to be watching their actions, but at that moment, they moved onwards, and clambering one of the cliffs by a winding path, entered the largest of the caverns. Effie now stood irresolute what course to adopt, for she felt that a further mystery was yet to be revealed, and her brother's apparent connection with the smugglers, filled her soul with new terrors.

"I will follow them," she at length muttered to herself, "even if it be at the hazard of bringing upon myself the severest displeasure of my brother. That he is engaged with these lawless men, there is no longer any reason to doubt, and it is therefore my duty to follow and warn him of the ruin that must follow, should he remain connected with these smugglers, who have so long been the terror and objects for the persecution of the whole neighbourhood. Yes, dear Paul, there is one who watches over thy welfare with sisterly affection—whose one heart, perhaps, is well nigh broken by the terrible revelations she has heard from a mother's lips, but who yet can feel for her brother's honour, and make one bold effort to snatch him from destruction."

Knowing the intricacies of the caverns, the maiden now cautiously followed the footsteps of those who had just before entered. For some distance she pursued her way in darkness, but at length arriving at an inner cave, she found a small lighted lamp suspended from the roof, by means of whose faint rays she could discover the entrance that led to another vaulted chamber, through whose dark recesses, her vision was unable to penetrate. She then directed her attention towards a piece of rock, which stood in the cave in which she stood, and advancing towards it, perceived that it was covered with warlike weapons, all of which she recognised as belonging to her brother.

"Alas! Paul," she sighed, " these are thine, and your presence here tell me but too truly that my worst fears are confirmed. Thou art leagued with men reckless and guilty of pandering to their own evil passions. And yet what has wrought this sad change in one who I had fondly thought was impelled by far nobler desires; who has sworn that he would draw his sword only to redress the wrongs of his country, and sheath it only when his noble purpose had been fulfilled. And now, how do I behold thee?— the companion of smugglers—mixing thyself with men who own no laws but their own will; scorning the actions of good men, and applauding on those which belong to the worthless. Alas! what a change is this! I find thee fallen when I had hoped to have found thee mounting towards honourable fame; thy name in danger of becoming dishonoured, and thy purposes directed against all that should make thee respected as I had once hoped to see thee. But why waste my time in idle surmises when it requires all my energy to turn the current of thy destiny? Why not hasten to trace whither he has gone with his guilty companion, and by my prayers and entreaties endeavour to bring him to a sense of the shame he would bring upon his family."

As she said this, Effie descended a flight of rugged steps cut out of the rock, and having reached the bottom, found herself in another spacious cavern, from whence she was guided, by a distant light, towards the place where the smugglers were assembled. Fearful of trusting herself, however, among men she dreaded to meet, she hesitated for a moment, irresolute what to do, but presently afterwards, she was startled by hearing loud voices in merriment, and then gathering all the resolution she could, she stealthily advanced towards the distant light, until she had reached the cavern adjoining the one in which the smugglers were met in wild carouse. Here she placed herself behind a piece of jutting rock, from whence she could overhear all that passed without being observed. Occasionally she would venture to look from her secret covert, but the grim visage of the men she gazed upon, filled her with terror, and at last, contenting herself by remaining where she was, she listened with eager ears to the conversation that followed:

"This is rare drink, my boys," she heard one of the smugglers say; " it drives sorrow from the heart and makes one feel like a man even if he was just going to mount the gallows. 'So here's success to free trade, lads, and down with all squeanish land-lubbers that would interfere to hinder us from getting an honest living, by assisting his Majesty's subjects to get a drop of choice spirits, such as this we're now drinking.'"

The toast was received with tumultuous applause, every can was emptied to do it honour, and when silence had once more been restored, another of the ruffians, whose voice betrayed how deeply he had been drinking, said :—

"The toast is a good one, comrades, but since we all of us like the sort of life so well, why do we stop idling here on land, when there's so much business to be doing afloat. It was not the way with Captain Transom, who was always for doing something, even if it was a bit of mischief; we could earn gold under him where we now only get silver, and never were there lighter hearts, or braver spirits, than the crew that own him for a commander."

"Aye, aye," observed another, "he was a lad of mettle, every inch of him. I remember some years since, when we had landed at this very place, he took it into his head to go to church, because he happened to hear that a wedding was going to take place; well, the bride and bridegroom were standing at the altar, the priest had got his book open before him ready to begin the ceremony, when our noble captain whips the girl up in his arms, and bolted out of the church with her before a man had time to say 'Jack Robinson.' Of course there was a terrible outcry at this violence as they called it, and away ran the bridegroom in pursuit, followed by the parson and the clerk, and a lot of other people besides, that bustled along because they saw the people running. But it was all of no use, Captain Transom got the wench on board, the anchor was weighed, the sails were out, and away went the little vessel over the dancing waters, whilst the poor devils on land were looking after them and raising a hullabaloo that might have been heard from here to the Land's End."

"Well," exclaimed Captain Starkie, who was at the head of the band of smugglers, to whose conversation Effie was listening; "it may be all very fine to be talking of the great doings of Transom, but did he ever beat what I have done? Was he ever known to take a king's ship, with double the number of guns against him, as I did off the island of Cuba? Talk of Captain Transom, indeed! why, I have done greater things in my time than ever he did. Did he ever treat his fellows better than I have, or did you ever know him fight longer and harder battles? But it's thirsty work, comrades, this talking in one's own praise, so let's drink another cup, and then I'll tell you what sort of an affair I was once engaged in."

This proposition was readily enough acceded to by every one present, and when due honour had been done to the liquor that stood before them, Captain Starkie commenced with a flourish :—

"You have all, no doubt, heard of Sir Andrew Rawdan and his handsome daughter, Edith; well, I had taken a mighty fancy to the wench, and though she didn't seem to care much about me, I was determined to have her in spite of the devil himself if he had said nay to me. So whilst my little vessel was riding at anchor in the bay, I used to go ashore and keep a good look out for an opportunity to put my plans in operation, and one day, as good luck would have it, she passed just by the place where I was lying concealed. Of course, comrades, I was not going to let a good chance slip, so I pounced upon her, and she was in my arms in a jiffy. Lord! how she screamed and shouted for help till I got her on board ship, and then I suppose the sea air served to bring her to her senses a bit, for she began to grow remarkable quiet when she found there was no help for her. So to humour her, one of our fellows shammed to be a parson, and we got spliced after a fashion, and as she fancied herself my wife, we found ourselves in smooth water, and going as gently as possible before the wind. At last, however, we happened to hear that the old curmudgeon of a father took her loss to heart, and, to make short of a long story, he died, leaving as pretty a bit of property as a man need wish for. But somehow or other money's always a curse, and so it proved in this instance, for I'm hanged if her ladyship didn't begin to ride the high horse as soon as ever she heard the news of the old fellow's death. She pretended to faint as dead as a nit, but I cured her of that with a bucket of salt water; then she cried, but I laughed her out of it; then she grew mopish and dull, and I rapped out a dozen or two of good round oaths; at last she got into a towering passion, and, snatching up a knife that was lying upon the cabin-table, she would have given me a finishing stroke if I hadn't been wide awake to her movements. But after that nothing would cure her, though I broke her heart in trying it."

"She died then?" said one of the comrades.

"To be sure she did, and to tell you the truth, the thing didn't grieve me much, for I was beginning to grow rather tired of her, and I fancied nothing would be so easy as to get the money the old man had left whenever I might return to England. But as the devil would have it, the lawyers were too cunning for me by half, and as they wanted to have proof of my marriage and a great deal more nonsense of that kind, I cut my cable, and left them to make a scramble for it among themselves."

"A very pretty adventure, but not a very profitable one," observed one of the auditors. "Now I knew a captain that took off a girl without ever thinking of asking her leave, and she went out with him the whole voyage as his wife, and when he got her to the Spice Islands, he sold her for a good handsome sum of money; that was a speculation worth hazarding something for, but then you see, comrades, it ain't every one that fortune favours in the same way."

"Fortune's like a woman, and, therefore, not to be depended on," exclaimed another of the men; "she's blind, too, they say, so who can expect that she'll give her favour to those that are most deserving of them?"

"Come, come, let's have no moralizing," interposed Captain Starkie;—"we are assembled here to enjoy ourselves, and hang the fool that would waste his time in preaching what he knows nothing about. So here's a toast comrades: 'Success to the lads of the wave, and confusion to all excisemen and guagers."

This and a great many other toasts that followed, began to have considerable effects upon the heads of the revellers, who, one by one, fell fast asleep; some falling back upon the benches, and others rolling under the table, where they lay like so many insensible beasts. Captain Starkie was the last to keep his seat, but at length the liquor he had consumed, began to grow too much even for his head, and after a few ineffectual efforts to swallow more, he followed the example of his worthy companions.

Having thus an opportunity to escape without being seen, Effie would have retired from a place so little suited to one like herself, but just as she was about to step from the recess which had concealed her, steps were heard approaching from another part of the cavern, and the next moment her brother and the person she had seen enter with him, paced within a few inches of the spot where they were standing. At the instant of their passing into the chamber where the revels had been going on, a beam of light fell on the countenance of the young man who accompanied her brother, and she immediately recognized in him Hugh Lorimer, a neighbour, and one who had hitherto borne an irreproachable character. Somewhat comforted by the discovery, Effie determined to remain yet a little longer where she was, in order to hear what had brought her brother and his companion to the haunt of these wreckless men. All was hushed, except the occasional snoring of the drunken Bacchanals, and as it appeared they were not likely to be interrupted, the young men resumed the conversation they had been occupied in previous to entering the cavern.

"It is a fair picture that you have drawn, John Ruthven," said Hugh; "perhaps too fair to be exactly after nature. We may rise to greatness, as you say, but on the other hand, the conquest is not easily to be obtained, and many will fall in seeking to obtain the freedom you seem so deeply in love with."

"I tell you nothing is more easy," answered John, impatiently; "there are some too high in the world, and some too low; some are born to command, others to obey, but those that have had the command, have grievously misused their power, and, therefore, it is high time that we, who are lowly born, should shake off our apathy, and prove that we are men like themselves."

"True," exclaimed Hugh Lorimer; "but men are not yet all of one mind; some are still content to place their necks beneath the iron heels of their superiors, and it is not all that either you or I could urge, that would raise their spirits above the level they have taken."

"You would passively yield, then," cried John, angrily, "because the minds of all men are not alike!"

"I would lend to the storm rather than fall in resisting it," answered the other. "Let us bide our time, and the day will yet come when man may assert his independence without fear of check or control. Such has always been my opinion, and I do not intend to change it, unless you can show good cause why I ought to do so."

"It is impossible that things can remain as they are," exclaimed John; "there may be difficulties in the way, but we are not yet such base slaves that we must meekly endure the injuries that are daily heaped upon us. I can understand why a man should be rewarded for any great service that he may have done his country, whether it be that he has defended it gallantly in war against his enemies, or by a powerful mind wrought improvements that must tend to the happiness and comfort of his fellow creatures. Such men ought, and always will be rewarded. But there are evils in the present state of things that must be eradicated; the heir's and successors of such men as I have spoken of have no right to become our hereditary legislators; they may be fools, or knaves, utterly unfit for the station fortune has placed them in, and calculated to bring a curse upon the very nation their forefathers have served. This is one of the abuses I would see wiped away, and if ever the time should arrive when men are bold enough to stand up in support of their own legitimate right, you shall see that I will be among the first to risk life, honour, and reputation in their behalf."

"There is much truth in what you have said," answered Hugh Lorimer, "and yet I cannot see that it is to be amended without a reign of anarchy and bloodshed that I shudder to think of. Men in power will not tamely yield to the voice of a turbulent mob; they will resist, and many among the middling and lower classes of society, will cheerfully assist them. Mankind is not prone to change; they take things as they find them, and are content with the lot that falls to their share."

"And it is that very blind servility that has produced all the evils of which I complain," exclaimed our hero; "apathy has produced intolerance, and thus our forefathers have gone on accumulating wrongs for their offspring, which are now too great for longer endurance. We will, however, drop this subject, for some of the sleepers I see are rousing themselves, and I have business with a few of them that will brook no delay."

"Why, John Ruthven," exclaimed one of the mariners, "who would have thought of seeing you here? We parted in America, and yet here are you almost as soon as myself. But you are after some of your devil's tricks, I suppose, so drink with us, if there is any whisky left, and then tell me what errand of mischief brings you here. But first taste our liquor, or your tongue will never find its proper use."

John did as he had been desired, and then Hugh Lorimer had to go through the ceremony; but this time Captain Starkie had roused himself, and looking inquisitively at John, he exclaimed, with impatience:—

"Why, who the devil have we got here?—Who is this, Andrew Foster, that has come unbidden to our feast, and looks as if he would not depart from it even at my bidding? Who is it, I say, sirrah?—Speak, or you'll have the contents of this pistol through your brain in another moment."

"You have forgotten me, it seems, Captain Starkie," said our hero, advancing a little nearer to the bully; "and yet," he continued, "I can scarcely wonder at it, seeing that you could hardly have expected to meet me here."

"I know you not," answered the captain gruffly; "you are none of my friends, so don't claim acquaintance with a man that never saw you before."

"Indeed!" cried John, "then, perhaps, I may be able to relate a circumstance that may serve to assist a short memory. Do you happen to recollect ever visiting the island of St. Domingo?"

"Aye, I have been often there,—but what of that?"

"You remember, perhaps, being on one occasion opposed by a young sailor when your were insulting a helpless woman? Does such a circumstance happen to be within your memory?"

"Aye, I do recollect some such thing," replied the other; "in fact, I have reason enough to do so, seeing that I have the marks now on my person left by that cursed sword of yours."

"I see," exclaimed John, smiling, "you remember me now."

"I have cause enough to do so," answered Captain Starkie; however, I am not one of those sulky fellows that bear malice for months and years. I was wrong, I dare say, and you were rather too quick upon me; but never mind, all that's gone by now, so here's my hand, and I drink to our better acquaintance, man."

But one cup was not enough for the captain, and having tossed of three or four in quick succession, he shortly afterwards began to show symptoms of drowsiness, and at length reeling from his seat, he fell insensible upon the floor. John now beckoned some of his sailors who had been listening to this brief conversation, and when they were gathered around him, he said :—

No. 8

"Andrew Foster, you, like myself, have lately visited the great American Continent; you have heard the words of liberty, that are there breathed by men who are resolved no longer to be trampled on as slaves. They have at length discovered the fact that the mother country would harrass and oppress them, and you have witnessed the stern determination with which they have sworn to rid themselves of the tie that unites them to England."

"Aye, aye, I know all about that, Master John," answered the mariner; "people over the water do seem to be in a bit of a ferment, to be sure; but what care I for that? My business is on the salt water, and landsmen may do just as they please, without my ever troubling my head with their affairs."

"But have you never thought of the reward that will be earned by those who have spirit enough to fight in the cause of liberty and independance?" demanded our hero. "Do you not thirst for gold, man, and if you do, will not avarice tempt you to draw a sword in so holy a cause as that I speak of?"

"Ah! now I understand you," answered Andrew Foster. "There's nothing like plain speaking when you've got to deal with a fellow that has only just sense enough to go through the world without butting his head against every post he meets with. The truth is, John, I have often thought the world was going wrong, and that people must be blind not to see it. A few men are rich, and good care do they take to keep all the gold they've got; but for the few rich men thrive, are millions that are starving for want, and yet those millions have a spirit enough to unite and say:—"Thus far oppression has had its own way, but now it is time that we should show a bold front and teach these haughty fellows that they must expect no more abject submission. I have often wondered, sir, how it is that things turned out as they have, but I suppose men have learnt to kiss the fetters that bind them, and if so, it is no business of yours or mine to tell them they are errant fools."

"Very true," replied Ruthven, "and yet, for all that, I have sometimes fancied that men only wanted some one to rouse them from their apathy. Once convince them of the wrongs they endure, and, like a hunted lion, they will turn round upon their pursuers."

"Perhaps so," answered Andrew; "but the lion does not always get off scot free. Sometimes he falls into the toils of the hunter, and then he becomes the slave and subject of his master. But you were speaking just now about the Americans,—not that I pretend to understand how the matter stands between them and the mother country, only people tell me they don't choose to be taxed by an English Parliament without being fairly represented in it. Now, all that seems to be right enough, to my thinking, and if the two countries should come to blows, I should like to see the old 'un get the worst of it. It would be a good example to other nations, and no doubt there would be more liberty than there is now;—for instance,—one might not be liable to the gallows for following an honest trade, and people would not be afraid of the exciseman if they happened to have a drop of contraband spirits in a snug corner of their cellar."

"And, suposing America should rise up in arms to demand freedom, would you, Andrew Foster, make one to aid in so holy a cause?"

"Why, that's a question I am hardly prepared to answer," replied the other; "not that I'm very particular, either, only I don't care to take up other people's quarrels, when I've got quite enough to do to look after my own affairs. But the Americans, it seems, have already made a beginning, for a hardy Scotchman has lately taken his vessel into one of their rivers, and if he only meets with a few brace of fellows like himself, there's a pretty fair chance yet that he will bear the British on their own element."

"How heard you this news?" demanded our hero, anxiously.

" It was spread abroad just as we set sail from the port of Boston, and, as everybody was full of it, I suppose the report was true enough."

Ruthven was about to reply to this, but at the moment Captain Starkie seemed to rouse from his drunken slumbers, and, in the opinion of our hero, he fixed upon him a look that augured anything but favourably to him. He therefore changed the high tone in which he had been speaking for one that was more subdued, and said :—

"The words I have given utterance to, Andrew Foster, do not exactly represent my own feelings on this subject. That the Americans will rise in their own defence, there is no doubt; but if they do, I shall follow my own peaceful course, leaving them to fight it out as best they can."

"You have altered your tone strangely," said Andrew, who was not aware of the reason for the change; " a little while ago you seemed to speak of the Americans as of brothers that you would fight and die for, and now you talk of them as of men that you care nothing about."

" I still regard them as men that have suffered more than they ought," answered Ruthven, anxious lest the other should misunderstand his real meaning. " I admire the spirit with which they have asserted their claims to equal rights, and, had I been a countryman of theirs, I should not long have hesitated about the part I ought to take."

"Aye, every man ought to fight for himself," exclaimed Andrew, " that's just my opinion, and for that reason, I don't see why you or I need take any trouble about it. They are a brave set of fellows, and, as all the fighting must take place in their own country, they will have a chance of showing the British that they are not to have it all their own way. But hark !—some one comes; so step aside with me, for I can guess who it is, and maybe he would not like that a stranger should know of his visit here."

Ruthven and Hugh Lorimer stepped on one side, as they had been directed by the mariner, and immediately a figure enveloped in a large cloak, made his appearance through an opposite door. Wondering who it could be, they gazed upon the stranger, and what was their astonishment when, on throwing off the broad brimmed hat that had concealed his countenance, they discovered the well-known features of Lord Dalmeny.

"By Heavens! tis he!" whispered Ruthven, utterly at a loss to conceive what could have brought him to the haunt of the smugglers. Hugh Lorimer observed the surprise of his friend, and he replied :—

"Yes, it is he, sure enough, Ruthven ;—but his visits here are not uncommon events, I can assure you. He is frequently at the cave, and as his associates bear not the best of characters, I doubt not his motives would not bear the light."

"What can be his object?" muttered Ruthven.

"That," answered the other, "is more than I can tell you. He is come, however, on a visit to Captain Starkie, and, no doubt, has a task for him to execute that few others would care to aid him in. Perhaps some love affair or other, for the captain is not over particular it seems, and some of his lordship's gold would not be refused, could he only secure it by doing his dirty work."

"You say," observed Ruthven; "that it may be some love affair in which his lordship is engaged; but what can that have to do with his presence in this place?"

"Simply," answered Hugh Lorimer, " that Captain Starkie has not got a very tender conscience, and if Lord Dalmeny should chance to wish a maiden to be carried off by violence, the man he now visits is the very one that would aid him.   He is, as you perceive, of brutal disposition, and the lord's gold would gain him over, even if it were to commit a murder."

"Murder!" groaned Ruthven, involuntarily.

"Aye, he is used to the sight of blood, and would not hesitate were such a proposition made to him," replied the other; "so far he has been fortunate enough to escape the gallows, but for the honour of humanity, it is to be hoped his course is almost run, and that the time is not very far distant when he will meet his just reward.   But come, Ruthven, we have been long enough in this dark place, so lead the way, and let us once more enjoy the freedom of the upper air.

"Would that I could remain and learn the secret business that has brought Lord Dalmeny here," answered Ruthven, without appearing to heed the latter words of his companion.   "That he comes for evil I have no doubt, and something seems to tell me that his affair with Captain Starkie most deeply concerns myself.

"I do not think so," replied Hugh Lorimer; "for, depend on it, my first suspicion of his intentions was right, and that it is some female that he wants to carry off with the aid of this reckless sea wolf.   Had it been a man that Lord Dalmeny had to cope with, he has courage enough to meet him sword to sword, but he is too much accustomed to the prayers and entreaties of the women that he has deceived, to care about encountering any more of them till they are fairly out of the reach of help.   So, no doubt, his next victim is to be carried on board ship, and Captain Starkie is to be the worthy instrument of his design.   But come, Ruthven, lead me from this place or we shall be discovered."

Ruthven silently followed his companions from their place of concealment, and then, taking the lead, he conducted Hugh through the mazes of the cavern to its entrance at the sea side.   Taking this opportunity, Effie also effected her escape without being seen; and, hurrying on, she soon afterwards found herself safe at the exterior of the cavern.

"What can all this mean?" she mentally ejaculated, on being thus free from the smugglers' haunt;—"why does my brother seek companions that at one time he would have shunned?   Lord Dalmeny, too, what could be the cause of his visit?   Mischief, I doubt, but against whom is yet to be discovered.   Yet the mystery shall be solved—I, myself, will not rest till I have found out the meaning of all this, for I feel but too well assured that my brother is in danger, and who is there but myself to rescue him?"

With this she turned away, and slowly pursued her route towards home.

CHAPTER VIII.

"Reason hath fled ;—
The mind is vacant, and you now behold
The wreck of what was woman !"
THE GOLD SEEKERS.

RUTHVEN and his companion, Hugh Lorimer, walked for some time in silence after leaving the cavern; their thoughts were directed towards the singular scene they had witnessed, and each seemed almost unconscious of the other's presence, until their arrival at a lofty head, from which a magnificent view of the ocean lay spread before them, and they paused to gaze upon a scene which they had so often gazed enraptured on before.   Ruthven was the first to speak, for his heart was always full whenever he looked upon his beloved sea, and grasping the arm of his companion convulsively, he said—

"Is not this a noble and exciting scene, my friend? Does not your heart warm as you look upon those dancing waves that seem to be rejoicing as if tempests never disturbed or lashed them into madness?"

"I am, perhaps, as much an admirer of the ocean as you are," replied Hugh Lorimer; and yet I cannot forget to what a savage pitch of fury I have sometimes seen it rise. Men trust to it, Ruthven, but thousands find a resting place beneath its wild and treacherous waves.

"They do so," answered our hero, thoughtfully; "my father lost his life upon the element he loved so well; he sunk beneath the waters, and yet, Hugh Lorimer, I never loved the ocean less, because it happened to deprive me of a friend ere I had the power to assist myself. I felt that fate had destined me for a sailor's life, and, as you know, I have followed it with some success."

"That's true enough, Ruthven," replied the other; "you seem to have a fancy for the sort of thing, and to enjoy that which would be anything but agreeable to many other persons. You are fond of a wild and roving life, whilst I, on the contrary, prefer the quiet which a landsman enjoys in his own snug home. But it is a mere matter of taste after all, for though there may be dangers to encounter at sea, there are also pleasures that I dare say fully make up for whatever I have, in my ignorance, set down to the black side of the question."

"It is for its dangers that I love it," exclaimed Ruthven with enthusiasm; "were it always smooth I should have grown weary of it long before this, and perhaps should have, ere this time, turned hermit, or committed some other extravagance equally unaccountable."

"But, as it is," observed Hugh, smiling, "I suppose you will become a dweller on the sea, and either win for yourself a glorious name, or die in the attempt."

"You jest, my friend," cried John; "but, perhaps, speak truly enough for all that. I do, indeed, hope to render my name famous to my future generations, and, unless I am much mistaken, an opportunity just now presents itself that will lead me to the highest point of my ambition."

"And pray what opportunity is it you speak of?" asked Hugh Lorimer.

"The war that has just broken out in America."

"You expect then to signalize yourself by taking an active part in the struggle that is to come?"

"I will do so," answered our hero, resolutely. "I am not, I believe, without my share of courage, and it shall be well proved if I am not fated to perish at an early period of the war."

"John," exclaimed his companion, earnestly, "I know your ideas respecting freedom and independence; you are a Republican in principal, yet I do hope you will never take up arms to fight against your native country. You have said that you hope to obtain honour and renown, but be assured you never can attain either unless you take the part of your sovereign against those who have broken out into open rebellion againt him."

"Very well urged, indeed, Hugh Lorimer," answered John; "you are a patriot, I see, and, therefore, I can pardon the narrow views you have taken upon this subject. I, however, see matters in a different light; I can understand the exact position in which these American colonists are placed; the mother country has assumed parental authority over them, and having first goaded them beyond further endurance, would now punish them for daring to remonstrate. We call them subjects of the English crown; we tax them for the support of the empire, yet refuse to allow them representatives in the English Parliament. This some people call justice, but for my own part, I am inclined to think with the Americans, that it is nothing short of an insolent assumption of power."

"Now all this may be very true," replied Hugh Lorimer; "there may be a little oppression on one side, but you must admit there is a great deal of insolence on the other. There are, no doubt, faults on both sides, and if they are determined to come to blows, let them do so, and settle it as the fortune of war shall turn out. For my own part, I have no wish to interfere in the matter, nor do I see what interest you can feel in the dispute, seeing that, like myself, you are but an humble individual without power or resources to benefit either side."

"You are mistaken, friend, as far as regards myself," answered John; "I am not without the means to take an important share in the ensuing struggle, and ere long you will hear of my having rendered some service to the cause I adopt."

"What mean you, Ruthven ?"

"More than I can at present explain to you," he replied. "I will, however, tell you, that I can have the command of a ship whenever I please, and that there are hundreds of gallant fellows who would be delighted at placing themselves under me. You smile at my words, Hugh, but I am not speaking as a mere visionary, and here twelvemonths have passed away you will acknowledge the truth of what I now tell you."

"And these men," observed the other; "who are so willing to place themselves under your command are enemies to England ?"

"They are," answered Ruthven; "and, to my thinking, none the worse for that circumstance. Be that, however, as it may, my mind is made up, and all I now desire is to prevail on you to become my companion in this search after renown."

"What! and fight against my own country ?"

"Aye, there's the difficulty; there are few of us that like to take up arms against our country, but, in this instance, we have a good excuse for doing so; England is no longer a land of liberty, and therefore I, for one, think it high time to cast off my allegiance."

"And by doing so become no better than a Buccaneer," answered Hugh Lorimer; "aye, Ruthven, disguise the truth as you will, the title is the right one, and not only England, but all other civilized nations will join in denouncing you as a traitor to the country of your birth."

"Let them," exclaimed Ruthven; "let them call me what they will, America shall henceforth become my adopted country, and there, at least, I will achieve honour, by gallantly fighting in her cause.

"Say rather that you will achieve dishonour," cried the other, reproachfully. "Is it not a crime to raise one's hand against a parent, and have not these colonists been too precipitate in drawing the sword when the quarrel that has arisen might have been made up by more pacific measures ?"

Tush, man !" ejaculated Ruthven, impatiently; "I am in no humour to argue further upon the subject; I have formed my own notions about it, and now I should like to prevail on you to join with me in obtaining renown; let it be recollected that this is a struggle to free a great and powerful nation from bondage, and that if the Americans succeed in affecting their object, they will not fail to reward those who aid them in their noble cause. For my own part, my mind is fully made up, and glad should I be to hear my friend, Hugh Lorimer, promise to join with me in the enterprise."

"The truth is," replied Hugh, "I look with dislike upon this rebellion, and no hope of enriching myself will ever make me forget the duty I owe my country."

"Humph!" exclaimed the other with a sneer; "perhaps you have no great stomach for fighting?"

"That I am no coward you have good reason to know," answered the other warmly. "In a good cause I am willing, at any time, to risk my life for the benefit of my native land; if soldiers or sailors are required to fight against the natural enemies of Britain, I will be among the first to offer my humble services. You, however, ask me to fight against my own countrymen, and, therefore, I at once declare that I will prefer being called a coward, to bringing upon myself the reproaches that must be consequent upon my adopting your proposition."

"I do not call you a coward," exclaimed Ruthven, "though I may perhaps have been a little too warm in advocating that I wish to prosper. Excuse the conduct of your own rulers as you will, still it must be acknowledged that the Americans have much to complain of; they have been goaded to resistance, and surely, since I can see the injustice they have endured, it would be cowardice to stand idly by when I have the power to aid them. I feel deeply interested in their cause, and if I have spoken thus urgently to you, it is because I would have made a convert of my own opinions.

"Be assured then that your labour will be thrown away," cried Hugh Lorimer. "I am equally resolved as yourself, and since nothing further can come of this, let us drop the subject and talk of other matters that may be less exciting. Our visit to the cave, for instance, may afford a subject upon which to exercise our conjectures since I can form no idea of the motive that could have induced the haughty Lord Dalmeny to visit the rough fellows we saw assembled there."

"Lord Dalmeny is a villain," exclaimed John, "and therefore we may well believe that his motives for visiting Captain Starkie were of the black nature. But we are interrupted, I see, for yonder comes poor May Grayson, whose fate must ever remind us of the fiend like impostor of her lordly seducer."

The maniac girl had by this time approached them, and the wild disorder of her dress, together with the wandering of her ever restless eye, told but too plainly of a mind utterly shattered and overthrown. Yet occasionally she burst forth with snatches of various songs, all of which had reference to the fate of maidens, who, relying upon the faith of man, had fallen into shame and dishonour. It seemed, too, that she had taken especial care in the arangement of her attire, for wild flowers of every hue and description were placed in profusion about her person, whilst pieces of straw and long grass were intermingled after a most fantastic fashion.

"A fair good day to you both," she cried, on approaching within a few paces of the young men; "I warrant me now you have come forth to see the bridal, and a bonny one it will be, for all will be welcome, and none shall depart, saying that we have been niggardly in our preparation for this happy day."

"Whose bridal are you speaking of, May?" enquired John.

"Whose should I speak of but my own?" she replied. "Have I not waited many a long and weary month for this happy moment, and now that it has come, all hearts shall be made as lightsome and cheerful as my own."

"And who," asked Hugh Lorimer, "is to be the bridegroom?"

"Hush!" she whispered, "I must not name him now, for he would be angry with me, and then there would be an end of all the fine doings I told you of. But he is of high name and station—I may tell you that—and he has a noble mansion to dwell in, of which I shall soon be the mistress."

"Where is his mansion?" asked John, willing to humour her in the wild otion she had taken into her head;—"is it anywhere in this neigbourhood, May Grayson?"

"No, it is far—far away."

"In which direction?"

"Yonder; far down in the deep blue sea. There dwells my lover, and there I am going to join him;—it is but to plunge from this rock, and then water sprites and fairy elves will guide me to the home of my husband."

"Nay, girl," exclaimed John, soothingly, "you had better wait till the bridegroom himself comes to fetch you; remember, the rock is very steep, and to plunge from it would be to precipitate yourself into certain destruction."

"Think you then," she asked, "the good people he dwells among will not watch over my safety?"

"I fear not," answered John; "at any rate, the risk is too great, and I would therefore prevail upon you to wait till the bridegroom comes to conduct you to the altar."

"But I have waited too long for him, already."

"Be patient, and he will yet come."

"He has sent for me, and I must obey," she replied; "I have had a summons from him, and he bade me put on my bridal attire, and meet him beneath the dark blue waters, where he would make me his wife and the mistress of all the treasures of the deep."

"Believe me, May Grayson, you are mistaken," exclaimed John; "this is some dream that you have had, for he who deceived and thus abandoned you, dwells not where you would so madly seek him."

"How know you that?" she asked quickly; "have I not told you he sent, bidding me no longer delay, for that he had surely repented the cruel wrong he had done, and was waiting for me in his chrystal palace? Oh, shall I not be a happy bride after all I have suffered, and yet you would persuade me that all this is but a dream."

"And so it is, my poor girl," exclaimed Hugh Lorimer; "we are your friends, and grieving as we do for the false step you have taken, would fain prevail on you to think no more of one who is unworthy of your love."

"Oh, you wrong him—indeed, indeed you do," cried the poor maniac, earnestly. "He has been thoughtless; and so, for that matter, have I; but even the worst of sufferings may have an end, and though I have sorrowed for the past, yet the time has at length arrived when I may hold up my head with the highest, and none shall even so much as whisper the shame that once came upon me."

"None ever speak of it, May Grayson," exclaimed Lorimer; "people pity even though they may blame the weakness that has produced all this misery."

"Aye, but I shall want their pity no more now that I am to be a bride," answered the distracted girl; "he will protect me from the sneers and scoffings of those that looked scornfully upon a fallen creature, and there will be some consolation, surely, in knowing that the proudest must acknowledge me their equal when once the marriage rites have been celebrated."

"But," observed Hugh Lorimer, "it seems you have taken a strange notion into your head that he you seek is to be found beneath the waves that are rolling beneath our feet. This, to say the least of it, is a wild thought of yours, and one that must end in disappointment."

"Oh, but he will be angry if I do not go to him," she replied; he is waiting for me, and will grow impatient if I make any longer delay."

And saying this, she was rushing towards the cliff for the purpose of precipitating herself into the roaring surge beneath, when the powerful arm of John was stretched forth to rescue her from an inevitable death.

"May Grayson," he exclaimed, "you would madly plunge yourself into destruction! Compose yourself, I entreat you, and suffer me to see you home to your cottage, before worse comes of this. You know us both; we are friends, and, therefore, you can have no reason to distrust us."

"Friends!" she cried, reproachfully; "you can be no friends of mine if you would step in to prevent my bridal. See, I am dressed in all my gayest clothes, and Nature has lent me some of her fairest flowers for the adornment and setting forth of my person. He that is to be my husband was ever fond of seeing me look gay and smart, and so I put those things on me to let him know that I have not forgotten former times."

"Well, well, girl," exclaimed John; "it's right enough, I dare say, to keep these things in your mind; it shows what a kind heart has been broken by this villain, who——"

"Oh, do not call him a villain," she cried, eagerly interrupting him. "I once thought him so myself, but I will never believe it of him again, because he is now going to make me his wife; so there's an end of my tears for the past, and as for the future, who can doubt but it will be a very happy one?"

"I dare say it will, my sweet May," exclaimed John, kindly; "but you must go home and remain very quiet till the time arrives that is to make you the wife of this young Lord of Dalmeny."

"Ah! you know the name, do you?"

"I do."

"Is he not a brave and noble youth?"

"He is a villain!"

"Ah! you called him so before," cried May Grayson; "this is the second

No. 9

time you have called him villain, and yet here I stay to hear the foul slander heaped upon his name."

"You have every reason to think him so," exclaimed John; "but for him you would now have been as happy as I once knew you to be; and how do I find you on my return from abroad—a changed and heart-broken girl, a mere wreck of the once pure and innocent May Grayson!"

"Let us prevail on her to go home," interrupted Hugh Lorimer; "together we may be able to withdraw her from this spot; it is, indeed, desirable that we should do so, for the sight of the ocean always affects her in this way. She knows that he sailed across the sea, and from the hour of his departure she has never ceased to watch for his return whenever a vessel is seen approaching the shores.

"Come, May Grayson," said John, coaxingly; "come with us and we will take you where you are more likely to see his lordship than by remaining here; it is said he is about to come home again from foreign parts—nay, perhaps he has already arrived, and in that case you will have an opportunity of seeing him sooner than you expected."

"You would deceive me," she exclaimed wildly; "it is yonder, where the waters roll and foam, that I shall see him, and I will go and seek him there, lest he should be angry at my long delay. Has he not bidden me to the marriage feast, and shall I listen to those that would deceive me with false stories about him? Oh, you know not how my heart yet clings to him, for though he deceived me, his heart is not so bad as people say it is, and for all that people say against it, I shall now be 'my lady,' and those that spoke ill of him will be made to confess that they have done him most foul wrong."

"At any rate," answered Hugh Lorimer, "it would be useless for you to remain here any longer. The Lord Dalmeny no longer thinks of you, and even were you to throw yourself in his way, it would only be to feel the additional mortification of seeing that he has not only forgotten his vows to you, but that he has also set his heart upon the ruin of other girls, even as he sought and effected your's."

"Oh, do not speak thus of him," cried May Grayson; "he has been wild and thoughtless, perhaps; but those days are past and over, and he will come back to be a blessing to the neighbourhood."

"Nay, girl," exclaimed John, "if the truth must be told, he is come back, and is now once more dwelling beneath the roof of his noble ancestors."

"Ah!" she sighed, "I have fancied myself that I saw him; but it was only in my dreams, for they say the ship he sailed in was lost, and that he dwells beneath the sea in a palace of gold and jewels, built up of the riches that have gone to the bottom, where vessels, and crews, and all have been plunged down amidst the mingled cries of drowning men, and the dismal moaning of the winds. There dwells he, lord of all—for, mark me, I have dreamed of all this, and it is as true as that you are both standing before me."

"And," exclaimed John, "you would just now have plunged into the waves, in the expectation of thus meeting him who is not worthy of a single thought."

"If I could but find him," cried May Grayson, "I should not mind any danger, however great it might be. I have dreamt of his ocean palace, and have fancied myself the lady of it all, and that he I love was kind at last, seeking by every means he could think of to banish from my mind the recollection of things that are past and ought to be forgotten."

"Yet these were but dreams after all, May," answered John, "and, therefore, ought to make no impression upon you. His lordship, I again tell you, is now in the Castle of Dalmeny, where you went to visit him when the mummery was going on last night."

"I dreamt of some such thing," she replied; "but the scene, instead of laying in the Castle of Dalmeny, was beneath the waters of the ocean. I thought myself in a spacious hall, and standing near to Lord Dalmeny, who was surrounded by fiends and demons, and all kinds of horrible forms. It seemed to me that he had given offence to some of them, for there was anger among them, and sharp words were spoken, and, perhaps, blows would have followed. But just then, a mighty tempest arose, that shook the building to its very foundation, and many trembled with fear, for it seemed as if the place would yield before the mighty force of the terrible tempest. But all passed over, and when I looked round for him that my heart worships, he was no-where to be seen, and I was left alone in the presence of fiends that seemed ready to tear me to pieces."

"The scene you have described was a real one," said John; "for it all happened last night within the Castle of Dalmeny. I was myself present, and saw the anger of which you speak; I also heard the tempest, and was a witness of its effects upon the ancient building, for the highest stone was levelled with the ground, and that brings about an ancient tradition that foretold the fall of the family whenever such an event should occur. I also observed the sudden disappearance of the young lord, but he returned again shortly after you had taken your departure."

"You would persuade me, then," she cried, "that Lord Dalmeny has returned to his castle, and that he no longer thinks of the vows he once took to make me his bride."

"He is now in his own castle," answered Hugh Lorimer, "and you have already heard from us that he is pursuing the same reckless course that he followed ere he went abroad."

"It is false!" she exclaimed, vehemently; "these are tales invented to make me believe that he has forgotten me, and that after all, I shall not be his bride. But I am not to be deceived, for he is true and faithful, and will not break the solemn promise he has given me."

"It is in vain to depend on one, the chief part of whose life has been passed in deceit," replied John. "Few who know Lord Dalmeny would be inclined to give him credit for good intention, and, therefore, would I prevail upon you to think no more of a villain, who, having betrayed a woman, leaves her to pine away her life amidst the cold neglect of a harsh judging world. Trust him not, May Grayson, or you will again be deceived by this fiend in human form."

"I will not hear him thus reviled," exclaimed May, angrily; "he has been false to his love, as I to my own cost have found; but he will repent the evil of his days, and when he remembers the time when he loved me, he will perhaps do me the justice I have a right to demand."

"You talk more rationally now, my poor girl," observed John; "your words and manner are less wild than they were but a little while since, and I would fain take the opportunity to prevail on you to return home, and forget the villain who has wrecked your peace and happiness in this world. Forget him if you can, or if you remember him, let it be only as one whose falsehood and pretended love have made you what you now are."

"Indeed, indeed, John, I will hear no more of this," she cried, half angrily; "you know how my heart loves to dwell on the days that are gone, and yet you cruelly remind me of the miseries that now afflict me."

"Then take a friend's counsel, and think no more of it," exclaimed John; "your mind will thus become calm; and perhaps in the course of time, reason will again resume its sway."

"Do you think, then, that he will never fulfil the vows he so often made me?"

"I am sure he will not."

"If I thought so," she muttered, gazing wildly round her; "if I thought so, I would seek speedy means to get that rest which I can never hope to find in this world."

"What mean you, May Grayson?" exclaimed John, alarmed at the tone and accent with which these words were uttered; "you speak of obtaining rest, and your words fill me with apprehension; tell me, girl, what are the fearful thoughts that are now occupying your distempered brain?"

"Death!" she replied, solemnly.

"Ah! but not by your own hand? you would not rush unbidden and unprepared into the presence of your Maker?"

"I am crazed," she exclaimed, "and again the image of Lord Dalmeny is before me;—see! he stands upon the brink of yonder precipice; he motions me to follow him!—John, I will no longer be restrained!—release me, for I will follow him, even though it be to death!"

With these words she sprang forward, and having broken away from the grasp with which John had held her, hurried onwards to the edge of the cliff that overhung the sea. Here she paused for an instant, and then hearing the footsteps of the two young men advancing, she leaped with a cry of triumph into the raging flood beneath!

Alarmed at this, John and his companion hurried down to the beach, and leaping into a boat, rowed out to the assistance of May Grayson, whose form might still be distinguished floating on the waves. After some exertion they succeeded in rescuing her at the very moment when she was about to sink for ever, and, having placed her in the boat, they returned to the shore, when they succeeded in restoring her to animation. This done, they procured further assistance, and the unfortunate May Grayson was conveyed to her own cottage.

CHAPTER IX.

"Grief has changed me since you saw me last,
And careful hours with Time's deformed hand
Hath written strange defeatures o'er my face."

SHAKSPERE.

John and his friend, Hugh Lorimer, could render but little more assistance to the unfortunate girl, and having ascertained that she was likely to do well, they took their departure from the cottage, and again continued their way homewards. And now their conversation turned once more upon Lord Dalmeny, and the misery he had brought into a neighbourhood, that but for him would have been blessed with peace and content.

"Would to Heaven he had never returned here," exclaimed John, after a pause of some minutes duration; "his presence seem to bring mischief with it, and sometimes I fancy he is some infernal agent, endued with a human form, that he may the more readily bring destruction upon those against whom his evil practices are directed."

"You are not the only one that has thought so," answered the other, "for I have myself had a notion of the same kind, and my only consolation is, that his own evil deeds will prove a certain antidote to a long continuance of them. He is hourly raising up more enemies, and by and by, he will fall by the hands of those he has injured."

"That is likely enough," exclaimed John through his clenched teeth.

"Ah! you have some thoughts then, it appears, that you may prove the avenger?"

"He affects to love my sister," answered the young man: "and should I see cause to believe that he means to add her to the number of his victims, I shall not fail to hurl upon him the full measure of my wrath."

"But he is your foster brother," observed Hugh Lorimer.

"He is, but the tie will be loosened the moment I've cause to suspect him. I am watching him narrowly, and, by my soul, I swear to sacrifice him to my vengeance if he dares but to imagine a thought of evil towards her!"

"You would slay him, John?"

"Aye, even though he were kneeling before the sacred altar, he should not escape from death!"

"But you would thus lay yourself open to the laws you had violated."

"That I should not care for," replied John; "besides, I have grown tired of this country, and it would not cost me a single pang to leave it for ever. My home is on the deep, Hugh Lorimer. Battle and strife are the elements I love, and though my name may be tainted with murder, yet will I do such deeds that people shall forget the crime in the deeds that are to follow."

"Let us hope that you will not be forced to carry your threats into execution," returned Hugh Lorimer; "the nobleman of whom we are speaking, may not intend treachery against your sister, and in that case you will be spared the commission of a crime that I shudder to think of."

"The wolf is not to be easily turned from the pursuit of its prey," answered the other; "Lord Dalmeny has determined ere this, whether my sister Effie is to be the next victim of his lawless passion, and his life hangs upon the course he may think proper to adopt. He knows full well I am not to be trifled with, and I will hunt him from one end of the world to the other but he shall die for any injury he may inflict on the fair fame of my sister."

"And yet, if I understand rightly, you have thoughts of leaving your native country for ever."

"Aye, such is indeed my intention."

"How then can you protect Effie from the acts of this lordly libertine?"

"My being at a distance," replied John, "will make no difference to him if he should basely accomplish his infernal purpose, I should hear of the disgrace were it to fall upon my family, and even from the uttermost bounds of the earth would I fly to avenge the dishonour upon the guilty perpetrator. This Lord Dalmeny knows: he has had proof of my resentment ere now, and therefore I hardly think he will venture to call down upon himself the fury he has every reason to dread."

"Hist, John, and let us change this subject," cried his companion; "we are now treading on holy ground where thoughts such as these should not find utterance."

"True, we are in a churchyard," answered John, pausing to gaze upon the numerous memorials of the dead with which they were surrounded. "Here lie those that have passed through this world of sorrows; their griefs are over, and they sleep in peace beneath our feet, little heeding the troubles that afflict those who have succeeded them."

"Who is it that comes to disturb the dead with their unhallowed steps?" demanded some one close at hand; "speak, whoever ye be, or take the curses of one who hates the whole race of mankind."

"Hark!" cried Hugh with terror; "it is the voice of Mabel Logan, whose grief for the loss of her daughter has driven her almost mad. Let us avoid her, or she will heap curses and imprecations on our heads."

"I care not for her maledictions," exclaimed John, resolutely: "she has spoken to us, and, therefore, I will not pass on till I have heard from her own lips the cause of her being in this lone and cheerless place."

With this he advanced a pace or two further, and then nearly concealed in the dark shadow of a tombstone, he beheld the form of Mabel kneeling upon a grave, and seemingly engaged in earnest prayer over the beloved form that the earth concealed from her view. She was, however, soon conscious of the two intruders, and glancing furiously towards them, she motioned with her hand for them to depart.

"Away!" she cried;—"leave me, I command, or my curses will fall upon and wither ye!"

"We are no enemies of yours, Mabel," answered John; "our path lay through the churchyard, and we knew not that in coming hither we should disturb your meditations."

"You have disturbed them," she answered; "I was thinking of my poor child that lies mouldering at my feet, and ye must needs come to bring back my thoughts to him that has brought me to misery and despair."

"Of whom speak you, old woman?" demanded John.

"Of whom else but that graceless villain, Lord Dalmeny," she replied; ' hath he not robbed me of the only comfort that was left me in this life, and yet he suffers me to live that I may endure the agony he has inflicted."

"Alas!" groaned our hero, "then you also have to bewail the presence of that fiend in human form."

"I have," answered Mabel; "he has wrung tears from my eyes, but at the same time, my lips can pronounce curses, and it shall be no fault of mine if I do not heap upon him such a load of misery that he shall execrate the hour when the demon of mischief tempted him to injure me."

"He will have little pity from us," exclaimed Hugh Lorimer, "even if your threats are fulfilled."

"And fulfilled they shall be," she replied; "aye, and upon yourselves, too, if ye do not instantly depart, and leave me to indulge my sorrows alone."

"Ere we go," exclaimed John; "I should like to learn the cause of your hatred towards Lord Dalmeny."

"Does not your heart tell you he is a villain?" asked the old woman.

"It does," replied the other, "but I would fain learn in what way he has injured you."

"He first deceived and then broke the heart of my poor child."

"You are not the only one that has to mourn the disgrace that has fallen upon their daughters," answered John.

"It may be so," she replied; "but who thinks of the misery of others when their own is weighing upon their heart?"

"You are right, woman," exclaimed her interrogator, "for we are all selfish alike in our sorrows, and think lighter of those that fall upon our friends and neighbours. But you were saying that your daughter lies in the sleep of death beneath our feet? Prithee, tell me how long she has been there?"

"I have scarcely heeded the time that has passed," answered Mabel, "but the hours have been long and weary, and though I have prayed for death to relieve me, yet here you see an old woman weeping and wailing like a child over the last relics of a well-loved toy."

"Was your daughter young?" asked John.

"She was."

"And yet you appear to be weighed down with years!"

"It is grief that has done it," replied Mabel; "two months of sorrow have been more to me than ten years of peace and happiness. Whilst my child lived in innocence I was joyous and content, but when I saw how deeply the canker worm of grief had eaten into her heart, my soul gave way to despondency, and I felt that death would be a release."

"What age was your daughter?" asked Hugh Lorimer.

"Scarcely twenty summers had passed from the first cry of infancy till I saw her laid in the grave that sorrow had dug for her," answered Mabel. "But ye must both have known the lass, for she was looked upon as the fairest flower of our vale; and in the pride of my heart I thanked Heaven for bestowing upon me a child that was the envy of all who saw her. Ah, me! Little did I think when gazing upon her with the delight of a fond mother, that the very beauty I was admiring would prove the destruction of her I loved so well."

"And so Lord Dalmeny saw the girl, and won her by his arts," exclaimed John.

"Alas! he did, indeed!" groaned the old woman.

"Are you sure you are not mistaken?" demanded the other; "the nobleman you speak of has many crimes to answer for, and I would gladly discover that he is at least guiltless of the one you charge him with."

"The false villain was the murderer of my child," cried Mabel, with rising anger.

"Nay," exclaimed John, "do not let my words cause thy wrath, for I do not doubt thee. Thou hast said thy daughter was beautiful; perhaps she was also vain, and, in that case, the flattery of her noble wooer would not pass by unheeded."

"She was fair, and knew it, as most other girls do," answered Mabel; "the young lord saw and was captivated with her charms;—he flattered her, she weakly yielded, and, when it was too late, found that he had deceived her."

"Did she reproach him for his perfidy?" asked John.

"Lord Dalmeny gave her no opportunity to do so," replied the old woman; "he left England to roam in foreign parts, and, as you may perhaps have heard, returned to this neighbourhood only a few days since. I have not seen him yet, but people say he has come back unchanged in heart, and, if so, I fear there will be many a sad spirit ere long among us."

"Your story has deeply interested me, old woman," exclaimed John. "I have myself been absent for some time, and, therefore, all you have been relating was unknown;—that Lord Dalmeny, however, was a villain, I had but too much reason to know, and I only bide my opportunity to crush him with the vengeance that his crimes so loudly call for."

"Ha! ha!" shouted Mabel, "you, then, have cause to hate him as I do? —He has sought the ruin of some one that you love;—nay, perhaps has accomplished his fiendish purpose, and thus has made one more enemy to seek his death."

"It will depend on his future actions," answered Ruthven, coldly.

"What!" cried the old woman, "will you wait till he has done all the mischief he meditates?"

"I said not that," replied John; "but I will watch him closely, and, should I see cause to fear the treachery I suspect him of, he shall feel that he has at length made one enemy too many."

"Aye, aye, revenge is pleasant," exclaimed Mabel; "I have often thought I would try to obtain it for myself; but his lordship has too much power, and he would crush me ere the hour I look forward to arrives."

"What hour is it you speak of?"

"That," she replied, "in which I shall behold him writhing on the brink of eternity;—when his thoughts shall turn back to the past, and when his guilty soul shall sicken at the dreadful punishment his crimes have merited. In that moment my revenge will be complete; and, if aught be wanting to add to his despair, he shall quit this world with my curses still ringing in his ears. That is the hour I hope to see, and to obtain the favour, there is no suffering, no privation that I would not cheerfully submit to."

"Perhaps," observed John, "the period you speak of is not very far off."

"Hah!—what mean you?"

"That my dagger may soon find its way to his heart, unless he discontinues his suit to one whose happiness is far dearer to me than my own."

"I see," cried Mabel, "he is endeavouring to supplant you in the heart of a mistress?"

"It is my sister," replied John, "that the villain would deceive with his honied words and false promises."

"Well," cried the old woman, "it matters not who the female may be, for the libertine deserves to die. Nay, I have myself, ere now, thought of taking his life;—aye, you start, and appear amazed, but again I tell you I had resolved to rid the world of a monster that seemed born to be a scourge to his fellow-creatures. For days and days, I carried a well-sharpened knife about with me, but Heaven thwarted my design, and no doubt, for some wise purpose of its own; at any rate, Lord Dalmeny still lives, though how long he continues to do so will depend on his future conduct."

"Enough of this," exclaimed John; "I have already spent too much time here, so now we part, though it is not unlikely I may seek you here again before many days have passed away."

"Stay," cried the old woman, taking his arm, and leading him towards the half-ruined church. "I was thinking of reading you a lesson upon pride, and the end of pride. Nay, it will not take me long, and surely you will stay to keep me company."

"Be brief then," exclaimed John, who found it would be in vain to resist. "I am already late, and there are those at home who will be uneasy at my absence."

"Well," began the old woman, "you see yonder pulpit, where many a holy man has got up to teach his hearers the way to climb to Heaven. I have known three of them in my time, and good men they were, but they had proud hearts and believed that none could be rewarded in another world for their good deeds unless they followed their advice. This was vanity you must allow, and there lie the three worthy men in the chancel, neither better nor worse than those they sought to teach."

"But what has all this to do with me?" demanded Ruthven, impatiently.

"I would warn you against pride," answered Mabel, "so now look at that fine gallery above where the pulpit stands; you see how handsomely the panels are carved with the badges of the family it belonged to, and how softly the seats are stuffed that the owners should sit easily, and then there are curtains made to draw around lest the cold air should blow upon those who were fortune's favourites. You perhaps do not recollect what a gay throng used to assemble there to hear the word of grace, but I mind it well, and methinks I now see the flaunting dames and the gay gentlemen that used to sit there as if they came to make a show of themselves and nothing more. And now where are they all? Look at yonder marble tomb, far beneath it lie the mouldering bones of the rich and powerful! What think you of that, youth, is it not a fall of pride?"

"It may be so," answered Ruthven, "and yet, for the life of me, I cannot see the use of my listening to it."

"It will not hurt you at any rate," cried Mabel, grasping him still more firmly as she saw he was about to leave her. "You have now heard a lesson upon pride of birth, and if you will turn your eyes towards yonder raised place in front of the pulpit, you will see the spot on which stood the stool of repentance. There I have seen many a fair creature, who in the pride of her heart

has forgotten herself so far as to yield to the seductive arts of treacherous man. And what brought them to this shame, think you? Why pride beyond their own proper station; they thought themselves better than their neighbours, and now how many of the poor giddy creatures have found an end to their sorrows in the cold grave!"

"I have heard enough," exclaimed Ruthven, impatiently.

"Nay, the best is to come yet," cried the old woman, detaining him by main force. "There was one who now lies in this churchyard; I mean Annot Lainson, the mother of the widow Ruthven, whose son has turned out such a wild slip—but you know them not, I dare say, and so I'll come at once to the story I was about to relate. Well, by yonder pillow sate old Annot Lainson for many and many a year, and if you might have judged by her demure looks you would have supposed she never knew what sin was; but you look uneasy young man, and perhaps my story is distasteful to you."

"Not at all," answered Ruthven, anxious to conceal his emotion, and yet desirous that she should continue her narrative. "Proceed, I prithee, good dame, and you shall find me a patient listener."

"Well," resumed the old woman, "I was telling you that yonder she used to sit as demurely as might be, and methinks I see her now, clad in her humble garb, and looking far more like a saint than a sinner, as she was. But pride was her undoing, for though of lowly birth, she was as proud as Lucifer himself, and few of her neighbours ever knew what it was even to get so much as a parting greeting from her. People knew not what to make of her, but all thought she was virtuous, and when the truth came to be told that she was frail like many others of her sex, there were none found to believe it. Yet for all that, I tell you, Annot Lainson was proved to be no better than many others that have fallen both before and since, and to make short of a long story, it turned out in the end that, for all her sanctified looks, she was a poor

No. 10

sinful, fallen woman.   There was pride for you! is it not enough to make you laugh at all who hold their heads as high as did Annot Lainson?"

"Perhaps," cried Ruthven, with difficulty concealing his emotion; "perhaps the world foully traduced her."

"No such thing, for it was all truth that I have told you," answered the old woman. "However, the subject does not seem very pleasing to you, so I'll tell you another story if you will only have a little patience. You must know then that a few nights since I dreamt that I was alone in this very churchyard, kneeling, as is my custom, on the grave of my child; and somehow I felt an awe that I had never experienced before, for a sudden darkness came on; the moon was veiled in heavy clouds, and I was going to hurry away, for fear a storm might rise, when I heard a dismal din, and presently a supernatural light shone forth so, that I could see every object as plainly as if it had been broad daylight. Then I heard another sound that thrilled me to the very heart, but I could not flee, for my feet seemed chained to the ground, and presently the graves opened, and from every one of them arose a corse, most of whom I had known in their lifetime. It was a fearful sight, young man, and the worst of it was that I was obliged to look on, because I was unable to stir from the spot. Well, I stood trembling, as you may suppose, and presently a funeral procession arrived, followed by a long train of mourners; and the priest mutters prayers over the corse, and then they laid it in the ground, there to remain and rot in the solitude of this dreary churchyard. Then the mourners departed without appearing to notice the grim spectres that were looking on at them, and no sooner were they gone, than there arose from the newly-made grave, a figure dressed in his shroud, and looking the most awful sight my eyes ever beheld. I could have screamed with terror, but at that moment who think you I recognized in the horrible figure before me? who think you was it but Lord Dalmeny, the destroyer of so much happiness. Aye, it was he, indeed; his crimes were ended, and they had brought his bones to moulder away in this lonely spot, where lie so many of his hapless victims."

"Psha!" cried John, "it was but a dream."

"True," she replied, "but such a dream never had I before; it seemed to be reality, and I trembled as I gazed upon the grim forms of those that surrounded me.   Then there were two other ghastly objects that stood just before him that appeared to be Lord Dalmeny; they were females, and each of them held a lighted torch in her hand, the flames of which cast a red and frightful glare over the whole scene. Well, I thought I should have sunk into the earth with fright, and presently afterwards, a perfect tempest of wind arose, the head gear of the two corses flew off, and I beheld the features of my mother and Annot Lainson, both of whom have been in their graves this many a long year.   At this sight I screamed aloud with terror, and then came a howling blast, that extinguished the torches, and when I looked around me again, the spirits had all vanished, and the moon was riding as calmly and serenely in the sky as if nothing whatever had occurred."

"Oh! you awoke from your dream, and found everything exactly as it had been before you fell asleep."

Mabel made no reply to this, and John sank into a reverie, occasioned by the wild narrative he had been listening to. But the circumstance that most excited his wonder, was that which related to Lord Dalmeny, and anxious as he was to make himself acquainted with every particular connected with that much-dreaded nobleman, he enquired of the dame whether she could tell him any more of one in whose dark career he felt so great an interest.   At this question Mabel raised her eyes from the ground, and fixing them stedfastly upon the countenance of the querist, replied :—

"I can tell you that he is ambitious, but that I dare say you knew well enough before ; that he is haughty, cruel, fond of power, a tyrant to those beneath him, and a heartless libertine. These are not half his evil qualities, but they are sufficient to show you that his presence in this neighbourhood is not coveted either by the rich or the poor. And for that matter," she continued, looking yet more earnestly at John ; " he is not the only one that may prove a scourge to those he ought to shield and protect. You have nearly the same base principles in your heart, though at present they have not been fully displayed ; yours is a restless, discontented spirit that will lead you into many a strange scene during life ; distinction and riches are within your grasp, yet ambition will lead you astray, and your name will be dishonoured, though it is in your power to attain the highest rank in society. You will become a traitor to your own country ; your sword will be drawn against those you ought to protect, and instead of advancing in life, you will lose the estimation of fellow men, and if I read your destiny rightly, you will go down into the tomb with the name of a Pirate !"

" 'Tis false, woman !" exclaimed John, fiercely ; " my spirit, I own, is a restless one that urges me seek glory wherever I can find it ; my place is in battle,—my element the sea,—and if I do not achieve honour, after ages shall at least confess that I was no pirate."

" I tell thee I have foreboded nothing but the truth," cried the old woman.

" Dost thou know me ?"

" Thy name I know not," answered Mabel, " but thy destiny is marked upon thy countenance. There is much that is good, and much that is evil about thee ; thou canst be a firm and steady friend, but against thine enmity none can stand ; thy fury is like the tempest, that sweeps away everything to destruction, yet in thy heart are many noble qualities that would confer honour upon the greatest in the land."

" Hear me, woman," cried John ; " hear me, I say, and —"

" I will hear nothing, now," she replied, wildly ; " I am bid to hasten away from hence. Hark ! hear you not thunder rolling far off ?—it is my summons to depart, and I dare not disobey it."

" Nay, but for one moment —"

" I cannot listen to you," she cried ; " duty calls me home, and I must go, whither you dare not follow me. Watch me not,—pursue me not, or my heaviest curses will fall upon and blight you !"

With these words she sprang from the ruined church, and in another instant was out of sight. For a few moments John stood wrapt in thought, for the words she had uttered filled his soul with wonder, and almost doubting whether she belonged to this world, he dreaded lest by pursuing her, he should bring upon himself the malediction she had threatened him with. At last, however, he roused himself, and hurrying into the churchyard, found Hugh Lorimer still waiting near the spot where he had left him.

" Upon my word, John," he exclaimed, " you seem to have picked up some strange company in our ramble. First we met with poor crazy May Grayson, and now you have parted with an old beldame, who seems to be almost as much beside herself."

John made no reply, but motioning to his friend, hurried away, and in a few minutes afterwards they were both of them once more on their way homewards.

CHAPTER X.

" The time was that I hated thee,
And yet it is not that I bear thee love,
Thy company which erst was irksome to me,
I will endure."   SHAKSPERE.

WHEN Lord Dalmeny found himself alone in the cavern with Captain Starkie, the smuggler, he stood irresolute a moment or two, and then beckoning the fellow a little on one side, he whispered :—

" I sought you, captain, in your wild retreat here among the rocks, to learn from your own lips whether I may rely upon that friendship which you have sworn on former occasions ?"

" I see no reason why you should doubt me, my lord," answered the smuggler ; " unless indeed you are conscious that you are about to ask more than I can accede to."

" What ! hast thou grown suddenly conscientious ?"

" Why, I don't know," replied the other, " that I can be accused of possessing more than my share of that commodity. But I happen to know your lordship has even less of it than I have myself, and perhaps you have something to propose that may startle even a rough-spun fellow like myself."

" Thou would'st not have spoken thus to me a short time since," exclaimed Lord Dalmeny.

" Perhaps not," returned the other ; " but then your absence from Scotland has not improved you much ; in fact, people say that you are more of a devil than ever, and it may be dangerous to mix myself up with one that is always scheming all sorts of myschief."

" But surely you don't believe all that people choose to say against me, captain ?"

" I do not," replied Starkie, " but if you are guilty of only half that I've heard, it's quite enough to make a man cautious how he is seen in your company."

" And think you not," exclaimed Lord Dalmeny, " that my character is as likely to suffer were it to be known that you and I have met together on a matter of business ?",

" I question whether it would," answered the smuggler ; " however, it's no use talking about these things now, so, if you have any question to ask, out with it at once, and then I'll tell you whether we can sail together in the same vessel."

" In the first place, then," returned Lord Dalmeny, " I would like to know whether I could have the use of your lugger for a few days ?"

" That will depend on the purpose you want it for."

" You shall know all in good time," replied his lordship ; " I have asked a plain, straitforward question, and I require a brief reply to it."

" Well, then," answered Captain Starkie. " I'll be as plain as I can ; the truth is my lugger is just now lying idle out yonder, and if you are not after any of your old tricks, she may be hired in exchange for a little of your lordships' gold."

" The gold shall not be wanting," exclaimed the young nobleman, " but if you and I come to terms, it may be necessary that you throw off some of this squeaimishness. I shall want the vessel for a few days, and the cabin must be placed entirely at my own disposal."

" Humph !" ejaculated the smuggler, " I begin to see which way the wind blows; there's a fair maiden in the case, and you intend to make her the companion of your voyage?"

"You have guessed rightly so far."

"I thought so," replied Starkie; "and if I am not greatly mistaken, the girl has no great opinion of your lordship, and would not, of her own accord, venture to trust herself with one whose character is none of the fairest."

"You are right again," answered Lord Dalmeny, gloomily: "she is, as you say, rather prudish in her way, and, therefore, I have determined to take her off, in spite of all her objections to the contrary."

"Has your lordship thought of the risk you must run in this affair?" demanded the smuggler.

"I have," replied his lordship; "but danger and I are old acquaintances, so that there is little reason why I should give up my present design, merely because a foolish girl takes it into her head that her character would suffer by the little adventure I have proposed."

"And yet the girl is right enough after all," exclaimed Captain Starkie; "she knows well enough the dismal fate that has attended all the wenches upon whom you have cast an eye of favour. Some of them have died, some gone mad, and others linger out a miserable existence, despised by those who once respected them, and hated even by themselves."

"Upon my word, Starkie," cried his lordship; "nature seems to have fitted you rather for a parson than a smuggler."

"Your lordship flatters me," exclaimed the other with a sneer; "and sorry am I that it is not in my power to return your compliment; however, such as we are there is no help for it, and I suppose as long as I remain a smuggler so long will you be the heartless libertine the world reports you to be."

"How, villain! am I to be insulted by a vile worm that I can put my foot upon and crush!"

"Fair and softly, young lord," exclaimed the smuggler; "there may be a difference between us in point of rank, but though I was born beneath a thatched roof, and you within the walls of your own proud ancestral castle, yet would I rather be as I am, than bear with me the mark of scorn that you do."

"And is it then the smuggler boasts his superiority over the high born peer!"

"Aye, and with good reason too," answered Captain Starkie; "for I do but defraud the revenue of some small portion of its profits, whilst you carry misery, despair, and shame, wheresoever you go, I therefore would not change places with you in spite of the empty title that your evil deeds have so often dishonoured."

"Villain!" exclaimed Lord Dalmeny, "wert thou alone, thou hadst not dared hold this language to me."

"If your lordship thinks so," answered Captain Starkie, coolly; "these men shall be dismissed without delay, and we will settle this affair with our swords."

"It seems, sirrah," retorted the other; "that you are trying to fasten a quarrel on me. If so, declare your object boldly, and you will find me ready to meet my antagonist, even though his humble rank may render him scarcely worthy my notice."

"Psha!" exclaimed the smuggler. "I want to breed no quarrel, unless, indeed, telling the truth in a plain way, should happen to give your lordship offence."

"Why then did you throw out such ugly hints about this affair of mine with the girl?"

"Merely because I think it's high time you should begin to reform in these matters," answered Starkie. "Besides, I was thinking your usual success with the lasses must be failing strangely since you are at last obliged to apply to me for assistance in the present instance."

"It is my own convenience," returned Lord Dalmeny, "that I consult, and therefore it is no business of thine to ask these questions."

"But this is not the way you used to carry on your courtship," exclaimed the smuggler; "I have known the time when you would have carried a girl off without asking for assistance, and now, because you have met with a rebuff, you leave your own stately halls for this rude cave of ours, and I am to be made a party in an affair that I've no great liking to."

"You can refuse it if you think proper," replied Lord Dalmeny, "but I suppose you will not turn round and tell the world what has passed between us?"

"Not I," answered the other; "your purse is sufficiently long for my purposes, and if you think fit to pay me a pretty tolerable price, my scruples will vanish as they have done with many a better man than myself."

"Will an hundred guineas satisfy you?"

"Aye, but my men will want something you know, or the secret will not be safe in their keeping."

"Well, they shall have fifty more, to be divided among them as you think proper."

"Come, now you begin to talk like a sensible man, and we understand each other," replied Captain Stardie. "It seems you want to carry on your courtship in this instance on salt water; so far so good, and when the money is paid down, the lugger shall be entirely at your service for the next month to come."

"And may I depend upon your keeping good faith with me?"

"Why, to be sure you may," replied the other; "I know how to behave honourably quite as well as those that happen to belong to a higher rank than myself; and so long as you give me no occasion to act otherwise, you will find me as true as the needle to the pole."

"But upon the first paltry provocation that occurs, you will turn round and do me all the mischief you can."

"If you think so, the better way will be to put an end to this affair before it goes any further," replied Captain Starkie. "I don't ask you any favour, remember, and if you can't trust me, I've no wish to join in any affair that may not end very pleasantly either to you or myself."

"Humph!" exclaimed the nobleman; "for a smuggler you talk with an air of tolerable independence!"

"Aye," retorted the other, "we learn what freedom is on the ocean; and men of our description are not apt to cringe much to our fellow men, merely because they happen to wear useless titles, that make them neither better nor worse than ourselves. If you want our services you must forget that you are a lord, and we, on the other hand, will try so to conduct ourselves as to give as little offence as we possibly can."

"Upon my word, sirrah, you carry off matters with a very high hand," exclaimed Lord Dalmeny. "But you forget, perhaps, that it is in my power to make you bitterly repent this insolence of yours."

"Aye, you could inform against me, and may be, send down a body of those cursed government fellows who would have no more mercy upon us than if we were so many wild Indians. But I'd have you beware, my lord, how you do that, for we are resolute fellows, and though some of us would be slaughtered, some few would still be left to punish the man that had perfidiously betrayed their comrades."

"Villain! do thou threaten me?"

"Villain in your teeth!" exclaimed the incensed smuggler, drawing his cutlass, and preparing to make a deadly attack upon his antagonist. Lord

Dalmeny, however, saw the danger he had provoked, and starting back to throw himself into an attitude of defence, his foot struck against a piece of rock, and he was precipitated with some violence to the ground. Recovering himself, however, he made an effort to rise, but before he could do so, the comrades of Captain Starkie sprang forward, one of whom placing his foot upon the breast of the prostrate nobleman, kept him in the position in which he had fallen, and holding a sword, so that the point almost touched his body, commanded him to remain still at the peril of his life.

"Am I to be murdered among you?" demanded Lord Dalmeny, fiercely.

"That must depend upon yourself," returned the fellow; "remain quiet and your life is safe, but if you stir till you have permission, you will have this sword through your heart."

"Let him get up if he chooses, Ned," exclaimed Captain Starkie, who by this time had recovered his usual coolness. "I was perhaps rather too hasty with him, and if he thinks fit to forget the past, he shall have my hand, and so the affair may go off quietly."

"You would have slain me, sirrah, when I was least prepared for your assault," cried Lord Dalmeny, who, by this time had raised himself from the ground.

"Nonsense," answered the smuggler, "it was all done in hot blood, and now I'm sorry that I so far forgot, so if you choose to accept that by way of an apology, the thing may drop and be no more thought of."

"Am I at liberty to leave this place without fear of being stabbed by your ruffians?" demanded his lordship.

"You have nothing to fear from them at present," answered Starkie; "but if you value your life, I would advise you to call them by less offensive names. The fellows are not used to it, and I don't know that it would be safe, even for myself, to say even half so much as you have ventured to do."

"You will answer for my safety then?"

"Aye," replied the other, "if matters go no further I will, so now let the past be forgotten, and if you are in the humour for it still, we'll arrange how this affair of yours is to be managed."

"How," demanded Lord Dalmeny, "can I longer entrust myself amongst men whose swords just now were aimed against my life?"

"Oh, never sulk upon the matter, my lord," exclaimed Captain Starkie; "the quarrel was a sudden one, and it has gone off as it begun; we no longer seek to do you an injury so, if you think proper, we may now be as good friends as ever we were."

"Aye," answered the young nobleman, "to have my life threatened again I suppose at the first trifling offence I may chance to give."

"Don't call us ugly names, or talk about the mischief you may have it in your power to do us, and there's no fear of our quarrelling again," replied Starkie. "The fact is, my lord, we are a rough and ready set of fellows, and when the blood's up, our swords seldom remain long in their sheaths. Why, even among ourselves, we fall out sometimes, and though the fellows know me well, they would not put up with it from me any more than from yourself, were I to call them names that they didn't like."

"Well, then, for this time I will think no more about the affair," answered Lord Dalmeny. "Your men seem to be great sticklers for their honour, and as I must in some degree rely upon it, we will bury the past in oblivion, and think only of the affair that is now to employ our thoughts."

A general manifestation of satisfaction might now be observed amongst the smugglers, and the one who had been foremost in the recent affray, stepped forward, and holding forth his huge hand, offered it to Lord Dalmeny, in token of his own willingness that the quarrel should be forgotten. The young peer, however, was not at first disposed to be upon quite such familiar terms, but remembering that it would be necessary to put on an outward show of reconciliation, he at length took the offered hand without exhibiting any very marked reluctance to the act of condescension he had submitted to.

"Come," exclaimed Captain Starkie, "things are now as they should be ; we're all friends again, and the first man that ventures to make strife among us, may be sure of receiving the contents of this pistol in his body. So now, comrades, you all understand me, and you may, therefore, retire just out of earshot, whilst his lordship and I finish the arrangement of the business that has brought us together."

Obeying the command of their captain, the men retired to the further end of the cave, where they were soon occupied in burying their late wrath in potations strong and deep. Lord Dalmeny watched them for a few moments, and then addressing himself to their leader, he said :—

"From the specimen I have already seen, Captain Starkie, I am inclined to think your fellows may do me good service in the affair I have got in hand. They are resolute I'll be bound, and I suppose you will undertake to answer for their good faith."

"Aye, to be sure I will," replied the captain ; "I have known the dogs both on sea and on shore for the last dozen years, and though they may be a rough set to look at, they know their own interest too well to neglect it, when there's such a pretty chance of putting money into their purses."

"I am not quite certain that I should require much of their services," answered Lord Dalmeny, "yet the sum I have agreed on shall be theirs on condition that they do not betray me."

"Why, you'll want them, I suppose, to assist in carrying off the girl ?"

"I have not yet made up my mind whether I shall or not," replied the nobleman. "The affair will require to be conducted with great caution and secrecy, and therefore I may deem it prudent to carry the wench off myself. That, however, I am not sure of as yet, so if I want the fellows' assistance, you will hold them in readiness against I see you further upon this subject."

"And when is it to take place, my lord ?"

"Perhaps to-night, if an opportunity offers," replied the nobleman ; " at any rate it will not be delayed for any long time, as the plot may get wind, and then all would be frustrated at a moment when success appears to be most certain."

"To make sure work of it," exclaimed Captain Starkie, "the best way will be to take half-a-dozen of my fellows, and then in the event of resistance being offered, you will be able to carry the girl off in spite of those that might wish to baulk you."

"But by so doing," answered Lord Dalmeny, "I might defeat my own purposes, for if a number of persons were seen approaching the house, an alarm would instantly be raised, and thus I should be disappointed in the hopes I have formed."

"And who pray," asked Captain Starkie, "is the girl you are going to carry off ?"

"One whom you little thought of, I dare say," answered the nobleman, and approaching yet nearer to Captain Starkie, he whispered a name in his ear, at which he started with evident astonishment, and an ominous frown passed across his brow, that showed plainly enough he was not best pleased at the task he had partly undertaken to assist in ; Lord Dalmeny watched his perturbation with uneasiness, and having waited some few moments for a reply, he said :—

"How now, captain ! the name I have just mentioned, seems to have had a different effect on you to what I had expected ; you look discomposed as if no longer willing to assist me in my designs."

"Why look you, my lord," exclaimed the smuggler, "I'm a man, as

you know, that don't stand upon trifles; but really this turns out to be such an
awkward affair, that I must take some little time to consider of it before I
agree to do an act that I might perhaps be sorry for afterwards as long as I
live."

"Fool!" muttered Dalmeny, "what matters it to you who the girl is?"

"Aye, you may call me a fool, my lord," answered the other, "but it may
turn out that I'm not quite such a villain as you take me for. I don't mind a
bit of a job now and then, if it comes in my way, providing the thing don't
go altogether against the conscience; but this affair has rather startled me,
and between ourselves, I think it will be much better if neither of us have
anything to do with it."

"Psha!" ejaculated the nobleman; "I, for one, am not to be turned from
my object by any of the conscientious scruples that seem to trouble you. The
thing is resolved on, so whether you think fit to assist me in it or not, the
girl shall be mine in spite of all the obstacles that may be thrown in my
way."

"But have you considered well the danger you will run in the present
instance?"

"To tell you the truth, I have thought very little about the matter further
than to make up my mind that the thing shall be done," answered Dalmeny.

"Aye," replied the smuggler; "but there is one at least who will hunt you
through the world should this attempt of yours prove successful."

"I know who you allude to," replied the other in a tone of indifference;
"and yet, in defiance of the dangers you would warn me of, I am resolved to go
on with it, even though I were sure that a violent death would be the consequence."

"And that it surely will unless you take my advice in time," exclaimed
Captain Starkie; "I know you have no child's play to expect from that

No. 11

quarter, and so surely as you pursue this matter further, so surely will you hereafter have to acknowledge that my warning ought not to have been rejected."

"It is hard to convince a man whose mind is made up to anything that may happen, exclaimed Lord Dalmeny; "and therefore it is but wasting time to say anything further upon that subject. I for one am not to be frightened from my purpose by the thoughts of who may feel aggrieved at the course I am about to pursue, and it shall be done, or I will perish in the attempt."

"Well," observed Captain Starkie, "there's no convincing an obstinate man, I know, but as I don't feel any great relish for this business, I believe, on second thought, that I shall decline having anything further to do with it."

"How!—you mean to betray me, then?"

"I didn't say that, my lord; though, between ourselves, I ought to do so, seeing that I have always had a respect for the girl and her family, and——"

"It is enough," interrupted Lord Dalmeny; "you have got the secret, and would now betray me."

"Never," exclaimed Starkie; "your secret is safe, my lord, but perhaps I may keep a watchful eye upon you to prevent the mischief you intend."

Lord Dalmeny was quite unprepared for this turn in the affair, and pacing up and down the cavern, he gave way to the fierce passions that were burning in his heart. At length, however, he subduced the tumult, and pausing abruptly, he exclaimed in a softened tone :—

"I know not, Starkie, whether I am henceforth to rank you as a friend or an enemy. If as the former, my purse shall be at your command, but if I find you are likely to do me a mischief, I will not fail to take immediate steps to prevent mischief to myself."

"I perfectly uuderstand you, my lord," answered the smuggler, unmoved by this threat; "you mean to warn me that I am no longer safe in this neighbourhood; that you will take steps to deliver me into the hands of my enemies; and in fact, that I shall fall under your vengeance for having dared to thwart your designs on this girl?"

"You have guessed my thoughts, sirrah," replied Lord Dalmeny; "but at the same time you have to remember that I will be your friend on condition that you serve me in this instance. Nay, I will double the reward I before offered, and you shall have another hundred guineas on the completion of the business."

"Another hundred?"

"Aye, I have pledged my word for it, and will not fail to keep it faithfully."

"Why, now your lordship begins to find out my weakest side," exclaimed the smuggler; "it must be confessed that the reward you now offer is irresistible, and therefore, upon second thoughts, I don't know but this affair may be managed to the satisfaction of both of us."

"And yet just now the bare name of the girl filled you with horror," cried his lordship.

"Yes, but you had not promised me so much by exactly one-half as you have now. Besides, a man is not to be bound down by the first notions of a thing, and as I have seen good reason to change my mind since we first began this conversation, you may now take my word for it that I will perform the business handsomely, on condition that you don't forget your own promises."

"I will trust to you," replied Lord Dalmeny; "and as for your men, I suppose they are to be depended on, provided the gold is forthcoming according to promise ?"

"Aye, aye, they are all right enough."

"Well, then I take your word for them; and now, as the affair is so far settled, I will go and make all the arrangements that are necessary, and when I have completed all this, you will see me here again to tell you how and when the affair is to be brought to a close."

With this he threw a couple of handsfull of gold among the smuggler's crew and retired from the cave. Captain Starkie watched his departure with a frowning brow, and when his men had finished picking up the coin that had been so liberally distributed, he said—

"There goes as big a villain as ever had the good fortune to escape the gallows! He thinks he has bought me with his gold, but I may yet serve him a trick that will prove I am not so bad as he takes me to be."

"You don't mean to keep your word with him, then, I suppose ?" exclaimed one of the men.

"You may take your oath of that, Ned," answered the captain. "The affair is one that don't suit me, and d—n me if I'm going to be the rascal he'd make of me just for the sake of the paltry reward he has promised."

"Why, you're not often so particular, captain," exclaimed the smuggler.

"No," answered Starkie; "and it don't often happen that I'm called upon to take part in an affair that's quite so villanous as this is. The truth is, I know something of the girl he wants to carry off, and as I'm not inclined to play her false, he may find some one else to do his dirty work for him."

"Who is the girl ?" demanded Ned.

"Don't ask me now," replied the captain, "because there are reasons why I should keep the thing snug. By and by, however, you'll know all, and then I think there's not a man among you but will say Lord Dalmeny is a greater villain than he took him to be."

"And that's hardly possible," exclaimed Ned; "for he don't bear the best of characters, and it's impossible for him to prove a greater scoundrel than he has always been reported by the folks hereabouts."

"Come boys, we'll say no more about him at present," cried Captain Starkie; "we have other business on hand you know, and when we have landed our cargo safely, we'll return here and meet Lord Dalmeny according to his promise."

A cup of liquor was now handed round to the smugglers, and taking advantage of the night, they left the cave, and in three or four small parties, took different routes towards the place where their cargo was to be landed.

CHAPTER XI.

" When midnight o'er the moonless skies
   Her pall of transient death has spread,
When mortals sleep, when spectres rise,
   And none are wakeful but the dead."
                              W. R. SPENSER.

WHEN Lord Dalmeny left the smuggler's retreat, he found that the moon had already mounted high above the horizon, and so brightly was she shining in the starry firmament, that each surrounding object was to be distinghished with almost as much clearness as in the broad daylight. But his mind was too much occupied with the project he had in contemplation to permit him to admire a scene so beautiful and calm, and passing onwards with hurried steps, he at length reached a lonely valley, which the superstitious peasantry of that neighbourhood had reported to be haunted by spirits of another world. On all other occasions Lord Dalmeny had laughed at the idle rumours that had been spread concerning the place, but now he approached the spot with an involuntary shudder, and quickening his pace, he resolved to make his way across with as little delay as possible. But an evil conscience is a bad companion for men in such a situation as this, and in spite of the forced courage he strove to inspire himself with, he found himself frequently looking round as if some sound had startled him.

At length he came to a part of the valley where the path ran along the side of a thick copse, the shadow of which served to render his way more obscure, and at the same time to fill the mind of the lonely wanderer with more gloomy thoughts. Again he endeavoured to redouble his speed, but scarcely had he proceeded half way along the solitary place, when the misty, spectre-looking form of an aged man glided from the deep shadow of the copse, and stood so directly in the path of Lord Dalmeny as to prevent his further progress. Horror-stricken at this, the other stepped on one side to avoid the figure that had occasioned him so much alarm ; but again the form glided before him so as to prevent his further advance. At the same moment the dismal hooting of an owl was heard at a short distance off, and then the spectral figure put forth its arm, and by a threatening motion, seemed to forbid his further advance. Lord Dalmeny was now completely under the influence of fear, and starting back a pace or two, he demanded of the figure why he had been thus interrupted in his way.

"I came here to prevent thy evil designs, Lord Dalmeny," answered the terrible form. "Repent ere it is too late, or thou wilt fall into the snare thou hast set for another !"

"Vile impostor, away !" exclaimed his lordship, in a voice trembling with emotion ;—"away, I command thee ! or my sword shall open for me the free passage thou would'st dispute."

As he uttered these words Lord Dalmeny drew his weapon, and would have made a stroke at the figure before him, but ere he could do so it had glided backwards beyond his reach ; and then a hollow laugh of scorn came upon his ears that made the blood curdle and turn cold within his veins. Still, however, the object of his terror remained in the path he was desirous of pursuing, and resolving not to be deterred from his design, he once more advanced, when the light of the full moon, falling upon the countenance of the figure, revealed to him the features of the aged parent of May Grayson, who, it was reported in the morning had died, a few hours before, of a broken heart, produced by the misfortunes that had driven his beloved child to madness and despair ! And now a thousand fearful thoughts rushed upon the mind of Lord Dalmeny, for he knew that he had been the cause of the sorrows that had bowed the old man to the earth ; and, frenzied with the reflections that pressed upon him, he turned to pursue his rapid flight across a rude wooden bridge that spanned a brook at the bottom of the valley, but ere he could reach the place the form of the old man again stood before him, and thus his object was again effectually prevented. By this time the terrors of Lord Dalmeny had driven him almost to madness ; every crime that he had committed rushed upon his memory with startling vividness, and making one more effort to pass over the bridge, he was seized by the throat with a grasp of iron, and hurled with fearful violence to the earth.

How long he had remained in a state of insensibility he knew not, but when at length Lord Dalmeny aroused from the stupor in which he had fallen, he found that the object of his terror was no longer present, but that in his place he was attended on by Hugh Lorimer, who, having found him in the helpless condition we have described, had rendered all the assistance in his power to restore him to his senses.

"Why how happens all this, my lord?" exclaimed the young rustic, as the nobleman at last revived under the care he had bestowed upon him; "how is it that I found you here lying in a swoon, and, as I thought at first, as dead as a herring?"

"I have seen a sight," answered his lordship, "that was enough to have killed a man of weaker nerves outright."

"And what might that have been, my lord?" demanded Hugh Lorimer, with surprise.

"Ere I answer your question," replied Lord Dalmeny, "I would know whether you have seen a spectral form since you have been in this place."

"Not I," answered the young man; "but I suppose you have, by the strange question you ask?"

"I have."

"Or rather you have fancied so, my lord."

"How! will you not believe me?"

"I am willing enough to believe that you have fancied that such a thing has appeared to you, my lord," answered Hugh Lorimer. "People have been deceived before now; but take my word for it, that no man ever yet saw a ghost, though many have fancied it."

"Again I tell you I have not been deceived," exclaimed Lord Dalmeny, impatiently. "At first I saw the form near yonder copse; then it followed me to this bridge, and as I attempted to pass across I was siezed by the throat and hurled to the ground with that violence which produced the insensibility in which you found me."

"By my faith," cried the incredulous Hugh Lorimer, "but the ghost must have been a strong one to have grappled with a man of sinew and muscle like your lordship."

"Dost thou still doubt me, Hugh?"

"How can I do otherwise when the story is such an improbable one?" demanded the other. "Anything in reason I can swallow comfortably enough, but when a man talks to me about ghosts, and all that sort of thing, I begin to think that one of us must be mistaken; either he for believing it, or I for not giving it credit."

"But surely my word is to be taken, sirrah, when I tell you that I distinctly saw the apparition of which I have been speaking."

"You have been mistaken, my lord," answered Hugh Lorimer, "for unless my eyes deceived me, I saw you not very long since making your way towards the smuggler's cave. Now, report says they keep a drop of rare stuff there, and as their hospitality has never yet been called in question, it's just possible your lordship may have taken a cup too much of one sort of *spirit*, which has given rise to *another* in your own imagination."

"Hugh Lorimer," exclaimed his lordship, angrily, "you presume upon the little service you have just now done me!"

"Upon my life you mistake me," answered the young man, "for if my speech may have appeared rude, I can assure you it was intended only to drive away thoughts that should never have been encouraged."

"But how can they be helped?" demanded Lord Dalmeny, "seeing that I am positive even now of the truth of what I have been telling you. The figure was plain enough to be seen, and the hollow tones in which it spoke to me even now thrill through my veins as if my blood had suddenly been changed into ice."

"What!" exclaimed Hugh, "did the ghost speak?"

"Aye, as plainly as you now hear me."

"Why this is better and better still," laughed Hugh Lorimer; "for though I've heard many people speak about ghosts and apparitions, yet I never heard of a speaking one, except those that appear to people in their sleep, and they of course are only imaginary ones."

" Still incredulous !" exclaimed his lordship.

" Aye, and so I always shall remain," answered Hugh Lorimer; " at any rate I shall not be inclined to believe in them till I chance to see one with my own eyes.   Why, if my own father was to tell me such a story as this, I should be apt to tell him my mind as plainly as I have done to your lordship ; for never yet did ghost walk on the earth, except in the imagination of people that are more inclined to be credulous than I am."

" Knave !" cried Lord Dalmeny, growing more and more warm, " this insolence is scarcely to be endured.   I have pledged my word for the truth of what I have uttered, and yet my assertion is to be doubted as if I belonged to your own common herd."

" Well," exclaimed Hugh Lorimer, in a tone of the most perfect indifference, " for aught that I ever heard, the word of a peasant is to the full as good as that of a lord.   However, that's nothing to the purpose, for all I mean to say is that no ghost has visited this place, and consequently your lordship has been most strangely deceived."

" Have you not heard," asked Lord Dalmeny, " that old Grayson died at an early hour this morning ?"

" Aye, I heard it certainly," replied Hugh Lorimer, " and I couldn't help saying to myself at the time that your lordship had sent him to his grave a few years before his right time."

" And how durst thou lay so heavy a charge against me ?" demanded the young nobleman, fiercely.

" Why the truth is," answered Hugh Lorimer, " that thoughts are free, and every man has a right to believe as he likes, so long as he don't spread his opinions abroad to the injury of other people.   Now I took good care to keep my thoughts to myself, so your lordship has nothing to blame me for in this particular instance."

" But how am I to be assured that you will not blab them to every idler you chance to meet with."

" My own prudence will be your best safeguard," answered the young man.   " I happen to know that your temper is fiery, and your sword keen, and that I should experience the truth of both if I was foolish enough to talk about affairs that I have no business with,"

" Thus far, sirrah," exclaimed the nobleman, " thou dost shew more wisdom than I gave thee credit for.   The affair I believe is tolerably safe in your hands, and therefore I will now tell thee that the spirit I have this night seen was that of old Grayson, the father of May, the poor demented creature that wanders about this neighbourhood."

" Hah !" cried Hugh Lorimer, " then of course the poor old man came to reproach you for the crime that had driven his child out of her senses ?"

" I know not what was the motive of his visit," answered Lord Dalmeny ; " but that a misty ghost-like figure presented itself before me I have already told thee.   He first stood in my path as I was passing by yonder copse, and when I turned to cross over this bridge he glided to the spot before I could reach it, and my further progress was arrested as I have before described."

" Well then," replied Hugh Lorimer, " all I wonder at is that he didn't serve you a still worse trick for the agony of mind you have caused him. Had I been him, and with the same power to appear before you after death, my fingers should never have relaxed their hold upon your throat till you had fallen a blackened and stiffening corpse at my feet !"

" Hah ! am I to be taunted by a vile worm like thee ?"

"Why, the truth is, my lord," replied Hugh Lorimer, "that when a man has plunged himself into crime he levels himself even with the very lowest dregs of society,—a man that you look upon with loathing and disgust, and who is yet rendered your equal by the crimes you have wilfully committed."

"Beware how you tempt me much further, Hugh Lorimer," exclaimed his lordship, with a fury that he could not control. "I have endured much from you; but, by Heaven! if you urge me thus with your taunting speeches, I shall not be able much longer to restrain the anger your words are calculated to give rise to."

"Aye, your lordship is armed with a sword, I see," replied the other. "You have thus, perhaps, an advantage over me; and yet, whilst I hold this good stout cudgel in my hand, I know not that there is much reason to be afraid of you; at any rate, I am well enough able to defend myself, as you may find to your cost if I should happen to be put upon my mettle."

"And yet thy vaunting might soon be changed into cries for mercy."

"I would never ask that from any man, much less from your lordship," answered the other, scornfully.

"Villain!"

"Oh!" exclaimed Hugh Lorimer, "all this rage is thrown away upon one who cares not for it. I have been used to see you in a passion many a time before now, and can, therefore, well enough bear the brunt of it on the present occasion."

"You presume upon my patience," muttered Lord Dalmeny, "because you chanced to do me a service just now when you found me lying here insensible upon the ground."

"Let not that be considered as any favour," retorted the other. "I ask no consideration from you on that account, since, had it chanced that I had seen my bitterest enemy as I found you, I should have rendered him all the assistance in my power, though, perhaps, only to renew my hatred when he had sufficiently recovered to defend himself."

"Well, well, I desire to have no further quarrel with you," exclaimed Lord Dalmeny. "At present I am in no humour to converse further with you, and, therefore, we will now part—friends, if you think proper, or enemies, should it happen to suit you better."

"That will depend upon your lordship," replied Hugh, in a tone of indifference; "so now, since it is your wish, we will part, and my most earnest wish is that you may see the evil of your ways, and repent the many crimes the world gives you the credit of having committed."

With these words, Hugh Lorimer strode away, leaving Lord Dalmeny to ruminate upon the few plain truths he had been compelled to hear. It was with no little difficulty that he could restrain the inclination he felt to follow and chastise him for the last words he had uttered; but, remembering the business he had on hand, he turned off in an opposite direction and pursued his way towards his own castle. But the most gloomy thoughts continued to haunt his imagination, for he could not forget the spectral figure that had crossed his path that night, and anticipating the most terrible results from the warning he had received, he approached the ancient home of his fathers with a heart loaded and oppressed with care.

The moon was shining brightly upon tower and turret as he advanced, and each portion of the antique dwelling was brought in in grand relief from the star-bespangled sky which formed the back ground. At another time Lord Dalmeny would have paused to gaze upon a scene that had often filled him with delight in happier days, but now the sight only served to remind him of the ruin which crime had brought upon his family;

and with an aching heart he hurried through the principal entrance, from whence he directed his steps towards the apartment usually occupied by his mother, the Lady Margaret Dalmeny. Here, contrary to his expectation, he found her anxiously awaiting his return, and with her was his fair cousin, the Lady Agnes Drummond, whose alarm for his safety would not permit her to retire to bed until intelligence had been received respecting him. Upon his entrance, both the ladies rose to welcome his return; but his haggard appearance soon arrested their attention, and it was in a voice that betrayed the greatest concern that his mother inquired what had happened to discompose him so much.

"Nothing, mother, I assure you," answered Lord Dalmeny; "unless, indeed, it be that I have taken a longer walk than usual, and, perhaps, the fatigue I have endured may be sufficient to account for my present care-worn appearance."

"These long walks, my lord, are ill-advised," observed the gentle Lady Agnes. "You have enemies, I fear, and there may be some among them who would not hesitate to carry their evil designs into execution, were a favourable opportunity to present itself."

"Nay, fair cousin," answered Lord Dalmeny, "there is, I believe, little cause to fear anything from them; I seldom appear out of doors without my trusty sword by my side, and in the event of any such ruffianly attack as you seem to anticipate, I should so punish the rogues, that none afterwards would ever venture to interfere either with me or my purposes."

"But this could not be done," replied his mother, shuddering, "without the spilling of human blood!"

"And if so," retorted his lordship, "the crime would lay against those who provoked the strife. I am not anxious, as you may be sure, to draw my sword against the mongrel herd; but if I am driven to it, then the consequences must fall upon themselves."

"My dear Dalmeny," cried the old lady, "let me entreat you to avoid these quarrels, lest the consequences should prove fatal to yourself. I have heard that the people in this neighbourhood are greatly incensed against you, and it is even said that old Donald Grayson, who died this morning, owes his death to the perfidy with which you have behaved to his unhappy daughter."

"Then the world lies most foully, mother," answered Lord Dalmeny. "It is my accursed lot to excite the enmity of almost all mankind, and now it seems that every idle story which is circulated against me is to be believed by those who should know me better."

"It is my anxiety in your behalf, my dear boy," cried Lady Margaret Dalmeny, "that prompts me to speak so plainly as I do. I know but too well that crime has reduced our once proud family almost to the verge of beggary and ruin; these crumbling walls hourly remind me that a curse rests upon our house, and when I see thee following in the same wild track that has marked the conduct of thine ancestors, I must own it fills my soul with apprehension that I cannot subdue."

"Canst thou make no allowance, then, for the follies of youth?" demanded his lordship.

"I can," she replied; "but, at the same time, I do not shut my eyes to the dangers you are continually exposed to. Many a hapless female I hear has fallen a victim to thy seductive arts, and depend upon it a day of terrible retribution will come, when thou wilt be made to suffer the vengeance of the enemies thou hast made."

"You are in a prophetic vein to-night, mother," exclaimed Lord Dalmeny, with an effort at gaiety that sat ill upon him; "your words con-

vince me that some one has been speaking of me, and that, too, not in the most favourable terms."

"You are wrong, my lord, I assure you," cried Lady Agnes Drummond ; "no one has been here since you left us ; but your mother, alarmed at your long absence, has been agitated with a thousand fears on your account, and thus arises the advice she has just given you."

"For which I scarcely thank her," replied his lordship, "seeing that it has been given in the presence of one who I would have blind to any faults that I may possess."

"Nay," answered Lady Agnes ; "but you should remember that she who has heard this conversation is one who is not likely to be prejudiced by any reports that may have been circulated against you."

"You believe them not, then ?"

"At present I am deaf to them," answered Agnes, with a faint smile.

"You have heard, doubtless, that I have had some few amours," exclaimed Lord Dalmeny ; "that I am not, in fact, altogether insensible to female loveliness. Yet, surely that can be no great crime, since the same feeling has rendered me the humble slave of your ladyship."

"Flatterer," cried Lady Agnes, "you would win my favour by this adulation."

"Your ladyship must e'en pardon me, since the fault has been produced by admiration for yourself."

"Would that I could see you wedded to each other," cried Lady Margaret Dalmeny ; "for then I could die content, whenever it may please Heaven to take me from a world that has grown wearisome to me."

"Marriage, my dear mother," answered his lordship, "is too serious an affair to be thought of by one who has not yet been tamed to domestic life. My cousin, I believe, is aware of my ideas upon that subject, and she

No. 12

will, I dare say, do me the justice to give me the credit of good intentions in the present instance."

"Well," sighed Lady Margaret, "it is in vain to urge the subject further at present; and yet I would once more implore you to abandon the evil ways you have fallen in with, and, if it be possible, to make reparation to those whom, in your thoughtlessness, you have injured."

"I have endeavoured to do so," replied Lord Dalmeny; "but the fools reject my money, as if the gold that comes from me were contaminated. It is their own fault, therefore, if I am prevented making whatever recompense may lay in my power."

"Can it be wondered at," cried Lady Margaret Dalmeny, "that fathers should utter their curses upon thee for the ruin thou hast brought upon their daughters? I have heard stories of thee that have made my heart weep drops of blood, and yet I have hitherto forbore reproaching thee, because I hoped thou wert not so far steeped in crime but thou wouldst soon see the error of thy ways, and become all that I could wish to find thee. But now I find myself becoming a prey to the blackest despair, and you will see me descend into the grave to which your career of crime and folly has driven me."

"Do you also turn against me?"

"I only seek to bring you to repentance," answered Lady Margaret; "yield but to my prayers, and I shall again be happy."

"Let us speak upon this subject another time, mother," exclaimed his lordship, wearied with the importunities he had been forced to induce. "At present I am in no humour to argue any further, and therefore if the affair is to be pursued it must be at some other time."

"Wilt thou not listen to the voice of one who has a right to be heard?"

"I have said that I am in no humour to be lectured any further to-night. I am already fatigued with the exercise I have taken, and my mind is occupied with an adventure that befel me in the course of my journey homewards."

"An adventure!" cried both the ladies in a breath.

"Aye, and one that has moved me much."

"Thou hast been waylaid by some who owed thee a grudge," cried Lady Margaret, anxiously.

"What it was I shall not explain further at present," replied Lady Dalmeny. "It may, however, account to you for the humour you now see me in, and with this I shall now respectfully take my leave till next we meet again."

Saying this, Lord Dalmeny bowed to the ladies and retired to his own chamber, where throwing himself upon his bed, he once more gave way to the distracting thoughts that passed through his brain. Sleep, however, seemed to have forsaken his eyelids, and it was not till the morning that he sank into a deep and disturbed slumber.

Nor were Lady Margeret Dalmeny and the Lady Agnes less agitated than the young and guilty nobleman, though the cause that affected them was a far different one; theirs was anxiety in behalf of him they desired to see repentant, and with tearful eyes they retired to their chambers to offer offer up prayers to Heaven for the change they so much desired to see in him whose career had hitherto been so reckless and sinful.

CHAPTER XII.

"As when a gryphon through the wilderness,
With winged course o'er hill and moory dale,
Pursues the arimaspion, who, by stealth,
Had from his wakeful custody purloined
The guarded gold."
PARADISE LOST.

THE sun had scarcely risen on the following morning when Effie Ruthven left her chamber, and descending to the lower chamber, found her mother already engaged in the household duties of the day. There was a look of sadness on the maiden's face, which was not unobserved by Dame Ruthven; but no sooner did the girl find that she was noticed, than assuming a more cheerful demeanour, she endeavoured to avoid the questions which she knew would be put to her should her gloominess last any longer.

But the widow Ruthven had already seen that something had occurred to oppress the mind of her daughter, and anxious as she was to ascertain the grief that oppressed her, she thought over a thousand methods by which to come at the truth she was so desirous of finding out. She observed, too, that Effie put on a more cheerful look when she saw that she was observed, and judging from this circumstance that the truth she desired to know was of some importance, she resolved at once to come at it by a plain, straightforward question.

"My dear Effie," she said, "you know I love you, and how deeply my heart would grieve were any sorrow to befal you. I have seen with grief that your heart is heavy this morning, and I would, therefore, know what has happened to make you so sad and thoughtful."

"Nothing, dear mother," she replied; but both the accent in which she spoke, and her downcast looks, belied the words she had uttered.

"Nay," cried Dame Ruthven, "it is in vain that you seek to deceive me; I know your heart, Effie, and conscious as I am that you only seek to keep that from me which would occasion sorrow"

"Indeed, mother, you are mistaken," replied the maiden; "it was shame only that prompted me to remain silent; but since you desire to know the truth, I will frankly own that I am at present under the influence of a foolish superstition."

"Superstition, child?"

"Aye, indeed, dear mother," answered Effie, "for, to confess what I am almost ashamed to speak, I have been half frightened out of my wits by a dream."

"A dream, girl!" exclaimed the widow Ruthven, and her own countenance grew deathly pale as the words of her daughter fell upon her ear.

"Aye, mother," cried Effie; "I knew you would think me a very silly girl for my pains; but you asked for the truth and I have told it, though at the expense of being laughed at for my pains."

"I am in no humour to laugh, Effie," answered the dame; "dreams are ominous things at times, and I have so often known them to come true, that I tremble lest yours should be one of those that are sent as warnings to those who are in great peril. So, tell me, dear girl, what the vision was that has thus disturbed you."

"Be not alarmed, and you shall know all," replied Effie: "I dreamed that I was lying in my own chamber, awake as I am at this moment, and that I heard a light footstep in the garden, as if my brother John had just returned from one of his midnight rambles. Overjoyed at this thought, I raised myself in bed, intending to go and open the door for him, but at the moment a vivid flash of lightning flashed across the room, and by its glare I saw the spectral form of a man standing by my bed-side."

"Proceed, my child, proceed," gasped the widow Ruthven, in a voice of the deepest anguish.

"Nay, be not alarmed, dear mother," cried Effie, "for remember, I am relating nothing more than what occurred in a dream."

"Did the form you speak of disappear as soon as you had seen it?"

"It did not, for by the light of another flash I saw it still standing in its former position, and its countenance had assumed a mournful expression me that I can never forget. It seemed to gaze upon me as if anxious to warn me of some impending danger, and though I tried to call upon your name my tongue clove to my mouth, and I was speechless."

"Horrible!" groaned Dame Ruthven.

"Aye, it was indeed, horrible," sighed Effie, shuddering at the remembrance of her vision

"Did the apparition speak to you?"

"It did."

"What were its words?"

"I almost forget them," answered Effie; "but their purport was to warn me of some terrible calamity that was about to befal me."

"Alas! my child," cried Dame Ruthven, "the warning I fear has come too late. Thou art in peril, and no caution of ours can ward off the danger."

"And yet, mother," exclaimed Effie, "all that I have been telling you was but a dream."

"Aye, girl," replied the widow, "but I also had a dream last night, and the warning was to the same effect as that thou hast told me of."

"And did the same mysterious figure appear to you?" asked Effie, anxiously.

"It did. I dreamed that I was wandering in a lonely glen, where nought disturbed the death-like silence save the wild roar of a distant waterfall. Then a sudden darkness came on, and anxious for thy sake, I turned to retrace my steps homewards, when the same apparition you have spoken of presented itself to me. Alarmed at the sight, I screamed aloud with terror, for I knew the form was an unearthly one, and that it was the messenger of evil tidings."

"And were you fears well founded?" asked Effie.

"They were," answered her mother, "for anon the figure spoke, and in sepulchral accents bade me beware of spirits that are yet unforeseen. Your name was mentioned, but when I demanded the nature of the peril that threatened you, the spectre shook its head, and as it slowly dissolved into air, I beheld in its place the form of Lord Dalmeny. At this sight I shrieked with terror, and awakening, discovered that all the horrors I had witnessed had passed in a dream."

"Then let that console you, dear mother," cried Effie, "for, like myself, you have been cheated by a vision, that after all, bodes not the evil you anticipate."

"It is in vain that you would persuade me so," answered the widow Ruthven, dejectedly; "for I feel assured that peril threatens us, or why should we both have been warned by a dream so similar? The same figure appeared to us, and therefore am I but too surely convinced that we have much to fear."

"And from whence are we to expect the danger?" asked Effie, with a a vain effort to smile.

"From Dalmeny Castle, girl."

"Nay, then perhaps you do an injustice to him whose name is already sufficiently odious."

"I am not mistaken," answered the widow sorrowfully, "for I have told you that the form of Lord Dalmeny stood in the place from whence the spectre had disappeared, and what else should I take this to be but a warning that the danger is to be expected from him?"

"Still dear mother, it was but a vision."

"Aye, child, but such a one as we are bound to take as a warning that great peril awaits us."

"But I have heard you say that these things sometimes foretell deaths and other changes that we are not prepared for," cried Effie.

"I have told you so," replied her mother; "but in this instance I believe it will be found that it was to give us a foreknowledge of some peril that threatens thyself."

Ere Effie could reply, a step was heard approaching the cottage, and as the door opened, Andrew Kenmuir, a travelling retailer of news and small talk, made his appearance before them.

"A fair good morning to you, dame," he said, "and you, my pretty Effie. By my troth, ye are early risers, for though I have passed the houses of many of your neighbours, nobody was up to hear the news I am the bearer of."

"What news?" eagerly asked both the females.

"Aye, ye have not heard then of the death of old Duncan Grayson?"

"Alas!" sighed the widow, "has he also been taken from us by the unsparing hand of death?"

"He has indeed," replied Andrew; "not that it was to be wondered at, though, for he was well stricken in years, and his neighbours have been looking for his end this long time past."

"But his death," cried Dame Ruthven, "was no doubt hastened by the cruel fate of his poor crazy daughter. This is another crime to be added to the long list that Lord Dalmeny has to answer for, and people will not fail to curse him for this new cause of hatred."

"Nay, mother," exclaimed Effie, "you are too severe upon the young lord; no doubt he has been gay and thoughtless, but surely some share of the blame is to be laid to those who have weakly yielded to his suit."

"Aye, girl, doubtless they were to blame," replied the widow; "but they were deceived by the glozing tongue of a flatterer, and who, I ask you, can beware of such a deep hypocritical villain as this Lord Dalmeny?"

"Aye, who, indeed?" chimed in Andrew Kenmuir; "the young lordling seems to make common property of all the girls that fall in his way, and lucky is the maiden who escapes his snares when once she has had the misfortune to meet his eye."

"I have often thought," cried Dame Ruthven, "that he must be an incarnation of the great fiend himself. He delights only in doing mischief, and sorrow and wailing follow his footsteps wherever he goes."

"But he may repent," cried Effie, "for report says he is soon to be married to his fair cousin, the Lady Agnes Drummond, and surely then he will retrieve the character he at present seems to have lost."

"Take my word for it, he'll not marry for many a long day to come," answered Andrew Kenmuir; "it's true the young lady is said to be rich, and that may be a strong temptation to a young nobleman, whose fortune, it seems, wants patching up by means of what the world calls a prudent marriage; but Lord Dalmeny is one that loves liberty better than matrimony, and whilst he can get a score of girls for the asking, without encumbering himself with a wife, he'll hardly think of tying himself to one woman till all his wild oats are sown."

"I fear you have prophesied but too truely, Andrew," sighed the widow; "at least," she continued, "I am afraid there is one more victim to be added to his list before he becomes the husband of Lady Agnes."

"Aye, aye," exclaimed the news-bearer; "and pray who is it in whose behalf your fears are excited?"

"My own daughter," cried the widow Ruthven.

"What! the good and gentle Effie!"

"Even so."

"Nay, then, you do her an injustice," answered Andrew, "for report gives Effie the possession of every virtue under the sun. I have heard light words spoken of many a maiden whose fair name has stood tolerably high, but never knew I of a word being uttered against your daughter Effie."

"The world has done her nothing more than justice," replied the dame, "and yet I cannot but fear the arts of Lord Dalmeny, whose name is sufficient to strike terror into the hearts of all those who have daughters that they love, as I do my fair and duteous child."

"But why, if she is duteous," asked Adrew, "do you fear the arts of the seducer?"

"Because he has betrayed so many," replied Dame Ruthven, "that even she might not be able to see through the cunning and wickedness of the heartless libertine. It is my thought by night as well as by day; peace seems to have fled from me for ever, and though I have sought by every means in my power to drive away the fear that preys upon my mind, yet still do I see the hated form of Lord Dalmney, and his fiendish laugh of triumph rings in my ears, as if exulting over the misery he has caused."

"Alas!" cried Effie, "you have little confidence then in me, if you believe that I would weakly yield to one whose vices are so well known."

"And what confidence can I have in thee, my daughter," exclaimed Dame Ruthven, "when I know the artifices that are employed by the cruel destroyer?"

"It's a thousand pities," observed Andrew Kenmuir, "but the lassie had a lover that was likely to take her soon off your hands. It would save her a deal of trouble and anxiety, and Lord Dalmeny, they say, never pays his respects to married ladies, however young and pretty they may be, for fear of having to encounter the anger of their jealous husbands."

"Effie has had many offers," replied the good dame, proudly, "but she has refused them all, rather than leave her poor widowed mother."

"I was not doubting it, my good widow," answered Andrew, who began to suspect he had gone a little too far. "In fact, I have been round the village several times to inform the neighbours that Effie had had an offer, and yet, after all, you see, it has turned out that I have been a little too fast, for your daughter has sent her lovers to the right-about almost as soon as they made their appearance, and thus my character for veracity has run no little risk."

"It is an affair that the neighbours have nothing whatever to do with," replied the widow.

"Very true," answered the supple Andrew Kenmuir; "but then we have no newspapers in this part of the country, and if it was not for a good-natured fellow like myself, the neighbours would be totally ignorant of each others affairs."

"And much better would it be were such the case," cried Dame Ruthven.

"Aye, so you think, perhaps," replied Andrew; "but there happens to be a general appetite for news, and though you may think my purpose a useless one, there are plenty, I can assure you, that would feel themselves quite at a loss without it. As an instance, here is the death of poor old Duncan Grayson, that has just taken place, and if it was not for a useful fellow like me, nobody would have heard of it out of his own family for no one knows how long a time to come."

"I am sorry to hear of my neighbour's death," replied Dame Ruthven, "and yet I know not that it is to be much regretted, since his life has been a continual torture to him ever since the sad fate of his daughter, and the madness that followed it."

"All of which," observed Andrew, "was brought about in consequence of the love of Lord Dalmeny for a pretty girl."

"Nay," cried Effie, "you are again too sweeping in your condemnation of a man who certainly deserves some of your censure; May Grayson herself always bore the character of being somewhat gay and thoughtless, but had she been firm in her own virtue, the miseries we now deplore would have been avoided."

"Upon my word, Effie," exclaimed Andrew Kenmuir, "it seems that you are candid enough at any rate, for it is few females, I believe, that would take the blame from a man like Lord Dalmeny, to throw all its weight upon one of her own sex."

"You have misunderstood me, Andrew," answered the maiden, "for though I have in part blamed poor May Grayson for her lightness of heart, yet I do not in the least excuse Lord Dalmeney, who, I believe, had behaved, not only in her instance, but in that of many others, in a manner that must draw upon him the condemnation of all persons laying any claim to virtuous notions. I blame him for many acts of the blackest perfidy, yet I cannot but confess that there is much to be said against those, who, knowing his character, have yielded to his delusive promises."

"Well," exclaimed Andrew, "judging from your words, I should say your mother has little to fear from any attentions Lord Dalmeny may show you."

"I fear nothing from his soft and flattering tongue," replied the widow Ruthven, "but Lord Dalmeney is apt to use violence when fraud is likely to prove unavailing, and I am afraid that he will endeavour to carry her off if all other means should fail him."

"Why you don't mean to say that you think he would be such a villian?" exclaimed Andrew Kenmuir, in a tone that expressed the utmost surprise.

"Alas! but I do," cried the dame, sorrowfully; "I have long expected it, and his visits here on two or three occasions of late, serve to increase my apprensions for her safety. Nay, more, we have both had a vision of fearful import, in which a shadowy figure appeared before us, warning us of secret dangers with which we were threatened."

"Well, all that's rather alarming, to be sure," cried Andrew; "but yet, though you may be threatened with danger, it neigther argues that Effie is the person who is in peril, or that Lord Dalmeny is the one that she has cause to be afraid of."

"But I saw him in my vision," answered Dame Ruthven, with a shudder; "he took the place of the apparition that had warned me, and then I knew but too well that he was the villain from whom I was to look for my future source of misery."

"Well, but it was but a dream after all, you know."

"I am aware of it," replied the widow, with a sigh; "but dreams, Andrew, are often sent as a warning to those who are willing to accept of it."

"And pray what sort of a person was the figure that you saw in your sleep?"

"That of an old man," answered Dame Ruthven; "and now that I come to recollect myself, his countenance bore a strong likeness to Duncan Grayson, who you have come to tell me is just dead."

"And such," added Effie, "was the exact description of the form I myself beheld in the fearful vision that haunted my sleep."

"Well, that's uncommonly strange too!" exclaimed the old man; "for in my way hither, I chanced to fall in with Hugh Lorimer, who you know is always an early riser, and he told me something about finding Lord Dalmeny last night lying upon the ground in a deep swoon. It seems, however, that Hugh contrived to recover him, and then his lordship began to tell him a wild story about having encountered an apparition that would not let him pass, and between ourselves, I should not wonder in the least if the spectre was the very same that paid you and your daughter a visit in your sleep."

"Ah!" cried the widow, "I already feel convinced it was; but say, Andrew, what effect had this affair upon his lordship? Is it likely to deter him from his further evil designs?"

"Why, that's more than I can possibly undertake to answer for," replied the old man. "All I can say is, that Lord Dalmeny is not to be very easily frightened out of his purposes, and if this one should happen to succeed, I should say that old Duncan Grayson has done more good after his death than ever he did in the whole course of his lifetime."

"But did his lordship seem to be much affected at the supernatural visit he had received?"

"Not much, I believe," replied Andrew; "for, from what I could gather, it seems he would at one time have taken Hugh Lorimer's life in spite of the service he had done; but Hugh, as you are aware, is as tough as a bit of oak, and when he found out what his lordship meant, he flourishsd a stout cudgel that he happened to have in his hand, which so far frightened the young nobleman, that he grew much more civil afterwards than he had been before."

"And they parted upon better terms, I suppose?" exclaimed Dame Ruthven.

"Why, I suppose they did, seeing that neither of them could get much by quarrelling. Besides, Hugh Lorimer, you know, is beneath the resentment of Lord Dalmeny, which, by the by, is exactly the sort of opinion I should like him to have of me if ever we should happen to meet together when he was in one of his quarrelsome moods. I have no great skill in managing a weapon, whether it be a sword or cudgel, as I believe you will give me full credit for, Widow Ruthven; and, therefore, you may very well conceive how awkward it would be to contend with a fiery young fellow like Lord Dalmeny, who no more minds running a man through the body, than I mind running through the neighbourhood to inform my friends of the latest news of the parish. In fact, both are pleasures to ourselves individually, though neither could, perhaps, very well participate with the other in so exquisite a delight."

"You are cheerful, neighbour, this morning," observed the widow Ruthven; "though Heaven knows there is cause enough for sorrow to those who know the ever-restless and mischievous spirit of Lord Dalmeny."

"Well, but I never could see the use of meeting troubles half way," exclaimed Andrew Kenmuir; "for my own part, I always think it's quite time enough to look them in the face when they are close before me, and if everybody would but think the same, there would not be half the misery in the world that we now see."

"You think, then, it is unnecessary to guard against dangers when we have every reason to expect them?"

"Why, no, dame, I don't exactly mean to say that; but there are many people that are fond of making troubles when there are really none that they need give a thought about; to such people I should say, 'don't put

yourselves in a flurry, but wait till you see the enemy approach, and then, when you have reconnoitred a little, either prepare to give him battle boldly, or run away when he comes too near, whichever may appear to youself the wisest course.'"

"Would that I could run away from this !" cried Dame Ruthven; "but unfortunately the peril is too close at hand, and all that remains for me to do, is to keep a watchful eye upon young Lord Dalmeny, and should he attempt to deprive me of my child, he will find that a mother will not relinquish her offspring whilst life remains to support her."

"Mother ! dear mother, talk not thus I beseech you !" cried Effie, timidly. "Remember, your words argue but little confidence in my prudence, and there is one present who will not fail to spread abroad every word that may escape your lips."

"Ah, Effie !" exclaimed the old man with a cunning leer, "I know you are meaning me all this time; but never mind, lassie, if I'm eager to tell the news, I always find plenty enough that are willing to listen to it, and so you see we are even on that score. But I have been forgetting myself all this while; the story of Duncan Grayson's death is hardly known to any one, and I shall miss the pleasure of circulating it unless I make haste and resume my journey."

"You'll stop and take a bite and a sup with us, Andrew," said the widow, throwing a snow-white cloth upon the table, and placing thereon the most substantial fare she happened to have in the house. "You have a long way to go, friend," she continued, "and a man that takes so much pains to inform and instruct his neighbours, should meet with hospitality wherever he goes."

"Aye, my good dame," replied the old man; "you are a true Christian, as well as a most considerate woman; but it's not everybody that treats me

No. 13

in this kindly fashion I can assure you, for, would you believe it, there are some that would as soon see the devil himself enter their houses as honest Andrew Kenmuir.   But the foolish bodies know not their own interest, or they would welcome with joy the name that sacrifices time and everything else, that he may let them know all that's passing in the country for miles round about."

And so saying, he set to in good earnest, partaking of most of the things that were placed before him, and praising everything with surprising volubility.   At length his appetite began to grow less voracious, and having satisfied himself, he concluded his meal by draining the ale-cup to its very bottom; after which he jumped up from his seat, again thanked the widow for the refreshment she had afforded him, and then declared that he must proceed on his journey, or somebody else would be before him with the news.

" It's not every day," he continued, " that I am the bearer of such tidings as these, and even the people that generally frown upon me when I enter their doors will listen to me with interest when I relate the manner of poor Duncan Grayson's death.   There is a mystery about it, dame, that will make it acceptable to everybody, and as it's pretty generally known that the old man's been drooping ever since that mishap of his daughter, the people won't fail to pour the execrations on his lordship which is neither more nor less than he richly deserves."

" Stay, Andrew, and take another cup of ale before we part," cried the widow.

" Not this time, my good dame," answered the old man; " I'm in a hurry to be off, you see; but perhaps I may give you a call on my way back, and then I can tell you any further news that I've heard in my rambles over another draught of that supernaculum of yours.   So farewell to you both, and may Heaven preserve you from the dangers you expect from that most incorrigible scapegrace, Lord Dalmeny."

Upon this the old man bustled out of the cottage to perform the errand he had undertaken, and Dame Ruthven and her daughter were once more left alone to talk over the affair that had occupied their attention previous to the arrival of their late visiter.

CHAPTER XIII.

" Tell me not of it friend. When the young weep,
    Their tears are lukewarm brine; from our old eyes
    Sorrow falls down like hail-drops of the north,
    Chilling the furrows of our withered cheeks,
    Cold as our hopes, and hardened as our feelings;
    Their's, as they fall, sink sightless; ours recoil,
    Heap the fair plain, and bleaken all before us."
                                                    ANON.

ON the day appointed for the funeral of Duncan Grayson, crowds of people might be seen journeying towards the house from whence the body was to be conveyed to its last resting place.   At that period it was a custom for all persons who thought proper, whether invited or not, to attend the burial of their neighbours, and, in fact, their presence on such an occasion was considered as a mark of high respect for the deceased.   The peculiar circumstances under which Grayson had died, and the strange stories that were afloat of his having appeared to several persons after death, had created the utmost interest throughout the country, and consequently a greater assemblage had taken place than was usual, for the house was crowded with persons of all degrees, from the wealthy gentry down to the beggars who wandered through the country to obtain a scanty subsistence from those who had the means to bestow their alms upon them.

Every room in the house was filled with guests, and even the out-build-ings were crowded with those who were unable to obtain more comfortable quarters in the principal edifice. But we must now enter the room where the dead man lay in his coffin, and in which were assembled his relatives and a few of those who had contrived to gain admittance there by the favour of their friends. At the head of the coffin sat the aged mother of the deceased, whose care-worn countenance betrayed the deep anguish that was preying on her heart. Yet her eyes were tearless, for the foun-tains of grief seemed to have been dried up, and her outward tokens of sorrow were uttered in groans and sighs, that moved even the callous hearts of those who usually felt little pity for the sufferings of their fel-low-creatures.

"This is a sad day," whispered Annot Teesdale to another old woman who sat beside her; "the poor old soul made a grievous end, for they say he died of a broken heart, and that he has rested so ill that his spirit has been wandering about ever since the moment of his death."

"Whist!" answered the other; "speak lower, Annot, or the old woman will hear you. She seems full of grief enough already, and it is not for us to be talking about things that don't concern us."

"And why need she grieve?" asked Annot; "her son has gone to his rest only a little while before her, and a blessed thing it is for him, to my thinking, seeing that his daughter has turned out so bad, and is nothing better than a poor wandering maniac. For my own part, I should wish for death a thousand times over if a child of mine was to turn out as May Grayson has."

"You are too hard upon the poor girl," answered the other. "May has been weak enough to yield; but what say you to the villain that deceived her with his false promises?"

"Aye, aye, he is bad enough," replied Annot; "but the girls know his character well, and it is their place to shun him instead of feeling proud, as many of them do, at the attentions he shows them."

"But they are inexperienced, you know."

"That's true enough," exclaimed Annot; "but their fathers and mo-ther are not inexperienced, and they should learn to take their advice, and then the mischief we complain of would cease."

"You don't blame Lord Dalmeny, then, for all the crimes he has com-mitted?"

"Lord Dalmeny is a fearful libertine, by all accounts," replied the other; "but we must not throw all the blame on him, when the fault rests as much with the foolish girls as with himself. They encourage him by their flaunting manners, and if they afterwards fall, who is to blame for it but themselves?"

"Aye, but all are not alike," returned her neighbour, "for poor May Grayson was deceived by a pretended marriage, and who should reproach her for the crimes of him who, with the art of a fiend, brought her to ruin and madness?"

"Very true," answered Annot; "but she had not much prudence, or she would have known that the proud Lord Dalmeny never intended to mate himself with the upstart daughter of a humble farmer."

"Nay, you are too severe upon her."

"Not a bit—not a bit," replied Annot; "for see what has been the con-sequence of her folly. Yonder lies poor Duncan Grayson, her broken-hearted father, in his coffin, and if all that people say is true, he's not yet at rest, for his spirit wanders upon the earth, as many people are ready to testify."

"I have heard something of this report before."

"You must have been deaf else," retorted Annot; "for every one is speaking of his having appeared to Lord Dalmeny a very little time after his death. Hugh Lorimer says he found him lying in a swoon upon the ground, and that his lordship confessed to him that he had seen the wraith of old Duncan Grayson, and that he was sure some harm to himself was about to follow."

"And the widow Ruthven is said to have seen him."

"Aye, and her daughter Effie," replied Annot; "but this may be taken as a warning to the lassie, for they say Lord Dalmeny regards her with favour, and we all know that if he once sets his mind on having her, that nothing will baulk him. But whist!—old Magdalen Grayson looks towards us, and is going to speak."

A death-like silence now prevailed, in the midst of which Magdalen rose from her seat, and stretching forth her hand towards the coffin, said, in a hollow voice that startled her hearers,—

"Yonder, my friends, lies all the remains of him who was the cherished object of my heart. He was my only son, and I loved him as never mother loved her offspring before; and yet death spared him not, and he was snatched from me, though I have so often prayed that I might be carried to my silent grave before him. Never once did he do ought to make my heart ache, and in my joy I have thought no such son was ever born to bring happiness to his mother. And now ye see what he has been brought to; death has laid his hand upon him, and he has withered away through the evil doings of her who should have been his pride and support when age came upon him."

Here an agonised sob interrupted her. For a moment the speaker paused and turned her eyes towards that part of the chamber from whence the sound came, but instantly recollecting herself she continued—

"Who that knew us a few years since could have believed the sorrow that has now fallen on us? And yet you now see how heavily grief has fallen on our house; here lies the father dead before you, and the daughter's shame is already but too well known. Oh, my friends, ye know not how the disgrace went to my poor son's heart; from that moment he was a changed and altered man; pleasure had for ever forsaken his roof,—and though he cursed not his child, yet silent grief was gnawing at his heart, and by slow degrees he pined away till he came to be what you now see him. He died, and his last prayers were offered up to Heaven that no more victims might fall through the means of Lord Dalmeny."

At this moment the loud tramping of a horse's feet was heard; then the sound suddenly ceased near the house, and when a few moments had elapsed the door was opened, and Lord Dalmeny, attired in deep mourning, entered the room. At this unexpected visit, a low supressed cry of horror was heard, and the assembled company shrunk back involuntarily as if dreading to come in contact with one whose name was connected with so much infamy. But the young nobleman appeared to take no notice of this, and, taking off his plumed cap, he advanced towards the coffin, and laying his hand upon the lid, shed, or affected to shed, tears for the departed. Thus deceived, the people began to think he had grown penitent; but the minister, David Cornie, was not to be misled by these outward tokens of grief, and advancing a few paces he said sternly—

"What is the reason of this unlooked-for visit, my lord?—Are you not satisfied with the mischief you have already done, but you must come here this day to insult with your presence those who charge you with being the cause of their present grief?"

"I am come to mingle my grief with yours," answered Lord Dalmeny, unmoved by the reproaches that had been thus heaped upon him. "I heard of the trouble that had entered this house, and hastened hither to offer what little consolation it was in my power to bestow."

"There is no need for it, my lord," exclaimed David Cornie, sternly;— "here you are regarded as an enemy; nay, as the fiend incarnate that has destroyed a father through the vile arts you have practised to rob him of an only daughter."

"They wrong me," exclaimed the nobleman, with hypocritical meekness. "The maiden was passing fair; and I must needs confess that, dazzled by her beauty, I was led astray. But you must make some allowances for the acts of an inconsiderate headstrong youth, who now sees the wickedness of his ways, and is willing to offer all the recompense in his power."

"That thou canst not do," answered the pastor, "unless thou canst descend from thy high estate and wed her whom thou hast brought to shame and disgrace."

"And even that may not be impossible," replied Lord Dalmeny, with assumed humility. "I have already repented the thoughtlessness I have been guilty of, and it now remains for others to say whether I shall make the recompense I am so anxious to do."

"Are you in earnest, my lord," asked the minister.

"I am, or you would not have seen me here."

"Alas!" cried David Cornie, "your lordship's repentance has come too late; the father now lies dead before you, and the daughter is bereft of reason. You should have thought of this before, my lord, and much of pain and agony would have been spared those who are now beyond the reach of kindness."

"But the girl may recover her senses," answered the nobleman, "and thus reparation may be made to one at least that I have injured."

"My lord," exclaimed the minister, "the more I hear you speak the more convinced am I that you come only to mock us. Repentance has not yet touched your heart, though you would fain make us believe it has in order to wipe away the odium that your crimes have brought on you."

"Wilt thou not believe me, priest?"

"I have seen but too much reason to doubt your word," replied the pastor, in a voice of reproach;—"the corse over which you stand reminds me of your former wickedness; and knowing as I do the depravity of your heart, I will not believe that you feel remorse for the crimes you have committed. That coffin contains all that remains of Duncan Grayson, whose simple and sinless life made him beloved by all who knew him. Him thou hast slain, through the baseness thou didst practice towards his daughter, and the curses of all good men will be upon thee for the deed that has robbed us of a friend and neighbour."

"Ah!" exclaimed Lord Dalmeny, "dost thou accuse me of causing his death?"

"I do, my lord," answered the minster; "a few months since, and who was so truly happy as Duncan Grayson? but then comes a fiend in the shape of a man, who poured his insidious words of love into the ears of this good man's daughter. The maiden was young and inexperienced in the artifices of the world; she believed the villain;—sinned, and went mad for very shame. You, my lord, I accuse of being the fiend I speak of; and you do I charge, in the presence of these people, with being the murderer of him we are about to bear to his last narrow resting-place."

"Thou dost accuse me falsely!" cried Lord Dalmeny, restraining his rage with great difficulty.

"How!" exclaimed the pastor; "wilt thou dare deny thy guilt in the presence of thy victim? Beware, my lord, for they say his spirit has walked upon the earth since his departure from us, and he may yet rise up before thee to confirm the words I have spoken!"

Struck by the earnestness with which these words were uttered, Lord Dalmeny stood pale and motionless for some few moments. His first impulse was to seize the offending priest by the throat and strangle him in the presence of his friends: but prudence came to his aid, and concealing his indignation as well as he could, he presently answered with a well-feigned appearance of calmness,—

"Thy words, old man, excite in me no anger, because I know, however imprudently thou mayest have acted, thy motives were such as I ought to esteem. Much of my wildness has been occasioned by my never having had so wise a counsellor as thyself by my side. This do I most deeply deplore, and yet thou dost refuse to give credit to my words when I say that I sincerely repent the error of my former ways."

"And why," demanded the minister, "hast thou chosen such a period as this to come amongst us?"

"To ask permission," replied Lord Dalmeny, "that I may follow the body of this good man to its last resting-place."

Lord Dalmeny had spoken with so much apparent sincerity, and his manner was altogether so subdued to what it had ever been before, that many who had previously regarded him with hatred began to believe that he was truly repentant, and, after a brief consultation, it was agreed that he should be permitted to join in the funeral procession. This decision being announced to him by David Cornie, preparations were immediately commenced for bearing away the coffin; but at that moment a piercing shriek was heard, and May Grayson, who had hitherto been concealed in a distant part of the room, rushed forward, and throwing her arms round the coffin that contained her father, gave way to the most heart-rending cries and lamentations. It was in vain that her friends interposed to prevail on her to retire from the chamber of death, for she was deaf to all their entreaties, and it was not till her grandmother, Magdalen Grayson, approached, that she would relinquish the firm hold she had taken.

"May—my beloved child!" cried the old woman, tenderly, "why dost thou appear before us at such a moment as this? Thy father is now beyond the reach of thy kindness, and his ears deaf to the cry of repentance thou wouldst pour into them. Leave us, girl, for they are about to remove the body, and thou knowest it brings evil upon the survivors to stay a corse when it is on its way to the churchyard."

But May Grayson seemed to be unconscious of the words with which she was addressed, and her eyes wandered about the room as if in search of some object that she expected to see. At length they rested upon the form of Lord Dalmeny, and then a sudden flash of light seemed to illumine them with unnatural fire, and springing forward, she seized him by the hand ere he had time to prevent her.

"Ah, my lord," she cried, "I knew you would be here, for there's to be a bridal at the church to-day; see you not how many are assembled here to do honour to the nuptials? You and I, my lord, are to be the bride and bridegroom,—nay, look not thus frowningly upon me, for thou hast often promised we should be wedded, and why not now, when such a gay party has met together to witness the vows between us?"

"See you not, girl," interposed the minister, "that all are habited in the garb of mourning and woe?"

"Aye, and 'tis better that it should be so," she replied, wildly; "for there has been much to grieve for since first Lord Dalmeny and I met together. Would you believe it, Davie, that some have told me I had lost my senses,—aye, that I was mad, and the cause of my madness was the inconstancy of him who had vowed to make me his bride?"

"May," exclaimed her grandmother, "this is no time to interrupt the solemn affairs of the day. Thou knowest thy father is dead, and those who are assembled here have come to accompany him to the churchyard."

"Dead!" shrieked the maniac.

"Yes, girl, thy cruel conduct—nay, I will not reproach thee, for thy sufferings are already too great for endurance; they have driven thee mad, and may the punishment thou hast received on earth satisfy the anger of that Heaven which thou hast offended."

"And do you, too, say I am mad?"

"Do not interrupt us further," interposed David Cornie; "already we have tarried beyond the appointed time, and the distance is far from hence where we have to deposit the remains of our friend."

"Ah, you do but deceive me!" cried May; "all of you speak of a funeral as if I knew not that ye are assembled to witness a bridal. Is it not so, my Lord Dalmeny? we are to be married you know, and just now I heard the bells ringing, though never did the sound come to my ears so mournfully."

"Girl!" exclaimed David Cornie, "it was thy father's funeral knell."

"Ah!" she cried, "you only tell me so to make me weep on my bridal day! But I know why you all seek to deceive me thus—you are envious because I am going to be the Lady of Dalmeny. Why else is my lord here? Would he come, think you, to a funeral?—*he* whose heart is light and joyous as my own."

"Alas! my child," sighed Magdalen, "thine, I fear, is heavy and sad enough; for thou hast been deceived by a villain, and yet, despite the curses of those he has injured, he dares to intrude himself into the house of mourning."

"You wrong me, dame," answered the young nobleman; "if I have injured you I am now truly repentant, and grieving, as I do, for my former misdeeds, I have come to pay the last tribute of respect to the deceased."

"I'll not believe your own assertion of repentance," cried the old woman; "your whole life has been one of deceit and wickedness, and your present appearance amongst us is only to carry on some base design that you have plotted."

"Woman!" exclaimed Lord Dalmeny, "I have already explained myself to the satisfaction of your excellent pastor, and he, at any rate, is willing enough to give me credit for better intentions in future."

"He has not such bitter cause to distrust you as I have," answered Magdalen, with deep emotion.

"And why shouldst thou do so?" asked his lordship.

"Canst thou ask me such a question?" demanded the old woman. "Look at that coffin and consider who it is that lies within it, and who it was that sent him there; and when thou hast feasted thine eyes with the sight of one of thy victims, turn them upon my poor grandchild, whom thou hast cruelly deceived and driven out of her mind."

"I have already told them I am sorry for the past," answered Lord Dalmeny; "unfortunately, however, my error cannot be entirely retrieved, but as far as lies in my power I will make ample amends for all the sorrow I have caused thee and thine."

"'Tis well to talk of what you will do," answered the old woman, bitterly; "but canst thou bring back my son to life, or restore my grand-child to her senses?"

"Thy son," replied Lord Dalmeny, "is beyond all human aid, but care and attention may, ere long, serve to recover poor May."

"Aye, to be even more conscious of her shame and disgrace than she is at the present moment."

"Nay," replied the nobleman, "if she recovers, as I hope she will, it is my intention to exalt her to that rank which shall make her the envy of thousands."

"Ha! wilt thou make her thy lawful wife?"

"I will."

"There, grandmother!" cried May, with childish glee, "you hear his lordship?—he promises to make me his bonny bride, and then I shall ride in my own coach, and you shall sit opposite to me; and those that scorned us before shall bow and cringe, and curtsey as we pass along; and I shall be called my lady, and——"

"Nay, my child, believe him not," interrupted the old woman; "there is some design in this deeper than we can see through, and he only seeks to make us his dupes. Besides, he is already pledged to the Lady Agnes, who has wealth and beauty as her dower, and you may, therefore, be sure he will not stoop to take a bride from among his own tenantry, at the risk of being laughed at by those who are as wicked and heartless as himself."

"Will you not believe him, then?" cried May Grayson, pouting like a spoiled child."

"It is time this subject should drop, Magdalen," whispered the pastor to the old woman; "take thy grand-daughter from the room, and we will proceed with the mournful business that has brought us together."

By means of entreaties and promises, Magdalen at length succeeded in coaxing the maniac girl from the room, and when the preparations were completed, the cavalcade set forth on its way towards the churchyard in which the remains of Duncan Grayson were to be deposited.

CHAPTER XIV.

"Mark me:—
Now will I raise the waters." MERCHANT OF VENICE

UPON reaching the outside of the house, Lord Dalmeny sprang upon his horse, which he had fastened by the bridle to a tree, and riding on towards the head of the procession, placed himself by the side of David Cornie, who, like many of the rest, was also mounted on horseback. Their way lay through a rocky and highly romantic country, and for some time the profoundest silence was observed, which was, however, at length broken by the young nobleman, who inquired of the pastor whether he had heard anything of a rumour which had been industriously propagated of his having been met by an apparition, supposed to have been that of the recently deceased Duncan Grayson.

"I have heard such a report," answered the minister, gravely; "but your lordship must be aware that it would ill-become a man like me to believe in superstitions that are credited only by the the most ignorant."

"True," replied Lord Dalmeny; "you at least know better than to believe such idle rumours, but I fear there are many who may be inclined to listen to this story, because it involves a marvel in which I am concerned."

"And yet," exclaimed the pastor, "one would have thought your lord-ship would care but little for anything that people may say to your pre-judice."

"Under other circumstances, I might do so," answered his lordship; "but prejudice has led to absolute hate, and it is provoking to see that people shun me as if I were the great fiend himself."

"And yet it is not to be much wondered at," returned David Cornie, "since you have not scrupled to make yourself as odious as possible to those who should have looked up to you as an example."

"For the future they shall do so," replied Dalmeny, "and, therefore, the past should be forgotten."

"Forgotten!" exclaimed the minister; "and does your lordship think then that parents can ever forget the daughters that have been sacrificed to your unhallowed love, or that brothers will overlook the shame and infamy you have brought upon their sisters. No, no, my lord, believe me you ex-pect that which is imposible."

"In other words, then," cried the nobleman, "you would tell me that repentance is too late, and consequently that I may as well keep on in the course I have pursued?"

"I say not that," replied the minister, "for it is high time thou should'st abandon the evil of thy ways, lest death should surprise thee in the midst of thy career. Besides, in time people may begin to believe in the sincerity of thy repentance, and then again thou wilt be honoured and respected."

"Thy counsel is most excellent," exclaimed the hypocrite; "it pleases me well to hear the good encouragement thou dost hold out; and, believe me, I will henceforth endeavour to profit by thy advice. Yet there are some, I fear, who are so deeply prejudiced, that no change will ever obtain for me their favourable opinion."

No. 14

"I admit that prejudices are not easily overcome," replied David Cornie; "but time worketh great miracles, and if thou dost continue steady in thy resolution, doubt not thou wilt ultimately gain the confidence and esteem of thy fellow-creatures."

"And in order to commence this happy reformation," cried Lord Dalmeny, "it will be necessary that I take unto myself a wife; I shall thus appear in earnest, and shall gain rapidly in the favourable opinion of the world."

"Your words remind me, my lord," cried the minister, "of a sort of promise that you made just now to wed poor May Grayson, in the event of her recovery from the dreadful malady she is afflicted with. Your words inspired my heart with joy, and I would now ask you, in all seriousness, whether you were sincere in what you said?"

"And what," asked Lord Dalmeny, "if I should confess that the words were only meant to comfort those who would look forward with joy to such an event."

"In that case," answered the pastor, "I should say you had added another crime to the long catalogue you have already committed."

"Then, suppose I act the hypocrite, and profess one thing while I mean another?"

"If your lordship does that, I have done with you," answered David Cornie, gravely.

"Nay, you must not take me too seriously," replied Lord Dalmeny, who began to see he was losing ground. "I was merely putting a case, that I might have the opinion of a man so experienced as yourself. As for May Grayson, she is a pretty wench enough, and gained my love, as you are aware, and at present I know not of any obstacle to prevent our union in case she should recover her lost senses."

"Which I am afraid is hopeless," cried the pastor. "Still, however, I rejoice in your repentance, and glad should I be to know for a certainty that it is not feigned to suit purposes of your own."

"How can I convince you of my earnestness?"

"That must be left to yourself," replied the minister. "Your acts may do much towards convincing me, yet still you may be playing the hypocrite, which few lookers-on can very well guard against."

"Suppose I were to present you with a piece of land, and materials sufficient for the building of a church; would not that look something like zeal in the cause of religion?"

"Outwardly it would, at any rate," replied David Cornie; "yet there are many who make a great display in the manner you have mentioned, whose hearts are black with sin. Such may not be the case with your lordship, and most earnestly do I hope that your conversion is as sincere I can desire."

"Well, I see it's a hard thing to make people believe in one's good intentions," answered his lordship, "and so, I suppose, I may as well go on in my old career, and let the world think as it will of me."

"I feared as much," exclaimed the pastor; "you have been laughing at us all this time, my lord, and, therefore, I must request that you leave us, for it is not meet that so great a reprobate should assist in a solemnity like this. Death should teach us a lesson, but your lordship makes light of it, though the man we bear to the grave has been the victim of your own unbridled and lawless passions."

"I see you do not yet understand me," cried Lord Dalmeny; "I am sincere, I tell you, and it only requires a little patience to convince you that I am a sincere convert to your own opinions. But a man cannot change all at once; and I may appear thoughtless and light of heart when most inclined to follow the excellent counsel you would give me."

" And yet they say," answered the minister, " that your heart has been set upon the possession of another maiden, whose virtue has been hitherto an example to her sex. I mean Effie Ruthven, and your lordship knows best whether there is any truth in the report that has been so industriously spread."

" Why, to confess the truth," replied Lord Dalmeny, " I have often been struck with the beauty of Effie, and have thought she was a prize worth the possessing; but I have made no attempt to carry her off, and that alone ought to be sufficient to convince you that I have no inclination to deceive her."

" Perhaps that has been because you have had no opportunity," observed David Cornie.

" Why, that is not exactly the reason," replied his lordship; " but the fact is, her brother John Ruthven, or Red Ruthven, as he thinks fit to call himself, is a sort of humble friend or companion of mine, and on that account, I have been rather more scrupulous than I should otherwise have been."

" Besides which," observed the minister drily, " her brother is reputed to be a man of fierce and violent passions, and it might be dangerous to do anything that would excite his anger."

" Think you, then, that cowardice restrains me ?" demanded Lord Dalmeny.

" I do not say it is cowardice," replied David; " but your lordship knows as well as I do, that John would never rest satisfied till he had washed out the foul stain in your own blood."

" John and I have quarrelled ere now, and have even measured swords together," answered Lord Dalmeny; " we have met in mortal strife, yet so equal was our skill in the use of our weapons, that the contest ended in nothing, and we parted as good friends as ever we were in our lives."

" Aye," replied the other, " but John Ruthven had not then to avenge the lost honour of a beloved sister; your quarrel was perhaps a slight one, and therefore he fought with less fierceness than he would have done had he been resolved to take your life."

" Be that as it may," exclaimed his lordship, " my own skill in swordsmanship is fully equal to his, and should we ever chance to meet again in mortal strife it is likely I may come of the conqueror."

" And thus," cried the pastor, " you will add the shedding of human blood to your other crimes !"

" But not unless I am provoked to it," returned Lord Dalmeny. " If I am spurred on by his insolence, I shall not fail to punish him according to his deserts; but if he knows his own place, and leaves me to follow the bent of my own humour, there will be little chance of my ever having to answer for the crime you have mentioned."

At this moment a man sprang from a high bank on the road-side, and the next moment Lord Dalmeny recognised in his countenance the well-known features of John Ruthven; he had scarcely, however, time to make this discovery, for his horse, startled by the suddenness with which this had taken place, began to plunge so violently, that the rider was scarcely able to keep his seat, though at all other times he had been remarkably expert in the management of his steed. Seeing the danger, several persons started forward to secure the bridle, but ere they could succeed in this, the animal reared upon his hind legs, and then falling upon his side, would have crushed the rider to death, had not the minister leaped from his own horse and dragged away the rider just in time to save him from the peril with which he was threatened. Lord Dalmeny seemed to be stupified with the danger he had so miraculously escaped, but recovering himself after a minute or two, he said, as he rose from the ground :—

"You have saved my life, David Cornie, and I thank you for the good service. It may be in my power to repay the service you have done me this day, and, therefore, I charge you to make a demand upon me at any time you may think proper, and you shall find that I am not ungrateful to the man who has been my preserver."

"My lord," replied the pastor, "the only request I shall make is, that you will repent the evil of your ways. Let your present escape remind you of the suddenness with which you may be called upon to account for the deeds you have committed, and I shall be amply repaid for the assistance it has been in my power to afford."

"We will talk of this another time," answered his lordship; "at present we do but delay the funeral procession, and when the solemnity is concluded, I may chance to be in a better humour to hear the serious matters upon which it seems you desire to speak."

"Have you received no hurt, my lord?"

"Nothing of any consequence," he replied; "a few sprains and a slight bruise or two, are all that I feel of an accident that had nearly proved fatal. My horse, however, seems to have fared worse than myself, for he is dying, and I shall lose one of the noblest steeds that ever submitted itself to the dominion of man."

"Nay, think not of your charger, my lord," exclaimed David; "he is past recovery, and we must, therefore, leave him to die by the wayside."

"And what," asked Lord Dalmeny, "has become of the man that caused this mischief?"

"That I know not," replied the minister; "he remained but an instant, and then, springing away, he disappeared whilst we were occupied in attending on your lordship."

"Did you know the man?"

"It was but a moment that I saw him," replied David, "but in that brief period I recognised the form and lineaments of John Ruthven."

"You are right; it was the person you have named, and his accursed presence had very nearly been the cause of my untimely death."

"And if it had," answered the clergyman, "there would have been small blame to him, seeing that his presence here was most likely the result of accident."

"It might have been so," replied Lord Dalmeny, "but the fellow ran away upon the instant, instead of stopping to see whether he could render any assistance after the mischief he had caused."

"But since the affair has terminated better than might have been expected," exclaimed David Cornie, "it will be your wiser course to forget the apparent neglect you complain of. So now we will proceed on our way, and conclude the melancholy duty we have been called on to perform."

The procession accordingly moved forward, but Lord Dalmeny soon found that the sprains and bruises he had received, occasioned more pain than he had anticipated, and the minister, who perceived this, would have dismounted from his saddle in order that he might ride the remainder of the distance. This, however, his lordship would not agree to, and at last it was arranged, as they had not much further to go, that the young nobleman should sit behind the pastor till they reached some cottage, where he might rest till the funeral ceremony was over.

But it chanced that their way lay through an arm of the sea, which, at low water, was easily fordable, though during the height of the tide the passage was not to be attempted without much danger. Aware of this, it had been arranged that the procession should leave the house of the deceased Duncan Grayson at a time that would enable it to reach the spot when the tide was nearly out; but delays had taken place, as has been seen, and by the time they reached the ford the water was running up with a strength that shewed the opposite shore was not to be reached without considerable danger. The business of the day, however, admitted of no delay, and those who were foremost dashed into the flood with a determination to reach the landing place ere the waters were much more swollen. The minister and Dord Dalmeny paused for a moment to watch the progress of these hardy pioneers, and were soon convinced that further delay would be dangerous; and urging the horse forward, doubly loaded as it was, they quickly found themselves in the middle of the stream, where the current was running with a strength that threatened destruction to both the horse and its riders. Their peril now became imminent, for they had lost all control over the half drowning animal, and there were none who durst venture to their assistance, as their own death would be almost certain to follow were they to attempt to rescue their companions. Thus abandoned to their fate the pastor and Lord Dalmeny gave themselve up as lost, for the horse had by this time become completely exhausted, and it was evident that with all their exertions it would be impossible to sustain him many minutes longer. Yet in this awful moment of despāir, when death appeared before them ready to seize upon his prey, a loud shout of joy was heard from those who had been fortunate enough to reach the shore, and looking round them they discovered a boat advancing swiftly towards them, rowed by a single man;—that man they saw at a glance was John Ruthven; but ere they could give utterance to their expressions of joy and gratitude the little vessel had darted towards them, and in less time than it would take us to describe it both the minister and Lord Dalmeny were safely seated in the boat. Not a word, however, did John Ruthven answer in reply to the thanks with which they would have overwhelmed him, but plying lustily at the oar he conveyed them safely to land, and then pulled his boat again into the stream without waiting to bestow a single word on them.

The first act of the minister was to fall upon his knees and offer up his gratitude to Heaven for his unexpected deliverance from death. This done, he ordered the funeral procession to move onwards to the church; and then, taking the arm of Lord Dalmeny, who was much less exhauted than himself, he led him towards a cottage that stood at the distance of a few paces from the place where they had landed. The rustic owner was standing at the door, and to him David Cornie addressed himself, asking permission for himself and his young friend to rest themselves after the fatigue and exhaustion they had endured. But the man gazed upon the young nobleman with an angry scowl, and then turning to the pastor he said—

" For yourself, David Cornie, there is room within my cottage; but I have daughters whom I love beyond all else that the world contains, and never shall my door be opened to receive one who would abuse my confidence, and tear from me the dearest treasure of my soul."

Lord Dalmeny smiled scornfully at these words, and the minister, turning sorrowfully away, directed his steps towards another cottage, and entering the open door, addressed himself to Dame Elsphat, who sat knitting by the window, requiring of her permission to rest themselves, and a change of raiment in place of their own dripping garments. But the dame was in no better humour than the cottager they had applied to in the first instance, and, scarcely raising her eyes from the work she was engaged on, she said:—

"You, David Cornie, are freely welcome to all that my poor cottage can afford; but you have a companion with you that I cannot but wish had been swallowed up by the hungry waters just now. He I cannot receive beneath my roof, and therefore I bid him begone and seek the shelter he requires from those who are as abandoned to wickedness as himself."

"Why, Dame Elsphat," exclaimed Lord Dalmeny, without appearing to be angry at her words, "surely you do not forget the many happy days and nights you have spent yonder in my old castle. Those were joyous times, and, boy as I then was, I used to think you loved me almost as much as if I had been your own son."

"And so I did," answered the dame, "but you have changed since then, and my love has turned to hatred."

"Aye, but you have not changed much, Elsphat," cried the hypocrite, "for in those days I used to think you the fairest and prettiest of all the lasses that used to come and dance in my father's hall. Years have passed since then, Elsphat, and yet Time has dealt so kindly that you look now as handsome as ever."

"Hear him!" exclaimed the old woman, whose vanity had been touched by the words of the flatterer; "is this the man that I have heard described by my neighbours as a born devil that should be shunned!"

"Aye, but I have been foully wronged by the envious," answered Lord Dalmeny, in his blandest tones; "men belie me, but it follows not that Elsphat, my old favourite and friend, should turn her back upon me."

"True," replied Elsphat, "I will not be harsh now that you require my assistance. So be seated by the fire, my lord, and you and our good minister shall be welcome to such poor fare as my house affords."

With this the table was spread, and whilst her guests were regaling themselves, the dame continued a conversation that was so flattering to her own vanity. In this she was well seconded by Lord Dalmeny, and they talked together of old affairs,—his lordship taking good care to advance still further in the favourable opinion she began to entertain for him. In the midst of this conversation footsteps were heard approaching, and as the door opened, John Ruthven, accompanied by Lady Margaret Dalmeny and Lady Agnes, entered the room. The elder lady, in particular, appeared to have been much alarmed, and falling on the neck of her son, she offered up her grateful thanks for the providential deliverance that had rescued him from the hands of death.

"We are also," she continued, "deeply in debt to John, who not only rescued you and this worthy minister from a watery grave, but immediately afterwards hastened back to the castle to assure us of your safety. We owe him much, my son, and I shall therefore leave it to your own generosity to reward his services as they deserve."

"Your ladyship may safely trust that to me," answered the young nobleman; "it must, however, be confessed that John had previously caused an accident which occasioned the death of my favourite steed, and had very nearly terminated in my own."

"The fault was none of mine," replied John; "I was at the time in pursuit of an object, and this may perhaps serve to account to you for my abrupt disappearance, when perhaps I ought to have staid to render whatever assistance was in my power."

"I have no wish to dive into your secrets," exclaimed Lord Dalmeny, but perhaps you will tell me how it was that you afterwards came to our assistance when we were struggling in the waters?"

"I know," answered John, "that you were about to cross the ford that led to the opposite side, and having previously ascertained that the tide had begun to flow, I was well aware of the danger that awaited you.

Upon this, I hurried to a part of the shore where I knew a boat was lying, and pushing out with all the strength I had, fortune so far favoured me, that I was able to rescue you and this good man at the very moment when you were about to sink beneath the raging waters. The service, such as it is, requires no thanks, and the only favour I shall ask in return, is, that you will never mention the subject again."

"Well, you are a strange fellow, John, that is certain," exclaimed Lord Dalmeny; "and so, as you will not accept of my thanks, I will bestow them on my fair cousin, the Lady Agnes, whose anxiety in my behalf has brought her thus far to ascertain the safety of one, who, I fear, is almost unworthy of her consideration."

"Nay, be not too vain on that subject," laughed Lady Agnes; "for if the truth must be told, I came with Lady Margaret, rather than suffer her to leave the house alone."

"You cared nothing for me, then, my fair cousin?"

"Why, I'll not go quite so far as to say that," she replied; "but the fact is, we had heard from John that you were out of danger, and therefore we had little reason to be alarmed on that account."

The tramping of many horses was now heard, and directly afterwards one of the mourners entered the cottage, and addressing himself to Daniel Cornie, said :—

"We have left the body of our friend behind us in the churchyard to become the prey of worms; he is now in his last resting-place, where the machinations of the wicked will no more reach him. And as the last sod of green turf was placed upon his grave, the form of an aged man stood before us, who, after gazing upon us for a brief space, said :—

"Ye have periled yourselves this morning in coming through the water, and death was hovering over you anxious to seize upon his victims; but you escaped, and all stand before me save two, who have lingered behind for shelter. They have escaped the peril that threatened them ;—but go back to them, and say from me, that they are both doomed,—the elder one to find a grave beneath the waters, and the younger to a life of infamy and a death of shame! Hie thee home, and obey my injunctions, for time presses on, and the warning will be short enough for both of them!"

"And was that all he said?" asked Lord Dalmeny, with a voice and look of scorn.

"It was."

"And what became of him after this?"

"He disappeared, no one knew how, and greatly troubled at the words we had heard, we left the churchyard, and mounting our steeds, hastened hither to deliver the message we were charged with."

"Then having executed your commission, you can now leave us with as little delay as possible," exclaimed Lord Dalmeny, and as the man left the cottage, his lordship addressing to David Cornie, said :—

"This is some foolish tale invented to frighten us; the knaves have some designs of their own to serve, but it shall go hard if I do not yet retaliate upon them in a way they little expect."

"Oh, be not too sure that the men seek to deceive you, my lord," cried Dame Elsphat, with terror. "The old man they saw was Archie Nixon, the seer, and take my word for it, he has good reason for the warning he has given. Take warning in time, Lord Dalmeny, for Archie seldom fails to speak the truth, and if you heed him not, sorrow and misfortune will be your doom."

"Why, you are almost as mad as Archie himself!" exclaimed the young nobleman. "Think you I am to be frightened by the words of a crazy, crack-brained old idiot like that?"

" I tell you again," replied Dame Elsphat, "the warning you have heard is intended for your own good."

"Very likely," replied his lordship ; "but as I am not inclined to take advice from any one, I shall e'en follow my own way, in spite of all the predictions that may be uttered to deter me from my own course.   So now, ladies, I wait but your further pleasure ;—we will leave this place on our return home, and in our way, visit the Beacon Hill, from whence so fine and extensive prospect is to be obtained.   You, Ruthven, I suppose, will remain behind, for we are seldom together, unless indeed it be to measure swords, by way of settling a dispute."

"On the present occasion I will go with you," answered Ruthven, "for I have myself heard much of the scenery you have been speaking of, and this may perhaps be the last time I shall have an opportunity of seeing it."

" Are you going to leave us, Ruthven ?" asked Lady Agnes.

" I am."

" Your resolution, then, has been rather suddenly formed ?"

"Perhaps so, my lady ; but I am a creature of impulse, and seldom know one day what I may do the next.   Besides, the land, beautiful as it is to some persons, has few charms for me, who love the ever restless ocean, which shews a perfect type of my own disposition."

"Oh, never attempt to question him, my fair cousin," exclaimed Lord Dalmeny, with a slight sneer ; " Ruthven is as wilful as a spoiled child, and quite as fond of having his own way.   Besides, the sea is the element he loves, for he believes he is destined to achieve great things there, and since such is his opinion, let him go, by all means, without further questioning, and my life for it he will by and by find out that he has been cheated by an empty vision."

So saying, Lord Dalmeny placed himself between the two ladies, and led them from the cottage, closely followed by John Ruthven and the pastor. The spot to which they directed their steps was at no great distance, nor was the ascent very difficult ; but on reaching the summit of the beacon hill, a scene lay spread before them that would have amply repaid for greater exertions than had been required of them.   Behind them lay a rich tract of country diversfied with every charm that could add loveliness to nature, whilst before them was spread the noble bay we have before mentioned, it's waters calm and placid as an infant's sleep, and sparkling with the last rays of the setting sun.   The ladies gave utterance to their delight in mingled accents of pleasure and astonishment, but John Ruthven gazed upon the smooth waters as one who would rather have seen them lashed into fury, and rolling their huge billows like giants battling with each other for mastery.   At length, however, a distant object arrested his attention. and gazing at it a short time, he took the arm of Lord Dalmeny, and drawing him on one side, said :—

"My lord, see you yon distant object dancing like a fairy upon the waters ?"

"Why, to be sure I do, John," answered the other, after a brief pause ; " 'tis a small vessel, if my eyes deceive me not, and that, between you and I, s no uncommon sight, that you need have directed my attention to it."

" But do you know what vessel it is ?" demanded John Ruthven, with agitation.

" At our distance it would hardly be safe to give an opinion," answered Lord Dalmeny, purposely avoiding too explicit a reply.   " I have, however, said that it is a small vessel, and by its build and form, I should say it is a lugger."

"You are right," exclaimed John ; " and now, perhaps, your lordship can give as shrewd a guess as to the owner of this lugger ?"

"Upon my life you have puzzled me there," cried the nobleman, with assumed gaiety.

"Shall I tell you to whom she belongs?" demanded the other, hoarsely.

"N—n—no,—that is y—y—yes," stammered his lordship; "either tell me or leave it alone, John, for upon my honour I have no wish to be enlightened upon this subject, that seems to be particularly interesting to yourself."

"Perhaps," observed John, "I am taking unnecessary pains when I inform you that yonder lugger belongs to one Captain Starkie."

"Starkie, Starkie," reiterated his lordship; "oh, I remember,—this Starkie is a smuggler;—and so yonder vessel belongs to him, does it?"

"It does, my lord, and I thought you, perhaps, might be able to inform me why she has been taken to the place she now occupies."

"What mean you, John?" demanded Lord Dalmeny, startled by the earnestness of these words.

"Nay, my question was put plainly enough, I believe," replied the other; "I asked if you could tell me why the lugger has been anchored in yonder creek?"

"How! do you think I hold communion with smugglers?"

"That remains to be proved," answered John, gazing upon him with a steady eye. "The creek where she lies is nearer to my mother's cottage than any other point she could have taken up. Perhaps you understand me by this time, my lord?—At any rate, my suspicions have been awakened, and if they were but confirmed, it is not all your titles or affected superiority over myself that should save you from my fury."

"Hark'ee, John," whispered his lordship, "this is no time or place to talk over such affairs; we have females in company; but name when and where we shall meet, and this business shall be settled in any way you think fit to propose."

No. 15

Here they were interrupted by the approach of their party, who, having watched them with some alarm, came forward to interpose between them.

"What is the meaning of this sudden change?" asked Lady Margaret Dalmeny; "you have had words together, and much I marvel at the cause, seeing that a few minutes since you appeared to be on good terms with each other."

"The truth is, my dear madam," replied her son, "that John and I have had a trifling argument about yonder small vessel that you see lying so snugly in the creek opposite. We can't agree as to the description of craft she belongs to, and—and—"

"Aye, but this is not all," cried Lady Margaret; "your confusion convinces me there is something more you would conceal from me, and I appeal, therefore, to John, who I know will not deceive me."

"His lordship is right," answered the young man, anxious to escape further questioning upon the subject; "we were speaking about the vessel you see yonder, and our opinions have not exactly agreed respecting her."

"What do you think of her, John?" asked Lady Margaret.

"That she is a smuggler."

"Well, that is likely enough, for it is said that our coast is much infested by such vessels."

"But I suspect," replied John, "that she is at present engaged in a very different pursuit."

"A more honest one, let us hope?"

"Scarcely so much so, if my suspicions are correct," replied the young man. "At any rate, they have been aroused, and should they prove well-founded, this business will perhaps cost the lives of at least two persons!"

"For Heaven's sake explain yourself, John!" cried Lady Agnes, with alarm. "Of whom do you speak?—Whose lives will be endangered, if these suspicions you speak of should be unhappily confirmed?"

"Lady," answered John, respectfully; "I have been foolish enough to utter more than I ought, in the heat of the moment. Perhaps no lives may be endangered;—nay, I trust there will be no occasion for it, since the cause—if it should arise—is one that I tremble even to think of."

"Will you not explain yourself?" cried Lady Margaret.

"Not at present," replied John. "I may have been mistaken in my opinions, and will therefore wait till I am better assured of the fact."

"You hear, madam, that he is not disposed to be more communicative at present," interposed Lord Dalmeny, anxious to change the conversation. "John, you know, was ever fond of dealing in mysteries, and it, therefore, is not to be wondered that he should refuse to enlighten us further upon this affair till he is in the humour for it."

"And will not you, my son," asked her ladyship, "tell what has given rise to this sudden storm of passion?"

"Upon my life, I know nothing about it," replied the nobleman, in a tone of the most perfect sincerity. "I can only say that John is a most singular fellow, and though we have known each other so long, hang me if I am able to make him out yet."

"Thou hast something to do with it, I fear," cried her ladyship, shaking her head.

"Indeed you wrong me."

"It may be so," she replied; "and yet, my dear, I do most earnestly wish you would forget the wildness of your former ways, and become worthy of the high rank to which you were born. You have wronged many, and, believe me, I would gladly see you make reparation to those who have received injuries at your hands."

"What!—would you have me humble myself at the feet of people that I despise?"

"I would have you do justice, my son, to those you have injured, whether they happen to be higher or lower born than yourself."

"Aye," cried David Cornie, who had hitherto remained silent; "listen to the voice of your parent, and you shall attain honour. Hitherto thou hast followed the counsels of a wayward and a wicked heart, but it is not yet too late to repent, and therefore do I call upon thee to renounce thy wickedness, and to make satisfaction unto those thou hast injured."

"Prating idiot!" exclaimed Lord Dalmeny, "have I ever injured thee?"

"Thine ancestors have," answered the minister.

"In what way?"

"By persecuting the Covenanters," replied the old man. "Aye, they slaughtered them with their swords; burned their houses with fire, and drove them forth naked and defenceless, to become companions with the wild beasts of the forest."

"Well," exclaimed Lord Dalmeny, "and dost thou ask me to make restitution for the acts of my forefathers?"

"It is not much I ask of thee," replied the old man; "but if thou wilt grant me one small request, I will be satisfied."

"Well, what is it?"

"Thou hast in thy castle a banner," replied the minister, "under which the Covenanters fought when they drew the sword in defence of their holy religion; it was taken from our people by an ancestor of thine, and hangs up in token of the triumph gained over us by our enemies in that day's fight. And now, Lord Dalmeny, I ask thee to return it to us; place it in my hand, and our people will never cease to pray for thee."

"I ask not for thy prayers," replied the nobleman; "yet, if it is thy wish, the banner shall be restored to thee."

"For that boon I thank you, my lord."

"'Tis a simple one enough," answered Dalmeny, "and therefore, if you will come to my castle with those friends whom you may think fit to bring with you, I will deliver up the bauble into your hands, as I have promised."

Whilst this was passing, John Ruthven had been engaged in conversation with the two ladies; but at length, perceiving some one approaching at a distance, he suddenly broke off the conversation, and hastened towards the person that was coming towards them. In an instant afterwards he recognized the man as a neighbour, who, hurrying close by his side, exclaimed:—

"Haste, John, haste, for there is sorrow and tribulation in thy home;— your house has been burned by a band of fierce and lawless men, who have carried off your sister. We heard her screams for help, but were not able to reach the villains ere they bore her to a boat, and rowed off to a vessel that was lying in the creek. Haste, John, for thy mother has need enough of all the assistance it may be in thy power to bestow."

John stood rooted to the spot at the fatal intelligence that had been brought him. His brain burnt and his heart swelled with a feeling of rage that he could not give utterance to. At length, recovering his speech, he would have questioned the man further, but at that instant the messenger darted from his presence, and rushing down the hill, was almost instantly lost to sight.

CHAPTER XV.

" The cronachs cried on Bennachie,
And doun the Don and a',
And hieland and lawland may mournfu' be,
For the sair field of Harlaw."

OLD SONG,

WITH a cry of vengeance, John sprang from the spot where he had heard this fatal intelligence, descended the declivity with the speed of a startled deer, and bounding over every impediment that came in his way, quickly gained the ford which had been passed in the morning with so much difficulty by the funeral train. Here he found the boat which he had moored immediately upon landing, and unfastening it, he pushed away from the shore, and with the speed of lightning glided over the glassy surface of the waters. Upon reaching the opposite bank, he sprang from the boat, and again resumed his rapid career towards the place where his mother's cottage had stood a few hours previously.

The fiercest rage burnt within the bosom of the young man as he thus flew along; a thousand thoughts of vengeance succeededed each other in his brain, as his mind recurred to the villany that had been practised on his sister, and rushing forward, unmindful of all obstacles, he at length reached the green lane that he had so often trod under happier circumstances. Here each object served but to remind him more and more of the afflictions that had fallen upon him, and writhing in agony, he gave free utterance to the fierce imprecations of vengeance that filled his soul. As he moved onwards he saw the dull glare of the fire, which was now nearly extinguished, and the sight seemed to inspire him with fresh motives for exertion; he dashed onward with yet more furious speed, crossed a field or two with the speed of a hunted hare, and at length stood by the ruins of the house where all so lately had been happiness and joy. Here John stopped to gaze for a moment on the scene of destruction; the fire was now nearly extinguished by the falling in of the roof, yet still there were black wreaths of smoke ascending towards Heaven, as if to whisper there the crime that had been committed upon earth. John's heart sunk as he looked upon this scene of desolation, but the sight quickly roused him to madness, and muttering his heaviest maledictions upon those who had brought ruin upon his home, he was about to turn away, when a groan of anguish fell upon his ear, and turning in the direction from whence the sound came, he beheld his mother upon her knees, her eyes turned towards Heaven, and her hands clasped together in prayer. For a moment he paused, as if unwilling to disturb her; but the vengeance he meditated admitted of no delay, and advancing towards her he laid his hand upon her shoulder. The touch was slight, but it was sufficient to rouse the widow from her meditations, and springing upon her feet, she threw herself with an hysterical sob upon the bosom of her son. The heart of John was completely subdued by the sufferings of his parent, and with a voice almost choked with emotion, he exclaimed :—

" Mother, I have come to avenge your wrongs ! Tell me—tell me who hath done this evil deed."

" I cannot tell thee, John," she replied, faintly ; " indeed—indeed I cannot."

" Hast thou no clue to the villains ?"

" Alas ! I have not."

" Didst thou not see them ?"

" I was from home when they came, and on my return I found the ruin thou now seest."

" And my sister ?"

" Ah! John, John!" groaned the widow, " there lies my greatest agony. They have borne her away I know not whither, and I am left to wear out the remainder of my days in hopeless misery."

" She has been stolen from us!" exclaimed John; " taken from her home by villains; but there is yet vengeance for them, and never will I rest till he who plotted this deed has atoned for his crime with his own blood."

" My son! my son!" sobbed the widow; " and must I lose thee too, as well as my poor Effie?"

" Her wrongs must be avenged mother," exclaimed John, hoarsely, " and who so fitted to hunt the monster through the world as myself?"

" But thou mayest fall, and thus shall I be rendered desolate indeed."

" I may fall, mother, as thou sayest," answered the young man; " the villain who has thus wronged us may triumph over me; but whilst I have an arm to wield a sword, never will I desist from my design till all who have been concerned in this base act have paid the full penalty of their crime!"

" Dost thou suspect, then, who has done this deed?"

" I do," he replied.

" His name?"

" Lord Dalmeny."

" Ah! I, too, have charged him in my own mind with the base act," cried the widow. " And yet, villain as we know him to be, he cannot have done it alone."

" I know it, mother; others are concerned with him, and they also do I already suspect."

" Hah! tell me their names, John, that I may blight them with a widow's curse."

" Another time, dear mother," cried the young man. " At present not a moment is to be wasted, or I shall lose the villains' track. Come, lean on my arm, and I will take you to the house of a neighbour, where you will receive the shelter and hospitality you so much need."

With some difficulty John prevailed on his mother to leave the ruined home she had so fondly loved, and having left her in the care of a friend, he again set forward at full speed in search of the villains who had carried off his sister. His first thought was to visit the smugglers' retreat, and hastening onwards, he at length entered the cave which we have before mentioned as being the hiding-place of Captain Starkie and his crew. Here, however, all was silent as death; but at the entrance of the cavern he discovered evident traces of a recent struggle on the spot, and pursuing his examination further, he found a handkerchief which he had seen in his sister's possession that morning. Here, then, was a full confirmation that she had fallen into the hands of Starkie and his men, and equally certain was it that the villains had been instigated to the crime by the gold of Lord Dalmeny. Thus far convinced, John continued his search till he was satisfied that she was no longer in the cavern, and then, hurrying from the place, he went down to the sea-shore, to ascertain whether the vessel was yet in view. But in this he was doomed to be disappointed; and almost frenzied with despair, he was pondering in his mind what next to do, when the sound of an oar roused him, and looking once more upon the waters, he beheld Hugh Lorimer approaching him in a boat. In another moment the little vessel ran upon the beach, when the young man, leaping out, inquired of his friend whether he had heard the full extent of his misfortunes.

"I have, Hugh," answered the other. "I have seen the house of my earliest infancy changed into a black and smouldering ruin; I have seen my mother weeping for the loss of her child, and yet I stand here as if Heaven had not given me hands to avenge the foul wrongs that have been inflicted on us."

"Whatever thou mayest do, John," exclaimed the other, "let it not be forgotten that thou hast a friend who will cheerfully sacrifice his life to aid thee in hunting out the monsters that have done this deed!"

"I know it, Hugh," cried the young man. "In thee I can repose my trust, and, believe me, I will not fail to engage thy friendship in my cause."

"But what step dost thou think of taking?"

"I will hire a vessel and pursue them," answered John; "they cannot have got far, and should I overtake them, I will either rescue my sister from their hands, or die in the attempt."

"It would be in vain to follow them," exclaimed Hugh Lorimer, "for I myself have just now returned from pursuing the vessel. They hoisted sail about half an hour since, and by this time are far out of sight of land."

"Alas!" groaned John, "then I fear my sister is lost beyond all hope of redemption."

"It is but a sorry consolation," answered Hugh Lorimer; "and yet if she is, indeed, lost, those who have been concerned in this affair shall not escape the punishment of their crime."

"Thou art a true friend, Lorimer," exclaimed John, grasping his hand firmly; "I have proved thee ere now, and can, therefore, trust thee. Thou shalt aid me in pursuing the villains; and by the Heaven above us! I swear never to relax my endeavours until ample vengeance has been executed. But I was far away when this cruel deed was accomplished, and, perhaps, thou canst tell me how it was effected."

"I can," replied Hugh Lorimer; "for it chanced that I was passing your mother's house about two hours since, on my way down to the rocks. On a sudden a loud scream startled me, and rushing forward, I saw your sister borne off from the cottage by a party of men, who, in spite of their disguise, I knew to be the crew of smugglers belonging to Captain Starkie. Unfortunately I had no weapons with me, but, determined to rescue her if possible, I ran with my utmost speed to overtake them; they, however, were soon aware that I was pursuing them, and increasing their speed, they reached the boat, and pushed off ere I could overtake them."

"And did my sister make no resistance?" asked John, anxiously.

"She did," replied the other; "I saw her snatch a brace of pistols from the girdle of the villain who was next to her; one of them she discharged at the man who held her, and which seemed to have taken fatal effect. The other she fired at Captain Starkie himself, who, though wounded, still continued to command the crew, and they rowed off with all speed towards the lugger, which was lying at anchor in yonder creek."

"I saw it from the opposite shore," cried John, "and my suspicions were aroused; yet, fool that I was, I took no steps to prevent the execution of this villanous design. And now they have robbed me of the treasure I held dearest in the world, and for whose sake I would have cheerfully submitted to endure the most cruel tortures that the ingenuity of man could invent."

"It is useless to lament the misfortune that has befallen us," exclaimed

Hugh Lorimer; "all we have now to do, is to seek measures of revenge, and it shall go hard if, between us, we do not bring retribution upon those who have thus foully wronged us."

"Aye," said John, fiercely; "the vengeance I will take shall be spoken of long after the present generation has passed away. I will have blood for this; but the method of my revenge shall be such as will strike terror into the hearts of all future evil-doers. I will hunt them through the world, Hugh Lorimer; no hole or corner shall hide them from my search, and if I perish in the attempt, so much the better; for since the misfortunes that have fallen on me, I have no wish to live a minute longer than that which gives me the vengeance my soul so eagerly pants for."

"I have been thinking," said Hugh Lorimer, "that Captain Starkie would expect to be handsomely rewarded for this service. The money may, perhaps, have not been paid yet, and if we can contrive to keep Lord Dalmeny here, the smuggler will grow tired of waiting for the promised gold, and it is not unlikely that he may bring your sister back again at an early period."

"It is a vain hope," cried John, in despair; "they have taken her away to a foreign land, and I fear there is little chance of their ever suffering her to return to her native country."

"What plan," asked Hugh Lorimer, "do you mean to pursue first towards the recovery of poor Effie?"

"I scarcely know what course to follow," answered the other, perplexed at the uncertainty that involved the affair; "I have thought of following these smugglers, but ignorant as I am of the place of their destination, I fear the pursuit would be in vain. There is one left behind, however," he continued, fiercely, "who is yet within reach of my arm, and he, at least, shall not escape the devastating tempest his own villany hath raised."

"Aye, Lord Dalmeny——"

"Name him not!" interrupted John, with the deepest emotion; "this last act of his has doomed him to destruction, for my sister's wrongs shall be heavily retaliated upon him by him who has sworn to have his blood. That thought alone sustains me in this hour of trial, and it will continue to support me till my terrible scheme has been fully carried into effect."

"Do you intend to seek him at once?"

"It would be in vain to do so," answered John, "for by this time he has returned to his castle, and I should be refused admittance. To-morrow morning, however, he is to receive a party of Cameronians, and I will take that opportunity to obtain an interview that would not be voluntarily granted."

"You will, at least, suffer me to accompany you?"

"I cannot," answered John; "if there is danger, I will encounter it alone, for I never will suffer my friend to risk his own life in any case where I can take the whole of the peril upon myself. In the present instance I shall meet Lord Dalmeny alone, and it will depend upon the answers he may give to my questions whether he lives to see the setting of another sun."

"But he will have assistance at hand," replied Hugh Lorimer, "and I fear lest your imprudence may go so far as to throw you into his power, that you will never have an opportunity of rendering that assistance to your sister which she so greatly needs."

"I am fully aware of him," answered John, "and, therefore, will avoid the consequences of any surprise."

"Yet I fear you may be overpowered by numbers."

"At any rate," exclaimed the other, "it will not be without a desperate resistance on my part. I will take care to arm myself well, and should they attempt any violence, the number of my assailants will be thinned ere I yield myself their prisoner. It is not the first time, Hugh Lorimer, that I have thrown myself into situations of peril, and in such a cause as this, I feel assured that I shall come off triumphant."

"Yet for all that, Ruthven," answered the other, "I cannot but wish you would suffer me to be your companion in this affair."

"You have heard my determination, and no entreaties will ever move me from it."

"Well," exclaimed Hugh, "it must e'en be so, then, I suppose; but you will at least accept my offer of hospitality for the night. Remember, you have now no home of your own to go to, and ——"

"I do remember it," cried Ruthven, with emotion; "my house has been made desolate, and the roof that once sheltered me has been laid level with the dust. Aye, and I remember, too, who has done all this, and that the monster yet triumphs in the hellish mischief he has caused. Yet the victory will not long be his, for ere this hour to-morrow, he shall have been made bitterly to repent the wrongs he hath done me."

"You will rest, then, for to-night, at least, in my cottage?" said Hugh Lorimer.

"No," answered the other; "I need no other roof to shelter me than the blue vault above our heads. It is sufficient for the wild beasts of the forests, and what better am I now that the inhumanity of man has made me what I am? I feel that my nature is changed, Hugh Lorimer; a boundless desire for vengeance has taken possession of my heart, and never shall I rest till the burning wish has been gratified."

"Come, come, Ruthven," exclaimed the other; "accept my offer of shelter for to-night, and we will talk over this affair together. We may arrange some plan that will better ensure success than the one you have at present resolved on, and then you will ensure the revenge you so eagerly thirst for."

"You have had my answer," exclaimed Ruthven, impatiently; "leave me, therefore, and do not again urge me to accept an offer that I have so peremptorily declined."

"Stay, John," cried Hugh, as he saw the other was about to leave him; "is it your desire that we should part on bad terms with each other?"

"Nay, there is my hand, Hugh," exclaimed John, with deep feeling; "it grasps thine, man, with all its former friendship; we will still remain to each other as we have ever been, and if my conduct on the present occasion has been more harsh than usual, attribute it to the right cause, and I am sure you will acquit me of any wish to break the bonds that have hitherto united us. So, now, farewell, Hugh, and should any evil befal me in my coming interview with Lord Dalmeny, I leave to you the protection of my widowed mother, and the avenging those wrongs that have been heaped upon the deceived and unfortunate Effie."

Again pressing the hand of his friend, John Ruthven rushed from the spot, and ascending the cliffs, made his way towards the forest, within whose solemn shade he had resolved to pass the night. For hours he paced up and down, meditating over the plans he had formed, and gloating with furious delight on the fearful retaliation he contemplated. It seemed, indeed, that his heart was entirely changed; that every spark of humanity had fled, and that the only purpose which remained for him to execute, was to carry death and desolation upon those who had wronged him; this done, he felt that he could cheerfully surrender up his life, even though it might be wrenched from him by the most horrible tortures. Thus meditating, John hailed with rapturous joy the first dawn of that day which was to light him to vengeance.

CHAPTER XVI.

"I know the penalty of failure
Is present infamy and death. Pause not;
I would have shown no mercy, and I seek none;
My life was staked upon a mighty hazard,
And, being lost, take what I would have taken." MARINO FALIERO.

MINDFUL of the promise that had been made him by Lord Dalmeny, the minister assembled his friends together at an early hour in the morning, and arranging them in something like marching order, he led them towards the castle, to claim the banner which had been taken from them in the defeat which the Cameronians had sustained under a former Lord Dalmeny. Previously to their setting forth, a long prayer had been offered up by David Cornie, and as the enthusiasts afterwards passed along on their errand, they exercised their voices in psalms, that might well enough have been heard from Berwick town to John o'Groat's house. Nor was their pious harmony suspended until they had reached the inner court-yard of the castle, when worthy David Cornie, lifting up his hands, commanded them to be silent whilst he addressed a few words to them.

"It is now time to cease, my brethren, for his lordship is no great admirer of sacred matters, and we may offend him if we continue to lift up our voices near his presence, and at such an early hour in the morning."

"If his lordship likes it not," answered one of his followers, "he can send out a message to that effect, and we will prepare ourselves to hear an exhortation from you till he thinks fit to receive us."

"Rest thee patient for awhile," returned the minister. "This is no

No. 16

place for exhorting thee, my bretheren, for the foul fiend is said to have taken up his abode within these walls, and we must therefore wait till we return to our own hill side. There I will address thee friends,—yea, and will continue my discourse from the rising of the sun even unto the setting of the same."

With this cheering promise the followers of David Cornie were obliged to be content, and forming themselves into little knots, they conversed together upon religious topics, just to pass away the time until it should be his lordship's will to see them upon the business that had brought them thus early to the castle.

The boisterous singing of the Cameronians had roused Lord Dalmeny from a troublesome dream, in which he had witnessed the abduction of Effie Ruthven, and had seen her carried towards the ship that was waiting for her reception. Exulting in the success of his schemes, he followed to the sea shore, but as he was in the act of stepping into the boat, the little vessel glided away with its fair burden, and at the same moment a loud roar of derisive laughter was uttered by the crew. It was in vain, too, that he called upon them to return, for the boat kept steadily on her way till she reached the ship's side; the female was then lifted on board, the anchor was weighed, the canvass spread, and in a brief space of time the bark was completely out of view.

From this dream Lord Dalmeny was roused, as we before observed, by the uproarious singing of the Cameronians who had assembled in the court-yard of his castle. But though he knew that it was nothing but a vision, the young lord was thoughtful and moody; in fact, so much were his thoughts occupied, that he was not conscious of the presence of his servant, Ronald, until he whispered in his ear :—

"My lord, he is come."

"Hah!" exclaimed his lordship, starting up in the bed ;—"let him be brought hither instantly."

"He'll not come alone, I'm thinking," answered Ronald.

"Who is with him?—the girl?"

"No, a score or two of psalm-singing knaves, that have roused the whole castle with their infernal noise, two hours at least before our usual time of rising."

"What mean you, sirrah?" demanded his master; "Captain Starkie does not usually associate with such people as you have spoken of."

"But it is not Captain Starkie at all, my lord."

"Who then, thou prating idiot?"

"David Cornie, my lord."

"Tell the knave I will be with him anon," exclaimed Lord Dalmeny, smothering his indignation as well as he could. "Bid them remain patient, and I will deliver into their hands the trumpery banner they have been at so much pains to demand of me."

Ronald obeyed his commands that had thus been given, and hurrying on his clothes with as little delay as possible, Lord Dalmeny hastened down to the court-yard, which he found nearly filled with the followers of David Cornie. Vexed as Lord Dalmeny had been at such an unlooked-for interruption, he could scarcely refrain smiling at the motley group which met his view. His presence, however, was hailed with vociferous cheering, which being silenced by their leader, he advanced, and with all due form, demanded the restoration of their banner, according to a promise made on the previous evening.

"I have not forgot it," answered Lord Dalmeny, "and since many of you have travelled far on your errand, I pray you to enter my castle, and accept the hospitality I am anxious to bestow upon you."

"Nay, your lordship must pardon us there," exclaimed David Cornie, "for we are all of us under a vow to Heaven never to sat foot within your castle till the banner has been again planted on the hill where we meet to pray."

"Thou hast then made a foolish vow," answered Lord Dalmeny, "since it debars thee from taking the rest and refreshment thou all stand so much in need of. However, I will press thee no further; the banner shall be re- stored according to promise, and then, since it pleases thee to be obstinate, thou may'st return to thy hills weary and fasting."

Upon this Lord Dalmeny retired, but in a few moments he returned with the much prized banner.

"Here is the bauble thou hast come for," he said, placing it in the hands of David Cornie. "As thou seest, it has not been much injured since it has been in the possession of my family; and now, friends, the best advice I can give thee is, to guard it safely in future, or it may chance to fall into the hands of those who will not be so willing to restore it as I have."

"We will take it to the appointed place," replied the minister, "and when our task has been accomplished, each man will return to his dwelling to implore its blessing upon you for the kindness you have this day mani- fested towards us."

Lord Dalmeny was about to reply, but ere he could do so, a great bustle was heard among the crowd, and the next moment John Ruthven suddenly presented himself before him. A single glance served to convince his lord- ship that he was now confronted by a deadly foe, and though little used to feel alarm, his countenace changed colour, and with a faltering tongue he demanded the reason of so unexpected an intrusion.

"Need your lordship ask such a question?" inquired John, hoarse with rage. "I am here to demand the restoration of my sister, who has been ruthlessly torn from her home. Give her back to me, my lord, pure, and virtuous as she was a few hours since, or I will take such revenge as your villany deserves!"

"Why, how now, John," exclaimed Lord Dalmeny, affecting surprise at the words that had been uttered; "what is the meaning of this rage, and why dost thou come here to demand her of whose whereabouts I know nothing?"

"'Tis false as thine own black and cankerous heart!" exclaimed John, furiously. "Thy minions have borne her hence, and, not satisfied with their violence, they have burned our house to the ground, and sent my widowed mother to wander homeless upon the earth."

"Why what dost thou talk of, John?" cried his lordship, affecting entire ignorance of the events that had taken place. "Thou hast brought charges enough aginst me, and yet I know no more of what thou speakest of than any of these honest men by whom we are surrounded."

"'Tis false!" vociferated John, "for thou, and thou alone, couldst have been guilty of so base and perfidious an act."

"I thank thee for thy compliment," answered Lord Dalmeny, maintain- ing all his customary coolness of deportment; "and yet do I again declare that I have been most foully charged with a crime that I have not so much as contemplated. Thy sister has something of thine own pride in her com- position, and though it must be owned I once looked at her with an eye of favour, yet did she treat me with more scorn than I could well stomach, and thus ended the whole affair between us. Besides, John, the friendship I have ever felt for thee would have prevented me from having any share in the burning of thy house, and driving forth thy mother from her home. Besides, it seems she has been carried on board a ship, and——"

"Hah! you have outwitted yourself," cried John, interrupting him;

"I spoke nothing of my sister being taken away in a ship, and yet it seems you know all about it. Your confession has condemned you, and now do I know that you are indeed the villain that has done me the wrong I would punish."

"Villain dost thou call me?"

"Aye, my lord, and in this instance it has been well applied. But why use time in idle words, when my errand here is to revenge the wrongs inflicted on me and mine? Come, my lord, draw your weapon and defend your life, unless you would have coward as well as villain attached to your name."

"Art thou mad, John?"

"If I am it is little to be wondered at," answered the other, hoarsely. "I have seen ruin and disgrace brought upon those I love; my house has been burned to the ground, and I am driven forth like a wild beast, without a roof to shelter me."

"Stay till thou art cooler," cried Lord Dalmeny, "and then perhaps I may be able to convince thee how much thy suspicions have wronged me."

"Where is my sister?" demanded John, without heeding these last words; "tell me where she is, for thou hast stolen her, and I am here to demand her back."

"Thou dost seek to incense one who pities and would fain spare thee," answered Lord Dalmeny. "Leave me, John, and when thou hast recovered thy senses return to me, and I will again essay to convince thee of the wrong thou hast done me by these suspicions."

"Once more I demand of thee," cried John Ruthven, "what hast thou done with my sister?"

"You hear him, David Cornie?" exclaimed Lord Dalmeny, appealing to the minister; "he is mad, it seems, and in his rage he comes here to accuse me of a crime that I never dreamt of committing."

"I am bound to take thy word, my lord," replied the minister; "and yet, having heard both the accusation and the denial, I ought perhaps to ask thee solemnly to declare that thou art as innocent as thou dost assert?"

"You have already heard me declare it," answered his lordship, "and if that is not sufficient, I know not that I ought to submit to further questioning. How, I ask you, does the affair stand?—This young man's sister, it seems, has somehow or other disappeared from home; the house has been burned down, and no one else, forsooth, is to be deemed guilty of all this violence but myself."

"Who else would have done it?" asked John.

"That is more than I can undertake to answer," replied Lord Dalmeny. "The girl, perhaps, had a lover unknown to you or the widow, John; she might have been afraid to mention the subject, knowing, perhaps, but too well that her chosen husband would be rejected. In such a case as that, it is natural enough to suppose that she would take the first favourable opportunity to elope, and that such has been the case I believe few persons will think improbable."

"This is a well-invented subterfuge," exclaimed John, "but the story will scarcely deceive one who knows the depravity of thy heart as I do. Thou hast stolen her away, and thou shalt either defend thyself with thy sword, or I will strike thee dead at my feet, without giving thee another chance to save thy life!"

"Young man," interposed the minister, "thou art too sudden in thy wrath. Thou seekest the blood of the man thou dost call thy foe, and therefore it becomes my duty to tell thee that if thou strikest the Lord

Dalmeny, we, who are now merely spectators, will array ourselves together to restrain thy fury."

"Nay, I ask not your interposition," exclaimed Lord Dalmeny, growing somewhat bolder at hearing these words of the pastor's. "I am willing enough to accept the challenge of this rustic, though he is so far beneath me, but ere I do so I should like to know upon what grounds he accuses me of having stolen away his sister, and set fire to his mother's house?"

"The life of crime thou hast hitherto led," answered John, "is alone sufficient to point thee out as the villain that has wronged me."

"And so, because my name happens to be in bad odour with thee, no one else but myself can have taken away the pretty Effie, John?"

"None other would have dared to do it," answered the young man, hastily.

"Indeed!" retorted his lordship;—"come, thou hast paid me a compliment after all in saying that I have done that which no other man would have ventured on."

"This is but idle talk, Lord Dalmeny," exclaimed John. "I came hither to seek redress, and will not depart from here till I have obtained it. Draw your sword, if you dare, and put this quarrel on the issue of the combat."

"Oh, I have no objection to fight, if need be," answered Lord Dalmeny. "I can indulge thee, my valiant stripling, only that instead of using swords, in the use of which I believe thou art well practised, we will try our hands at pistols, in which, perhaps, I may have an equal chance with thine own."

"As you please, my lord," returned John; "it is indifferent to me what weapons we use, so that we bring this matter fairly to an issue."

"Now then, take your choice of one of these," said his lordship, offering a brace to his antagonist, which had just been placed in his hand by Ronald. "They are charged, John, so take your place now, and we will quicky see whose skin is bullet-proof."

"This affected coolness, my lord, does not deceive me," cried John, as he took one of the pistols and examined the priming. "Had you been innocent of the crime you would have betrayed some feeling for the unfortunate, but the levity with which you have treated the affair proves that you were well acquainted with all the circumstances ere I presented myself before you."

"Aye, aye, think of me as you will, John," answered his lordship, "for I am already so loaded with charges of this nature, that the weight of this one will hardly make any difference to me. And now, David Cornie," he continued, addressing himself to the minister, "this young man and I have a little affair to settle, of which, perhaps, you have no wish to be a spectator. You and your people therefore can retire, if you think proper, for I promise you this business will not terminate till one of us has fallen mortally wounded. Go; you have got your banner, and the piece of ground I promised you to build a church on shall be yours, if I am fortunate enough to survive this encounter."

"My lord," exclaimed John, "I would speak once more before we meet in mortal conflict. "That you have instigated others to take away my sister, I am well aware. But, your triumph is a short lived one, for Captain Starkie has sailed away with your prize, and means to keep her for himself. You have been cheated, Lord Dalmeny, and the villany you plotted against others has fallen on your own head."

"Wretches!" vociferated his lordship; "have they dared to trick me thus?"

"Hah! you confess, then, at last?"

"I do," exclaimed Lord Dalmeny, furiously. "Concealment is no longer necessary; but should I survive this fight with thee, Captain Starkie and his crew shall feel the vengeance that I can pour upon their devoted heads."

"Nay," answered John, "they will have little cause to dread the fury of your lordship."

"What mean you, sirrah?"

"That I am here to punish the many crimes thou hast committed," replied John, "Aye, thou may'st smile scornfully as thou wilt, but never will I remove from this place till I have seen thee perish."

"Let me entreat you to forbear the sinful deed you both seek to commit," interposed David Cornie. "You have quarrelled with each other, and yet consider how much better your time might have been occupied in seeking after the maiden who has been carried away. She may yet be within your reach, and therefore do I again conjure you to seek means for her restoration."

"Leave us, old man," exclaimed Lord Dalmeny, impatiently. "I was not the first to propose this method of settling our quarrel, but since I have made up my mind to it, my antagonist shall find that I am not the coward he had the insolence to call me. Stand back, therefore, I say, all of you, and interpose no more between two desperate men."

With a temerity natural to men of peace, the whole party of Cameronians stepped aside, upon which the two combatants took their places, at the distance of a few feet from each other. In another moment their pistols were raised; the report came from each at the same instant, but neither of the duellists had received even the slightest wound. Ruthven was now without any weapon of defence except his sword, but, unmindful of this, Lord Dalmeny snatched another pistol from the hand of his servant, and he was in the act of discharging it with a fatal aim at the bosom of his antagonist, when David Cornie, rushing forward with frantic speed, raised the arm of the nobleman, and the weapon was discharged in the air. Infuriated at this interruption, Lord Dalmeny was about to turn his wrath against the offending minister, but at that moment Lady Margaret, followed by the Lady Agnes, flew to the spot, the former of whom, throwing her arms round the neck of her son, implored him, in accents of terror, to leave the place and return with her to the house.

"Leave me, mother," exclaimed Lord Dalmeny, sullenly; "leave me I say; this is no place for women, nor will I be prevailed on to depart till I have chastised the insolence of yonder low-born villain, who has dared to apply to me the most villanous epithets."

"Tell me, my son," cried her ladyship; "how has this quarrel originated?"

"It matters not," answered his lordship; "nor, indeed, is the affair worth explaining; let it suffice that I have been insulted, and that I will not leave this place till I have wiped out the stain of dishonour with his blood."

"Nay," cried David Cornie; "let me add my entreaties to those of your good mother; reflect, my lord, and——"

"Away, thou whining priest!" interrupted Lord Dalmeny, furiously; "away, I command you, and take with you the canting hypocrites that have accompanied you hither; you have obtained that which you have come for, and never let me see your faces again within the walls of my castle."

David Cornie saw that his presence could do little service in the present humour of his lordship, and gathering his people around him, he conferred with them for a brief period, and then retired without the ceremony of leave-taking.

By this time a number of domestics had come to the assistance of their young lord, and seeing Red Ruthven, who they knew had been their master's antagonist in the late affray, they advanced for the purpose of making him their prisoner. He was, however, aware of their purpose, and drawing his sword, he placed himself against the wall, so as to afford him as much protection as he could from the numerous assailants by whom he was threatened. But Lady Margaret had perceived these indications of renewed strife, and commanding the domestics to retire, she addressed herself to Ruthven in a tone of reproach.

"Why is it," she said, "that you have come hither to seek the life of my son? Hath he ever injured thee in thought or deed, that you have intruded yourself within his castle to murder him in cold blood?"

"Ask him no questions, mother," exclaimed Lord Dalmeny, anxious to prevent a reply, that he feared would unfold too much of his own recent evil practices; "fortunately he has done no mischief, and therefore I can easily pardon what has passed."

"Thy words, my son, fill me with apprehension," cried Lady Margaret; "for that thou hast not forgiven him I am well satisfied, since thou dost seldom pardon those who have ever offended thee; speak, therefore, for I will know all ere I cease urging thee."

"Let the answer come from him, then," exclaimed Lord Dalmeny; "and I dare say he will give thee a well garnished tale of wrongs that he has endured, which will call forth thy pity for him, and thy reproaches on your most unlucky son."

"Since his lordship is present to hear it," cried Ruthven, "I will tell thee that he hath employed ruffians to carry away my sister to some distant place; that they have burnt down our house, and turned my widowed mother forth to wander through the world without a roof to shelter her. These cruelties, lady, inflicted upon those I love, provoked me to come hither for revenge; I met his lordship, shots were exchanged between us, and my only regret is, that either he or I was not slain in the conflict."

"Ruthven," cried the Lady Margaret; "I never knew thee guilty of a falsehood, and yet do I again ask thee if thou hast spoken truly in this instance. Is thy sister stolen from thee, and thy once happy home given to the devouring flames?"

"All is exactly as I have told your ladyship," answered the young man. "My sister has been conveyed on board a smuggling vessel, which instantly set sail with its fair prize; our house is now a smoking ruin, and my mother, but for the kindness of a neighbour, would be a homeless wanderer."

"And dost thou charge my son with being the instigator of all these crimes?"

"I do."

"And didst thou not follow to see whether aid could not be given to thine unfortunate sister?"

"I did, my lady, but the vessel had sailed some time ere I was aware of the extent of my misery. Enraged at the villany that had been practised against us, I wandered all night in the woods, and this morning came hither to retaliate upon the evil doer the crimes he had committed. For the present I have been foiled in my design, but vengeance is deeply rooted in my heart, and I will hurl retribution upon my enemy, or perish in the attempt."

"You have heard the heavy charges that have been brought against me," observed Lord Dalmeny, with much apparent indifference. "I am accused of carrying off this girl and burning down his mother's house, and yet Ruthven himself knows that I was with him some miles off when the news was brought of the calamity that had befallen him."

"His lordship so far speaks the truth," answered Ruthven; "but I do not accuse him of having done these things with his own hands. My sister was carried away by the crew of smugglers under the command of one Captain Starkie,—a most worthy companion of your son's,—and they it was who set fire to our house."

"Perhaps you wrong him by this suspicion?" cried the Lady Margaret.

"His lordship knows well that I have spoken nothing but the truth," replied Ruthven. "He has acted in this affair by his agent, and my sister has been carried away to some place where he will be able to find her whenever he can leave this place without creating suspicion as to his real motives. He has trusted them, but perhaps he may hereafter find that they have deceived him."

"Again I say thou mayest have judged him wrongfully," exclaimed her ladyship. "He may be innocent of the crimes you have charged him with, and therefore I implore thee to let this quarrel go no further till you are better assured of the truth of your suspicion."

"His lordship knows that I am already convinced, and his own conscience will tell him how justly," replied Ruthven. "He, however, knows my intentions in the affair; I have challenged him to mortal combat; we have been interrupted, but he knows that I am not to be trifled with, and if he refuses to meet me, I will slay him like a coward where he stands."

"Forbear," cried Lady Margaret, imploringly; "forbear I say, and if an injury has been done to thee, learn to forgive it with Christian charity. That your wrongs have been grievous ones I admit, but whatever lies in my power shall be done to redress them. I will endeavour to learn where your sister has been carried to, and if I succeed in that, a vessel shall be despatched at my expense to bring her back. Thy mother, too, shall not long be the houseless wanderer thou hast described; her cottage shall be rebuilt on the same spot where it formerly stood, and I will add a pension from my own purse to render more easy the latter days of her life. Thus, you see, Ruthven, matters are not so bad as they might have been, and therefore do I again entreat you to suspend your wrath until we have ascertained the fate of your sister."

"I will make no promise," answered Ruthven, doggedly.

"In that case," returned Lady Margaret; "I must insist upon you both accompanying me before a magistrate, who shall hear the case fairly between us, and who will probably bind you to keep the peace towards each other. This you surely will not refuse me, since it will serve to appease the alarm that now agitates me."

To this no objection was offered, and leaving Ruthven in the court-yard, where he chose to remain, her ladyship and Lord Dalmeny entered the castle to prepare themselves for the visit they were about to pay the magistrate.

CHAPTER XVII.

" He turned him right and round again,
   Said, Scorn na at my mither;
Light loves I may get mony a ane,
   But minnie ne'er anither." OLD SONG.

THE house of Tony Gripple, the justice to whom Lady Margaret Dalmeny had proposed to leave the decision of this affair, stood at the distance of two miles from the castle, and thither her ladyship and Agnes repaired in the carriage as soon as possible after it had been arranged that the arbitration should be left to the wisdom of the man of law. The worthy to whom we are now about to introduce our readers, was one of those distributors of justice who can always find a good plea for punishing a poor man, and an equally satisfactory one for letting the rich escape through any of the thousand loopholes that are generally to be found when wanted. Among beggars and petty larceny rogues he was looked upon with great terror, for never were such persons allowed to escape the punishment awarded by the law to their particular cases. Fines or imprisonment, pillory or the stocks, were the ready weapons which he had always at command, and never did he fail to make the best use of them for the immediate punishment of those who were unlucky enough to be brought before him, and the terror of those who might at any time be inclined to follow their example. Some there were who said he was not above receiving a bribe for any particular favour that they might wish to obtain from him, but these might be idle reports, raised to the prejudice of a man whose rigid administration of justice had raised against him a great many enemies.

No. 17

As the carriage approached the house, Lady Margaret had ocular proof that some of the reports at least were not without foundation, for just without the gate was an unfortunate wight, who that morning had been convicted of the high crime and misdemeanour of begging for a crust of bread to keep him from starving. For an instant her ladyship ordered the carriage to stop, and throwing the poor fellow a small sum of money, bade him be of good comfort, for that she would use her best interest with the justice to obtain his release as soon as she possibly could after her arrival at the house.

In a few moments the carriage stopped at the door of the justice, where Lord Dalmeny and John Ruthven were waiting their arrival. David Cornie, too, who by some means or other had heard of the intended visit, was also there, and when the two ladies had alighted, the whole party were conducted by a shabby-looking livery servant into the room where his worship usually decided upon the merit of the cases that were brought before him. Gripple was already seated in anticipation of his visiters, whom he had seen approaching from the parlour window, and whispering to his man of all work, he desired him to prepare a couple of warrants, as he had fully made up his mind to commit both the young fellows, as he called them, as rogues and vagrants.

Whilst he was yet speaking, Lady Margaret Dalmeny and her niece entered the room; and now, for the first time, he discovered that one of the young men he was going to send in such a hurry to prison was no other than Lord Dalmeny himself! Hereupon a wondrous change came over the justice of peace, and applying his mouth once more to the ear of his factotum, he desired him not to be in a hurry about making out two warrants, as he had discovered that one would be quite enough for all present purposes.

This being so far arranged, he hemmed twice or thrice, tried to look very big—in which, by the by, he failed most wofully,—and, throwing himself back in his chair, addressed himself to the minister.

"Well, David Cornie," he exclaimed, "so we have got you here at last, have we? Couldn't keep out of mischief, eh? Well, well, all in good time—all in good time, man. I've been looking to see some of your psalm-grinding crew brought before me ere now; but you have been lucky, though your turn has come at last, and I shall have the pleasure of sending you to repent of your folly in the county jail. Ah, Lady Margaret, your presence here warms my heart with the recollection of old times when—but stay, we'll talk of those matters another time, when there are not so many gaping idiots about to swallow up every word that passes. Lady Agnes, too! beshrew me, but I'm highly honoured to day to be visited by rank and beauty such as this. And my Lord Dalmeny has deigned to favour me with his presence! Your lordship is welcome;—ah! I see, you have come on business? You have a charge to make against this vile Cameronian who——"

"Mr. Gripple," exclaimed the minister, offended at the rudeness of the official, "ye may cast your jeers on me as much as you please, for I happen to be a man of peace, and to be utterly beneath my contempt. Nay, never frown at me, sir, for you cast the first stone, and if in return I utter a little piece of plain truth, you have yourself only to thank for it. By insinuations, you have charged us Cameronians with being disaffected and unworthy the protection of the law which you are placed there to administer; this I utterly deny; but since you have reminded me of a circumstance that made us enemies years ago, I will now relate a story about your own evil doings that happened——"

"Silence, sirrah! or I'll instantly commit you as a rogue and vagabond," interrupted the justice, who knew well enough the story to which David Cornie alluded, and the relating of which in the present company would not redound much to his honour.

"Your worship, I'm thinking," answered the minister with perfect composure, "must have some charge brought against me before you can get rid of me quite so easy as you would wish. However, I have no desire to bring up an unpleasant subject, and so, if you think proper to allow me, I will go on with the affair that has brought us all before you."

"Go on, David Cornie," said the justice, with much more civility than he had thought it necessary to exhibit before. "Go on with the matter you have to state, and I will listen patiently to its end."

"Well, then," exclaimed the minister, "I have a charge to make against John Ruthven, or Red Ruthven as he calls himself, and Lord Dalmeny."

"Lord Dalmeny! impossible!" vociferated his worship. "I can readily enough comprehend that one of these young men has offended against the law, but that a man of Lord Dalmeny's rank should have done so is utterly to be discredited."

"If you will but have a little patience," returned David Cornie, "I will explain the matter fairly. John Ruthven accuses Lord Dalmeny of carrying off his sister by fraud and violence, and of burning down his mother's house. This is a serious charge, your worship, and is not denied by his lordship; in fact, he owns that though the deeds were not committed by his own hands, they were executed by those whose services he had purchased with gold. The consequence of all this is, that the peace is likely to be broken, for one duel has already been prevented, and unless your worship withhold them by the strong arm of the law, there will be bloodshed between them as surely as you are now sitting before me. Now, I am willing to be surety for them both; and when they have been bound to keep the peace towards each other, the affair will end, and all further danger be prevented."

"Humph; this is a very serious affair," cried the justice, with as much dignity as he could command; "a very serious affair, indeed. And, pray, David Cornie, who is this John Ruthven, that has had the presumption to fall out with a gentlaman of his lordship's rank?"

"The son of the widow Ruthven," answered the minister; "your worship knows the widow Ruthven, who, though poor in pocket, bears a character for honesty that might well be envied by greater folks."

"Hah!" vociferated the justice, in a voice of thunder; "and has this son of a poor widow dared to affront so great a man as Lord Dalmeny."

"I forgot to observe," answered David Cornie, "that I myself see the heniousness of the offence he has committed. He had no right to imagine that his honour had been wounded when his sister had been forcibly carried off, and his house burned by a lord! He ought to have submitted mildly and patiently to it all, and I am not quite sure but it would have been seemly for him to have gone cap in hand to his lordship, and have thanked him for the high honour he had been kind enough to bestow upon his sister. This would have been submitting with a good grace, and then there would have been no occasion for our troubling your worship to bind them over to keep the peace."

This was spoken in a tone that could not be mistaken, but Justice Gripple was just wise enough not to take any notice of it at the time, resolving on some future occasion—if a lucky chance offered—to pay the minister off all the old scores that he owed him. Swallowing the insult, therefore, as well as he could, he turned his attention to the most humble of the two defendants.

"John Ruthven, or whatever other name you choose to go by," he cried; "you have to answer for an affair that may get you into a good deal of trouble. It is stated that you have libelled his lordship grossly; accused him of carrying off your sister by force of arms, and burning down your mother's house; both of which are great crimes, of which I am sure Lord Dalmeny would not be guilty."

"And that he is guilty of both acts I still maintain," answered John, resolutely.

"Humph! and pray, sir, who was the landlord of the house that your mother inhabited?"

"Lord Dalmeny"

"Very well," exclaimed the man of justice; "then there the charge against his lordship falls to the ground; for I never yet heard of any law that deprived a man of the right to burn down his house at any time when he may think fit."

"This may be your notion of law, sir," answered John Ruthven, "but I, at least, am not one that is inclined to abide by it."

"But you have no remedy, sirrah," exclaimed the magistrate; "and so listen patiently, whilst I proceed to the second part of your accusation against his lordship. You have the unparalled audacity, it seems, to charge him with carrying off your sister, as if the honour of such an occurrence was not a full equivalent, even supposing all you have stated to be true. I, however, have formed a different notion of it, which is this: your sister, I dare say, was a pretty interesting girl for a rustic, and his lordship, who is acknowledged to be one of the finest men in the country, sees, and falls desperately in love with her. She, of course, is vain of the honour, but conceals the fact of their acquaintance from her friends; this is all natural enough, you see, and in the end they both run away, to the great indignation of those who have not looked fairly at the matter. The consequence of all this is, that his lordship is accused of having forcibly carried her off, and in a violent passion you go to his castle, vowing death and destruction against the man who has so far honoured your sister as to fall desperately in love with her."

"I see," cried John, with difficulty restraining his indignation, "it is your interest to pervert the truth when a lord chances to be arraigned against a commoner."

"What's that, you say, sirrah?"

"It matters not," replied John; "but this I tell you—though justice has been denied me here, I will obtain it elsewhere, or my own hand shall secure that which others would withhold from me."

"What, villain!" roared the enraged justice, "do you dare talk in this way to a man that has been entrusted by his sovereign with a commission of peace? Do you know who I am sir?—that I am a justice?—and that I can at my own will and pleasure send you to cool your heels in the county jail for having dared to insult the representative of your lawful king."

"Really," replied John, with as much gravity as he could assume, "I was not before aware that I was in the presence of so dignified a personage. Your conduct led me to suppose that you had formerly been one of those pettifogging rascals who are a foul disgrace to the law, but who sometimes contrive to step up the ladder of preferment instead of one that leads to the gallows. I am now, however, fully aware of the mistake I have made, and henceforth I will endeavour to conduct myself with more propriety in the presence of so august a personage as the king's representative."

"Take, care, sirrah! take care what you are saying," cried the incensed magistrate, "or I may presently feel it my imperative duty to commit you for utterring treasonable words. Remember, sir, I do not sit here without power, and that power may be exercised in a way that you will not like, unless you can conduct yourself in future with propriety and respect."

" I have no desire to wrangle with you," answered John, boldly. "The eagle stoops not to make a prey of flies, nor have I any desire to hold further converse with you, since it appears that I am denied that justice which I have a right to demand."

" But you will not depart from this place until I have done with you," vociferated the justice. " I have clearly shown you that Lord Dalmeny had a right to burn the house that was inhabited by your mother, since it was his own property ; and as for the story of his carrying off your sister, it's my opinion that she rather prevailed upon him to run away with her. So now, all the charges against his lordship being settled, I have next to inquire by what right you went armed to a nobleman's castle, and threatened to take away the life of one of his majesty's most illustrious subjects ?"

" I acted," replied John, fearlessly, " as every man would who had been wronged by a villain."

"Villain !" exclaimed the horrified justice ; " and have I lived to hear a nobleman called a villain by such a base-born hound as thou art."

" Aye," cried John, " you may call me what you please ; but in spite of your one-sided justice, I again accuse Lord Dalmeny of forcibly carrying off my sister. Not that he did it with his own hands, but that he engaged others to do an act which he was ashamed to commit himself. This, sir, I am prepared to prove, and knowing the fact to be as I have stated, I swore to have revenge for the gross outrage that had been offered, and arming myself, I certainly challenged Lord Dalmeny, which he was cowardly enough to decline till he could do so no longer without bringing upon himself a charge of cowardice."

" You hear his story," whispered Lady Dalmeny to her son ; " and though I would be the last to turn against you, yet, if there is truth in his words, I would say that thou hadst done a deed that has brought shame and dishonour on our house."

" It seems, then, madam," muttered his lordship, " that this vile peasant has succeeded in turning your heart against the son you lately professed to love ?"

" It is because I love you so well," answered Lady Margaret, " that I would now see you make restitution for the wrongs you have done this young man. Restore his sister without delay, and I will see that the widow's cottage shall be rebuilt with all speed."

" And what if I chastise the insolence of this peasant by suffering the affair to take its own course ?"

" In that case you will lose my favour."

" And mine too," added Lady Agnes ; " aye, my lord, I know you have it in your power to restore Effie to the arms of her mother, and if you refuse to do an act of justice like this, you cannot wonder if I henceforth regard you as a cruel and inflexible enemy to those who I believe have never injured you."

" My fair cousin will, I am sure, think differently of me when she reflects calmly," answered Lord Dalmeny ; " at any rate, I hope she will do me the justice to believe that I am not so black of heart as has been represented."

During the time that this brief conversation had been passing, Justice Gripple was sitting in profound thought, and by the working of his countenance, it was easily enough to be seen that he had not forgotten the words of defiance that had been uttered by John Ruthven, and that his judgment would be biassed by the offence he had himself received. As Lord Dalmeny, therefore, concluded his last few words, the magistrate leant forward in his chair, and frowning yet more awfully, addressed himself to the person who had raised his ire :—

"John Ruthven," he exclaimed, "or whatever other name you think fit to pass by, it is my duty to inform you, that after a very patient hearing, there can be very little doubt of your guilt in the mind of any reasonable man. The charges against you are many. In the first place, you are found with unlawful arms in your possession, and in the second place, you go to the castle of Dalmeny, and threaten the life of his lordship. These are heavy offences, and must be heavily punished. In the third place, you discharge those unlawful weapons, to the imminent danger of the person you have sworn to murder. Fourthly, you are a mere peasant, a slave of the soil, as I may say, and, therefore, undeserving the protection of the laws. Fifthly, your mother once had the insolence to offend me, and I vowed at the time to have my revenge at the first opportunity. Sixthly, you have dared to affront me in the judgment seat, and that is an offence that demands a speedy and terrible example to all future evil doers. And, seventhly, your conduct has been so infamous throughout this whole affair, that neither justice nor his lordship will be satisfied unless you are made to suffer the severest penalty I have the power to inflict. I shall, therefore, order you to be committed to prison, where you will have time to reflect on the enormity of your offences."

"Call you this justice?" demanded John, scornfully. "Am I to be sent to gaol as a felon, because I happen to be humbly born, whilst his lordship escapes through the title he so unworthily bears?"

Justice Gripple was about to make an angry reply to this, but he was interrupted by the opening of the door, and Mr. Johnston, another magistrate of the district, entered the room, and took a seat by the side of Justice Gripple. His looks were mild and benignant, and his manner so courteous, that John began to hope he had now a better chance of obtaining the justice that had been hitherto denied him. At the request of Mr. Johnston, the evidence was briefly gone over, and then, addressing himself to his colleague, he said :—

"It seems to me that both the parties that have been brought before us are equally in fault. I see, however, that you have made out a warrant for the committal of only one of them, and, therefore, as I like to see equal justice, I shall make out a second warrant for the committal of the other."

"Nay, my dear friend," cried Gripple, in the utmost consternation, "only think of the rank and ——"

"I shall take nothing of the kind into consideration," interrupted Mr. Johnston ;—and then, addressing himself to the young nobleman, he desired to be informed who and what he was.

"You know me well enough, sir," answered the person who had been addressed ;—"we have met often enough before, and, therefore, your question is superfluous."

"I know neither persons nor rank when I sit in a judicial capacity," replied the worthy magistrate, "and, therefore, you will be pleased to answer my question."

"Well, then," answered the young nobleman, "I am the Lord Dalmeny, and may, perhaps, have it in my power before long to punish the insolence you have thought proper to treat me with."

"Come, come, my lord," exclaimed the magistrate, "all this fury and bluster will not deter me from doing my duty. You, it seems, have thought fit to stoop from your lordly dignity, to do a great wrong to those who you ought rather to protect than persecute. You have committed an act of injustice, my lord, and, therefore, I shall feel inclined to show that the poor man is to be protected as well as the rich."

"Beware, sir, how you act, or ——"

"I shall take care of that, depend on it," replied the magistrate, calmly; "and, at the same time, I will take it upon myself to caution you as to your future actions. Hitherto you have borne the name of being a libertine, and the scourge of all those who love virtue and honour good deeds; it is time, however, that you should reflect, for infamy does not always triumph, though it may chance to do so for a little time. Why, my Lord Dalmeny, the whole county rings with your evil deeds, and it needs but little more to bring down upon you the hatred of even those who now profess to be your friends."

"And I to be told that," cried his lordship, fiercely, "by a man who owes his elevation to the bench through the influence of my father."

"That may be true, Lord Dalmeny," answered Mr. Johnston, "but I should never have been entrusted with the authority I possessed, if those who bestowed it on me had not believed that I would hold the balance of justice with a fair and impartial hand. You have committed a crime of a heinous nature against those who were unable to protect themselves against your violence. Helpless women have been wantonly injured;— one has been carried off no one knows where, and the other has had her house burned down, and she herself is driven forth, either to become a houseless wanderer, or to depend upon the charity of those who, perhaps, scarcely have it in their power to afford the aid she requires. These offences I look at with an impartial eye, and I must confess that the crimes you have committed deserve to bring down upon you the loathing and execration of all honourable men."

Lord Dalmeny listened to these words with an impatience that was observed by every one present. His brow was contracted into a portentous frown; his bosom heaved violently, and his hands were clenched, as if he meditated an attack upon the person who had spoken to him so freely. Still, however, he restrained himself till the concluding words of Mr. Johnston's address, and then, uttering an exclamation of fury, he snatched forth a dagger that he wore in his girdle, and aimed a blow at his heart, that must have proved fatal had not John Ruthven sprang forward at the moment, and seized his arm just in time to prevent the perpetration of murder. As it was, however, Mr. Johnston received a slight wound, which, on examination, proved to be of little or no consequence. Lady Margaret Dalmeny and her younger companion were dreadfully agitated at witnessing this scene of violence, and when it was ascertained that the injury inflicted on the magistrate was of a trivial nature, the former, addressing herself to Lord Dalmeny in a tone of reproach, said :—

"My son !—my son! to what a fearful height has thy rashness urged thee! It has been foretold that thou wilt bring ruin and disgrace on thy family, and now, alas! I am but too well assured that I shall live to see thee perish by a death inglorious and ignoble."

"Let him who urged me to this violence take the blame upon himself," answered Lord Dalmeny, gloomily. "He it was that raised the fierce tempest in my heart, and had he perished for it, the fault must have rested entirely upon himself."

"I acknowledge that I have been in error," said the magistrate, calmly. "I certainly overstepped my duty in speaking of matters that were unconnected with the business that had been brought before us. The fault, therefore, is my own, and I do not hesitate to ask pardon for any wound I may have inflicted by the words I uttered."

"You hear, my son?" cried Lady Margaret Dalmeny; "an apology has been offered for what has passed, and surely you will not refuse to act with equal courtesy towards one whose life had well nigh fell a sacrifice to your ungovernable passions?"

"There is no occasion for it, my dear lady," answered the magistrate, with all his accustomed mildness and composure. "Lord Dalmeny, I dare say, is too proud to ask pardon of one so far beneath him in rank as myself, and I have too independent a spirit to require any concession from him. In time his hot blood will become cooler, and he will then learn that it is the duty of the young to pay some respect to those whose hair has become grey through length of years. He will then regret the violence he has this day offered me, and may, perhaps, often think of it with sorrow when I am mouldering in the grave."

"Come, my son," cried Lady Margaret, "you hear the forgiving spirit of the man you would have slain, and surely you cannot hesitate to express some contrition for an act that, if fully accomplished, would have terminated in your meeting an ignominious end."

"I require nothing of the kind," answered the magistrate, "for I have already acknowledged myself in error, and, therefore, having taken the blame of the whole affair upon myself, I will remain perfectly satisfied if matters rest where they are. At present his lordship is heated, and his proud stomach cannot yield quite so humbly as you wish. I am content that it should be so, and most earnestly do I entreat your ladyship to say no more about it."

"But you are wounded, sir, and may need some assistance?"

"Nay, 'tis a mere scratch," answered the magistrate, "and not worthy of a moment's thought. At any rate I will return home before I have it looked to, and therefore I will now take my leave of you, with a fervent wish that the events of this day may terminate to the equal satisfaction of both parties."

So saying the old gentleman left the room, and entering his carriage, which was waiting for him at the door, he drove away from the place which had so nearly been the scene of his own death.

Justice Gripple was not perhaps the least alarmed at the affair that had lately taken place in his presence, but he was a cautious, prudent man in all things, and therefore he deemed it best in every point of view to sit calmly by and take no part either on one side or the other. He therefore listened with the utmost composure to all that was passing, and it was not till the departure of his brother magistrate that he again found the use of his tongue. But when Mr. Johnston was fairly out of hearing, he roused himself from the sleepy posture he had maintained, and addressing himself to Lady Margaret Dalmeny, said oracularly,—

"That's a most extraordinary man, my lady,—a most extraordinary man, I assure you. He's full of oddities, and, between ourselves, a most unfit person to be entrusted with a commission of the peace. He's too humane by half, for I've actually seen him pity the wretches that have been brought before him, and it's scarcely a month ago that he let off a villanous mendicant that had been brought before him, because the old hypocrite made up a wry face, and told him that he had a wife and ten small children depending on him for support. So you see how utterly unfit he is for the office he bears, though there are people who are foolish enough to think him a very worthy and humane man. *Humane*, indeed!—let him follow my example, and I'll warrant you we would soon rout out all the rogues and vagabonds that at present infest our neighbourhood."

"And yet, with all his oddities," observed Lady Margaret, "I wish he had remained to assist you in the decision of this case of ours."

"Aye, aye," exclaimed Gripple, "you have rightly enough reminded me of the business we have on hand. But, really, the incapacity of my neighbour Johnston is so notorious, that I must be excused for rambling from our subject in the manner I have."

"Perhaps," interposed John Ruthven, "you will now be pleased to come to the point. My patience can brook very little more delay, for I must take my departure from hence immediately, since I have things to do that must be performed instantly, or——"

"Hark'ee, young fellow," interposed the magistrate, sharply; "you have committed sundry offences, which I was enumerating just at the time when my brother justice entered the room. I told you, if I remember rightly, that there were no less than seven reasons why I should hold you to be a most dangerous character, and one upon whom the whole weight of the law ought to fall, in order that others may be deterred from following your evil courses. You have outstripped yourself a little in this affair, young man, and it is now my duty to restrain you from all further acts of violence."

"Well, sir," replied John, "there is one present who has already expressed his willingness to be my security."

"That's not sufficient," exclaimed Justice Gripple, with affected astonishment; "and what security can I have, think you, that you will not make a bad use of your liberty?—that you will not, in fact, go with arms in your hand and take the life of Lord Dalmeny?"

"You are resolved, then, to send me to a prison?"

"No; I have been thinking of something else that may meet the justice of the case, and suit you better than the confinement of a prison. What say you to going to sea, young fellow?"

"It is the life that pleases me better than any other," answered John.

"Why, that's well said," exclaimed the magistrate; "and as we all agree pretty well upon the matter, you shall go on board a ship of war this very night!"

"To-night?"

"Aye; doesn't that exactly suit you?"

"It does not," replied John. "If I go to sea it must be with my own free will, and not through any compulsion on your part."

"Nevertheless," exclaimed Justice Gripple, with the most provoking coolness, "I say again that you must go, and that, too, this very night."

"It is impossible," answered John Ruthven; "I have arrangements to make ere I can leave England, and there are, besides, a few friends to whom I would say farewell, previous to my departure."

"Aye, and no doubt you have got mischief in your head as well," cried the magistrate. "You think to slip through my fingers, and after committing some heinous offence against his lordship, to leave England, and thus escape the punishment of your crimes. But I am aware of you, my fine fellow, and shall take care that you go on board the frigate this very night."

"But I again tell you——"

"It's useless to say anything more about it," interrupted Justice Gripple; "because my mind is made up, and nothing will ever turn me from it. The king wants good sailors to fight for him, and a stout well-built fellow like you will exactly suit the service. You will thus have an opportunity of retrieving the former errors of your ways, and if you should be lucky enough not to be killed in any of the actions you will be engaged in, you may by-and-by return to England a much better man than you left it. So make your mind easy, for this night you go on board his Majesty's frigate, the Fury."

"And is this the power you possess over a free-born subject like myself?" exclaimed Ruthven, furiously. "Am I to be sent away like a convicted felon, because I come to complain before you of the villanies that have been practised against me by the lord?"

"Don't put yourself in a passion," exclaimed the magistrate, "for it will do you very little service here, I can assure you. Besides, you have only to wait with a little patience, and you will return and——"

"Aye, I shall return," interrupted Ruthven, "and when that moment arrives, I would have all those beware who have now wronged me. I shall return, sir, and if by that time you have not found a refuge in the grave to which you are hastening, you will be made bitterly to repent the injuries you have heaped upon me. My only crime consists in resenting the wrongs that have been done to those who are the dearest to me, and yet you banish me from my native land, and send me as a slave to serve under a taskmaster who is not of my own choosing. But, mark me, a day of reckoning will come, and heavily shall you then repent the tyranny you have this day exercised!"

"Aye, aye, rave away, young fellow," returned the justice, with a cold smile of scorn. "Threaten as much as you please, for you are privileged now to say or do just as you please; this is the last hour of your liberty, and I can well afford to indulge you in so harmless an amusement as this is."

"Recollect that I have vowed to be revenged for this," cried Ruthven; "remember it, I say, for when the time arrives, there will be little warning of the punishment that is near at hand. And so," he continued; "I am to serve as a common sailor, though my pride revolts at being placed in the servile situation you would doom me to. I am to be the slave of some upstart fellow, who, being armed with authority, may play the tyrant, and even sentence me to endure the lash for the most trivial affair that he may be pleased to construe into a breach of discipline. This you may call justice, but, give it what name you please, I will be revenged for it, and that too before you expect my return."

"Come, come, sirrah," exclaimed the magistrate impatiently, "you have had your say out, I suppose, and now let me advise you to be more civil in future, for I have handcuffs for the wrists, and fetters for the ankles, and I may be induced to use both of them unless you think fit to restrain the anger you affect to feel."

"I care not," answered Ruthven; "do with me as you please, for I have already endured so much wrong, that I can put up with a little more till the time comes for paying off all at once. The thought of that serves to sustain me, though you have small reason to wish for my return to England."

"Nonsense man!" exclaimed the magistrate; "this is not so serious an affair, after all, and it only wants a little philosophy to carry it off lightly enough. Besides, only think what an honour it will be to fight for your king and country, and to belong to a ship that never yet lowered her colours to an enemy. Here is honour thrust upon you, man, and yet you are ungrateful enough to think that you have been very hardly done by."

"Am I not forced to this service against my will?"

"And what of that?" demanded Justice Gripple; "if it was not for being forced, I'm thinking, there's very few that would be induced to fight under the banner of their king. Besides, just now you said that you preferred a sea-life in preference to any other; and yet now, when I am going to oblige you by sending you off without delay, it seems you think yourself very cruelly treated."

"I see it is not convenient to understand me," exclaimed Ruthven. "However, it is your turn to triumph just now, but do not forget what I have before told you, that a heavy day of reckoning will yet come, when you will bitterly repent the course you have thought fit to adopt against me."

Lady Agnes had hitherto remained a silent spectator of this scene, but now she was no longer able to restrain her indignation at the injustice that was contemplated, and stepping forward, she addressed herself to the magistrate in a tone of reproach.

"It seems, sir," she said, "that you have wholly mistaken the object for which we have come before you. A quarrel, likely to be attended with dangerous consequences, had occurred between the two young men, and we wished to have them bound to keep the peace towards each other. You, however, have thought fit to suffer one of them to escape even without reproof, whilst the other is to be sent on board a ship against his will, for no other purpose than that you may gain favour in the eyes of a great man."

"Upon my word, young lady," exclaimed Justice Gripple, as soon as he could recover from the surprise into which he had been thrown by this unexpected reproof, "you would have made an admirable advocate had you happened to belong to our own sex. You have spoken up bravely for the young fellow, but as it happens that I have the power, under an act of parliament, to do as I have proposed, he must go to sea, and that, too, at the short notice I have given."

"And what think you the world will say," demanded Lady Agnes, "when it is known that this act of scandalous injustice has been committed for no other reason than to serve your own purposes? You would obtain some favour from Lord Dalmeny, and have taken this method to place him under an obligation that you know he will be but too happy to repay on the first occasion that offers."

" And pray," asked Gripple, " why need you take so great an interest in the fate of this youngster ?"

" Because I cannot endure to witness such a scandalous perversion of justice," answered Lady Agnes. " This person, who has never wronged you, comes to complain that he has sustained serious injuries from Lord Dalmeny ; into this, however, you think it unnecessary to inquire, and without any cause being assigned, he is to be sent on board a ship like a felon."

" Humph !" muttered his worship ; " you have come here, I suppose, to teach me the law ?"

" Nay," she replied, " I merely ask you for justice ; he hath been wronged, I tell you, and, therefore, you have no right to punish him in the way you propose."

" Psha !" exclaimed Gripple, peevishly ; " I don't set here to be told what is law and justice. I am to decide upon that myself—aye, and will do so, too, whoever I may happen to offend. And now, young lady, take a little piece of advice that I can give you ; return home, and let your attention for the future be directed to household duties, rather than to things you don't understand ; dive deeply into the mystery of making puddings and pies, attend to embroidery, and such like feminine qualifications ; but never again come to tell me in what way to administer justice to the evil-doers that are brought before me."

" For your discourtesy, sir, I was well prepared before I came here," answered Lady Agnes, reproachfully. " However, I am not to be baffled because you are angry ; and, therefore, do I again entreat you to reconsider this business before you send away this young man, perhaps never to return to his native country."

" I'll not be turned aside by a woman's tongue, and so there's an end of the affair," cried the justice, resolutely. " My mind is made up ; the warrant is made out for sending him on board the Fury, and this very night he shall go, in spite of anything that you or anybody else can say against it."

" Aye," exclaimed John Ruthven, furiously, " it is your turn to triumph now ; but the time is not far distant when I will pour upon you such vengeance for this day's injustice that shall be remembered for years to come. I go forth alone, but many months shall not pass away when I will return as the leader of a gallant band, who will carry fire and devastation wherever it shall be my command to send them. Then you will repent the tyranny that has banished me from my native land, and yet your supplications for mercy will be rejected, even as you now reject the entreaties that have been made in my behalf."

" Constables," vociferated the justice to a couple of men who now entered the room," seize your prisoner, and convey him with all speed on board the Fury, which now lies in the bay. Here is your warrant for executing your task, and remember, that if he escapes, the consequences will fall upon yourselves."

Promptly obeying this order, the men advanced, and each laid a hand upon the collar of John Ruthven, who calmly submitted himself, though for a moment it seemed doubtful whether he would not have resisted the attempt to make him their prisoner. Addressing himself, however, once more to Justice Gripple, he said, in a tone almost choked with fury,—

" You see, old man, that I have yielded myself quietly, though it was in my power to have overcome all the obstacles you have thrown in my way. I, however, seek not the blood of those who are only the intruments of your tyranny. For the present, therefore, I submit myself quietly; but ere I go, let me again warn you of the consequences that will follow the act you have this day committed. You yourself shall be driven forth from house to house, nor will one be found to pity the heartless villain who has ever proved himself to be the oppressor of those whom it was his duty to protect. Yet I will be their avenger, and——"

"I'll hear no more," interrupted the magistrate; "bear him away, fellows, and let me never see him again, as you value your lives. Away with him to the ship, and when he has been safely put on board, return here, that I may know we have fairly got rid of him."

Scarcely resisting the rough usuage he was now subjected to, John accompanied the two constables from the house. At his departure, a weight of apprehension seemed to have been removed from the mind of Justice Gripple, and he attempted to be very facetious with his aristocratic friends; but both Lady Margaret and her niece instantly retired in disgust, leaving Lord Dalmeny to confer with the partial administrator of the law on certain other proceedings that were to follow those we have just described.

CHAPTER XVIII.

"You shall not force me, sirs, to leave this place,
For I'll resist you till the latest moment,
Rather than yield to tyranny."   OLD PLAY.

JOHN's heart was nearly bursting at the injustice he had been made to endure, and as he eyed the two men into whose custody he had been committed, he endeavoured to form an opinion of the sort of customers he had to deal with. The justice was himself an instance of what might be done by bribes and corruption, and there was some little reason to hope that the men in whose care he now found himself would not prove more difficult to prevail on by promises than their employer had been. It was, however, not quite certain that the constables would dare to accept a reward for such services; for Justice Gripple had a notion that he alone was to make a profit by the sale of his favours, and it was pretty certain he would not fail to punish his unfortunate subordinates in the event of its ever coming to his ears that they had accepted money for letting the prisoner escape. Under the circumstances, it would be extremely hazardous to make them an offer; but when he came within view of the sea, where the vessel that was to bear him away to a foreign clime was lying at anchor, he saw that only one chance presented itself, and if he let that slip, he should be borne away without even the consolation of bidding his mother a last sad adieu.

Under these circumstances he determined to run the risk, and having conversed with them for a little while upon various indifferent subjects, till he brought it to bear on the one he felt most interest in, by pointing out the ship which lay before them,—

"Yonder," he said, "is, I suppose, the vessel that is to bear me away from my native land, and a right noble-looking ship it is; yet it must needs be confessed that I do not go very willingly, seeing that no choice has been left me in this matter."

"And what has that to do with it?" demanded Jamieson; "England has need of a few good able-bodied fellows like yourself, and I suppose his worship thought, rightly enough, that he could not do better than make all safe and sure by sending you abroad till your blood grows a little cooler."

"There was no need of it," answered John, impatiently; "the quarrel between me and Lord Dalmeny was a private one, and we were well enough able to settle it without appealing to an ignorant justice, who knows scarcely so much of the law as I do myself."

"An ignorant justice!"

"Aye, or a dishonest one, whichever you please," replied John.

"Young man," exclaimed Jamieson, in a tone of indignant surprise, "are you aware who it is that you are speaking about in this insulting manner?"

"I know him better than he perhaps thinks for," answered the other haughtily; "he is one of those that will sell justice, as he calls it, to those who can best afford to put money into his pockets, and at the same time will punish all those who are unfortunate enough to be poor;—a great crime in his eyes, and one that is sure to bring down the full measure of his resentment."

"Ah!" exclaimed Jamieson, "I see well enough how it is;—you don't half like going to sea, and, of course, you think it very hard to be forced there against your inclination."

"I certainly do think it hard," replied the young man: "but you are mistaken in supposing that I have a dislike to the sea, for it is my favourite pursuit, and the one which it was my intention to have voluntarily followed."

"Well then, what difference can it make?" asked the constable; "why, by your own confession you like the life well enough, and yet you think it very hard because the justice happens to have sent you off a little sooner than you intended to go."

"He sends me as if I was a felon, and that thought alone is sufficient to give me a distaste for it."

"Psha!" exclaimed Jamieson; "he has only done it to keep you out of mischief."

"In that case," cried John, "why did he not take the same precautions with Lord Dalmeny?"

"Lord Dalmeny!—why you didn't expect that he was going to send out his lordship as a common sailor?"

"I expect equal justice to be administered," replied John; "but in the present instance I have been most foully deceived, and the man who chances to possess a title has been suffered to escape harmless, whilst he who is unknown and unfriended is to be sent away by force, as if he had committed some heinous offence."

"Well, we know nothing at all about it," replied the man; "we are only doing our duty, and as there's no help for you, the only way is to put up with it quietly. Remember, you are going to fight the battles of your country, and, with a good share of prize-money, you may come back one of these days with gold enough to make you bless the chance that sent you off to sea."

"But I have no quarrel with those you call my enemies."

"Perhaps not," replied the fellow, "but your country has, and that's about the same thing. The French are the foes of old England, and you'll have a chance of helping to give 'em a good drubbing, and, by way of a change, you may now and then fall in with the Americans, who, they say, have been very saucy to us of late, and if that's the case, they must be taught to treat us with more respect."

"Neither the French nor the Americans are foes of mine," replied John, impatiently; "they have never given me cause to consider them as such, and perhaps I might feel quite as much inclined to fight on their side as the other."

"What!" exclaimed the other, with surprise, "would you draw your sword against your own countrymen?"

"They have wronged me," answered John, "and therefore I have every right to consider them as my foes. One of them at least, has this day injured me, and now I only look forward for an opportunity to return at the earliest opportunity to revenge myself."

"Nonsense, man!" returned Jamieson, "you'll think better of this by and by, and when you come back again you will have forgot this day's little affair. It will all wear off by and by, and then——"

"It will never be forgotten while I live," replied John, fiercely; "I am not one of those that forget injuries, and the one I have now received is unlikely ever to be forgotten until I have had my vengeance."

"Why, you surely would not come back to do old Justice Gripple an injury?"

"That he will some day or other find out," replied the young man. "It may, perhaps, not be very long first; but, happen when it may, I will be as sudden and terrible in my revenge as he has been cool and deliberate in injuring me."

"Then I can only say that the sooner you are out of the country the better," exclaimed Jamieson. "So, there, you see, lies the vessel, and close to the shore lies a boat that is to take you off to her."

"I have been thinking," said John, after a brief consideration, "that you, at any rate, can have no ill-feeling towards me, and that, of course, you would rather assist to do me a good turn than lend your aid towards forwarding an act of oppression that would include yourself in the sweeping retribution I mean to secure."

"Humph!" ejaculated the other, "why, the fact is I am rather tenderhearted in these matters, but where a fellow has got a task to do, he must go through with it, however disagreable it may chance to be."

"You are determined, then, to obey the unjust commands you have lately received?"

"Why, there's no help for it, that I can see."

"At all events," replied John, "I have been thinking that a couple of golden guineas that I happen to have in my pocket might as well be in your possession as in my own."

"Halloa!" exclaimed Jamieson, "why, you are not going to offer us a bribe, are you?"

"You can do as you please about accepting it," answered John Ruthven, with an appearance of unconcern. "I, of course, shall not persuade you either one way or the other; but you are aware that Justice Gripple is not above accepting a reward, and, therefore, I see no reason why you and your companion should be very nice in this instance."

"Aye," replied the constable, "but it depends upon whether you offer enough to make it worth our while to run the risk. Justice Gripple ain't a hard-hearted man, provided people have got money enough to put him into a good humour, and perhaps you would find us something like him, only it's not to be expected that we can injure ourselves for a trifle that would not be worth our acceptance."

"I have offered you all I at present happen to possess," answered their captive; "I have no more in my pocket than the two guineas I just now spoke of, but if you think proper to let me slip off, you shall have ten more in two or three hours, and when I come back to England you will find me a friend instead of an enemy."

"But promises won't do for us," exclaimed the constable; "we must either have the money or you shall go off to yonder ship, and then, I'm thinking, we shall not be troubled with you again for some years to come."

' "Have you no pity for one who has never injured you?" demanded John.

"Yes, we both of us pity you," replied Jamieson, "but we should pity ourselves a good deal more if we had to return back to the justice with a lame story."

"There is no occasion for a lame story," answered the young man ; "say that I resisted you, and broke away from your custody, as soon as we approached the sea-shore. There can be no help for that, you know, and though the affair may create a little surprise at first, the thing will soon wear off, and be no more talked of."

"And we are to do all this for the paltry consideration of two guineas?"

"Nay, I have told you that more shall be given you within a few hours afterwards."

"And I again tell you that we can't do anything of the kind upon trust," answered Jamieson. "The risk is a great one, and unless we have money enough to enable us to leave the country, we must do our duty, according to the orders of Justice Gripple."

"If you are so resolute," exclaimed John, "you will, perhaps, accompany me to the house of my mother, for we may never meet again in this world, and I would fain embrace her ere I go upon this forced voyage."

"And so, perhaps, give you chance of escaping from us, eh?" retorted the constable.

"Nay, if I was resolved upon that," replied John, "it would be quite as easy to do it now as by and by."

"Why, you wouldn't think of giving us the slip?"

"I don't know that," answered the captive, "for there are few men that like to be forced into exile, and I am one of those who would rather perish than be sent away from my own country as if I was a felon. I have already told you that I desire to have one more interview with my broken-hearted mother, who has been victim of the same wretch whose artifices have brought upon me the troubles that now send me forth to become a wanderer upon the face of the earth."

"Why, to hear the young fellow talk," exclaimed Jamieson to his companion, "one would suppose he was going to make a desperate attempt at escape."

"Aye," answered the other, "but he will find his mistake out if he should happen to try it on, for we are both of us armed, and if he makes the least attempt we must shoot him as we would a dog."

"Indeed!" exclaimed John, resolutely, "then it's time I should show you how one man can successfully oppose himself against superior numbers. I would have prevailed on you to have some little fellow-feeling towards the unfortunate, but since that hope appears to be a vain one, I will no longer hesitate to protect myself from the violence you would offer me."

"Take care what you do," replied Jamieson, drawing a pistol from his pocket, and presenting it at the head of his prisoner ;—" take care what you do, I say, or you will be a dead man in less than another minute."

"Shall I!" exclaimed John, breaking away from them with a sudden effort, and at the same moment, snatching the weapon from Jamieson's hand, he sprang a few paces off, and levelling it at the constable, said,—

"We are now placed upon more equal terms, you see, and be the consequences what they may, I will never again submit to become your prisoner!"

The other constable, however, who still retained possession of his pistol, instantly raised the weapon towards John and discharged it in the direction where he was standing. But fortunately the aim was not so true as had

been intended, and John, who was conscious of the advantage he now possessed, advanced a few paces nearer to them, saying,—

"You must now see how dangerous it would be to carry this affair between us any further. You would have taken my life, but, having failed, I have it in my power to be terribly revenged for the rough treatment I have received at your hands. Leave me, therefore, and when you return back to Justice Gripple, say that I have left England without the violence he intended, and that I shall return ere long to fulfil the promise I this day made him. He will understand the message well enough, and you may tell him that the vengeance I have sworn to shall be as was certain the provocation that led to it."

"You are mistaken, John, if you think we are going to be frightened from our duty by your blustering words," replied Jamieson. "We are two to one against you, and, let the consequences be what they may, we will not return until we have placed you savely on board yonder vessel."

"Humph! you are resolved, then, to rush upon certain death?"

"We are," replied the constable; "so now either yield yourself our prisoner, or we will close in upon you, and thus prevent the mischief you threaten us with."

John saw that they were preparing to rush in upon him, and having looked to the priming of his pistol, he said, in a voice almost choked with rage,—

"Madmen, as you both are, you are tempting me to do a deed that I would fain avoid. I would have spared your lives, but since no alternative remains, you must e'en take the consequence of your own wilfulness."

"What say you," demanded Jamieson to his companion, "shall we laugh at his threats, or save our lives by getting away from this place as soon as possible?"

No. 19

"You may do as you like about it," replied the other; "but I don't feel inclined to have a bullet through my head when it may so easily be avoided, and so, leaving you to do as you please about it, I shall make my escape with all possible dispatch."

And in pursuance of this resolution the fellow scampered off with all the speed he could, leaving his comrade to shift as well as he was able for himself. Jamieson, however, was not possessed of any very large share of courage, and finding himself thus deserted by his ally, he also made a hasty retreat, leaving John Ruthven in complete possession of the victory.

Thus relieved from all present danger, the young man paused for a few seconds, to consider what he had best do. That England was no longer a place of safety for him he felt quite convinced, and resolving, therefore, to take his departure with as little delay as possible, he turned his steps towards the spot where his home formerly stood, in order that he might bid his mother adieu ere he left, probably never to see her again.

Leaving him, however, for the present, we must now return to Justice Gripple, whose visiters having all of them taken their departure, he was left to ruminate on late events, and put what construction he pleased upon the words of John Ruthven, who had threatened him with his vengeance. Yet there was one consolation for him,—John was, in all probability, by this time, on board the vessel that was to bear him away from his native land, and as the war was just then raging furiously, there was a fair chance that he might be slain in an action with the enemies of his country, and thus all future danger in that quarter might be avoided. This was Gripple's only hope, and, faint as it was, he caught eagerly at it, and already began to consider himself safe from the man he had so much reason to fear. In the midst of these cogitations, however, he was disturbed by a terrible loud knocking at the door, and scarcely had he time to jump up and run to the window, when Jamieson and his comrade came rushing into the room.

"Why how now, fellows," exclaimed the justice, with surprise; "have you seen a ghost, sirrahs, that you come running back as if you were both mad?"

"Worse, worse, squire," answered Jamieson;—"we have been put in fear of our lives, and the only wonder is that we are here to tell you what has happened."

"Happened!" shouted the justice; "and pray what has happened that you come back looking more like a couple of scarecrows than christian men?"

"Ah! we are afraid to tell you what has happened."

"Afraid!—why, if I thought—but no, you never could have been such fools as that either—and yet, if it should turn out that you have suffered John Ruthven to escape, I'll—I'll—I'll have you both hanged as sure as you are now alive."

"The truth is, you have guesed it, your lordship," exclaimed Jamieson, gasping for breath; "yes, the prisoner has escaped, and we are both ruined men."

"Escaped!" roared Justice Gripple.

"Yes," answered the constable who had last spoken; "he has got off, and little wonder too, considering that we were attacked by a dozen men, who would have murdered us both, if we had not escaped by taking to our heels."

"What's that you say?" demanded the justice, who was extremely fond of anything that was marvellous; "attacked, were you, by a dozen men that rushed out to rescue the prisoner?"

"Aye, sir," replied Jamieson, who was well pleased at the success of his abominable falsehood; "there were at least a dozen villains, though we didn't stop to count them; and good reason we had, too, for taking to our heels, seeing that if we had not we should have been murdered."

"And so," exclaimed Gripple, as soon as he could recover himself a little,—" and so you were cowards enough to let your prisoner escape, because you happened to be attacked by a dozen villains?"

"Aye," answered the constable, "and I don't think you would have acted very differently if you had been in our places,"

"Sirrah! how dare you libel a justice of the peace in this manner?" shouted the man of law; "do you forget that you are speaking to the representative of majesty, and that if I do my duty I shall send you to prison on your own confession, that you have commited a high crime and misdemeanour?"

"You know better than to send me to prison, Justice," answered Jamieson, instantly.

"And why do I know better, sirrah?"

"Because it so happens that I could tell a good many things that would not make folks think any the better of you," replied the constable; "you don't bear a very excellent character in this neighbourhood. and if I was to think it worth my while to set my tongue going, there would be——"

"Villain! do you dare to threaten me?"

"I dare do anything, if you take a fancy to send me off to a prison for what I couldn't help. The young fellow, I tell you, got off through a number of friends that came to his assistance, and as I and Christie were not a match for thirteen of 'em, we thought the best thing we could do was to run away as fast as we could."

"Thirteen! why you said there were only a dozen just now."

"Ah! and so you think you have caught me out telling lies, do you?" exclaimed Jamieson. "I said there were twelve men, and so there were, but when John joined them, as he did directly afterwards, that of course made up the thirteen; so you see I have told you nothing but the truth, as you'll find out if you like to inquire about it."

"Or if you don't believe us," added Christie, who thought it necessary to say something, "you had better get somebody else to do your dirty work the next time there's anybody to be got out of the way that you don't like."

"I'll tell you what it is, sirrahs," exclaimed Justice Gripple, "here's the king's representative insulted by a couple of infernal rascals, and if you don't both fall down on your marrow-bones and ask pardon, I shall send you off to the county gaol on a charge of suffering a prisoner to escape. That will bring you to your senses, I think, and I shall have the satisfaction of punishing you for daring to speak slightingly in presence of a great man."

"If we had known that," replied Jamieson, "you would not have seen either of us here again, I'll warrant you. Why, we were offered a bribe by Red Ruthven to let him escape, and yet, when we have done the best we could to take him off to the ship, we get blustered at, and may think ourselves well off if we escape a prison."

"Did you say the fellow offered you a bribe to let him escape?" demanded Justice Gripple.

"He did."

"The rascal!—and why, I should like to know, didn't he offer it to me?"

"Because," replied Jamieson, "I suppose he thought you would take his money and leave him in the learch."

"Come, come, sirrah," growled the man of law, "remember who you are speaking to, if you please, and let your words be a little more civil, if you can, or I shall be obliged to show my authority, and the end of it will be that you will find out how dangerous a thing it is to deal with men that can send rogues to gaol whenever they like."

"That's as much as to say the truth ain't agreeable to you."

"The truth, fellow, is not to be spoken at all times," answered the magistrate, "nor are little fellows like you to be insolent to great ones such as myself, who have authority to punish all trangressors against the law."

"But I'm no transgressor against the law," replied Jamieson.

"What! haven't you let a prisoner escape that was entrusted to your care?"

"Aye, we did that; but how could we help it, seeing that a dozen en came to rescue him."

"You may be telling a parcel of lies for aught I know about it," exclaimed Justice Gripple; "besides, you have let the man go, and that's quite enough for me; so mind what you are saying, or I shall be under the disagreeable necessity of sending you and your companion to prison."

"Oh, you can do as you like about that," replied Jamieson; "send us to prison if you please; but remember, if you do so, I shall not fail to let the world know that there is an infernal villain in it, and your worship may pretty well guess who the rascal is that I mean."

"Scoundrel! you shall pay severely for this."

"Perhaps so; but I can tell the truth for all that. You have taken bribes where you ought to have punished those that deserve it, and I'm not much out when I tell you that this very day you have tried to get a poor man out of the country, whilst a nobleman was suffered to escape, because you thought it would be more to your own interest to let him."

"Hush!" interrupted the magistrate, "not a word about that, if you please; it's a dangerous subject to speak of; for though I am innocent of taking bribes for doing my duty, yet if such a report got abroad, there are ill-natured people that might perhaps be ready enough to believe it."

"And if they did," returned Jamieson, "they would only believe that which is quite true."

"Nonsense, man! you are prejudiced against me, and say things that have no foundation."

"I say no more than all the world knows as well as I do myself," replied the constable; "here's Christie has heard the same of you, and if people will do such things, they must make up their minds to be found out some day or other."

"Who says I was ever guilty of taking a bribe?" demanded the justice.

"Who?—why, everybody, to be sure."

"But they have no proof against me."

"That's very likely, because I dare say you take pretty good care to do these things upon the sly. But recollect, a stir may be made when you least expect it, and let that time come when it may, you will find that something will turn up to show the world what a pretty game you have been carrying on this long time past."

"I tell you there's no truth in these abominable charges," cried the magistrate, who by this time began to grow terribly alarmed at the turn things were taking; I never took a bribe for doing a service to any man, and what's more, I'll trounce the first fellow that dares utter such a falsehood against me."

"I'm not afraid of your threats, Squire Gripple," exclaimed the constable; "you may talk as large as you like about what you're going to do, but this affair between John Ruthven and Lord Dalmeny will be talked about, depend on it, and people won't shut their eyes to the fact that a poor man has been treated with injustice because his opponent happened to be a man of rank. Besides, John's sister has been carried away, his house burned down, and his mother turned into the wide world, and though all this has been done by Lord Dalmeny, yet the poor young fellow is to banished by your orders, whilst his lordly opponent gets off scot-free, to do as much more mischief as he thinks proper."

"And what is it to you whether John Ruthven gets into trouble or not?" demanded the justice. "He is a dangerous fellow to have about the place, and I was glad of taking the first opportunity that offered to send him out of the country."

"Why, to be sure I have not much reason to speak well of him," replied Jamieson, "and so, perhaps, the best thing we can do is, to say nothing more about it."

"I don't know but what you are pretty right there," exclaimed Gripple, glad of an opportunity to get rid of a subject that was anything but pleasant. "You and I have no reason to like the fellow, certainly, and, therefore, I should advise you to look after him, that he may be got out of the country as speedily as possible."

"Which is not so easy as you seem to expect," replied the constable; "to be sure he may take it into his head to go away of his own accord, and if he don't think fit to do so, I have no wish to be employed against him."

"You are a coward, Jamieson."

"Perhaps so, your worship; but at any rate I have no wish to get myself into trouble, merely because you and Lord Dalmeny want to get rid of him. You have both your own reasons for it, I have no doubt, and he has sworn to come back one of these days to burn down your house, as a punishment for what has lately taken place; but I have no desire to be turned out of house and home, and, therefore, shall take especial good care to have nothing further to do in the business."

"But it is my command, sirrah, that both you and Christie go in search of him without further delay."

"Humph! and where do you suppose we are to find him?"

"Wherever his mother has taken refuge you will be sure to find the villain."

"And so, 'squire, you would deprive a son of the consolation of taking leave of a parent that he may never see again?"

"Why, what does he want with his mother?" demanded the magistrate; "the fellow has no more feeling than the chair I am now sitting on, and since he talks of burning down my house, and perhaps murdering me into the bargain, the sooner we get him out of the country the better it will be for all of us."

"I don't know that, your worship," replied Jamieson, "for at present he may not think it worth his while to trouble his head about me, but if I take any part against him in this affair, it might not be long before he would take it into his head to serve me in a way that I should not like."

"You are afraid of him, then?"

"Perhaps I am," answered the constable; "and it's not without good reason, too, for John is known to be a devil, if once his passion has been roused; and it don't follow that I should get myself into a dilemma, because you have thought fit to offend him. Besides, he never offended me in his life, and so, of course, I can have no reason for hunting after him."

"But you are a constable," retorted Justice Gripple, "and having suffered him to escape from your custody, it is now your duty to take him again, in order that we may fairly rid ourselves of a rascal by sending him out of the country."

"And if all the rascals were sent out of the country," retorted the constable, "it would be the means of clearing away some that I should not be sorry to be rid of."

"You are insolent, sirrah!"

"What; for merely speaking my mind a bit?"

"The mind is not always to be spoken so freely," answered the magistrate; "and henceforward I shall know how to regard you. You have insulted the king's most excellent majesty through me, and—and——"

"Well, well, there's no occasion to get into a passion about it," exclaimed Jamieson, interrupting him; "the fact is, the sooner we end the business the better; and so I'll take my leave, by merely saying that if I'm wanted in the morning you'll know where to find me."

And with this, the two constables took their departure, leaving Justice Gripple anything but pleased with the turn affairs had taken.

CHAPTER XIX.

"You witch me in it;
Surprise me to the very brink of tears.
Lend me a fool's heart and a woman's eyes,
And I'll beweep these comforts.—TIMON OF ATHENS.

WHEN John had contrived to escape from the custody of the officers of justice, he took his way, as we have already seen, towards the place where his mother had found a temporary asylum; but his heart was heavy with grief, for he knew that his present parting would most likely be for ever; and loving his mother as he did, he felt that to leave her was like separating himself from all that he held most dear in the world He reflected, too, on the cruel uncertainty in which the fate of his sister was involved, and again his heart swelled almost to bursting as he thought of the villany that had torn the gentle Effie from her once happy home. Upon this revenge again inspired him to acts of desperation, which at any other time he would have shuddered at, but the honour of his family had been tarnished by the base conduct of Lord Dalmeny, and he resolved, let the consequences to himself be what they might, to pour his full wrath upon the man who had thus wantonly injured him. He knew, also, that he should be compelled to leave the country of his birth in order to avoid the persecution that would otherwise be certain to follow him; and remembering that this banishment would be through the instrumentality of Lord Dalmeny. he resolved yet more and more to punish the author of his miseries to the full extent of his means.

In this manner he had proceeded some distance, perfectly unconscious of all around him, and it was not until a friendly voice had hailed him three or four times, that he looked up and perceived before him his favourite companion, Hugh Lorimer, whose look of solicitude showed that he had come forth purposely to meet him, and endeavour to subdue the angry feelings which had now taken possession of his soul. For the first time in his life, John would have turned away without speaking to his friend, but Lorimer perceived his design, and stepping up to him, said:—

"Why, how now, John? this is not the way you were wont to greet your old companion and friend."

"True," replied the young man, "but the world and I are now at enmity, and I know not now who are worthy to be ranked among my friends."

"Nonsense, man; you must not give way to these gloomy thoughts," exclaimed Hugh Lorimer. "I have heard all that has taken place, and that you have just now had the good fortune to give the slip to those who were going to take you on board the vessel."

"I have," replied John, gloomily; "and now let those beware who have driven me to this extremity."

"Nay, you must not think of committing violence John," cried the other, in a voice of kindness. "You have been cruelly wronged, I must own, but do not suffer the reflection of what has passed to urge you to a step that you would aterwards repent."

"It is well for you to talk thus coldly, who have not been injured as I have," replied John. "You may believe it possible to endure the heartless oppression of mankind without a murmur, but my blood is of a warmer temperature, and never will I rest satisfied until I have had revenge for all the bitter wrongs I have received from my oppressor."

"You allude to Lord Dalmeny," replied the other, "and I must needs acknowledge that you have endured heavy injuries from him. All this is bad enough, but consider how much worse you may render matters by seeking that revenge which you seem so eagerly to covet."

"I care not," answered John; "I am prepared to suffer a great deal more, and can do so on condition that I am not disappointed in the scheme I have formed. Thus far Lord Dalmeny has triumphed over his humble foe, but the day shall yet arrive when the peasant will obtain the full retribution his heart yearns for."

"I have heard," exclaimed Lorimer, "that you have an idea of entering some foreign service."

"You have not been misinformed, then."

"But have you considered, John, the crime of joining with the enemies of your country?"

"Those whom I shall join," replied the other, "are brethren of our own. The Americans are now at war with England, and I will give them my services against a country that I no longer love."

"And so, because a paltry fellow like this Justice Gripple has offended you, the land of your birth is to be deserted for ever, and your sword drawn against those whom it was your duty to protect."

"You do not recollect the injuries I have received, Lorimer," answered John, sorrowfully. "Think of the fate that has befallen my sister, and the cruel act that has driven my widowed mother to become a houseless wanderer. These were the acts of Lord Dalmeny; yet when I asked for justice against the oppressor, I was treated like a felon, and condemned to be forced on board a vessel, as if I was the party who had committed all these wrongs I complain of."

"But, having escaped from these fellows, your best course will be to leave this place as soon as possible; your absence will create no great deal of surprise, and after a short time you may return without fear of further persecution."

"And think you I can ever consent to go sneaking about the country like one who has committed a great crime, and is afraid of the consequences?" asked John, haughtily. "I have been wronged most cruelly, and never will I cease to hunt the monster until I have revenged the injuries he has inflicted upon those who are dearest to me."

"His own conscience will be the severest punishment that can be inflicted on your oppressor," replied Hugh Lorimer; "let him pursue his own evil course for the present, and, depend on it, a time will soon come when he will be the prey of such harrowing thoughts as will serve to embitter the remainder of his days. This surely ought to be sufficient revenge for you, and thus the disgrace of fighting against your native land may be avoided."

"There is no disgrace in joining a good cause," answered John; "the Americans are a brave people, and will not fail to reward those who draw the sword in their defence. At any rate, I have never been wronged by them, and if I join their cause, I may hereafter have it in my power to procure that vengeance which I so ardently long for."

"Nay, let me again implore you to reflect a litttle ere you resolve upon this fatal project."

"I have reflected," answered John, "and my resolution is irrevocable; I linger but to take farewell of my mother, and when that is done, a few more hours will serve to take me from a country that has proved so utterly unworthy of my regard."

"You are determined, then, to do an act that will hand down your name with odium to the latest posterity?" exclaimed Hugh Lorimer.

"There is no fear of that," answered John; "for honour is to be gained by bravery on whichever side a man is inclined to fight. Besides, let those who blame me remember the provocation I have received; let them recollect that I had injuries to avenge, and that I might never have been tempted to take part against my country but for the injustice I have this day endured. Here I am no longer safe, for the myrmidons of the law are by this time in search of me, and unless I quit this place of my own accord, I shall be forced on board the ship that now lies anchored in yonder bay. The thought of this has served to confirm me in my resolution, and no persuasion will ever induce me to swerve from the determination I have come to."

"But thus far you have not lost you honour," replied Hugh Lorimer. "People will be ready enough to acknowledge that you have been wronged, and whilst they execrate the tyranny that has driven you from a once happy home, they will pity the victim who has fallen for a time through the evil machinations of a powerful foe."

"I demand no man's pity," answered John, haughtily; "justice is all I seek, and since it has been denied me by those who have the means of punishing the author of my wrongs, I will take the affair in my own hands, and future ages shall acknowledge that I procured for myself an ample vengeance."

"Aye," answered Hugh, "but you will not obtain for yourself the respect of those whose esteem you might otherwise have procured."

"That I care not for," replied the other coldly; "my own injuries will be avenged, and in that respect, at least, I shall be satisfied to my heart's content."

"But your mother will be left behind, and she will have to endure the scorn and reproaches of those who will call you a traitor to your country."

"Let them beware how they say aught that may offend their neighbour," exclaimed John; "let them beware, I say, for a short time hence I will return to my native land, and then woe unto those who may have given me cause for anger! They shall find me a scourge, and bitterly shall they rue the hour that they offended one who is far dearer to me than my own life!"

"All this you may do," replied Hugh Lorimer; "but do not forget that you may chance to fall into the hands of those who will adjudge you to an ignominious death for the deed you thus contemplate with exultation."

"Aye, I am aware of all that," answered John Ruthven; "I know that my enemies will be glad to hurl upon me their fiercest wrath, but let that be as it may, I shall, at least, have the satisfaction of knowing that my own revenge will have been fully accomplished."

By this time they had reached the ruins of his late home, where the

Widow Ruthven was seen gazing with silent grief upon the blackened walls within which she had passed so many of her happiest hours. Indeed, so deeply were her thoughts occupied, that she heard not the approach of the young men, and it was not till her son had come within a few paces of her and spoken, that she became aware of his presence; then, with a cry of joyful surprise, she sprang forward, and throwing herself into his arms, exclaimed,—

"Ah! my son, my dear John, you have come to bring me news of your sister Effie. She has been discovered and will soon be restored to us."

"Indeed, mother," replied the young man, "I know no more of her now than I did the first moment that she was carried away from us. All I know is that Lord Dalmeny is the villain who has robbed us of our dearest treasure, and that I will be revenged for it at the very earliest opportunity that offers."

"But, alas! she is in the hands of villains, my son, and I fear you will not be able to rescue her."

"Be comforted, my dear mother," answered John, "for bad as her situation is, there are yet some who will perish in her defence. The men amongst whom she is thrown are, it is true, smugglers, but they are many of them neighbours of our's, and will protect her from the villain who has employed them to carry her away."

"In that case," cried the widow, "why did they engage themselves in this cruel business?"

"That is a question," replied John, "that I can hardly answer. It is likely, however, that they saw no other way of rescuing her from the hands of Lord Dalmeny, and that they have taken her where he will have but little chance of finding her. Besides, they are under the command of Cap-

No. 20.

tain Starkie, who we know to be a man of violent passions, and it is likely he might deliberately murder all those who refuse to obey his orders."

"Then I fear, John, she has little reason to hope for favour or protection where all are under the subjection of a man like Captain Starkie. He, as you remember, was once a suitor of your sister's, and when she refused to listen to his propositions of marriage, he swore she should be his in spite of any opposition that might be offered him."

"But it is likely enough we may meet together sooner than he expects," replied John.

"What mean you by these words, my son?" asked the dame, anxiously; "you speak of meeting with Captain Starkie ere long, and yet we know he is now sailing with his prize on the broad bosom of the ocean."

"I know it," replied John Ruthven; "but I will follow him there, and should our vessels chance to come near each other, I will pursue him till I have destroyed the villain who has thus dared to become the guilty instrument of Lord Dalmeny's treachery."

"Alas! John," cried the widow, in despair, "am I then doomed to lose you as well as my daughter?"

"There is no help for it, mother," replied the young man. "Fate urges me on with resistless force, and I should be unworthy the name of man were I to hesitate for a moment when my sister's wrongs call aloud upon me to redress them. I am driven to adopt the course I have spoken of, and let those who have made me what I now am, take upon themselves the blame of that which will follow."

"Nay," exclaimed the widow earnestly, "take time to consider ere you have gone too far."

"And what time have I for consideration?" asked John; "is not my sister torn from us by the hands of ruthless villains, whilst I myself am in momentary fear of falling into the power of those from whom I have only lately escaped?"

"Escaped, John!" cried his mother; "have you, then, also been the victim of our enemies designs?"

"I have."

"And what cause have you given them for persecuting you, my dear John?"

"The only cause I know of," replied the young man, "is, that I went to Lord Dalmeny and demanded satisfaction for the injuries he has done us. But the villain only laughed at my complaints, and when, at length, I urged him to defend his life, we were interrupted, and the whole blame of the affair thrown upon myself."

"And you have thus rendered yourself liable to punishment for provoking a deadly feud with Lord Dalmeny?"

"I have so, mother, and narrowly escaped the doom awarded against me by Justice Gripple," replied the young man. "They would have sent me on board of the king's ships, which is now lying in the bay, but I contrived to escape from my guards, in order that I might see you once more ere I leave this place for some time to come."

"Must you, then, really leave us, John?"

"There is no help for it, mother; I am in danger of falling again into the hands of my foes, and should I do so a second time, there is little chance that they would suffer me to escape again. You see, therefore, the necessity for immediately taking my departure, lest I should become a prisoner to those who are eagerly seeking my destruction."

"He speaks truly," observed Hugh Lorimer, who had hitherto been a silent auditor of the preceding conversation; "he is in danger if he should chance to remain here, though I should be glad if you have influence enough to prevail on him to abandon the design he at present entertains."

" You know his designs, then ?"

" I do."

" Are they such as will bring dishonour upon his name ?"

" Aye, the blackest dishonour."

" You hear his words, John," cried the widow, anxiously ; " he tells me that which fills my soul with apprehension, and I would hear from your own lips whether you can deny his words ?"

" I deny nothing," replied the young man ; " Hugh Lorimer speaks, I dare say, as a friend, and he is at liberty to tell whatever he knows as to my determination."

" Tell me, Hugh," exclaimed the widow, almost distracted by her fears —" tell me, where is he going, and what are the pursuits that take him from hence ?"

" His present destination is, I believe, America," answered Lorimer, " and, if I may judge from the words that have fallen from his lips, he has some idea of enlisting in their cause against his own country."

" Is this true, John ?" demanded his mother ;—" does your friend truly state your intentions when he says that you are going to turn a traitor to your native land ?"

" He does," replied the young man ;—" this is no longer a place for me, and I will go where I may have some chance of attaining the eminence I aspire to."

" Eminence !" cried the widow Ruthven ; " and have you, then, forgotten that your name will become a bye-word for dishonour, and that future generations will mention it only as belonging to a man who forgot all other ties that he might rank himself on the side of his country's enemies ?"

" What country have I got ?" demanded John ; " am I not compelled to flee from it as if I had committed a heinous offence that deserved the severest punishment ?"

" There is no occasion to flee, John," replied the widow ; " all that is passed may be forgiven, and it is even possible that the dark clouds which at present obscure our happiness may give way to the sunshine of which we have thus long been deprived."

" Can my sister be restored to the home from whence heartless villany has forced her ?"

" I hope so," replied the widow ; " at any rate, I have spoken to Lady Margaret Dalmeny, and she has promised to use her utmost influence with her son to restore our beloved Effie to my arms."

" And our cottage," observed John ; " you see its black and tottering ruins before you, and yet can talk of future happiness as if we had never felt the iron grasp of oppression."

" My dear John," replied his mother, " I came hither to gaze upon and mourn over the desolation that has fallen upon our house. I behold its ruins, and yet, melancholy as the sight is, there is one consolation in the midst of all the wretchedness that surrounds us."

" And what is that, mother ?"

" Our cottage, John, is to be rebuilt on its old site, and in exactly the same form as it stood ere the ruthless hand of man levelled it with the dust."

" Aye !—and who has told you this, mother ?"

" The Lady Agnes Drummond."

" And how knows she this ?"

" Because she has obtained permission from Lord Dalmeny to rebuild our cottage at her own expense, and upon whatever part of the domains she may think proper. You may, therefore, judge, John, that he has repented his former violence, and let me hope you will now change the determination to leave your native land."

"It is in vain that you ask me, mother, for never will I again seek shelter beneath any roof that owns Lord Dalmeny for its master. Besides, I have told you that I am in danger here, that men are hunting after me, as if I had committed some terrible crime, and should I remain here much longer, you may chance to see me dragged away by the officers of justice to a prison."

"Nay, there is no likelihood of it," replied the Widow Ruthven, "for Lady Margaret Dalmeny has promised to obtain your pardon from her son, and, therefore, you can have no further reason for refusing to stay with me during the brief time that remains to you in this world."

"It almost breaks my heart to refuse you," exclaimed John, in a tone of deep emotion, "and yet I feel that nothing which can be urged will ever prevail on me to change the project I have formed. This land is no longer a home for me; nay, my mind has been made up to quit it, and at this moment a boat, well manned, lies waiting my signal behind yonder point."

With these words John applied a small whistle to his mouth, and blew a shrill tone that was instantly answered, and almost at the same moment a boat filled with men darted round the promontory he had spoken of. As its keel was heard grating upon the shore, Ruthven threw his arms round his almost fainting mother, and kissing her pale cheek, gave her to the care of his friend, Hugh Lorimer, and then breaking away from them, darted down the steep declivity with the speed of an antelope. In a short time he was on board the boat, which was immediately rowed towards a vessel that lay at no great distance off. As Ruthven ascended the side of the vessel, loud huzzas could be heard from those who seemed to be expecting his arrival, and directly afterwards, the anchor being weighed, the ship was wafted away, and in less than half an hour not a trace of her was to be seen by those who had been so sorrowfully watching her departure.

CHAPTER XX.

"There cannot be a pinch in death
More sharp than this.
Should we be taking leave as long a term
As we have yet to live, the loathness
To depart would grow."   CYMBELINE.

TWELVE months passed away after John Ruthven had left his native land, and Lord Dalmeny was still the same reckless, daring villain that he had ever been. Occasionally he was absent from his ancestral halls for weeks together, and none knew whither he had gone, or what was the business that led him from his home. Lady Margaret Dalmeny showed evident symptoms of uneasiness at the increasing waywardness of his disposition, and many were the anxious hours that she passed in pondering over the conduct of that son who seemed destined to bring disgrace and ruin upon the family. Yet her anguish was confined within her own bosom, and none knew the secret thoughts that were preying upon her heart, and bringing her slowly to that grave where alone she could hope for that peace which was denied her while living.

Even Lady Agnes was not aware of the full effect of the grief which was thus tormenting her kind protectress. She was aware, indeed, that she felt deeply the wild conduct of her son; but she believed that time would assuage her sorrows, and anxious as she was not to remind her of them, she seldom mentioned any circumstance which might serve to open afresh those wounds which she trusted would ere long be healed. The frequent occasions of Lord Dalmeny's absence was to her a source of much self-gratulation, for it released her from the necessity of being frequently in his society, and she even began to entertain some hopes that he would, in the course of time, cease to regard her in the same light he had been accustomed to do. Still, however, when he was at the castle he took every opportunity to throw himself in her way, but his language was seldom that of flattery, and at times there was a sarcastic vein in his conversation that almost proved he would not be sorry to find occasion for releasing himself from an engagement from one who, he could not but see, held him in abhorrence.

As we have said before, twelve months had passed away since John Ruthven had left the shores of his native land an angry and disappointed man. Lady Agnes had often thought of him, but rarely mentioned his name, for strange rumours respecting his course of life had reached her ears, and she was unwilling that it should be thought she felt an interest in the man who, it was said, had linked himself with pirates. One evening, however, as she was sitting with Lord Dalmeny on the battlements of the castle, which overlooked the sea, her thoughts were again fixed on the wanderer, and almost unconscious of what she was saying, she inquired of his lordship whether any news had lately been heard of his former enemy, John Ruthven.

"Your ladyship's consideration," replied Dalmeny, with a sneer that was only half suppressed, "does too much honour to a worthless villain who is not satisfied with turning traitor to his country, but he must needs become a leader of pirates, and thus place himself beyond the pale of civilized society."

"I have heard such rumours of him," replied Lady Agnes, in a tone of equal severity with his own; "but John Ruthven is not without enemies, and it may suit them to raise reports to his prejudice, even as they did ere he was driven an exile from his country."

"That, my fair cousin, I know nothing about," answered his lordship, with more good humour than he had hitherto shewn; "but had John Ruthven been a better man, it would not have been in the power of his enemies to make him leave Scotland; I would have been his friend, as you must be well aware; yet his pride urged him to repulse my well meant kindness, and now he has become just what his natural disposition best fits him for."

"And does your lordship think never to see him again?" asked Lady Agnes.

"To speak the truth, I have hardly given the subject a thought," he replied. "People do say, indeed, that he has vowed vengeance against all belonging to the neighbourhood, and that he will come some day with fire and sword to burn and destroy all within his reach. But that was a vain boast, my gentle cousin, and you may take my word for it he will never venture to show himself where a rope and a gallows awaits him on his first arrival to fulfil his threat."

"Make not too sure of that, my lord," answered the lady; "for John Ruthven rarely breaks his word or promise, and if he has once vowed to revenge himself for former wrongs, you may be sure he will never rest satisfied till he has accomplished all that he has sworn to. We shall see him yet, and I shudder to think of the blood that will be spilt when next he sets foot upon the land of his birth. You have more cause to fear his coming than any one else, for to your lordship he owes his exile and disgrace, and dreadful, I fear, will be his vengeance should it ever be your luckless chance to meet together!"

"Your ladyship's words are oracular," observed Dalmeny, with his usual coolness; "but let me hope that in this instance at least, you will prove false in your predictions. I wear a sword, Lady Agnes, "and have a stout arm to wield it, and should John Ruthven ever meet meet me as a foe, we will never part till either he or I have bit the dust. At all events, the chances between us will be equal, and better would it be for him to perish by my hand than that his body should rot upon a gibbet as a warning to all future traitors."

"And why should you wish such a fate to the man you have deeply injured?" asked Lady Agnes in a tone of reproach. "But for you he might have been happy and contented in his own country, and following the peaceful occupation that gave bread to his forefathers. But you have wrought him all this mischief and yet can exult with fiendish joy in the reflection that a death of dishonour will terminate his hapless career."

"Why am I ever to bear the blame of his misdoings?" asked Dalmeny, sullenly. "Did I ever seek to injure him, or was it at my instigation that he committed the deeds which ended in his being obliged to flee his country,"

"Those are questions, my lord, that you can answer much better than myself," she replied. "All I know is, that you were ever the bitter foe of John Ruthven, though you sought to conceal your enmity beneath the mask of friendship. Even he was aware of your evil designs against him, and he would have taken care to foil them long ago, but that he regarded your mother, and forbore to commit an act which would have embittered the remainder of her days."

"And perhaps," said Lord Dalmeny, with a sneer, "he was somewhat checked by the great respect in which he held your ladyship. Nay, frown not, my fair cousin, for 'tis truth I speak, and there are other persons besides myself that think John Ruthven had presumption enough to hope that he might one day wed the peerless Lady Agnes Drummond."

Her eyes sunk beneath his steady gaze as he uttered these words, and scarcely knowing how to reply, she instantly changed the subject of conversation.

"Your lordship is ever too much for me when sarcasm comes to aid your argument," she replied; "and now, as we have spoken quite enough of John Ruthven, perhaps you will oblige me by saying what has become of his sister, who you ordered to be borne away and carried off to sea?"

"It is but little I have heard of her," answered Dalmeny; "and even that little is veiled in mystery. It is said, however, that Captain Starkie had the insolence to fall in love with her because he knew I was not present to punish his presumption. And as he made no secret of his passion, the rest of the crew thought proper to follow his example. The poor wench was thus sorely beset with lovers, and finding there was no other way to escape them, she jumped out of the cabin window, and of course found a grave at the bottom of the ocean."

"Horrible!" cried Lady Agnes, shuddering; "and you, my lord, can speak thus coldly of this dreadful event, though you have the poor girl's death to answer for! Think of it as you will, my lord, this act of your's was a murder, and the sin lies upon your guilty soul!"

"Psha!" he exclaimed impatiently; "am I to bear the blame of her death? Was it any fault of mine that she leaped into the water through some mad notions of her own?"

"It was by your orders that she was dragged away from home," cried Lady Agnes, reproachfully. "She found herself among men of lawless habits, and seeing the danger of her situation, preferred death by her own hands to dishonour."

"Well, turn and twist the story which way you will, it cannot be said that I was instrumental in her death," he said. "Nay, I would rather anything had happened than this, and should Captain Starkie and I ever meet again, he will dearly answer for the conduct which urged Effie Ruthven to the rash deed. So you see, cousin, I am not so bad as you imagined, and you may yet have to acknowledge that Lord Dalmeny is not the villain that he has been represented."

"And what answer can you give her brother when he calls upon you to account for the unfortunate victim of your violence?" demanded Lady Agnes.

"Why, as that is a thing that may never happen," he replied, "I have not given it a thought. Ruthven may talk about returning to seek for vengeance, but take my word for it, he will never revisit a place where he is so likely to meet the reward of his treason. Every man's hand would be raised against him, and the certainty of that will be quite enough to keep him at a safe distance from me."

"You know not the man you speak of," answered Lady Agnes. "He thinks less of danger than you do, my lord, and should he have an opportunity to revenge his sister's wrongs, he will suffer no selfish thoughts to deprive him of the vengeance his sister's fate so loudly calls for."

"But, this story of her death may be false," replied Dalmeny. "At any rate we have no other evidence of it than that of Captain Starkie and his crew, and it is by no means unlikely that they have spread the rumour for purposes of their own. She may yet live, and in that case Ruthven may have her restored to him, if he only thinks proper to make application."

"And that will be a poor consolation to a fond brother," answered Lady Agnes. "Besides, he has now become as a raging tiger that thirsts for blood; persecution and injustice have, it seems, forced him to become a leader among pirates, and heading, as he does, those men of blood and rapine, he will not be easily intimidated from landing on this coast to carry fire and bloodshed among those that he conceives have wronged him. You, my lord, are one of those he has least reason to respect, and heavy would his wrath fall, should he chance to meet the man who has driven him to his present reckless career."

"I am not one of those who either preach or profess virtue," exclaimed Lord Dalmeny, "but you must talk a long time, my pretty cousin, ere you convince me that I have anything to do with the step he has taken. Ruthven turned pirate to suit his own restless disposition, and now, if all I hear is true, he has joined the Americans in their war for independence against this country. The latter act is at least his own, and should he ever be caught on our English soil, he will meet that fate which he justly merits."

"And has he obtained rank in their service?" she asked.

"He has had the command of a ship given him," replied Lord Dalmeny, "and to do the fellow justice, he has shown some judgment and gallantry in the new profession he has adopted. Already several of our vessels have been taken by him and his crew, and so well satisfied are the American's with his conduct, that Congress has passed a vote of thanks to him, and recommended his advance on the first opportunity that offers."

"What you have been telling me, my lord," she exclaimed, "convinces me more than ever that Ruthven will be here sooner than you expect. He thirsts for revenge against those who have wronged him, and woe unto those upon whom his anger slights. You, Lord Dalmeny, have much to fear from, and therefore do I caution you to fly ere it may be too late. He may be here ere many hours have passed away, and should you be near, you will meet your death at a time when you have much need for repentance. Depart, therefore, from the castle ;—let not a moment be lost in idle deliberation, for the moment of dread may be near, and what arm stretched forth in your defence would avail against the fury of your foe ?"

"Think you I am a coward, Lady Agnes ?" he asked bitterly, "that you would bid me fly from a worm that has once been beneath my heel, and may be so again should he dare show his face again in the country that no longer owns him !"

"Would you face the avenger of a sister's wrongs ?" asked Lady Agnes, reproachfully.

"I fear no man," answered his lordship in a tone of resolution. "Ruthven knows that I never yielded superiority to him, and where he to appear before me this moment, I would never part from him till one of us was laid dead at the feet of the conqueror."

"Oh, speak not so, my lord !" exclaimed his faithful attendant Ronald, who, as he approached, had overheard the latter words. "John Ruthven has a name that few men would covet, and I have just heard that his ship was seen, not two days since, sailing towards this coast."

"You hear that, my Lord Dalmeny !" cried Lady Agnes, alarmed at the intelligence she had just heard ; the avenger comes, and yet you would madly stay here to meet that fate which he has sworn to accomplish."

"Is this news true ?" demanded Lord Dalmeny, of his vassal.

"It is," answered the other.

"And is the vessel he sails in a frigate or a man-of-war ?"

"A frigate, my lord."

"How many guns carries she ?"

"That I have not heard."

"What number of men ?"

"I know not that either," replied Ronald ; "but they say she carries more than the usual number of men, and there are some desperate fellows among them, too. There's Charlie Johnston, the smuggler, that used to be down at the cave yonder, and Robert Deverel, the poacher, that they say has slain as many men as heath-cocks ; and what's worse than all, Andrew Foster has joined him, and I believe he owes as little good-will to your lordship as does Ruthven himself. By the by, they call him Red Ruthven, now, for he has spilt much blood in this new cause that he's taken up,— more shame for him ; seeing that he's fighting for an enemy against his own countrymen."

"But let it be remembered," interposed Lady Agnes, "that Ruthven was not a traitor from choice. He was driven hence by persecution ; Scotland no longer afforded him home or shelter, and if he has found that kindness among strangers that was denied him among his countrymen, who can wonder that he has taken up arms in their cause. He has been driven to do wrong, and woe upon those whose malignity forced him to become an exile from his home."

"You are still severe upon me, Agnes," exclaimed Lord Dalmeny ; "and yet I know not why you should take part with a traitor like this, against one whose worst crimes are trifling in comparison with those of a man who could sell his country because a few may have offended him. Ruthven, I say, is a villain, and my most earnest wish is that it may be my lot to punish him for the base part he has acted."

"I have no more kindness for him than your lordship has," said Ronald, "and though I have not drawn a sword or handled a musket for many a

long year, I shall not forget my duty should these Americans, with Red
Ruthven at their head, make their appearance here."

"Do you think," asked Lady Agnes, "there is any truth in the report
you have heard?"

"I have no doubt about it," answered Ronald, "for the vessel was seen
by the crews of some of our fishing boats, and as the wind was favourable
there is no doubt we shall have them in sight within a very little time.
And if every man is of my way of thinking, when they do come upon our
coast, they shall have such a reception that the Americans shall never send
another ship to this part of our island."

With these words Ronald left them, and both Lord Dalmeny and his fair
cousin were too much occupied with their own thoughts to speak on the
subject which threatened them with so much danger. Lady Agnes was
alarmed at the news which she had just heard, for of Ruthven's approach
there could be no doubt, and equally certain was it that his return to that
place was caused by his desire for the revenge he had determined to inflict
upon those who had driven him from home and country. She feared also
that the destruction of the castle would be among the first objects of his
visit, and fearing lest Lady Margaret Dalmeny should perish in the flames,
she was about to implore his lordship that he would convey his mother to
a place of safety, when her eye detected the white sails of a vessel in the
distance, and gazing upon it for a few minutes with intense anxiety, she
felt but too certain that it was making towards that part of the coast.

Lord Dalmeny's attention was also attracted towards the same spot, and
it was easily to be seen by the constantly changing expression of his countenance, that he watched the object with no less anxiety than his cousin.
He at once conjectured that it was the vessel commanded by Ruthven,
and knowing how little the castle was prepared for any attack that might

No. 21

be made upon it by armed men, he was about to hurry away for the purpose of giving the necessary directions to his servants and dependents, when he saw another vessel that was evidently giving chase to it, and as the second one shewed the British colours, there was some hope that the daring invader of his native land would fall an easy prey to the bravery of our own gallant sailors.

The vessel they had first seen now made towards the bay, and by a series of manœuvres got the advantage of the one that was in pursuit. The English, however, shewed no inclination to be dispirited by this circumstance, and though night was fast closing in, preparations were instantly made on both sides for an engagement. At length a discharge of cannon announced that the battle had commenced, and from that moment the strife became terrible in the extreme. Even Lady Agnes watched it with an anxiety that made her regardless of her own safety, and she thought not of the peril she was in till Lord Dalmeny approached and offered to conduct her to a place where she would be less exposed to the cannon balls of the conflicting parties.

"Your lordship's advice is well meant, I have no doubt," she replied, "but I feel an irresistible desire to witness this conflict, even though I know the death and destruction that must be the consequence. Many a brave man that witnessed the setting of the sun will find a grave in yonder waters, ere the glorious orb again rises to shine upon the scene of blood and slaughter. The thought is, indeed, a sickening one, and yet I cannot leave the place till the noise of battle is hushed in silence."

"I have warned you of the danger, Agnes," he said, "and would still urge you to seek safety in your own chamber on the other side of the castle. But I see you are bent on seeing this mischief to an end, and, to say the truth, the scene is an exciting one, though little fitted for a young and delicate female."

Lady Agnes made no reply, for her soul was intent on the object before her, and regardless of the cannon balls that were flying about, she stood unmoved and fearless, as she gazed upon the strife that had now grown furious in the extreme. Nor was Lord Dalmeny a disinterested observer of what was going on, for he felt assured that Ruthven was the commander of the hostile vessel, whose appearance had first attracted his attention. Anxiously, therefore, did he look forward to the termination of an engagement that would either render his hatred rival an exulting conqueror, or drive him for ever from the coast which he had come to plunder and destroy. Much indeed depended upon the result of this conflict, and it was with dismay and disappointment that he saw the tide of battle turn in favour of the enemy. Still, however, the crew of the British vessel fought with the greatest courage and heroism, and there was yet a chance that they might retrieve the disadvantage of their situation, when a loud cry of horror was heard, and it became evident that the English ship was rapidly sinking. Lord Dalmeny watched the terrible scene with feelings that may be more easily imagined than described, and when at last he saw the hull sink beneath the waters, he turned away his head and looked towards the spot where Lady Agnes had been but a few moments before. She had, however, disappeared, and believing that in her terror she had hurried to her own chamber, he quitted the battlements, and proceeded to the apartment usually occupied by his mother, in order that he might soothe the alarm into which she must have been thrown by the unusual event which had passed within so short a distance from the castle.

But Lady Agnes, instead of seeking safety in her own chamber, had hurried down to the beach, that she might render assistance to any of the unfortunate seamen who might be washed ashore. On arriving at the place, she found crowds of the peasantry collected there; some instigated by a desire to afford aid to those who needed it, and others to help themselves to any portions of the foundered ship that were driven on the beach. There was much indeed to tempt the dishonesty of those who went there for the purpose of plunder, and several dead bodies were lying upon the beach, which, under the direction of Lady Agnes, were conveyed to an outbuilding belonging to the castle, where they were to remain till they could be decently interred. But no living being had yet reached the shore, and the trembling girl had almost despaired of saving even a single life, when a loud shout was heard from some of the people, and hurrying towards the spot where they were congregated, she, by the little light that remained, saw a man clinging to a spar, and urging his way to the shore with what strength remained to him. A reward was instantly offered to any that would assist in saving him, and no sooner was this made known than a number of men threw themselves into the water, and swimming towards the struggling mariner, succeeded in bringing him safely to the shore. The poor fellow was nearly exhausted; but being laid upon the beach a little brandy was administered, under the judicious direction of Lady Agnes, and in a short time the poor fellow was sufficiently restored to walk, with the aid of one of his preservers, to a cottage that was situated close by, where, being put to bed, the place was cleared of all strangers, and Lady Agnes returned to the castle to account to her protectress for her absence, and request such medicines and nourishment as were necessary for the man who had thus been rescued from the horrible fate that had befallen so many of his brave companions. These were immediately sent to the cottage, and having thus administered to the wants of a fellow creature, she retired to her own chamber, not so much to sleep as to think over the events of the day, and ponder upon the probable results of a victory in which she felt but too certain John Ruthven had been concerned.

At an early hour on the following morning she again visited the cottage, and found the mariner so far recovered that he had been able to leave his bed, and partake, with his widowed hostess, the humble breakfast it had been her care to provide for him. In an instant he recognised in Lady Agnes, the generous female who had been the chief means of saving his life, and rising from his seat, he, in a rough and homely language, expressed his gratitude for the benefit she had conferred upon him, and offered to devote the remainder of his days in the service of her who had exhibited so much zeal to preserve him from a fate which had appeared to be inevitable. She, however, soon put an end to these expressions of gratitude, and turned the subject of conversation by inquiring about the battle which she had witnessed on the preceding evening.

"Why, as for a battle ma'am," he replied, "it was not so much of a one as a mere looker on might fancy. The skirmish was a sharp and pretty one enough, and all my brave companions have perished by the sinking of the ship just as we were preparing to give the enemy a broadside that might have turned the victory on our own side. But what's done can't be helped, and the remembrance of this defeat will only serve to make our countrymen the more determined when next they have a rub with the enemy again."

"Who were they you fought against?" asked Lady Agnes, anxious; "I mean, were they French or American?"

"They wern't French for certain," answered the sailor; "as we shouldn't have had half the trouble with them, nor have lost the battle as we did. They fought under the American colours, but if I might give my opinion about it, I should say they must have been some of our discontented English people that can't be satisfied with our own laws, and must enlist with the enemy to fight against their own countrymen."

"Know you who commanded them?" asked Lady Agnes, trying in vain to conceal the breathless anxiety with which she availed his reply.

"Ah, ma'am!" answered the sailor; "that's just what I should like to know myself. But, be who he might, I never saw such a dare devil fellow as he was in the whole course of my life. He was the first to board our ship and cleared our decks in no time, for our captain fell by a pistol shot that he fired into his hull, and in the confusion that followed, we retreated like so many frightened sheep. At last, however, we rallied a bit, but by that time it was of no use, for he had then swarms of his own fellows about him, and as they knew what would be their fate if they happened to be made prisoners, they fought with such desperation, that the deck was soon covered with our own dead. It was an awful sight, ma'am, and yet I believe, if the ship hadn't sunk at the time it did, we should have driven the fellows overboard, and gained a victory for our country, instead of losing it to those American chaps."

"Should you know their captain if you were to see him again?" asked Lady Agnes.

"Aye, that I should, ma'am," he replied; "for he gave me good cause to remember him as long as I live."

"Was he an Englishman?"

"I should say he was by his courage," answered the sailor; "and yet we would hardly think so brave a fellow would turn traitor to his country. But he was not an American I'm certain, or he'd never have shown the courage he did in that action. However, I shall not be likely to forget him, and if he and I ever happen to meet again, whether it be in battle or otherwise, I shall not fail to pay him off our old scores."

"Nay," exclaimed the ancient dame, who acted the part of his hostess; "do not seek vengeance for the past, for your own life has been spared in the moment of peril, and surely that might teach you the mercy you owe to your fellow-creatures. The man you speak of is a countryman of my own, and if he has forgotten his duty, it is not for such as us to bear the sword of justice. Spare him then I say, or I shall curse the hour when you were saved from the waters that yawned for your destruction."

"You know something of this man it seems?" returned the sailor, with surprise.

"I do," she replied; "for who else should it be but John Ruthven, who was forced to flee from Scotland because she was no longer a home for him."

"John Ruthven!" cried Lady Agnes, faintly; "are you sure it is he, dame? And yet why should I doubt it, since where is the man that will not vengeance against those who have oppressed and injured him? Are you certain, I again ask, that the enemy's captain was John Ruthven?"

"Aye, my lady," replied the woman, "I am as certain of it as that I now see you standing before me. My nephew went in his boat while the battle was raging, and there, sure enough, he saw John Ruthven, sword in hand, and his clothes drenched in the gore that had flowed from the enemies he had slain. And who can wonder at his fighting against his own country since he was driven forth to become a wanderer and an exile upon the face of the earth?"

"I can answer for his devilish courage," said the sailor; "for though I have been used to battle since I was a boy, yet never saw I a man so like a demon as this was. Our guns were aimed at him in vain, and those that ventured to approach him, sword in hand, did so only to meet that fate which had laid low so many of our brave fellows. I like not your traitors that turn against their own country, but this man seems to have been driven away, and if ever he made a vow to revenge himself he seems in a fair way to make his enemies tremble for their misdeeds towards him."

Lady Agnes had heard sufficient to convince her that her worst fears were realized, and having desired the dame to continue her hospitable attentions to the object of her present care, she went forth from the cottage, sorrowing for the cause that had robbed Scotland of a brave man, and converted him into a curse that would be remembered even by the latest posterity.

CHAPTER XXI.

Fantastic passions' maddening brawl,
And shame and terror over all!
  Deeds to be hid which were not hid,
    Which, all confused, I could not know
  Whether I suffered, or I did;
    Fall seemed guilt, remorse or woe;
My own or others, still the same,
Life stifling fear—soul stifling shame!

               COLERIDGE.

On the evening when these events occurred, the aged mother of Ruthven was seated at her cottage door, to watch the calm and gradual close of day, and to ponder over events which, though long passed by, were still thought of with anguish by the widow Ruthven. It is true a neat though small house had been erected, as near the site as possible to the one which had been burned down, on the night when poor Effie had been carried away by ruffian hands, and Lady Agnes had superintended the fitting of it up, till everything seemed to be so comfortable that she hoped the poor old dame would cease to remember the violence which had been committed towards her. But dame Ruthven could not forget that on the night in question she had been deprived of a son and daughter, and that she was now desolate, in spite of the kindly efforts that were made to render as light as possible the misfortunes she had endured. Joy seemed to have forsaken her heart for ever, and often would she sit, as now she did, gazing up the sea that lay widely spread before her, and wondering whether its waves would ever bear home to her the lost treasures, for whom she had never ceased to mourn.

On the evening in question she was more than usually pensive, for her thoughts still ran upon the object of her cares, and a sort of presentiment of approaching ill oppressed her heart. So occupied was she, indeed, in these reflections, that she saw not the vessels which had attracted the notice of Lord Dalmeny and his cousin, and she was unconscious of the threatening danger, till the loud thunder of the cannon roused her from the reverie into which she had fallen. In an instant she directed her glances towards the spot from whence the sound came, and terrified at the scene of blood and carnage that had commenced, she hastily rose, and hurrying from the porch, entered the cottage to shut out the dreadful sight which she shuddered to think upon. But the heavy roar of artillery still reached her ears, and falling upon her knees she earnestly besought the interposition of Heaven to stay the deadly strife which thus urged man to destroy his fellow creature.

At length the firing ceased, and once more she ventured to leave the cottage, but by this time evening had closed in, and a thick white smoke rested upon the spot where the battle had been raging, and stood like a veil to conceal the horrors which had there been perpetrated. Still, however, her mind could conceive all that had occurred, and sighing, as she thought of the many poor wretches now lying dead, but who an hour before had been in the full enjoyment of life and health, she returned to her lonely cot, and seating herself at a table, pored over those pages of Holy Writ, which at all times, and under all circumstances, afforded her the only consolation that had now been left her in the world. That night she sought not her usual rest in bed, and when the morning was far advanced she was still employed in the same religious occupation. At length, however, she was aroused by the raising of the door latch, and looking up she saw a figure advance, wrapped in a large clock and his brow shaded with his hat, which had evidently been disposed so as to conceal his features from observation. But a mother's instincts are quick, and springing from her seat she rushed forward with a wild cry of delight, and welcomed to the humble cot her long lost son.

"Welcome, welcome to me, my loved boy," she cried, "and may this hour unite us never more to be separated, till that moment when death tears me from a world which till now was as a cheerless desert. Deeply have I sorrowed for you, my son, till at length it seemed that we were never more to meet together, and then resigning myself to the sad destiny I yielded with submission to a destiny which brought with it grief and loneliness of heart. But you have grown darker, and your countenance looks full of care, which never was the case, dear John, ere you left Scotland to become a wanderer on the face of the earth."

"I have seen and endured much, mother, since you and I last saw each other," he replied. "Now, however, we have met again, and if it is your will we shall never part more."

"It is my will that we never part more, dear John," she replied; "but why are you thus armed with deadly weapons? Think you to meet with enemies here, that you have sword and pistols, as if foes were now to be met with where friends only dwelt before. No, boy, it is in vain you try to conceal them beneath your cloak, for mine eyes have already seen them, and much I grieve that you could not enter your mother's peaceful cot without weapons that have been made by man for the destruction of his fellow creatures."

"Arms, mother, are necessary for him whose profession is war," he replied. "I am now engaged in active service, and these pistols which seem so much to have alarmed you, are necessary in a time of war like the present."

"But not when you are visiting your mother's house," she said. "However, I will not find fault with thee, my son; so give me your cloak, for thou wilt stay with me awhile, and——"

At this moment Dame Ruthven uttered a scream of horror, for as she snatched from his shoulders the cloak which he wore, she perceived that his regimentals were not those which belonged to his own country.

"What means this, my son?" she cried, in a tone of mingled terror and reproach. "This dress belongs to the enemies of thy native land! I have heard that thou didst turn traitor to thy country, and when people whispered the rumour in my presence, I told them to their teeth they lied, for never thought I to see the hour when a child of mine stood the acknowledged hireling of his country's foes! Speak, John, if shame hath not tied thy tongue; speak, boy, I command thee, and say this is but some trick of thine to make me believe my love for thee has been thrown away upon a worthless rebel."

"Hear me, mother——"

"I will hear nothing from thee," she interruped, "unless thou canst, with unblushing cheek, declare that thou art not yet unworthy to be my son."

"Can my mother have forgotten the wrongs I have endured?" he asked. "Has the lapse of a few months served to take away the remembrance of wrongs which have been inflicted, and are yet unavenged? Was I not driven from home by the persecution of my enemies, and is it to be wondered at that I am now leagued with the common foe?"

"I have not forgotten the injuries you received, nor the act that drove thee an exile from your mother's roof," she replied. "All that I remember; but how do I see thee return to me now? Are not your hands stained with the blood of those who should have been as brothers to thee; and has not your sword been drawn within the last few hours against those whose only crime is that they were true and faithful to their sovereign? Fie upon thee, boy! and if thou canst not prove thyself free from the foul taint of treason, take thy departure from hence, and never more let me behold thy face."

"Be calm, my mother, and listen to me," he said. "My country now lies far from this place; America claims my allegiance, and from this time forth I will live and die in her service. I have come across the broad ocean that I might again behold thee, and, if my prayers could further my wishes, to prevail on thee to go back with me to a land where you will be honoured and respected. Come, mother, my ship lies at anchor not far off, and it was not without peril to myself that I have ventured to land upon a shore where all are enemies to me."

"I cannot curse you, John," she exclaimed; "and yet the remembrance that you were in last night's battle against those for whom your sword should have been drawn, makes me curse the hour when first I brought thee forth to be a blight upon my old age. You have broken and seared my heart, boy, and all I ask of thee is to depart in peace, and never again to present thyself before one whom thou hast dishonoured by thy base acts. Away, boy, and let none see thee, for I should blush to have it known that John Ruthven has boldly stood before his mother and confessed that he is a traitor."

"It is no secret, mother," he replied; "for my name is already known to your people as a scourge upon that element which till this time they have dared proudly call their own. The battle last night was none of my seeking; I came hither to take you back with me to the land of my adoption, and was pursued by one of the king's ships; an engagement was thus rendered necessary, and the gallantry of my crew secured a victory which will at once mortify your proud English, and exalt the growing fame of those whose uniform I now wear. So come with me, mother; bid farewell to this land, and follow me to that which will receive you with honour and esteem."

"And do they regard *you*, John?" she asked.

"They do," he replied; "for though I have not long been in their service, yet have I obtained victories that have done more for the securing their liberties than all the battles put together that they have fought on land."

"The greater your deeds," she answered, "the deeper in the shame that lights on you. Let the Americans fight their own battles and win independence if they can; it will be to their glory if they can do so: but is it not a shame for one like thee to take up arms and strike a blow at that country in which thou and thy forefathers were born?"

"These reproaches are all in vain," he said, "for the act you condemn has been done, and having once drawn my sword against England, I have thrown away the scabbard till an honourable peace has been concluded between the two countries. This country, however, can never be my home again, for the deed I have done will not be forgotten, and even if it were, I have now friends in America; and where could I so well enjoy the tranquillity of peace as in the land which I have aided to throw off her fetters ? Come with me, therefore, dear mother, and repine no more that I have thrown off my allegiance to a country from which I was thrust by the cruelty and oppression of my fellow men."

"Stay, boy," she said, irresolutely; "wait but till to-morrow, and after considering your proposition I shall be better able to say whether I can follow you to the land of the stranger."

"To-morrow night would see me in the hands of my enemies," he replied. "Already the country is up in arms about this victory that I have gained within musket shot of your shores; Lord Dalmeny and Justice Gripple both owe me a grudge for the slippery trick I played them before, and depend on it they will not give me another opportunity to escape should I chance to fall into their power. My gallant ship is ready to sail at a moment's notice, and if you will accompany me, we have a fair wind to carry us far enough off before my foes will have time to follow in pursuit."

"If I must give my answer now," she said, "it shall be to tell thee that I will not leave this place where I have dwelt from infancy even to the present day. Go, then, John,—or Red Ruthven, as men now call thee,— leave me, and I will endeavour to forget that I ever had a son that has brought sorrow and disgrace on my old age. Thou wert brought forth in affliction, boy, but never did I know what real anguish was till I saw thee in the garb of our enemies, and heard thee exult at having become a scourge to those whom it was thy duty to succour and protect. I will not curse thee; but my hope is, that this may be the last interview between a broken-hearted mother and the son that has infamy and dishonour on his name !"

"These are harsh words, mother," he said, "but hardly more so than I expected from one whose prejudices are against the course I have been driven to adopt. You have refused to go with me, and my own safety demands my immediate departure from a place where I can expect to find none but enemies. Still, however, though I may be far distant, I shall not cease to keep a watchful eye for your protection, and should any dare to harm the mother of John Ruthven, they shall find that though he may be far distant, yet has he still the power to strike down those that would harm the lonely and unprotected widow."

"There thou still showest thyself to be my son," she cried, "and now do I feel more bitterly the cause of that eternal separation that must take place between us."

"At least," he exclaimed, "you will do me the justice to admit that it was the persecution of my inveterate foes that compelled me to turn my sword against the country of my birth. I may have acted rashly—imprudently; but however that may be, the step has been taken, and it is now irrevocable. Farewell, then, and may Heaven spare you the affliction which I fear the course I have adopted has brought upon your heart."

As he spoke the latter words he hastened towards the door; but ere he had reached it, Lady Agnes entered the cottage and stood before him. For a moment his limbs seemed palsied at this sudden apparition, but quickly recovering himself, he said, tremulously,—

"My lady, you have arrived in time to witness the tears of one who seldom yields to the impulse of grief. I came hither on an errand of peace, but my mother has joined with my enemies, and instead of receiving her blessing, I have met with nought but reproaches for that step towards which fate has urged. But I am wasting time in idle words, for there are

foes abroad that would gladly capture so good a prize as John Ruthven, and I do but endanger myself by remaining after the refusal of my mother to accompany me to a foreign land. Before I go, however, you will, perhaps, take my hand in token that you have not judged of me so harshly as those do who know not the provocation I have received."

"I cannot take your hand," she said, stepping back with horror; "it is still stained with the blood of my countrymen, and though thou mayest triumph in the victory thou didst last night gain, I can regard it as nothing less than a murder committed under the most aggravated circumstances. You have heard me, sir, and be assured that my voice has but recorded the opinions of all honourable persons."

"I need no words of thine to assure me that such is indeed the fact," he replied; "my mother has already said as much, and I myself feel that I should justly deserve these reproaches had it not been for the cruel oppression that drove me forth a homeless exile from the land of my birth. You feel that I have done wrong, and join the common cry in calling me a traitor to my country."

"And what worse name couldst thou be called?" asked Lady Agnes. "Does it not render you unworthy the friendship of your fellow men?— Hast thou not stained thy hands in the blood of thine own people, and canst thou ever wipe away the foul spot that will prove a mark by which all men shall know and loath thee?"

"That may be," answered Ruthven; "and yet there may be arguments brought forward on the other side of the question. I was not the aggressor in this quarrel with my country, and even you must admit that never did man receive greater injuries than were inflicted upon me by those who sought my ruin. But you know all the argument I could bring forward,

No. 22.

and much as you may condemn my actions, yet would Lady Agnes be the last that would wish me to suffer either death or imprisonment."

"The latter I do not wish thee," she replied; "but death in battle is a punishment for thy crime which none could regret. May such be your fate, though, Heaven knows, the chances are that your end will not be so honourable a one."

"You are still severe upon me, and reflect not that I already endure tortures which my enemies would glory at did they know how much I suffer. To part from my mother is affliction enough, and the more so when I know that she will let me leave her in anger. You, too, whose regard I once esteemed beyond all price, now despise me; and knowing that I would go forth and forget in the active duties of life those miseries which are too much for endurance."

"I once thought you possessed a noble and independent spirit that would one day raise you in the esteem of your fellow men," answered Lady Agnes. "I respected you, and even now would have prevailed on you to throw aside your errors, and by submission to the king's will, deserve the pardon which there is no doubt he would have granted. But I now see that you are bent upon persuing the path of dishonour, and my advice is that you leave this place ere you are found here by those who will triumph in having captured the traitor, John Ruthven."

"You think, then," he said, "that no action, however gallant it may be, will serve to wipe away from my name what you conceive to be a foul stain?"

"If spilling more human blood may do it," she answered, "there is little doubt you will achieve what the world, in its blindness, calls honour and renown. You may take ships, destroy towns, and thus earn fame. But who will envy you, save the bad man whose ambition would lead him to the same end through the same means? Rouse yourself, John Ruthven, and prove your honour by breaking the sword you now wear—cast aside and burn the garb which now disgraces you — swear allegiance to the monarch you have insulted, and when you have done all this your treason will be wiped away, and you will rise to that eminence in your country's service which you in vain seek for among those who have taken up arms against us."

Ruthven was evidently moved by these words, but he had not time to answer them before footsteps were heard approaching, and as no means of flight were heard in any other direction, he sprung into an inner chamber, where, however, he was quickly followed by a soldier, who, accompanied by three or four others, at that moment entered the cottage. In another instant the report of a pistol was heard, and others of the military were rushing to the assistance of their comrades, when Dame Ruthven, throwing herself between them and the inner chamber, earnestly besought her son to fly whilst he had yet an opportunity. Nor were her entreaties made in vain, for Ruthven immediately sprung through the window, and urging his way towards a deep ravine, continued his flight till he felt pretty well assured that his pursuers had for the present lost scent of him.

The soldiers gave utterance to the rage in curses loud and deep, and returning to the room they would have inflicted summary vengeance upon the widow Ruthven had she not already quitted the cottage and pursued the path which she knew her son would take towards the cavern by the sea side.

The soldiers also had followed towards the same spot, though by another direction, and with such speed did they urge their way, that Ruthven began to see that all hope of escape by flight was at an end; he, therefore, stooped down behind a thick bush, and having got his pistols in readiness for any sudden need, he waited with tolerably calmness any attack that might be made upon him by the enemy. In a short time, he heard the voices of two of the soldiers as they approached, and from their conversation he became convinced that he would not be suffered to escape till he had had a conflict with them in which he would have to encounter odds that rendered his chance of escape extremely doubtful.

"He can't be far off," said one of the men, "for I caught a glimpse of him just now, and then all of a sudden he disappeared, as if he had sunk through the earth."

"He must have the devil's luck and his own too, if he gets clear away from us," said the sergeant; "for we know he's close by, hiding himself somewhere, and I'll stay here all day but I'll find him yet."

"Take my advice and leave him to his fate," said the other; "he's a desperate chap, they say, when he's put upon his mettle, and if we lose our lives in this affair, it will be a very poor consolation for our wives to be told that we fell in the performance of our duty."

"You may do as you like about it," answered the other, "but I've sworn to take Red Ruthven dead or alive, and I'll never go back to quarter's with a lame story that we have had the misfortune to miss him."

"But suppose he shoots you?"

"In that case I shall die in the discharge of my duty," replied the sergeant. "I have been in battle and never yet shrunk from danger, and it ain't from one man that I'm going to fly now because he happens to have got a name for being a desperate chap. Besides, we know he discharged one of his pistols in the cottage, and if it happens that he's got but another, we are certain, at the worst, that he can but kill one of us."

"And that one may happen to be myself," observed the other fearfully.

"And if it should be so," exclaimed the sergeant, "his majesty will lose one of the rankest cowards in his service. So, I'll tell you what—I'll remain about this place, because I know he's not far off, and you can go yonder and be prepared, if he should happen to make a start in the direction. But remember, you must shoot him like a dog if there's any chance of his escaping."

The soldier instantly went towards the place which had been pointed out, and the corporal advanced so near to the place where Ruthven was concealed, that another pace or two must have led to his discovery. At that moment, however, a pistol was fired, and as the man sank wounded to the ground, the fugitive darted from his hiding place, and was still making towards the cavern, when Andrew Foster suddenly presented himself before him.

"That shot told well for your safety, sir," said Andrew. "I was lying concealed all the time, and when I saw the fellow approaching too near where you were lying, I sent a ball through his right arm, and gave you the opportunity that I'm glad to see was not lost.."

"It was bravely done, at any rate," exclaimed Ruthven; "and since it's likely I owe my life to you, I shall be ready at any time to return the favour whenever you think proper to demand it."

"We'll not talk of that just now, captain," said the other; "so, as there's not much time to lose, perhaps you'll tell me what you mean to do next?"

"That's more than I can very well tell you," answered Ruthven, "for this chase has put everything out of my head, and I scarcely know what step to pursue. It seems likely, however, that they'll give up the pursuit for to-night, so as I've a few things to do on shore, I shall not go on board till the first thing in the morning."

"Don't be too sure, captain, that the pursuit is over," exclaimed Andrew

Foster, stooping his head almost to the ground as he spoke. "I can hear footsteps in the distance, and if we don't mind, those cursed soldiers will be upon our heels before we're aware of it."

"And if they do come and press us too closely, we must be prepared to give them a warm reception," answered Ruthven in a tone of careless indifference. "We are both armed, my friend, and though I seek not to shed the blood of my fellow creatures, yet self-preservation is the first law of nature, and the blood hounds must e'en perish."

"Aye, aye, captain," said the other, "if the odds don't happen to be too much against us, I think there's very little to be afraid of from these fellows. I can pop down a couple of them with this brace of bull-dogs, and you, I know, can settle the business for two or three more of the fellows in case we should be put upon our mettle."

Whilst they were thus speaking, they mended their pace, and at length reached the sea shore, where they again paused to listen, but every thing around them was quiet, and having pretty well ascertained that they were not in danger from their enemies, Ruthven said:—

"It seems, Andrew, there is not so much cause for uneasiness as we expected, for the soldiers have no inclination to peril their lives in a conflict with a desperate man like Red Ruthven, and have wisely enough returned to the town, where, I suppose, will spread more marvellous tales of the daring fellow they have had to deal with. The poor devil's are not over-paid for their services, and in my opinion, they act wisely in refusing to risk their lives when they can comfortably walk home with an excuse for not capturing me."

"They have done well, captain," answered the other, "and have saved us something in the cost of gunpowder, so they are welcome to go home and raise what reports they please about us. But I suppose we are to part here, so give me your orders, and I'll prove my love of good discipline by obeying you to the very letter."

"Then return to the ship, Andrew," said the captain, "and tell the lieutenant to anchor off yonder headland. Say that I would have all the boats ready for immediate use, and desire every man to be well armed with cutlass and pistols, for it may happen that there will be warm work for them sooner than they expect. In a short time, I may be on board, and when I come, there must be no delay, or my schemes will be frustrated, and a pretty night's work spoiled."

"I'll see that everything's done according to your wish, sir," exclaimed Andrew; "but mind what you are about, captain, for you are not upon very safe ground, here, and if you should happen to fall into the hands of any of the people they would hang you like a dog."

"Thanks Andrew, for your care of me," replied Ruthven, "but the fellows will not be able to lay their hands upon me quite so easily as you imagine. So now leave me, for as this may be the last visit I shall ever pay my native place, I would be alone, to think, without interruption, of the past, and to find, if possible, something in the future to console me for the mental sufferings I now endure. Away, Andrew, and tell the men to be prepared for my coming, which will be sudden, and at no great distance of time."

Andrew Foster departed, and Ruthven, deeply pondering upon the trials and vicissitudes it had been his lot to bear, wandered up and down the sea-shore, utterly reckless of the danger to which he was exposing himself.

The alarm which had been occasioned by the battle was quickly spread around the neighbourhood, but there was no one who felt more terror at the circumstance than did Tony Gripple, the magistrate, who had taken so unfair a part against John Ruthven on a former occasion, which will be within the recollection of our readers. He had, on this occasion, dined late, in consequence of some professional business, in which he had been engaged, and was seated with his wine before him, when an unusual sound met his ear, and after listening some little time longer, he could come to no other conclusion than that the noise was produced by cannon; consequently, that a battle was going on nearer to the English coast than was agreeable to a man whose nerves were none of the strongest.

"Why, what's the matter now?" he muttered to himself; "what's in the wind, I should like to know that a man can't sit down to enjoy himself quietly after being occupied the whole of the day in the service of his country? But I suppose the revenue officers have fallen in with the smuggler's lugger, that they say has been lying off the coast for the last two or three days, and if so, there will be warm work among them, for they owe each other a grudge, and only wanted an opportunity like this to square up their differences. And what need I care about it, since they are fighting it out on the sea, and as my jurisdiction don't extend so far as that, I suppose they'll let me have my after-dinner nap without coming to press me into a service of danger."

With this comfortable hope the magistrate threw himself back in his chair to sleep away the next half hour, but scarcely had forgetfulness began to steal over him, when a heavy footstep was heard in the passage, and as the door flew open, his neighbour, Mark Bowman, hurriedly approached him.

"Friend Gripple," he exclaimed, "this is no time for a man to be sleeping as if nothing was the matter. The enemy is upon our coast, and is likely to sink or carry off one of our ships, and the people round about here are alarmed lest the foe should land and burn and destroy all they come near."

"What enemy are you talking about?" demanded Justice Gripple, whose terror had been excited by this intelligence. "I thought it was only a fight between the smugglers and our revenue officers, but —"

"Then you are mistaken, Gripple, interrupted the other, "for the battle is between one of our own vessels and the ship commanded by the traitor, John Ruthven."

"The devil!"

"Aye, you may well say the devil," exclaimed the other, "for he fights like a fiend of darkness, and, from what I hear, is likely to pay us a visit on shore when he has finished beating our countrymen at sea."

"In that case," said Gripple, starting up from his seat, the sooner you and I look to ourselves the better. I've a friend that lives about twenty miles off, and as he has often invited me to go and see him, I think it would be as well to accept his kindness now that there's danger in staying at home."

"And be called a coward for your pains!"

"What care I about that, if I can only get beyond the reach of this Red Ruthven?" exclaimed the magistrate. "Besides, my profession is one of peace, and, of course, it can't be expected that I am going to take any part in the battle."

"But it's expected that you will collect together all the force of this neighbourhood, answered the other; "and if you fail to do so, the consequence must fall upon yourself."

Upon this Mr. Bowman took his departure, leaving rather an awkward impression upon the mind of the justice that he must either take an active part in attempting to repel the foe, or run the risk of being dismissed from his office in disgrace. He, therefore, chose the former alternative, but took especial care to take his party of constables to a part of the coast where he believed there was little chance of the enemy attempting a landing.

~~~~~~~~~~~~~~~~~~~~~~~~~~~~~~~~~~~

CHAPTER XXII.

" I'll seek for other aid—Spirits, they say,
Flit round invisible, as thick as motes
Dance in the sun-beams. If that spell
Or necromancer's sigil can compel them,
They shall hold council with me."

JAMES DUFF.

ABOUT the period to which the events of the preceding chapter belong, Lord Dalmeny spent a short time with a bridal party in the neighbourhood of his castle. It is true he was an invited guest, because the bridegroom could not very well omit the compliment without giving offence, but he was watched with suspicion, for it was known that he had expressed his admiration of the maiden who had that day given away her hand in marriage, and his libertine habits rendered him too dangerous a rival to be lightly thought of.

Her mother, Dame Horrock, was reputed to be a witch, and often had she warned Lord Dalmeny to beware how he tampered with the happiness of her child; but he merely laughed at what he called the folly of her suspicions, and with his usual plausibility assured her that his intentions were perfectly honourable. On the night in question, however, it was easy to see that his presence was far from being pleasant to the dame; and when the dance began, she watched him with a jealous eye to see whether he paid any marked attention to the bride. This did not pass unnoticed by Lord Dalmeny, who began to find that he must proceed with more caution; and when the next dance was over, he seated himself next the dame, and with an assumed expression of sincerity, congratulated her upon the marriage of her daughter.

"If we may judge from circumstances," he went on to say, "Kate has secured for herself a good husband, and well does she merit as great a blessing, for the world reports her virtuous, and I can myself offer testimony that she is beautiful."

"And beauty, my lord, is a dangerous commodity to possess whenever the owner chances to come within your knowledge," answered the dame, in a tone of severity. "Poor May Grayson is one example of your toosuccessful treachery, and if one thing more than another could give a pleasure this day, it is the certainty that my child is now protected from your arts by the watchfulness of your husband."

"Your opinion of me," he exclaimed, "it must be admitted, is not a very favourable one,"

"It is not," she replied, "and your lordship may thank yourself for whatever evil I suspect you of."

"And yet," exclaimed Lord Dalmeny, "the same voices that have denounced me are also raised against yourself. In fact we both serve the devil, though in rather a different manner, and it, therefore, ill-becomes us to utter reproaches which are no less deserved by one than the other."

"It may or may not be as your lordship has said," answered the dame, "but at any rate your crimes have brought sorrow and misery wherever you have gone, and the curses of many a one will follow you to the very grave."

"And who, I pray, you dame, have I injured so much?"

"There is May Grayson, for one," replied the old woman; "hasn't her reason fled for ever, and who is to blame for all that but the man whose station in life should have taught him that humble poverty, if virtuous, is far better than the glare and tinsel that deceive so many who look no deeper into life than the surface? Poor May Grayson, my Lord, is a living monument of your perfidy, and nothing that you can ever do will serve to wipe away the remembrance of the wrongs that most unfortunate girl has been made to endure."

"Upon my life, dame," exclaimed Lord Dalmeny, lightly, "you have read me a very pretty homily, and a dare say it will not be long before I make use of it to my own advantage. And now, having made this promise, you will perhaps oblige me by saying who else I have wronged."

"Effie Ruthven."

"Nay," he cried, with well feigned indignation;—"that is a charge that I must stoutly contradict; for Effie Ruthven has been carried off by other persons, and it is hard that I should bear the blame of doing that of which I am innocent."

"Lord Dalmeny, you are not innocent?" exclaimed the dame. "It is true that so far you have been careful to keep in the back ground, but you have accused me of being a witch, and I may prove myself to be one before we part. Your lordship's gold fee'd the men that took her away, and I am much mistaken, if they do not play you a trick yet, which will make useless all your arts and villany against Effie Ruthven."

"What mean you, woman?" demanded Lord Dalmeny, with an expression of impatience that he could not control. "Who will play me false, and in what manner shall I be made the laughing stock of the people I have trusted?"

"I will mention no names," replied the old woman, "because, perhaps if I did so, you would still think it impossible that any other man can break his word with as much ease as yourself. However, to come to the point,—Effie Ruthven has already found favour among the rough fellows to whose care you have entrusted; and I am much mistaken if they do not carry her off with them in their vessel; and, in that case, I leave your lordship to judge how small a chance remains of their ever returning here with the prize you have been so anxious to obtain."

Lord Dalmeny made no reply to this, for at the moment a young female entered the room, whose extreme beauty immediately attracted every eye towards her. She was a perfect stranger to all who gazed on her, but the rich garb in which she was attired, gave proof that her visit to the bridal party was premeditated. Lord Dalmeny instantly advanced towards her, and having introduced himself to the strange lady with all his accustomed ease, he was shortly engaged with her in the dance, which by this time was proceeding with the greatest spirit.

Dame Harroch had watched the last comer with a look of anxiety that somewhat startled the few who happened to be directing their glances towards her; for there was an expression in her countenance so peculiar, that it was no difficult matter to guess the feelings of awe and wonder with which she observed the new comer. Unconscious, however, of the attention she had attracted towards herself, the old dame at length advanced towards Lord Dalmeny and his mysterious partner, and as she passed the latter, she muttered two or three words in her ear that had an instantaneous and almost electrifying effect;—a half-suppressed shriek of horror burst from the lips of the fair unknown, and staggering backwards a few paces, she fell fainting into the arms of Lord Dalmeny.

This incident, as may naturally be supposed, occasioned the greatest

consternation amongst the visitors, but the female quickly roused herself by
an effort, and making a confused apology for the singularity of her conduct,
she begged that it might not interrupt the festivity that was going on; and
then whispering something to Lord Dalmeny, she set the example, and the
dance was resumed with as much mirthful hilarity as if nothing had occurred to disturb the harmony of the evening. Lord Dalmeny was not
among the least curious to ascertain who his partner was, and by engaging
her in a constantly changing conversation, he hoped so far to put her off her
guard as to obtain some clue by which the discovery might be affected.
At length, finding that he was not likely to gain the knowledge he required
in this way, he became more bold in his mode of questioniong her, and in a
speech full of compliments and admiration of her beauty, he inquired to
whom it was that he had the honour of addressing himself. The question
thus abruptly asked, seemed to fill her with momentary confusion, but
quickly recovering herself, she said :—

"Lord Dalmeny will, I am sure, pardon me if I hesitate to reply in the
present instance, for the secret is of some importance to myself, and must
therefore be kept till I am at liberty to disclose my name and from whence
I came."

"If there is indeed any occasion for the secrecy," exclaimed the nobleman, "I will, of course, urge you no further upon this subject at present.
You will, however, perhaps admit that your mysterious appearance here
may give rise to many awkward suspicions, and it was for your own sake
therefore that I have sought to obtain this explanation."

"There are none here who have any right to know more of me than I
may think proper to permit," answered the female. "That my arrival
among them was unexpected, I am well aware, but these wedding festivities
are open to all comers, and surely those that give the entertainment will
not depart from the custom by inquiring the name of a guest who relied
upon their hospitality?"

"You have nothing, I believe, to fear on that score," replied Lord
Dalmeny, "nor should I myself have ventured to put the question had it
not been that I feel deeply interested in one who has come among us under
such singular circumstances."

"Your lordship must suspend your curiosity for a time," she exclaimed,
for I know not yet whether I ought to give the required explanation, since the
doing so may bring me into no little danger. Besides, we are now surrounded by a crowd of curious observers, and this is no place to talk upon
a subject of so much importance."

"There I must confess you have raised an unanswerable objection," replied Lord Dalmeny. "This is indeed no fitting place in which to continue
our conversation, and you will perhaps indulge me by naming some other
spot where we may meet and speak together in privacy?"

"Your request is rather a bold one, my lord," she exclaimed, "considering this is the first time we have ever chanced to meet each other."

"Well, I will confess there is much truth in your observation, exclaimed
his lordship, "and yet you will perhaps pardon me the presumption, since
it has been caused by the deep interest you have thus suddenly excited in
my heart. You have, I dare say, heard me spoken of as a gay thoughtless
libertine, but my wild oats have now been sown, and it only remains for
yourself to declare whether I shall from this moment throw off the evil of my
ways."

"Really, my lord," she replied, "I must again remind you that this is
no place for such a declaration as you have just made. We are surrounded
by anxious listeners, and as I am a total stranger among them, they will

not put the most favourable construction upon my conduct, should it appear that I permit too much familiarity."

"But you will not leave me," he said, "without affording some information by which I might be able to find you?"

"Upon so short an acquaintance," she replied, "it can matter very little whether we ever meet again or not. We have seen each other for half an hour, and yet your lordship would fain make me believe that your heart is already overflowing with love."

"Had the opportunity been better," exclaimed Lord Dalmeny, "I might, perhaps, have convinced you that love at first sight may be as powerful and sincere as when it is produced by a long acquaintance. That, however, cannot be done now, and I therefore entreat you to give me a meeting this night where we may converse together without being observed."

"And would you not think me over-bold and forward were I to comply with your request?"

"By no means," he replied; "I have ventured to ask the favour, and shall be most happy if you will comply with it."

"In that case," she said, "I will, for once, exceed the modesty which should ever mark the conduct of a female, by granting the favour you have requested. In two hours I will meet you in the Hunter's Glen; but you must remember that I shall be there in full reliance upon your honour, and that the least approach to familiarity will be received with all the anger of an indignant woman."

"Rely upon me," he exclaimed, "and I will not give cause for the anger with which you have threatened me. In the Hunter's Glen we will meet, and, perhaps, ere we part again, we shall have pledged ourselves to each other, and thus secured the happiness which it is the lot of those to possess who love truly and sincerely."

No. 23

Whilst Lord Dalmeny was thus speaking, the company rose from their seats to commence the dance, and in the slight confusion which had been thus occasioned, the mysterious lady disappeared, no one knew how or whither.   The circumstance, however, occasioned but little wonder to any one, except Lord Dalmeny, who, retiring to the further end of the apartment, had leisure and opportunity to reflect upon the singular adventure in which he was engaged.   But at length, perceiving that he was observed, he roused himself from the meditative train of reflection in which he was engaged, and bidding the bridal party a hasty adieu, hurried away, and took the direction which led towards the castle of Dalmeny, which he entered by one of the private gates, in order that his return might not be noticed.

Here he remained for about an hour, and then having changed his dress for one less conspicuous than that which he had worn at the bridal, he left the place with the same secrecy that he had entered it, and directed his way to the Hunter's Glen, where it had been arranged he was to meet the singular being who had obtained so strong a mastery over his heart.   She was not there when he reached the place, and throwing himself beneath a tree, he was insensibly lulled into composure by the beautiful moonlight view that lay spread before him, and was, in fact, almost forgetful of the object which had brought him there, when a slight sound was heard, and raising his eyes towards the spot, the mysterious female stood before him, looking more like a spirit of light than one belonging to this earth.   In an instant he sprung upon his feet, and rushing forward, would have clasped her in his arms had she not glided on one side to avoid him.   A slight flash of anger was instantly visible upon her countenance, and regarding him with a look of offended modesty, she exclaimed with some severity :—

"It seems, my lord, that you have already forgotten the pledge that I extorted from you ere I consented to this meeting.   You are little mindful of your promises, it seems, and I now warn you that a second offence will occasion our immediate and final separation."

"Pardon me, fair lady," he exclaimed, "and you have my solemn word for it that I will not again give you cause for anger.   Nay, look not thus coldly upon me, for the error was not premeditated, and I will endure any penance it may be your pleasure to command."

"Your repentance is accepted," she replied, "though I know not whether it is sincere.   You, however, understand the terms upon which this meeting has been granted, and I shall not fail to resent any breach of the contract by disappearing from your sight with the same suddenness that I did when we separated on the last occasion."

"I have expressed my contrition," answered Lord Dalmeny, "and you shall find it is sincere ; and now, having thus made my apology, I have to request that you will favour me with the name of her who has honoured me with this interview."

"Nay, that formed no part of our previous contract," she exclaimed, "and I have already told you that the secret must remain with myself till circumstances permit me to be more explicit upon the subject."

"Do you dwell far from hence ?"

"I do ;—so far, indeed, that I much question whether your lordship's travels have ever taken you to the place."

"What," he exclaimed, "am I to understand by all this ?"

"It is in vain to attempt to penetrate the mystery so long as I think proper to keep it," she replied.   "I have motives for doing so at present, and in the meantime you must be content to know me only so far as you have seen me.   And now, having thus far explained myself, I suppose your lordship has no further questions to ask."

"The mystery is still wrapped in obscurity," he replied, "and I understood, when this meeting was appointed, that it was your intention to afford me some clue by which I might learn to whom I have the honour of being thus singularly introduced."

"From me you will at present learn nothing," she answered; "but at the same time I must tell you that a few days may serve to clear up this mystery."

"But is it necessary," asked Lord Dalmeny, "that there should be any mystery?"

"That you will hereafter learn."

"From whom?"

"Your questions grow troublesome, my lord," she replied, with some warmth. "You are aware that our introduction was the result of chance, and if I have complied with your request to permit this interview, I have done quite enough, without being required to enter into explanations."

"Shall we meet again soon?"

"Perhaps we may; but it will depend entirely upon yourself."

"At least you will permit me to see you back to the place where you are at present residing?"

"That is impossible," she replied, "since it would lead to a disclosure which I do not feel inclined to make."

She retreated a few steps as she spoke, and Lord Dalmeny, resolving to arrest her progress, sprang forward to catch her in his arms, but ere he could reach the place, the figure had vanished from his sight, and though he gazed wildly around him in every direction, the form of the mysterious female was no longer to be seen.

CHAPTER XXIII.

"Now would I give my fortune but to know
The end of all this mystery.   No one
Can tell from whence she came, or why
This visit has been made.''

THE SISTERS.

IT was some time before Lord Dalmeny could recover from the surprise into which he had been thrown by the marvellous disappearance of the unknown lady; but at length, deeply musing upon the occurrence, he began to retrace his steps homewards, with a determination of using every exertion to penetrate the mystery in which he found himself involved. He had not, however, proceeded very far, when his attention was arrested by the sound of footsteps, and in another moment his former antagonist, John Ruthven, stood before him. But he quickly subdued any emotions of anger that he might have felt, and holding out his hand, he exclaimed :—

"This is a fortunate meeting, Ruthven, for I have been in strange company to-night, and was just wishing that chance would throw some one in my way to whom I might relate my adventure, and who would be able to afford me counsel and advice."

"And would your lordship," demanded Ruthven, sternly, "seek the counsel you speak of from the man you know to be your sworn enemy, and who has even now come forth that he might seek you out, and inflict upon you the punishment your many evil deeds have justly merited?"

"'Psha!" exclaimed the nobleman, "I was in hopes our quarrel had ere this time been forgotten, and that we might have been friends again, as we were in the days of our boyhood."

"That is impossible, whilst my mind retains the memory of the wrongs I have endured," answered Ruthven, and taking a brace of pistols from his girdle, he presented them to Lord Dalmeny, as he added :—"you will take your choice of these weapons, my lord, and should I chance to fall, I shall at least have the satisfaction of knowing in my dying moments that I perish in the cause of a sister whom you have deeply wronged."

"Ruthven," exclaimed the nobleman, "you will do me the justice to admit that I am no coward, but I am resolved that I will not accept your challenge to-night. There is in fact something on my mind that disturbs me, for I have just seen that which fills my soul with doubt and suspicion."

"I have nothing to do with what you have seen," answered Ruthven, "since the wrongs I have endured are rankling in my heart, and I feel that nothing must arrest the course of that vengeance I have sworn to take. You will, therefore, take one of these pistols, lest, in scorn for your cowardice, I shoot you as I would a dog."

"It is in vain that you thus seek to urge me upon this subject," returned Lord Dalmeny, "for I am resolved that neither taunts nor threats shall provoke me to seek your life at present. And now, having expressed my firm determination, I will ask whether, in your progress hither, you met a female hurrying from this direction ?"

"I did," answered Ruthven, sullenly.

"Was she young ?"

"She was not : on the contrary, she was old, and, therefore, unlikely to be the person you are inquiring about. She spoke to me as she passed, and telling me that my enemy was here, wished me success in the ensuing strife, and then went on her way. So now, my lord, since we have met, we must not part again till the quarrel between us has been fairly settled."

"You have heard my determination," exclaimed Lord Dalmeny, "and once more I repeat my hand shall not be raised against you this night. I have seen a vision of loveliness, Ruthven, that at present occupies my every thought, and there was a mystery in her appearance before me that I am resolved to unveil ere I risk my life in a duel that may probably end in my own destruction. She of whom I speak stood beside me, but when I stretched forth my arm to clasp her to my bosom, she glided away, and then a suspicion first crossed my mind that she I had been speaking to was a spirit of air."

"I am not superstitious, my lord, and therefore cannot give you my belief in so marvellous a story," answered the other. "I come here with deadly intent to meet you, but it seems you refuse my challenge to-night, and I am not coward enough to raise my hand against the life of a man who will not even make an effort to defend himself. Depart, therefore, in peace, Lord Dalmeny ; and remember, that when next we see each other, the quarrel between us must be brought to a conclusion. But hark ! some one approaches, and should it be an enemy to take me, I am fortunately well armed, and will defend myself to the very last."

"Keep your own counsel and all will be well," returned Lord Dalmeny, glancing towards the direction from whence the sound came. "I can see several persons approaching on horseback, and if, as I suspect, they come in search of you, I will presently afford you proof that I am both willing and ready to give that assistance which your necessity may require."

He had scarcely finished speaking when a party of troopers galloped up, the chief of whom, advancing towards Lord Dalmeny and Ruthven, said abruptly :—

"Gentlemen—we are out in search of some enemies that are reported to have landed, and are supposed to be prowling about the country with a hostile intent. You will, therefore, please to tell me your names, that I may know whether to arrest you on suspicion of being two of the persons we are seeking."

"And what if we refuse to answer your question?" demanded Lord Dalmeny.

"Why, in that case," replied the officer, "it will be my duty to make you prisoners till full inquiries have been made to ascertain whether you are good men and true."

"Humph!" retorted the nobleman, "and where, I pray you, are we to be imprisoned till it is the pleasure of your superiors to make the inquiries you speak of?"

"In the castle of Dalmeny," answered the officer; "the owner is known to be loyal to his king and country, and he will be well pleased to prove his zeal by undertaking the duty with which I shall entrust him."

"You have done Lord Dalmeny no more than justice," replied the nobleman; "and since it is not my intention to disclose my name at present, you can convey us to the place you have mentioned as soon as you please."

"At any rate," exclaimed the soldier, "you have given us good ground for suspecting that our notion about you is correct. You will, therefore, please to accompany us to Dalmeny Castle, and should it turn out that we have been mistaken in our men, you will have only yourself to blame for the inconvenience, since you have refused to tell me your name."

Lord Dalmeny made no reply to this, and some of the soldiers having dismounted, the two prisoners were marched off without either of them offering any resistance to the proceeding that had been taken against them. A short time served to bring them to the castle gate, where three or four rustic sentinels were pacing to and fro, one of whom recognised Lord Dalmeny, and would have greeted him by name, had not a sign commanded him to silence; and the party thus proceeding onwards, entered the state chamber, where Justice Gripple was seated, and enjoying himself over a bottle of wine. The approach of these persons seemed scarcely to disturb him, so intent was he upon the enjoyment of his glass, and it was not till the officer had informed him that he had brought a couple of prisoners for examination that he was conscious of being called upon to exercise his magiterial duties. He then, however, assumed a look of profound wisdom, and throwing himself back upon his seat, demanded the nature of the charge against the two men. But Lord Dalmeny began to think he had now carried the affair quite far enough, and scarcely suppressing the laughter in which he felt inclined to indulge, he explained who he was, and jestingly thanked the officer for being so kind as to conduct him and his friend to the castle.

"I was in no humour, captain," he continued, "to enter into any explanation when you came so suddenly upon us, but since I have no discourtesy to complain of, I beg to tender you my best thanks, and in return for your kindness, shall insist upon your remaining to pass the rest of the night with me in conviviality. Our friend the justice is a good man for the bottle, and I doubt not we shall pass away a few hours to the content of all parties."

"I can answer for myself," said Justice Gripple, who was always willing enough to enter into the spirit of an affair like this; "and since there are four of us, I see no reason why we should not make a glorious night of it.'

"My friend, I believe, will decline the invitation," answered Lord Dalmeny, "for he has business that takes him elsewhere, and I have pledged myself not to press for his company."

"You say he is a friend of yours, my lord," said the justice, glancing towards Ruthven, who had purposely turned his back in order to avoid a recognition, "and such being the case, I should be happy to make acquaintance with him."

"Another time I shall be happy to comply with your wish," answered Lord Dalmeny, "but as he is at present engaged in business of a private nature, I must decline the proposition you have made."

"And you can of course answer for his loyalty?"

"Justice Gripple," replied his lordship, "should know me too well to suppose that I would hold friendship with any man whose loyalty and honour were not well confirmed. This person is above all suspicion, and as a friend of mine, it is my request that you treat him with courtesy."

As he said this, he led Ruthven from the room, and conducting him to the court-yard of the castle, proceeded towards one of the posterns that was but little used, he threw it open, and pointing towards the sea, exclaimed :—

"Your way now lies before you, and it will be your own fault if you do not make good use of the opportunity I have thus given you to escape. That I am not your enemy you will perhaps at length admit, and should chance ever throw us in each other's way again, I may be able to explain the mystery which at present involves the fate of your sister. For the present, then, farewell, and may our next meeting be under more favourable circumstances."

Ruthven sullenly took his departure, and Lord Dalmeny immediately returned to the hall, where he found his friends waiting his arrival; and it may be scarcely necessary to observe that Justice Gripple was soon asleep, under the influence of the wine he had swallowed.

CHAPTER XXIV.

"Would that I knew his secret lurking-place,
That I might yield him up to that stern fate
Which now awaits him. That were indeed
A glorious and most excellent revenge."

                                        CONSTANTINE.

WHEN Ruthven quitted the presence of Lord Dalmeny, he darted down the steep side of the hill upon which the castle was situated, and then, directing his footsteps towards some rising ground at no great distance off, he soon found himself standing before an ancient cottage, at the door of which he hesitated to knock, as if doubtful whether he should disturb the inmate at that late hour of the night. At length, however, his mind seemed to be made up, and applying the hilt of his sword to the door, he was quickly answered by an old man, who no sooner recognized him, than, uttering an exclamation of joyful surprise, he bade him enter.

"You are welcome to my roof again, John Ruthven," he exclaimed, "for I have long wished to see you; though, when they told me you were gone abroad, and that honours had been conferred upon you, I almost began to fear my hopes were vain."

"I can never forget a friend, Murchieson," answered the other; "and even if the officers of justice had been at my heels, I believe I should have risked the danger rather than take my departure without coming to say farewell. Besides, I would offer you a better home, for this place is scarcely habitable, and I fear you are in poverty and distress."

"Nay, I shall never leave this place whilst I am alive," replied Murchieson, "for beneath the roof that now covers my head I have passed some of the best years of my life, and here will I spend the few hours that may remain to me. Though old, I am still able to obtain fish from the sea for food, and never will I accept of charity whilst I am able to put forth a hand towards procuring the little that is required for keeping life and soul together."

"But surely you may accept the proffered services of a friend?" exclaimed Ruthven, "and the more especially since I have been under so many obligations to you in former days. You want society, too, my good old man, and I would fain prevail upon you to take up your abode in the village, where there are many who would gladly hail your return among them."

"It is enough to know that I have one friend in you, John Ruthven," answered the old man, "for I have now grown weary of the world, and have little feeling in common with my fellow men. A brief period will suffice to bring my life to a close, and well pleased shall I be if existence lasts long enough to hear of your success in arms."

"And if I should obtain the reward you speak of," exclaimed Ruthven, "it will be owing to the inspiring tale of honour and renown that in early youth I heard from your lips. Often have I hung in admiration upon your words, and when manhood began to dawn, I eagerly panted to become somewhat greater than fortune seemed to have intended. Already I have achieved some renown, and who can I thank for it but him who roused my soul to deeds of daring and enterprise?"

"It is true I loved to dwell upon the deeds of my youth," answered Murchieson; "but the vanity has passed away, and I now seek to obtain reconciliation by devoting myself to the service of Heaven. Ambition appears to be a bauble scarcely worth the trouble we take in seeking it, and often do I wonder that men can be found who are willing to risk even life itself in endeavouring to attain useless honours."

"Well," exclaimed Ruthven, "we will speak no further upon this subject, since youth and age can scarcely be expected to agree upon it. I came to bid you farewell, and to endeavour, by what little influence I possess, to prevail upon you to enter once more into the world you have forsaken."

"It is a vain attempt," replied the old man, "for this is my haven of rest, and no persuasion shall ever induce me to quit it. You, however, it seems, have turned against the country of your birth, and are now engaged in affording assistance to the enemies of our land. Doubtless you have received ample provocation, and I shall therefore offer no reproaches, though I could have wished your arm had been raised in a better cause."

"That is impossible," answered Ruthven, "for I am now endeavouring to exalt the banner of freedom in a land that has been too long tyrannized over by the mother country. America had loudly demanded her liberty, and ere long you will see her raised to a level with the first nations of the world."

Murchieson was about to reply to this, but ere he could do so the latch was lifted up, and as the door opened a man in the garb of a sailor strode into the room. Ruthven would have left the place, had there been an opportunity of doing it without being observed, but the stranger gazed upon him with a look of curiosity, and as the other did not wish it to appear that he sought to shun his notice, he seated himself by the window, and gazed out upon the broad expanse of ocean, whilst the visiter explained the motive that had occasioned his visit.

"Now, old man," exclaimed the sailor, "I am come to try whether your craft is as great as folks say it is. In fact, I am going to make a trip once more over the blue waters, and I should like to know whether our good ship is likely to come back safe and sound to the shores of Old England."

"I am no practiser of the mystic arts," answered Murchieson, "and therefore cannot give the information you desire. I believe, however, you belong to Captain Starkie's crew, and if my guess is a right one, I should say that, as a smuggler, your life is scarcely worth a month's purchase.

"Humph! that's tolerably plain speaking, too," exclaimed the sailor; "but as you don't think proper to tell me what sort of a voyage we shall have, perhaps you won't mind saying who this stranger is that sits here listening to our conversation."

"He is a friend of mine," answered Murchieson, "and one that you have nothing to be afraid of."

"And so you are quite sure he will not give information that the smuggler's lugger is lying off the coast ?"

"I am sure he will not."

"Well, then, now to business," continued the sailor ;—"we have come back after a short trip, and are going to make another in the course of a day or two; but as we men of the salt water are rather apt to be superstitious, I thought you might be able to tell me what sort of success we shall have."

"Captain Starkie is a man of dark and treacherous soul," replied Murchieson, "and therefore little deserves the good fortune he is so anxious to obtain. All good men are against him, and though he has triumphed thus far in villany, the period is at hand when he will meet the punishment he merits."

"Come, I like your honesty, old man," exclaimed the sailor, "though I should have been glad if you could have been a little less severe in your remarks about our captain."

"I speak my mind openly and fairly," replied the other. "Captain Starkie has been engaged in carrying off one of our maidens,—he has been largely bribed to do it, and from that moment he has drawn down upon himself the curses of all those who are not as worthless as himself."

"Why, it must be confessed he was engaged in an affair of the sort," replied the sailor, "and for my own part I can see no great harm in it, since, if he had refused, somebody else would not have been quite so particular. The girl was pretty: we set fire to her mother's cottage, and bore the damsel away."

"For which a speedy punishment awaits you," answered the old man. "Aye, you frown, and half pluck the dagger from your vest, but I have spoken the truth, and you will yet have reason to acknowledge it. See you not with what a look of anger yonder stranger regards you, and need I say that you will be consulting your own safety by leaving the place as quickly as you can."

"It is her brother, perhaps?" whispered the sailor, after glancing round inquisitively at Ruthven. "I knew something of him when he dwelt in these parts, but fortune has sent us on different errands, and I now only hear of him sometimes as gaining laurels abroad by fighting in the cause of another country. That will not gain him much applause in this place, and if he should happen to fall into the hands of those that are seeking him, I rather think his life will be a shorter one than you have said my own will be."

"But his foes may not be able to reach him," exclaimed Murchieson, "for Ruthven knows what he has to expect from them, and will take care to keep out of harm's way. Besides, a battle was fought not long since between the pirate, as they call him, and one of our own ships, and Ruthven, it seems, contrived to gain the victory."

"Aye, but success may not always attend him," replied the sailor; "and, between ourselves, if I thought yonder man was the one we are speaking about, I should not long hesitate about giving information in a quarter where it would be acceptable."

"Would you be villain enough to betray a fellow-creature, when you have so much need for secrecy yourself?" demanded the old man.

"To be sure I would," answered the other, "since, by doing so, I could make a good bargain for myself, and perhaps get a free pardon. Besides, I don't forget that John Ruthven and I had a quarrel when we were boys together, and I then swore to be revenged upon him some day or other, and I'm not one to forget a thing of the kind."

"And if he knew you had such an intention, what course do you think he would pursue against you?"

"Oh, it's not very hard to guess what he would do," replied the sailor. "No doubt he would lay wait for me, and if I didn't prove the stronger of the two, I suppose he would send me to Davy Jones, and then the gallows would be cheated of its prey."

"I question whether John Ruthven would think you a foe worthy of so much trouble," answered Murchieson, "for he would rightly judge that you can do him but little harm, and being rather nimble in his motions, he would hoist sail and bid farewell to our shores before the people hereabout would have an opportunity of commencing a pursuit. But you may chance one day or other to meet him on his own favourite element, and in that case I warn you to beware of him, for he can be terrible in his wrath, as many a better man has found ere now to his cost."

"Well, I'm obliged to you for the hint, old gentleman," replied the sailor, carelessly, "but as two of us can play at that game, I don't know that there's any great deal to be afraid of. So, as you can't tell me much

No. 24.

more than I knew before I came here, I'll take my leave, and if I should return home safe from this next voyage, I'll pay you another visit, if it's only to let you know that my life's not held on so short a lease as you seem to believe."

Saying this, he rose suddenly from his seat, and striding towards the door, passed through it and instantly disappeared. As he departed, Ruthven approached the old man, and said,—

"That fellow I suspect has gone on an errand of mischief, and therefore this place no longer affords me the shelter you would give me."

"Your suspicions exactly agree with my own," answered Murchieson, "for I also have a notion that he means to give information of your being here, and in that case he will return presently with half the neighbourhood at his heels. Away then, John Ruthven, and may my prayers for your safety be heard."

"There is another that I have more reason to dread," exclaimed Ruthven, as he prepared to depart. "I have this night seen Lord Dalmeny, and though he professes to mean me well, and has even assisted my escape, I believe there is mischief lurking in his brain, and that he seeks only a better opportunity to betray me into the hands of my foes. But let him beware, for I know him to be a villain, and though I was foiled in my vengeance just now, the time is not far distant when the wrongs I have endured shall be dearly answered."

With these words he hurried from the house, and once more directed his steps towards the sea shore. Murchieson then threw himself upon a seat and gave way to the gloomy reflections that chased each other through his mind.

CHAPTER XXV.

> " The gods, in bounty, work up storms about us,
> That give mankind occasion to exert
> Their hidden strength, and throw out into practice
> Virtues that shun the day, and lie concealed
> In the smooth seasons and the calms of life."
>   CATO.

ON reaching the shore, Ruthven found that a boat was lying there in readiness for him, and leaping into it he was quickly rowed to his ship, where his return was hailed with vociferous acclamations by his crew. He, however, soon silenced their uproarious joy, and stepping upon the quarter deck, ordered his officers to be summoned to a council, and no sooner were they assembled around him than he addressed himself to them in the following words :—

"You are aware, gentlemen, of the circumstances under which I have taken up arms against my native land ;—that I have received injuries from those I once esteemed my dearest friends, and that, in disgust, I have transferred my allegience to the American government? Our object at present is to terrify these islanders by approaching their coasts, and thus compel them to employ a considerable part of their navy in watching our movements. This we have so far been successful in doing, but it must be admitted that our position begins to grow perilous, and that we must sail from hence with as little delay as possible. You must not, however, imagine that I have any intention of leaving with dishonour, for, on the contrary, I have resolved upon executing a bold project, which, if successful, shall be talked of long after we have ceased to live. In short, gentlemen, we will attack one of their towns, and thus prove to the world that we have courage enough to combat with our foes even upon their own boasted land of freedom!"

These words were listened to in silence, but it was evident, from the cheerful countenance of his auditors, that they heard him with satisfaction; and scarcely had he concluded ere active preparations were commenced for trimming the vessel and getting it under weigh. At length, just as the day began to dawn, a ship was descried at no great distance off, and as the light increased, it was recognised by John Ruthven as the one which was commanded by Captain Starkie, whom he had long wished to meet, in order that he might retaliate upon him certain injuries of which he had to complain. The vessel moved rapidly onwards, and in a few minutes Starkie came alongside, and seizing a speaking-trumpet, he summoned the Americans to surrender. This, however, the others made no reply to, and as the two vessels had by this time approached side to side, Starkie addressed a few hurried words to his crew, and leaping on board the enemy's ship, he was promptly followed by the greater part of his men, all of whom were inspired with an ardour which it seemed vain to resist.

But the Americans were no less resolute than was the foe, and no sooner did they see their decks filled in the manner that has been described, than sword crossed sword, and a fight was commenced that for some time was waged with so much equality that victory was quite uncertain. At length, however, Ruthven and Captain Starkie met together, and, as a grim smile of satisfaction passed across the countenance of each, they advanced a step or two nearer, and the next moment saw them engaged hand to hand, with the desperate determination of either conquering or falling beneath the sword of his foe. For some time the chances of victory were equally divided between them; but at last a slight wound that Ruthven received from his adversary seemed to add still greater fury to his rage, and from that period he fought with such overpowering determination that Starkie began to give way and retreat inch by inch towards the side of the vessel, when, springing upon the bulwarks, he leaped upon his own deck just in time to avoid a fatal blow that was aimed at him by his infuriated enemy. But he only escaped death for a moment, for his men were exasperated at seeing him flee before his foe, and scarcely had he leaped into the vessel than three or four of his crew rushed upon him with their drawn cutlasses, and no sooner had he fallen mortally wounded at their feet, than he was lifted up in the arms of one of his men and thrown overboard, when he sunk never to rise again.

When this was done, Ruthven and nearly the whole of his crew rushed on board the enemy's vessel, and, after a short but severe conflict, succeeded in taking it. Elated at his victory, the American captain rested for a moment on his sword, while he contemplated in silence the scene of death and slaughter with which he was surrounded. From this brief state of listlessness he was, however, soon roused by his old acquaintance, Andrew Forster, who, having assisted to defend his own ship as long as there was a chance of saving her, was now willing to transfer his services to the conquering foe.

"Captain Ruthven," he said, "I've done nothing more than my duty in fighting against you as long as I could, but fortune seems to have deserted us to-day, and as I don't wish to be stowed away under hatches as a prisoner, you may, if you please, have my services from this time forward."

"I accept your offer, Andrew," replied Ruthven; "and now, since our bargain is complete, the first command I shall give you is to lead me to that part of the vessel where Captain Starkie has stowed away his ill-gotten gains."

"His riches!" exclaimed Forster, with surprise.

"Aye," answered the other; "my men have fought well to-day, and the gold and silver of your late captain must be fairly divided among them."

"Then I'm afraid they'll get but little here," exclaimed Andrew Forster; "for the truth is, Captain Starkie had a secret place where he used to hide it ashore. Here he never kept anything that might tempt his men to mutiny against him, or it's likely he would not have lived to this day to perish for his cowardice when he ran away from you. But the ship herself is a pretty one, and the cannon and other stores that you have taken in her will prove well worthy the trouble you've had in making her your own."

"That I grant," answered Ruthven; "but the vessel I have taken will belong to the government under whom it is now my pride to serve, and as the country is at present a poor one, the men will have but little to expect over and above the wages for which they serve the republic. Had Starkie's gold been on board, it would have proved an incentive to urge them to deeds of bravery on another occasion, for avarice will ever tempt men to deeds of danger and peril, even though death stares them in the face."

"And what chance is there of a man rising in your navy?" asked Andrew Forster.

"There are chances such as you know nothing about in this country," answered Ruthven. "In the new world men rise through their merits, and not as they do here, through high birth and patronage. All that are brave will be rewarded according to their deserts, and a common sailor who shows talents that fit him for command will attract the attention of his superiors, and be transferred to the quarter-deck."

"Well, and after all, that's the only fair way of managing such matters," observed Andrew. "For my own part, I should have entered the British navy years ago, instead of joining a band of smugglers, but I saw no chance of bettering myself, however great the risk might be, and so I thought, as many others have done, that if they want sailors they had better look out for them among the sprigs of nobility, who are at present so fond of large pay with nothing to do. Turn and turn about is fair play, you know, and the rich ought to learn from experience what hard toil the poor man has to go through for a bit of bread."

"And America is setting an example that will, one day or other, be followed by other nations," answered Ruthven. "I do not say the change will take place in our time, Andrew; but it will occur, and men will then wonder how the world could so long have been governed by laws so unequal. But see, they have already cleared the decks of the bodies of those who have fallen in this day's encounter, and after giving the command of our prize to my first lieutenant, I shall return to my own vessel, and we will then shape our course towards Dormer Island, where I have a little business to settle that will serve both to put money in our pockets, and to fulfil a vow of revenge that I made some time ago."

Ruthven now busied himself in giving the various necessary orders for the management of the vessel which had thus fallen into his hands, and having entrusted the care of all this to the next to himself in command, he returned to his own vessel, followed by Andrew Forster, and ere many minutes had elapsed, the necessary arrangements were made for sailing towards their place of destination.

As the ship passed onwards all tokens of a warlike nature were carefully concealed, and the British ensign was kept flying, in order that no danger should be apprehended from the foe they were endeavouring to lull into the full confidence of security. Ruthven himself stood upon the deck, which he paced with the air of a man whom no perils could appal, and occasionally gave signals to the helmsman whenever any alteration of the ship's course was to be made. By his side walked a noble-looking youth, who gazed upon his commander with looks expressive of eagerness and anxiety; but the captain seemed scarcely to heed him, for his thoughts were bent upon other objects which at that period filled his mind. The youth was armed with a brace of richly ornamented pistols in his belt, and altogether his countenance bore upon it traces of military ardour, which promised at no very distant period to raise him in the highest rank in his profession. At length Ruthven seemed to awake from the all-absorbing thoughts that filled his mind, and directing his keen glances towards the youth, he said,—

"I have been meditating, Henry, upon the past, for this coast is well known to me, and every place I look upon is the scene of some story, that almost makes me regret the circumstances that have driven me from England to seek a country and a home in the new world. In yonder island that we are now passing I have spent some of the happier years of my life, and yet, were I to set foot upon it now, I should be looked coldly upon by those who were once my friends, and who would doubtless shun me as a traitor to my country. But they know not the wrongs I have endured, or they would scarcely blame me for taking up the sword of vengeance, even though the weapon may have been placed in my hand by an enemy."

"And what need you care, sir, for what men say or think?" demanded the youth. "You are now on the road to fame and glory, and though England may term you a traitor, yet all good Americans will praise you as a hero."

"True, boy," answered Ruthven; "but the character seldom fails to suffer when some men praise and others blame. And yet why should I think of that which cannot be helped, since I am in a fair way of attaining the height of my hopes, and can laugh all the evil rumours of my enemies to scorn? Let them say as they will, it must after all be acknowledged that I have had cause for the step I have taken."

"And, at all events," observed his youthful companion, "you have the satisfaction of knowing that the gratitude of America will not be wanting should you carry out the intentions you have so well begun. There, when the war is over, you will find an honourable home, and the reward of your exertions will be equal to your merits."

"I ask for no other reward than the esteem and approbation of my fellow men," answered Ruthven. "From some I know I can never expect it; but future generations will do me justice by acknowledging that I am not the depraved villain my enemies have sought to represent me to be. However, let people say of me what they please, my course is shaped out, and I will follow it out unshrinkingly."

Upon this he turned abruptly away, and his companion, seeing that he desired to drop the conversation, moved to another part of the vessel, where he stood gazing over the blue and sparkling waves that were everywhere rolling around him. He would have spoken further to Ruthven upon the subject of his future intentions, but to do so at present would be vain, and he therefore determined to await a more favourable opportunity.

CHAPTER XXVI.

" Hast thou no mercy?
Or wilt thou go, for the mere lust of gold,
To frighten women with thy lawless presence,
And plunder them of all?"   THE CORSAIR'S BRIDE.

RUTHVEN had been occupied some little time in his ruminations, when he was suddenly interrupted by Andrew Forster, who, hastening towards him, said abruptly,—

"Do you see, Captain Ruthven, how the sloop, that you have been at so much trouble to make your prize, is bearing away from us. By jove, she's scudding away with all her sails set, and something strikes me the person you've entrusted with her command means to go back to America and get all the credit for taking her."

With a look of anger, Ruthven turned his gaze in the direction alluded to, and saw that the instructions he had given to his lieutenant had been totally disregarded, and that the vessel was pursuing a route very different from what he intended. His first command was to throw out signals, but these were totally disregarded, and finding that he must now adopt a resolute course, he ordered all sail to be crowded, and having a favourable wind, he pursued his prize with so much speed, as in a short time to decrease the distance between them in a very considerable degree, and within half an hour afterwards he ran up so close that their sides nearly touched. By this time Ruthven's passion had somewhat abated, but he was still determined to assert his superiority, and having summoned the officer in command to his presence, he exclaimed in an authoritative tone,—

"How dare you, sir, disobey my orders? Explain yourself, or I shall take care your conduct is reported to government immediately on our return to America."

"I have yet to learn, Captain Ruthven," answered the other haughtily, "by what right you dispute my authority to do as I please. I am now in command of this vessel, and I shall not resign my right except into the hands of Congress."

"Are you not an officer under me?" asked Ruthven.

"I was," replied the other; "but you have made me your equal, and I know how to make use of my advantage. I belong to a free country, where no man is suffered to domineer over another, and you, sir, will yet find that I know my own right much better than you do yourself."

"Come, sir," exclaimed Ruthven somewhat more soothingly, "I must request that you will listen to reason, and I believe you will find no difficulty in acknowledging that strict discipline is absolutely necessary, both in the army and navy; without it disunion must take place among our people, and in such an event as that, we should become an easy prey to our enemies."

"I know nothing at all about that," answered the other; "but the rights of man must be maintained whatever the consequences may be. I have the honour to have been born in a land of freedom, and where is the American, I should like to know, that would submit to bow with submission to a native of the old country, where they are all slaves?"

"You have heard my orders, sir, and I shall expect them to be obeyed," exclaimed Ruthven, firmly. "This expedition has been entrusted to me by Congress, and I will perform my duty with zeal and determination. You will, therefore, follow my vessel, sir, or the consequences may be more serious than you expect."

Ruthven, however, soon saw how little attention was paid to his commands, for the British flag under which they had been cruizing was pulled down to give place to the American flag, and immediately afterwards the vessel was once more in full sail. This at first excited the anger of Ruthven, but a little consideration served to convince him that he had met with a good riddance in losing an officer who was so little under discipline. His own vessel now moved steadily along till they came near Dormer Island, which was to be the scene where their next attack was to be made. Here Ruthven called his men together, and addressed them as follows,—

"My friends, we have been entrusted by Congress with a perilous but an honourable duty, and it now remains for us to prove that the confidence of your country-people has not been misplaced. You are aware that many of our citizens are prisoners in the hands of the enemy, and that some have already been led forth to the gibbet and executed as felons. It now, therefore, becomes our duty to seize upon the noblest people we can find, and to hold them as security for those who are captives in the hands of the English. He whom we are now about to take is Gordon, who dwells on yonder island, and the possession of whose person will afford security to many of our own people. He must be ours; but let it be remembered we go to make a prisoner, not to shed the blood of our fellow-creatures."

About twenty of the mariners instantly began to arm themselves, and when everything had been prepared, a couple of boats were lowered and the men descended, Ruthven taking the command of one party, and the other being entrusted to his young friend Henry. A short time served to bring them to the island, when, springing ashore, they left a couple of men in charge of the boats, and proceeded in silence and order towards the mansion, which stood at some little distance before them.

A rustic, employed at his daily labour, was the first to see their approach, but he little suspected the hostile intent that had brought them there, and quitting his work for a moment, he advanced towards them to inquire the occasion of so unusual a visit.

"Ye'll all be welcome at the mansion, I dare say," he exclaimed, "if you are going to my lady with a message from her husband, for she is sore troubled at his absence, and news from him will be like giving a fresh lease to her life."

"The Gordon is from home, then?" said Ruthven.

"Aye, truly is he," answered the man; "he heard that the king was ill at ease about these American rebels that have been making such a stir of late, and so he has gone up to London to offer his majesty advice. And if the king can only be persuaded to take it, I fancy it will not be long before the traitors meet with their deserts."

Some of the men could scarcely refrain from drawing their swords and punishing the plain-spoken old man on the spot, but Ruthven foresaw their design, and beckoning for them to follow him at some little distance, he said,—

"Our object, as you hear, has already failed, for Gordon is absent from home, and it would therefore be cowardice were we to go up to the mansion and terrify a helpless woman who has never given us any cause of offence."

"What would you have us do, then, captain?" inquired Paton, one of his lieutenants. "Are we not in the land of an enemy, and shall we now turn back, when I dare say the mansion contains gold and plate enough to reward us all for our trouble?"

"I know not what your feelings may be, Mr. Paton," said Ruthven, sternly, "but for my own part I war only against those who are able to return blow for blow. We have heard that Lady Gordon is the only person left in charge of the house, and a hand of mine shall never be raised against her."

"But no doubt the house is well guarded by men that are able to offer resistance," answered Paton; "and as none of us wish to war against women any more than you do yourself, we will undertake that no harm shall befal her ladyship."

"I will have no hand in it," exclaimed Ruthven; "for I never yet warred against those who are unable to defend themselves. My native country, as a nation, I have learnt to despise, and I have even accepted service under the banner of America, but never will I strike where there is no power of resistance."

"You forget, captain," interposed Henry, "the violence that has been committed by the English on our own coasts, where nothing has oeen spared whenever they could obtain a landing. I myself have suffered from them, for they set fire to my father's house during my absence, and when I came back, what a scene of sorrow and desolation did I behold; m ymother and my sisters were kueeling and weeping by the ashes of their onc eloved home, and from that moment I vowed to draw the sword of vengeance, and neve to sheath it again till my country had shaken off the fetters that bound her to this nation."

"Very sensibly spoken, my youngster," exclaimed Paton; "for I can't see why we should hesitate about trifles when the mansion we are in search of lies just before us. There's gold and silver enough, no doubt, and I, for one, shall not turn back till I have seen an end of the day's work we cut out for ourselves."

"Will nothing prevail upon you to abandon this cowardly enterprise?" demanded Ruthven.

"Nothing," answered Paton. "Gordon is in London, it seems, and from what I can understand, there are no male domestics left to guard the place, so that we have only to show ourselves in the house, and I warrant you her ladyship will not be long before she gives up all the valuables that happen to be in the place."

Ruthven would have resisted this design had there been the faintest possibility of frustrating it, but he saw that the general voice was against him, and yielding to the necessity, he resolved to have nothing to do with an affair which could only reflect dishonour upon those engaged in it. He, however, resolved to make one more effort with his men, and turning away from Paton, he said to them,—

"Comrades, we have often fought together, and I have reason to know that you are brave and resolute when engaged in honourable strife. Now, however, you have been called upon by one or two of our number to engage in a business which I am sure you will blush to think of during the remainder of your lives. Remember, it is a helpless woman that dwells in vonder mansion; one, in fact, who deserves our merciful consideration rather than the cruel injustice you seek to inflict. I speak thus feelingly upon this subject, because I have a mother and sister who have suffered from the villany of those who can commit injustice even for their very sport. I have seen them become the victims of treacherous men, who should rather have been their protectors, but the hour will yet arrive when vengeance shall be mine, and terrible will be the retribution I pour forth upon their guilty heads. It is true, if you go, there is silver and gold to repay you for the villainous task you undertake; but will that purchase you peace of mind when, in sober seriousness, you come to reflect upon the occurrences of this day? Back, then, with me, my friends, and when you return with me to America, I will not fail to reward you amply for the mercy you this day show."

The men listened to him with sient attetion , but few of them seemed.
to be struck with the arguments he used in favour of their retreat. Indeed
it was only three or four who appeared willing to depart with him, and
even those few Paton endeavoured to prevail on to accompany him to the
mansion.

"It's all very well," he said, "for the captain to preach about the thing
being dishonourable, but he himself brought us here to seize upon Gordon,
and now he is the first to try and persuade us against it. But I shall to
the house, if I go alone, for though we own him to be our captain on the
sea, we have a right to be our own masters on shore ; and be the consequences what they may, I shall not go on board again till I have levied con-
tribution of the money and plate of Lady Gordon."

"Henry," exclaimed Ruthven, "I see that all remonstrances are in vain,
but do you go with them, and by your presence endeavour to restrain their
violence as much as possible."

"Had you not better go with them yourself?" asked Henry; "for they
are accustomed to obey you, and will be more likely to be checked if you
happen to be present."

"The affair is so discreditable," answered Ruthven, "that I must refuse
to accompany them, even though my being with them might chance to restrain their violence. But I would have them beware how they break my
orders in this respect, for should any insult or violence be offered, I shall not
fail to let them see that I have not lost the power over them which was
given to me by Congress. Tell them this, Henry, and bid them act with
caution."

He turned away as he spoke, and without even glancing at those who
had thus braved his displeasure, he descended the hill, and made his way
to that part of the shore where the boats had been left when they landed."

No. 25

CHAPTER XXVII.

" We come against you as an enemy;
  As men who know no law, save their own will,
  And that necessity which all obey when force
  Or inclination drive them to it."—Lorenzo.

At the period when Paton and his companions were advancing towards the mansion with their ill-omened design, Lady Gordon, with two young female visiters, were seated at the breakfast-table, totally unconscious of the terrible visitation they were so soon to experience. They were, indeed, occupied in the light conversation which usually takes place on such occasions, and were laughing over the several little incidents which each had in turn to relate, when they were startled by a loud knocking at the principal entrance door, and almost at the same moment a harsh voice demanded admittance to the house. Lady Gordon, however, quickly recovered from her surprise, and speaking to the serving woman who was in attendance, she said :—

" Hasten, Martha, and see who it is that so roughly demands to be admitted to our presence. Perhaps, girl, it may be some one requiring my aid, and if so, bid them come in, for I would not have the unfortunate turned harshly away when it is in my power to relieve the sufferings of my fellow creatures. Go child, and bring me word back quickly who it is, for a thought now strikes me that it may be a messenger from my lord with news from London."

Martha staid for no further bidding, but instantly quitted the room, and in a short time returned pale and out of breath. Lady Gordon observed her terror, but wishing to conceal her own apprehensions from her guests, she inquired, in a tone of assumed indifference, what was the matter.

" Oh, my lady !" cried the alarmed girl, " I can scarcely tell you what's the matter, but the hall is nearly filled with a number of armed sailors, and as soon as I heard them demanding to see you, I ran back to entreat your ladyship to hide yourself."

The voices of a number of men were now heard below, and almost at the same instant, the door was thrown open, and a youth of noble aspect ran in, and taking the hand of Lady Gordon, exclaimed hurriedly :—

" Oh, my mother, the peace of our house is threatened, for strange men have forced their way into the hall, and I fear some terrible mishap is about to befal us."

" Have you not heard who they are ?" asked her ladyship.

" I have not," he replied; " but it is said a press-gang landed this morning on our island, and I think it may be them. At any rate, I will go and demand their business, and should it be as I suspect, I will insist upon their leaving the house, and then convince them that we are not to be thus invaded by ruffians, even though my father happens not to be at home."

Ere Lady Gordon could lay her commands upon him to remain where he was, the youth had rushed from the room. But in another minute he returned with a flushed and agitated countenance, and again addressing her ladyship, said :—

" I have seen them, mother, and their numbers, I should think, amount to from fifteen to twenty. Two among them seem to be superior to the rest, and I questioned them as to the nature of the errand that had brought them here, but I could get no other answer than that they were sailors, and desired to speak to you without delay."

"Go, then, my son," she replied, "and say I will see them immediately. Their business must be of importance, or they could hardly have visited us at so early an hour in the morning, and in such numbers."

Before the youth, however, could leave the place, footsteps were heard ascending the stairs, and in a short time Paton and Henry entered the room. The ladies rose to greet them, and Lady Gordon, recovering from her surprise, said :—

"You are welcome to our house, gentlemen, though I am ignorant to what circumstance I owe the honour of this visit. Our doors, indeed, are ever open to those who serve the king, but whoever you are, I welcome you to our roof. If you are shipwrecked, or have need of aid, say so, and it shall be freely granted."

"Lady," exclaimed Henry in a mild tone, "we have neither been so unfortunate as to be shipwrecked, nor do we serve the king of whom you have spoken. In fact, we are Americans, and have come hither with no peaceful intent."

"Americans!" cried her ladyship with mingled terror and surprise; "then I can indeed believe that your purpose here is to murder and destroy all that comes within your reach."

"There you have wronged us," answered Henry, "for our object is to capture your husband, in order that he may be prevailed on to use his influence with the King of England, and procure for us that honourable peace which can alone bring with it the tranquillity we desire."

"My husband is happily from home," replied Lady Gordon, "and, therefore, as your object has been foiled, I have to request that you and your companion will quit my house."

"As far as I am concerned, my lady," exclaimed Henry, "I shall have no hesitation in obeying so reasonable a request." Then, addressing himself to Lieutenant Paton, he said :—"You hear what has been said, and I propose that we return to our ship without further delay."

"And leave our work unfinished?" exclaimed Paton, with a half suppressed sneer. "No, no, Henry, we go not away till the rest of our object is accomplished, for though his lordship may have given us the slip, his money and jewels may yet be ours."

"Why surely you would not plunder the house in the absence of its chief?" cried Henry, indignantly. "Besides, you remember the injunctions of our commander, and if we disobey him, we well know what will follow."

"If you are afraid of that," muttered the other, "you had better leave our company, for my mind is made up, and be the consequences what they may, I shall not quit this place without taking with me that which will reward our toil. So now, my lady, since you have heard our purpose, you will perhaps spare us any further trouble by bestowing upon us whatever valuables you may have in your possession."

"If you are robbers you will take it from me by force," answered Lady Gordon, "and your conduct certainly goes far to prove that I have little mercy to expect at your hands."

Paton was awed into temporary silence by this rebuke, but at length resuming his customary insolence of deportment, he said :—

"Your ladyship applies hard names to us, and yet we deserve them not, for it must not be forgotten that our country is at war with yours, and that whatever we take must only be regarded as a lawful prize. We are in excellent force, too, my lady, and you shall yourself be a witness that we have numbers sufficient to take that which you seem unwilling to give voluntarily."

At the same moment he called upon to advance, and immediately upon his doing so, a number of sailors entered the room, and by their manner showed plainly enough that they were ready to obey any command that was given, however unjust it might be, against the inmates of the house. Paton observed their approach with evident satisfaction, and when they arranged themselves about him, he said :—

"You are aware, comrades, that we came to enrich ourselves with whatever we might chance to find in the house. Her ladyship seems to doubt our right to do so, and as she may adopt measures for our being pursued, I rather think our safest plan will be to convey her on board our vessel, and take her with us to America, where she will find honourable treatment till her husband thinks proper to use his influence with the king for procuring an honourable peace between the two countries."

Lady Gordon heard these words with dismay, but ere she could make any reply to it her son Percy rushed from the room, and forcing his way through the sentinels that guarded the door, he quitted the house, and with hasty footsteps made his way towards the sea-shore, resolving to make his way over to the mainland, and return with such a force as should speedily put the invaders to the rout. In his passage, however, he had been nearly intercepted two or three times by persons who had been placed to guard every avenue leading to the house ; but he was light of foot, and the danger with which he had seen his mother threatened added considerably to his speed, so that in about ten minutes after leaving the house, he found himself near the sea-side, when a stranger suddenly stepped before him, and demanded whither he was going.

"I am hastening on business of life and death," he replied, "and if you stay me even for a moment the life of my mother will be sacrificed to the fury of a number of lawless men who have just invaded our peaceful home."

"Nay, you pass me not at present," answered the other, "for your errand threatens mischief, and I will bar your further progress till the men you speak of have left the island."

But the youth was not to be thwarted thus, and though his adversary was evidently superior to him in the use of his weapons, he instantly drew his sword, and endeavoured to force a passage for himself. The other, however, quickly disarmed him, and then, handing back the weapon he had wrested from his grasp, he exclaimed in a tone of gentleness :—

"You see, my young friend, how vain it is to contend against one who has more strength and greater experience in the use of his weapons. I am no enemy, though circumstances may certainly be against the assertion, and in proof of what I have said, you have only to return with me to your house, and you shall see how soon I will clear it of those who have dared disobey my orders."

The youth was convinced, by the earnestness with which these words were spoken, that he could rely upon the man who had uttered them, and following him at a rapid pace, they soon reached the house, where ready access was yielded by the sentinels who had been placed about it on duty. Ruthven, for he it was, paid little attention to them, however, and striding up the stairs, he entered the apartment just as Paton was seizing upon Lady Gordon to force her to accompany him to the vessel. In an instant his cutlass was drawn, and he furiously approached his lieutenant, with the intention of sacrificing him to his ungovernable rage ; but the other foresaw his design, and stepping back among the sailors who stood beside him, he appealed to them whether he was to be butchered for merely plundering an enemy of a little gold and jewellery.

"Hark'ee, Paton," exclaimed Ruthven ; "if I spare you now, it is in the hope that you will gather wisdom from experience, and learn that my orders are not to be disobeyed with impunity. We war with men, and not with women; yet you would have seized upon yonder helpless female, though by so doing you would have widened the breach that already exists between our country and this."

"You needn't make such a fuss, captain," retorted the other, "about a few old silver spoons, and the like of them. Her ladyship will be willing enough to give them up, and surely we are not obliged to refuse a good offer when it is made."

"You would have taken them from the house by force and violence," answered Ruthven, "and such an act as this would have brought upon us the highest indignation of Congress. You will, therefore, now retire with me, and I trust her ladyship will not be unjust enough to blame a whole nation for the lawless conduct of a few avaricious Americans."

Paton made no reply to this, but he looked anxiously round upon his companions, and seeing that none of them were inclined to back him in any disobedience of orders, he sullenly disengaged himself from among them, and instantly hastened from the room. Ruthven then offered the best apology he could to Lady Gordon for what had taken place, and having seen every man leave the house, he immediately quitted with Henry, and the whole party proceeded once more towards the sea-shore.

Here they found the boats which had been left there till their return, and the men who had been entrusted with the charge of taking care of them no sooner observed their approach, than the little vessels were rowed close in among the rocks, and the whole party embarked without the delay of an instant. And well it was for them that they did so, for scarcely were they seated at their oars than several soldiers were observed advancing rapidly towards the beach, and scarcely had the Americans proceeded a hundred yards from land, than a volley of musketry was discharged after them, though without effect. This served to inspise the rowers with fresh energy, and pulling with all their might, they were shortly on board their own vessel.

CHAPTER XXVIII.

"The spirit of the storm is out to-night,
To pour forth vengeance upon mortal man;
Black roll the clouds, and angry lightnings flash,
To illumine all beneath."

THE OCEAN CAVE.

No sooner had Ruthven set foot upon his own deck, than it became evident to every one that looked upon him that he had not forgotten the conduct of his men on shore, and those who had offended him looked with fear at the consequences which they were pretty certain would follow. For some little time he paced up and down in moody silence, but at length, seating himself as Paton advanced, he pointed towards a chest at his feet, and said sternly :—

"What is this, sir? I observed you bring it on board from the boat with much care, and I have my doubts that you have been mad enough to barter your honour and that of your country for what it contains."

"Why, to tell you the truth, captain," answered Paton, somewhat abashed at these words, "the trunk contains the plate and jewels that we brought with us from Lady Gordon's."

"And did I not tell you, sir," demanded Ruthven, "that no violence was to be committed?"

"You did," replied the other, "but our orders were to seize the master of the house, and as he was not in the way, I thought we could not do less than leave convincing proofs that we had been there. Besides, a prize don't fall in our way every day, and it would have been madness to let slip such an opportunity as this to put money in our pockets,"

"It is your duty to obey, and not to set up yourself as a judge in such matters as this," exclaimed Ruthven, angrily. "You have, however, thought proper to disobey me, and, by so doing, set an example that, if practiced in a few more instances, would prove fatal to the country you profess to serve."

"Captain Ruthven," cried the other, "you know not yet the sort of men you are called upon to command. We are free-born Americans, and if we fight and risk our lives for our country, we conceive that we have a right to enrich ourselves with the spoil belonging to an enemy."

"Humph!" muttered Ruthven; "this is a principle in warfare that Europeans happily know nothing about; in this quarter of the globe there is such a thing as honour even when we have to deal with our foe, and those who are placed under my command must observe the same custom, or I shall take such steps as may appear somewhat too severe by your countrymen, who profess such a veneration for liberty. Your conduct, sir, has justly merited the punishment of death, but for this time I am inclined to pass it over without further comment. Now, sir, listen to me;—word has been brought that two ships have been sent to give us battle, and if you do your duty to my satisfaction, I will not only pardon the past, but honourably mention you to Congress. But, if, on the contrary, you show any disinclination to serve your country faithfully, I will take it upon myself to punish you with that death which you have already deserved."

Ruthven abruptly rose from his seat as he said this, and turned away with the evident desire of finishing the conversation. But the haughty spirit of Lieutenant Paton could not brook this insult, as he termed it, and turning angrily away, he shortly afterwards met Henry, to whom, however, for certain reasons of his own, he did not think proper to mention the cause of his wrath, and assuming a confidential tone, he said:—

"I know not how you feel, young man, with respect to the person that has been set in command over us, but for my own part I cannot help thinking that he is wasting time that might be more profitably employed. What advantage, for instance, have we gained after a long and wearisome cruize; and yet now it seems a couple of armed ships have been sent against us, and the chances are that in the course of a few hours we shall fall into the hands of our enemies."

"You have not very thoroughly explained yourself, lieutenant," answered the young man, "but I understand enough to know that you are tired of his command. I, however, know the value of discipline, and can give him all due praise for having acted with judgment and discretion. If you are dissatisfied with him, transfer your services to the captain of some other American vessel, and I dare say the parting will be no less welcome to yourself than to Captain Ruthven."

"And why should you not accompany me?" demanded Paton. "Honour, though it is not to be gained here, may be found somewhere else; and if your opinion of Ruthven is no better than my own, you must longace have learned to hate and despise him as much as do myself."

Henry heard him with surprise, and it was some little time before he returned an answer. At length, however, in a tone of scorn, he said:—

"Your words, Lieutenant Paton, have filled me with wonder, yet you have to learn, sir, that I can despise the man who has the baseness to undermine the respect which all men should entertain towards those who are placed in authority over them. Captain Ruthven is an honourable man, and you may well be ashamed of having acted so base a part towards him."

"And what, pray, are you, sir, that I should hear such words as these?" demanded Paton, haughtily; "a boy, scarcely yet freed from his mother's apron-strings, and yet you have dared to speak as if your were my equal."

"You have reminded me, sir, that *here* you are my superior," exclaimed Henry, angrily; "but you will remember that the time will come when we shall meet elsewhere, and whenever that period arrives, I shall not forget the insult you have passed upon me this day."

"Away to your duty, sir!" cried Paton, in a tone of authority. "Leave me, and do not fail to remember you owe it to my clemency that you have not been punished for using such language as this to your superior officer."

Henry paused, for he knew not whether to obey the order that had been given with so much insolence, or resent the affront which was to be conveyed by it. Pride, however, in the end got the better of him, and he had grasped the handle of his sword to unsheath it, when Andrew Forster stepped up, and addressed him in a whisper:—

"Hold, sir," he exclaimed, "and don't give advantage to a man that will be glad enough to make use of it. Remember the lieutenant is your superior officer, as well as he is mine, only I am better able to cope with him if it comes to drawing swords, and all I want is an opportunity to let him know that his conduct since I've been aboard this ship has brought us to a level with each other. Aye, you may frown upon me, Paton, but no man need be ashamed of the truth, and if I've said more than is pleasing to you, sir, you know how to resent it."

And as he spoke, he half drew his cutlass, and returned the look with one of defiance that the other could not misunderstand. Paton regarded him for a moment or two with an expression of surprise that he could not conceal. But he knew that Andrew Forster was a man of his word, and was far superior in point of strength to himself, and affecting to regard his adversary with sovereign contempt, he turned upon his heel, and paced to and fro upon the deck to meditate fresh plans of mischief, and contrive some method by which he might avenge himself for the reproof he had met with. Andrew, however, took little heed of this, and while the lieutenant was at a distant part of the vessel, he hastened towards Ruthven, whom he interrupted in the midst of the ruminations he was engaged in.

"I don't know whether you observed it as well as myself, sir," he exclaimed, "but the sun went down in a bank of suspicious-looking clouds, and from the low wailing of the wind, I rather expect we are going to have more than a breeze before another hour is over."

"I scarcely observed the indications you speak of," answered the other; "but now I can see that your fears are not groundless. Lieutenant Paton, too, I perceive, has forseen it all, for he is busily engaged with the men in preparing the vessel against the tempest. But tell me, Andrew, how long has the sound I hear continued?"

"Ever since the sun went down," replied he other; "and the moment I heard it I knew what we had to expect."

Whilst he was yet speaking, a thick fog was observed rolling towards them, which in a short time completely enveloped the vessel, and left the mariners uncertain what course to pursue, or how to avoid the rocks which they knew were thickly scattered over that part of the sea. There was no wind, and the water was motionless, yet all felt that the greatest danger surrounded them, and every man prepared himself for the worst, in case a sudden change should take place.

"Now," exclaimed Andrew Forster, "it is necessary that every man should be at his post, for I happen to know this coast well, and many a brave vessel has been lost upon it in a less storm than we are likely to have to-night. But hark, comrades, what sound was that?"

"I heard no sound, Andrew," exclaimed Henry, "except, indeed, the croaking of a raven that seemed to come landwards."

"And ravens are birds of fearful omen," answered Andrew, with superstious awe; "they never bode good to man, but are always to be seen and heard whenever death or carnage is about to take place."

Ruthven, cool and collected as he usually was, could not help feeling alarmed at the indications of an approaching tempest. At length upon a sudden a smart gust of wind was felt that sent the fog eddying around them, and for a short space the mariners could see the distance of some few furlongs around the vessel. But this was only the commencement of the storm, for the waves began to lash themselves into fury, and in the space of a few minutes they rose, threatening destruction to the ship.

"Now, captain, my words have come to pass," exclaimed Andrew Forster, "and I'm not sorry the storm has begun in earnest, for I'd rather know the worst at once than be kept for hours in fear of my life."

The captain paid no attention to this, but seeing Henry approach, he said to him :—

"This is a raging tempest, young man, but you must not fear it, for ours is a good ship, and there must be more wind than this before a plank about her starts."

As he spoke a furious sea struck the vessel, threatening her and all on board with instant destruction; she, however, proved herself well worthy the commendation that had just been passed upon her, for in a moment afterwards she recovered from the shock almost as harmless as she had been previous to the accident, and again she rode like a cork floating upon the waters, and seeming proud of the triumph she had gained over a powerful and treacherous enemy.

"'Tis a good ship," exclaimed Andrew Forster, "and it would be a thousand pities if she should go to the bottom after proving herself so worthy of the trust confided to her. She floats as light as the sea-foam itself, and with skilful men to work her, I believe even such a storm as this will do her no further harm than just rending a few of her sails."

"I believe we shall ride the storm out safely enough," said Ruthven; "but I much fear the sloop we took from Captain Starkie will sink, and carry with her a score or two of our brave fellows. Should the storm continue, our masts must go, for they are shivering in the blast, as if they knew the danger that threatens us."

Of all who watched the fury of the tempest, none regarded it with more terror than did Lieutenant Paton, who looked upon the raging billows as if expecting each moment to be swallowed up in them. He heard the howling of the winds with uncontrollable alarm, and listened to each word that was uttered by the sailors around him, as if expecting to hear from them the fate he so much dreaded to encounter. To his horror the tempest seemed rather to increase than diminish, and a fear insensibly stole upon him that he was unable to conceal. This was quickly perceived by Andrew, who, creeping to his side, said,—

"People may talk as they like about having no fear of death; but place them in a situation like this, sir, and we shall soon see what all their boasting comes to. For my own part, I, perhaps, think of these things

as little as most folks, yet I must confess to you, lieutenant, that I'm afraid
we are almost at the end of our last voyage in this world. This sea is a
dangerous one for a lighter vessel than ours, and as we are not likely to see
the light of morning, would it not be as well to stave in the heads of two or
three brandy casks, and drink to our pleasant passage into the next world?
Do you feel uncomfortable, sir, at the prospect before us?—for, to my thinking, you seem as if you would rather have gone to any other grave than
the one that lies some few fathoms beneath us."

"I have scarely had time to think about it at all," answered Paton, who
saw that the other was jeering, in spite of the perilous situation they were
in.   "But it seems, Andrew, you think the ship is in danger?"

"It don't want much thinking about, sir," he replied, "because the
thing's plain enough to be seen. However, sir, I don't wish to alarm you,
only I fancied it might be as well to let you know that a few minutes may
serve to send us all to the bottom of the sea."

Meanwhile Ruthven, though he saw the danger, exhibited no signs of
fear or perturbation, but moved about from one part of the ship to another,
giving his orders with perfect coolness and self-command, and issuing such
commands as were most likely to save the vessel from destruction.   On the
other hand, the crew laboured cheerfully, though the toil was almost too
much for endurance, and for some weary hours they toiled on with the one
cheering prospect that morning would at length arrive, and that when it
did come the storm might lose some of its violence. At length the first
streak of daylight appeared in the horizon, and as it increased, the crew
saw, to their horror and dismay, that they were rushing impetuously towards a long ridge of rocks which threatened them with instant destruction.
In an instant Ruthven sprung to the helm just in time to change the vessel's course and save her from destruction; and within an hour afterwards,
the wind had so much abated, that the peril seemed to have passed away,
and the crew once more resumed their usual occupations.

No. 26

CHAPTER XXIX.

" I love the raging battle in its height,
For then the heart grows warm, and lurking fear
Is driven from the soul. There's honour in't,
And I would rather die a thousand deaths
Than live to see our foes victorious."

HANNIBAL.

LIGHT and cheerful were the hearts of the mariners when they saw that the peril of the tempest had passed away, and even Lieutenant Paton, whose fears had been so great, began to recover his spirits and confidence as the raging of the ocean gradually subsided; and rousing himself once more to exertion, he set himself cheerfully about the duty of seeing the vessel restored to the trim condition in which she had been previous to the storm which had threatened them with destruction. Indeed, so courteous was he in his demeanour towards the men under his command, that most of them forgot the cowardice he had displayed in the moment of danger, and it was only Andrew Forster and Henry that bore in their remembrance the utter prostration of energy which had marked his conduct at a moment when the utmost coolness and self-possession were required.

"Well, after all," whispered the former to Henry, "that Lieutenant Paton is but a coward when a little bit of danger stares him in the face, for just now he was trembling with fear like a young girl, and now he's all smiles and sunshine because the worst part of the business has been got through."

"I have been thinking the same thing," answered Henry, "and could not help contrasting his conduct with that of our captain, who never lost his courage for a moment, even when our danger was at its height. But it's the way with all bullies,—they can show off famously when there's nothing to be afraid of; but only wait till things turn against them a bit, and you will see them ready to sink into their shoes."

"Aye, aye," replied Andrew; "and those that live longest will see something more to prove him unworthy the confidence that Congress has placed in him. We shall have a brush with the enemy soon, and I expect our lieutenant will be the first in the ship to show the white feather."

"I'm almost afraid your anticipations about meeting the enemy will end in disappointment," replied Henry, "for we have been cruizing about this coast some time, and no armed vessels have yet ventured to come in pursuit of us."

"Have patience, man," exclaimed Andrew, "and you'll see that the British are not quite such cowards as you take them for. A few hours will serve to prove the truth of my words, and when the battle begins we shall find an enemy to cope with that will supply us with work to our heart's content."

"You are right, Andrew," answered the young man, "and I have indeed done an injustice to the men we call our enemies. As an American, I glory in having sprung from these islanders, and glad shall I be when the honour of both parties will permit two great nations to be at peace with each other. But the world acknowledges that we have been wronged, and having drawn the sword, our country will never sheath it again till justice has been done us."

"There your people are right enough," exclaimed Andrew; "and you may be sure I think so, or I should never have joined Captain Ruthven when I knew the object he had in view."

"The fact is, we have been oppressed by the tyranny of the mother country," returned Henry, "and we should have been worse than cowards had we hesitated to assert our equality with your English people. We have adopted a bold course, and ere long the world will see that the Americans can fight bravely when liberty is the watchword."

At this moment a cry was heard from the mast-head, announcing that a vessel was in sight, and having awaited a few moments to ascertain the particulars, Henry descended to the cabin to arouse Captain Ruthven, who had thrown himself upon a couch to rest himself after the wearisome night he had gone through. The young man touched him lightly on the shoulder, but it failed to rouse him from the deep slumber into which he had fallen; but no sooner had he uttered the magical words, " A sail, captain, a sail !" than Ruthven sprang upon his feet, and, without waiting to make any inquiries, rushed upon the deck, where he found all the mariners intently occupied in observing a vessel at some distance off, and which the man at the mast-head declared to be a frigate mounting sixty guns.

"The odds are against us," exclaimed Ruthven, "and yet, were they twice as great, I would not seek to avoid an engagement. Is everything ready to give yonder vessel a warm reception when we come near enough to her ?"

"Everything is quite ready, sir," answered Lieutenant Paton.

" 'Tis well," exclaimed Ruthven; " and now let it be remembered that not a gun must be fired till you receive the order from my lips, and when I give the word to board, let there be no laggards, for if the ship belongs to an enemy she must be ours at all hazards."

"I rather think we may spare ourselves all trouble on that account," interposed Andrew Forster, who had been eyeing the vessel through a telescope, " for she bears the ensign of France, and, of course, on a friendly errand."

"You are right, Andrew," exclaimed Ruthven, who had snatched the glass from his hand, and carefully examined the approaching vessel. " She belongs to our ally, and no doubt has been sent by the French government to my assistance."

Shortly after this the vessel came within hail, and the satisfaction afforded by this meeting was mutual on both sides. A signal was then displayed for Ruthven to go on board, which was promptly acceded to; and no sooner had he and a few of his men set foot on the deck of the French ship, than a loud shout welcomed their arrival, and Captain Durand, advancing towards the English leader, received him in the most gratifying manner.

"Captain Durand," exclaimed Ruthven, "this meeting is a most welcome one, since it will enable me to carry out the orders I have received from Congress. I expect to be engaged with the enemy within a very short time, and you will, therefore, be good enough to show me the instructions you have received by those who sent you to my aid."

"I am sorry it is not in my power to oblige you," replied the ceremonious Frenchman; " but the truth is, my instructions are sealed, and I received orders to open them in a certain latitude. It happened, however, that I was asleep at the time, and as we have now passed the place, I dare not break the seal for fear of the consequences."

"And would you, then, risk the safety of our cause by standing on so paltry a point of etiquette ?" demanded Ruthven, in a tone of indignant surprise. " If the case was my own I should not think anything about consequences, but would break open the seal and then act according to the instructions, just the same as if all had been done in strict conformity with whatever orders I might have received from the director of naval affairs."

Captain Durand looked astonished at this, for he belonged to a country which sacrificed everything to certain set forms, and he could scarcely believe it possible that any man could be found to disobey orders, however necessary it might be to do so in a case of emergency. It was, indeed, some time before he could find words to reply; but at length, with much bowing and grimacing, he begged to assure Captain Ruthven that it was utterly impossible for him to break the seal under such circumstances as these.

"In that case, sir," exclaimed the American captain, "it is necessary that you should thoroughly understand our position. Here are my instructions, which I am bound to obey; they are written, as you will observe, by our minister at the court of France, and are signed by your king. By this you are directed to take command under me, and you will therefore take charge of my vessel whilst I take that of yours, and together we will endeavour to take the homeward bound British fleet, which I believe will arrive hereabouts very shortly."

The Frenchman listened to these words with a sullen air of offended dignity; but the signature of his king could not be doubted, and under these circumstances he was compelled to submit with the best grace he could. He therefore coldly bowed his acquiescence, and shortly afterwards proceeded to the American vessel, with such a number of his own men as had been agreed upon between him and Ruthven, who followed him to the ship by way of compliment.

"Captain Durand," he said, "I now commit this vessel to your keeping, and I believe you will find all the appointments in such excellent order that you will have very little to feel dissatisfied with on that account. The crew consists of brave men, who will fight to the very last for the honour of their country, and never will they leave the vessel whilst a plank of her remains entire. You, I have no doubt, will prove a worthy leader, but should your conduct prove that I have been deceived, I will brand you as a coward, and proclaim your disgrace from one end of the world to the other."

Durand was not best pleased at the words he had heard uttered, but he could not betray his wounded feelings just then, and shaking the hand of Ruthven with feigned warmth, he assured him that nothing should occur to give an unfavourable opinion either of his seamanship or his courage.

Ruthven made no reply to this, for he was busily engaged in gazing through his glass upon that part of the horizon from whence the prize was expected to appear. At length a cry of exultation burst from his lips, and moving the telescope from his eye, he joyfully exclaimed,—

"They are in sight, Captain Durand, and I must now leave you to go on board the vessel I have to take charge of. Be vigilant, I entreat, and should you be at a loss what to do my signals will put you right. Their ships of war, that are sent to guard the merchantmen, must be the first objects of our attack, and you will therefore lay yourself muzzle to muzzle with the smaller vessel, whilst I engage with the stronger one. And remember, sir, the victory must be ours, or before the battle ends you and I must find a grave at the bottom of the ocean."

Saying this, he and his men hurried into the boat that was lying alongside, and in the course of a few minutes afterwards the sails of both vessels were spread, and with a favouring breeze they started forward on their course, having first of all hoisted the colours of England, in order that they might deceive the enemy till they came within range of their cannon balls. It, however, soon became apparent that they could not easily gain such an advantage over the commander of the English ships, for he instantly gave orders for the merchantmen to retreat and make for land; and having seen this done, his vessel and the one that accompanied him advanced, with the evident intention of giving battle should his suspicions prove correct.

Ruthven, who had been anxiously watching every movement of the enemy, stood boldly, and with an undaunted mien, in the midst of his crew, for everything was in admirable fighting order, and he felt confident, notwithstanding the superior size of the advancing ships, that the victory would be his.   On the other hand his men were no less vigilant in the discharge of their duty, and as nothing further remained to be done till the battle commenced, they stood round their leader impatiently awaiting the command which was to begin the engagement.

At length a gun fired from one of the English ships, but it was evidently not intended to hit any particular object, for the ball was seen scudding along the surface of the sea till its strength was spent, when it sunk harmless to the bottom.   Ruthven was apparently unmoved by this, for, as if nothing had happened, he followed on his course, with Captain Durand close by his side, awaiting any commands that he might have to give relative to a commencement of hostilities.   The English vessels, it now appeared, were nearly equal to those of the enemy, but if any advantage existed it was with the Americans, who carried a little more weight of metal, though scarcely sufficiently to turn the tide of battle in their favour.

It was not long before Ruthven ran up, as he had undertaken to do, to the larger English ship, and as he did this a simultaneous broadside was poured in from both of them.   At the same moment the other two vessels were engaged together, but scarcely had the first broadside been fired when it became evident that the Frenchman grew uneasy, for he commenced manœuvring in order to avoid the mischief which was intended by the foe; but all his efforts were in vain, for the English captain would not suffer him to flinch so easily from the strife, and after some little time he found himself compelled either to fight resolutely, or yield to the superior bravery of those he was engaged with.

In the meantime the battle was hotly carried on between Ruthven and his antagonist, for the former knew what his fate would be in the event of his becoming a prisoner in the hands of the English, whilst his adversary fought for the honour of his native country, and to keep up the old boast that England was rarely beaten by the enemy whenever there was no great disadvantage against them.

After many broadsides had been exchanged between the ships, the captain of each sought to come to closer quarters, and the Englishman, calculating upon the courage of his men, pushed suddenly a-head, with the intention of raking his adversary fore and aft; but Ruthven foresaw the design and was prompt in his endeavour to thwart it, and so quick was the movement he made that they were almost immediately side to side, and then a shout of defiance was sent forth by both parties, that was plainly heard by the persons who were watching the conflict from the shore.   By this time the American vessel was so pierced with shot that it was with difficulty she could be kept above water.   Nor had the English ship escaped much better, for her planks were terribly torn and shattered by the destructive fire she had sustained from the enemy, and the crew, as well as the Americans, were nearly exhausted by the increasing toil they had so long been forced to endure.

As for Ruthven, he had scarely time to think much of passing events, for his soul was bent on the strife in which he was engaged, and notwithstanding the desperate condition of his vessel, he was still determined to fight to the very last, though the advantage appeared by this time to be rather against him.   But liberty was the watchword, and in spite of all, he determined either to gain the victory or perish in the attempt.

CHAPTER XXX.

" The battle was a fierce and bloody one:
  And many a gallant spirit there, 'tis said,
  Was silenced in the sleep of death.   Yet this
  It is that kings make sport withal, and think
  'Tis honour."   THE RIVAL MONARCHS.

WHILST the battle was thus raging on the sea, a number of anxious
spectators were assembled on shore to watch an event in which all felt so
great an interest.   At last darkness began to set in, and those who were
desirous that victory should reward the efforts of their English brethren,
felt some hope that night would give an advantage to their countrymen,
which their enemies would vainly seek to counteract.   But in this they
were disappointed, for both the commanders were determined that the victory should be decisive one way or the other, and as it was impossible that
the battle could be continued at night, hostilities were suspended for awhile,
and the ships moved a little way apart, in the hope that the moon would
presently yield sufficient light to bring this sanguinary battle to an issue.

During this short interruption assistance came to both parties;   that
which came to Ruthven consisted of a French frigate, which, though almost
useless in every other respect, afforded aid to Captain Durand, and thus
prevented his vessel from falling into the hands of the foe he was engaged
with.   The aid which came to the English captain was of a different sort,
and will take some little time describe.

Among the many persons who had watched the sea-fight from land, there
were two who regarded it with more than common interest;   one of these
was Lord Dalmeny, and the other Hugh Lorimer, both of whom were well
acquainted with John Ruthven, and knowing his daring spirit whenever
danger was in the way, they looked forward with anxiety to the result of
the hard-fought battle.   At length, when the night had fairly set in, and
the sound of cannon was no longer to be heard, the former, addressing
himself to Lorimer, said,—

" I know not how you feel after the excitement has passed away, but for
my own part I cannot help thinking that this darkness is very awful, and I
would give almost everything to have light enough to see what is doing
among the late combatants.   The moon will not rise for some little time
yet, and I've been thinking, Hugh, that we might find an opportunity to go
on board one of our vessels, with fifty or sixty stout fellows at our back,
and so teach this John Ruthven that he is not to come upon our coasts and
do all the mischief he can, without finding that we have spirit enough left
to drive him back to the country of his adoption."

" My lord," answered the other, " your proposition is an impracticable
one, for we might as well venture to approach a legion of devils as go near
John Ruthven and his band of desperadoes.   Besides, there is a chance
that the English captain would mistake us for enemies, and in that case
he would blow us out of the water long before we could get near enough
to his ship to explain who we were and the purpose we went upon."

" What course would you adopt, then ?" demanded his lordship.

" It is scarcely for me to give advice to one so much above myself," answered Lorimer;   " but if I may be allowed to give my opinion upon the
subject, I should say the best plan will be to wait till the moon rises, and
then we shall have light enough to see our way clear."

" Well, I will follow your suggestion for this once, at any rate," exclaimed
Lord Dalmeny.   " But who, in the name of fortune, have we here ?   What

strange animal is this that appears to have just dropped down from the clouds ?"

The man who had been the subject of these remarks, was, indeed, a singular being, dressed in a most extraordinary manner, and denoting by his conduct that he was either mad, or assumed an appearance for the purpose of deception. His clothes were a mixture of the fashions of the last and present century, and the style in which he walked along seemed to declare that he thought himself far superior to the forty or fifty fellows that followed him, more out of joke than for anything else. Even Lord Dalmeny could scarcely forbear laughing as this strange figure came before him, but he contrived to restrain his mirth within bounds, and with as much gravity as he could assume, inquired what had brought him out from home that night.

" I am called upon to defend my country," he replied.

" Your name ?"

" Martin Stewartson."

" A tailor, please you, my lord," exclaimed a bystander by way of explanation. " He has left his shopboard to play at soldiers, and I have followed to persuade him to go back and mind his business instead of troubling his head about a parcel of foolish things that don't concern him."

A rap on the head, administered by Martin Stewartson with no little force, reminded the rustic that he was going too far, and taking advantage of the pause that ensued, Hugh Lorimer said to Lord Dalmeny,—

" The moon will rise in a few minutes, my lord, and the boats are all ready for us. I can just distinguish the ships at a distance, and if any thing is to be done, I think the sooner we get out to sea the better."

As he said this he sprang into one of the little vessels that was lying upon the shore, and his example was followed by Lord Dalmeny, who quickly jumped into another of the boats, both of which were soon filled by as many of the multitude of spectators as could get into them. Martin Stewartson chose to go by that which carried the nobleman. By this time the moon rose bright and unclouded, and as she became visible above the horizon, the English and American ships recommenced the battle, which had been broken off by the darkness of the night. Again the air resounded with their cannon, and the two boats, with their crews, were placed in a dangerous position, from which it was not very easy to escape.

" Hugh," exclaimed Lord Dalmeny, " can you tell me which of those ships belongs to John Ruthven ? Look for the American banner, and point out to me where he is to be found, for where he is there will I be also. We are now sworn enemies, and my dearest wish is that I may meet him sword in hand, and then settle the differences that have so long been between us."

" Yonder," answered Lorimer, " is a light English vessel bearing the colours of our native land. She has borne the shock of the contest bravely, but if I may judge from her appearance she will not be able to endure the fight much longer. Let us board her, my lord, with these volunteers, and perhaps we may turn the tide of battle in her favour."

" Then bend to your oars, lads," cried Lord Dalmeny, " and we shall soon be in the thick of the glorious action. When we come alongside, spring on board without delay, and then let your muskets do the work of death amongst those traitors that have dared come and invade our native soil."

The bowsprit of the English ship lay partly over the deck of the American, thus presenting, as it were, one deck, and so fast locked together, that they moved as if there was but one keel between them. It was in vain that the English commander endeavoured to release himself from the jeopardy into which he had fallen ; the anticipated result of all his previous manœuvres was now lost, and after a desperate struggle to set the vessel free he gave up the attempt, and prepared to renew the fight, however great the disad-vantage might be against him.

In this interval Ruthven had formed his own plans, and calling his men around him, he rushed on board the English vessel, followed by the bravest of his sailors, and forced his way onwards in spite of all the obstacles with which he was opposed. Two of his enemies fell beneath his sword as he thus sprang among them, and pointing towards the British ensign, which still hung proudly above him, he called upon his followers to tear it from its place. But this was a task of greater difficulty than he expected, for the English were resolved to be spared that humiliation as long as possible, and terrible was the slaughter which took place in the contest which ensued. Yet the colours would have been lowered in spite of the gallant defence that was offered, had not Ruthven been suddenly assailed by a new enemy, and turning round to see who it was that had thus come to the defence of his country's emblem, he discovered Lord Dalmeny with his sword reeking with the blood of his slaughtered foes, and glancing a look of proud defiance at him whom he had come to fight against as an enemy. For a moment Ruthven was rendered motionless with surprise, but recovering himself, he waved his new assailant away, exclaiming, in an agitated voice,—

" My lord, at this moment I am not warring against you ; leave us, then, and suffer this contest to end amongst those by whom it was begun ; another time we shall meet again, and then either Lord Dalmeny or I will bid farewell to this world for ever."

But the nobleman to whom these words were addressed paid no heed to them, for he was infuriated at seeing some of his best men fall, and rush-ing upon his enemy, he soon convinced him that he had at last found one to deal with who would never sheath his sword till the purpose for which he had come on board had been accomplished. In the midst of this contest Andrew Forster drew a pistol from his belt, and held it with a certain aim at the head of the nobleman, when Ruthven, striking the weapon from his hand, commanded him in a voice of anger to leave the issue of the combat to himself.

As Andrew slunk away, the battle was renewed with more fierceness than ever,—the deck ran with human gore,—the smoke hung like a thick cloud above them, and the vessels rocked from side to side as the combatants rushed backwards and forwards, according as circumstances required their presence in one or another part of the conflict. Yet, with all the bravery that had been displayed by the English, it soon became evident that they were losing ground, and the battle would scarcely, perhaps, have lasted five minutes longer, had not a number of cartridges exploded and destroyed many of the Americans, by which means Ruthven was deprived of the services of some of his best men, and was thus compelled to retreat to his own ship.

Here he recommenced a most destructive fire upon his foe, mowing down the seamen like grass, and directing chain-shot against the masts. But on the other hand he was attacked by a devastating fire from the men who had accompanied Lord Dalmeny, and at the same time his vessel was torn and mangled by another broadside, that threatened to send the already nearly sinking vessel to the bottom. Now, therefore, was the time to make a last vigorous effort, and calling upon his men to follow, he led them once more with the determination of ending the fight by such an assault as his foes should not be able to withstand.

During the whole time that the battle lasted, no one had seen anything of Lieutenant Paton, who, trembling with fear, had betaken himself below,

where he remained till the repeated broadsides compelled him to hasten up on deck, where he saw nothing but English faces, and imagining that the victory had been declared against his countrymen, he hastened to the place where the American colours were suspended, and instantly struck them.

No sooner had this unexpected occurrence taken place than a loud shout announced the cowardly act to Ruthven, who, raising the pistol which he held in his hand, presented it towards the traitor, and almost ere the report was heard Paton uttered a loud cry of mortal agony, and, sinking upon the deck, he quickly yielded up a life which had been so foully disgraced by his last act.

Sorely pressed as they were by the foe, the English were soon compelled to retreat to their own vessel, and Lord Dalmeny now found that out of the numbers who had accompanied him, two only had escaped the devastating attack to which they had been subjected. He himself had escaped without a wound, though in no instance had he shrunk from placing himself in the post of danger. He was, however, soon attacked by Ruthven, and in the contest that ensued, the issue was so dubious that Andrew Forster, believing his captain was in danger of falling beneath the sword of his antagonist, seized upon a boarding spike, and struck the nobleman a blow that instantly precipitated him into the sea.

From this moment the contest may be said to have ended, for the English vessel had been rendered unmangeable, and more than half the mariners had fallen in the deadly strife. To maintain the contest longer would have been useless; the British ensign was lowered, and the captain delivered his sword into the hands of John Ruthven. But the victory was purchased dearly, for within half an hour afterwards the American vessel sank, barely allowing time for the crew to escape.

No. 27

CHAPTER XXXI.

" Man's bravest actions meet with little praise
From those who envy deeds they dare not do ;
Yet there are some with spirits less ignoble,
Who deal laudations where they are deserved."
                                        THE BANISHED DUKE.

AFTER the events recorded in the last chapter, Ruthven sailed for France, where he was received with honour, and entertained by most of the chief people of the kingdom as a hero who deserved the best praises of mankind. Here he remained for some time, but at length growing weary of an inactive life, he determined once more to go to sea and make his way towards America, where the news of his victory had inspired the people with a frenzied admiration of his bravery and talent.

It was towards the evening of a summer's day when Ruthven once more returned to his vessel, weighed anchor, spread his sails to the wind, and made his way from the shore where he had spent so much of his time in useless frivolity and idleness. Now again his heart seemed free and light, for he was in the midst of the waters that he loved, and he beheld around him those well known comrades who had followed his fortunes with so much pleasure and satisfaction to themselves. He gazed around him with delight, and visions of future glory again visited his ever fertile brain.

Nor was Andrew Forster less delighted than his superior, for he had long been dissatisfied with the indolence of the life he was leading, and as he beheld the land fast receding from his view he could not forbear giving expression to the joy that filled his heart at the thought of returning to what appeared to him his native element.

It is not our intention, however, to follow them through the whole of the voyage, and it will, therefore, be sufficient to say that the mariners sailed on for many a day and night without meeting with any adventure that would be worth recording. At length they passed some of the West India islands, where the air became warmer and more oppressive ; but the voyagers knew that they were approaching home, and the inconvenience was scarcely heeded by men who were anticipating the joy they should experience upon once more seeing their families and friends, from whom they had been so long separated.

At last, after sailing many a league further, the whole ship's company was thrown into an ecstasy of delight by hearing land proclaimed from the mast-head, and soon afterwards a cry of " Boston—Boston !" was heard ringing from one end of the vessel to the other. At this sound Ruthven, with the aid of his glass, looked in the direction to which all eyes were turned, and then placing the telescope in the hand of Andrew Forster, he asked him to say what he saw before him.

" I see ships of war in the harbour, captain," answered Andrew ; " and if I might give my opinion upon the subject, I should say the place is beseiged."

He then took another long look through the glass, and having gazed intently upon the object for some time, he said,—

" I'll tell you what it is, Captain Ruthven, there's been hot work at Boston, and we are just too late to lend a hand to these Americans, who, I dare say, have been fighting like so many devils, for I see several hulls of ships that look as if they had been burnt to the water's edge."

Ruthven could not conceal the surprise these words had occasioned, and once more following with his eyes the direction alluded to by the mariner, he perceived that he had indeed spoken nothing more than the truth ; for at a distance the sea was covered with floating fragments of ships, which had, doubtless, been shattered by some fierce conflict that had recently taken place between the English and Americans. He, however, made no further observation, but approaching Henry, who just then came in sight, he desired that the vessel might be ready for battle, in case of any sudden emergency when they reached the harbour towards which they were steering.

A couple of hours more brought them to an end of their voyage, when the anchor was dropped, and after giving a few directions to the lieutenant who was to be left in command of the vessel during his absence, he proceeded to the shore with a party of his men, and no sooner had he landed than he saw quite sufficient to prove to him that the Americans had succeeded in repulsing the English, by whom the town had been beseiged. In almost every street were marks of the bombardment which the town had undergone, and all around showed fatal proof of the destruction that was spread in every direction by bursting shells and other missiles that had been poured in upon the beleaguered by an exasperated foe. Proceeding onwards to the town-hall, where it was expected the council was assembled, it was easy to see that they were looked upon with suspicion by a large party of men who had been for some time watching their movements, and dreading an attack from them, the captain addressed himself to the man that seemed to be the principal among them, saying,—

"My friend, you will, perhaps, go on a message from me to our governors, and tell them John Ruthven has just landed in Boston, and craves an immediate audience."

No sooner had Ruthven pronounced his name, than a marked difference might be observed in the demeanour of those who but a few moments before had regarded him with doubt and suspicion. In fact, the daring deed performed by Ruthven had already reached the States, and all men looked upon him as a hero little less than Washington himself, and to whom the country owed much of the success which had now placed them in a fair way to obtain their independence. He was, therefore, received with loud cheers—way was made for him through the assembled multitude—and in a few minutes afterwards he found himself in the presence of those who had been intrusted with the government of the town till a more permanent form could be arranged. Here he was received with the utmost enthusiasm; every member rose at his approach, and he then found himself the observed of all observers, and raised to a pinnacle of greatness and honour that he had never anticipated even in his wildest dreams of future glory.

"Ruthven," exclaimed an old man, who appeared to be the chief of the council, "thou art welcome to the land which has struggled thus long and successfully for liberty. Here thou shalt find a home, and shame be to the American who forgets the deeds thou hast done, and the honour which thine arm has wrought for the country of thy adoption."

"Welcome is almost too cold a word for the hero who has thus come among us," cried a younger man, whose admiration appeared to have been excited to the highest pitch. "It is true we have ourselves defeated the enemy that would have driven us from this city and levelled our homes to the very earth; we have sunk their ships, and proved to them that having once drawn our swords in defence of our rights, we will not sheath them again till our land is free. But here is a stranger fighting for us because we are engaged in a just strife, and what honour I ask of you is sufficient for the man who has thus boldly stood forward to assist in our noble struggle."

"My son," interposed another venerable-looking man, "your words breathe the pride of victory, yet I would entreat of you to endure our success with moderation and calmness. The foe has been beaten, but is not yet vanquished, for many a hard-fought battle must yet take place between us and the enemy, and much blood will be spilt ere we attain that glorious object for which every true American yearns."

This speech was received with silence, for all were sanguine of success, and there was not a man in the assembly but believed the last speaker to be at the best a lukewarm friend. After a pause of a few minutes duration, another of the council arose, and with violent words and gestures, denounced the English as tyrants and blood-suckers. He was, however, interrupted by another of the citizens, who proceeded to address the assembly in a calmer tone.

"My friend," he exclaimed, addressing himself to the last speaker, "thy words are violent, where temperance would much better serve our cause. I wish for peace with England, because we have ourselves sprung from her people, but the peace must be one of honour, and such as will give satisfaction to our countrymen who have boldly stood forward in defence of their rights. But I like not this calling upon foreign powers for aid ; France sides with us, not because she loves liberty, but because she thus hopes to cripple the resources of Great Britain, whom she has long regarded as her natural enemy. Neither do I like the assistance which has been afforded us by this John Ruthven, for he has been a traitor to his own country, and who shall say that he will not prove equally treacherous to ours. Trust him not, therefore, lest ye be betrayed and sold to the enemy ; we are ourselves strong enough to cope with them."

These words were listened to with evident impatience, for there was not one among the assembly that could coincide with him, and the speaker was instantly regarded as one who had not the interest of his country at heart. In fact, the assistance given by France was at that time looked upon as the certain means of bringing the War of Independence to a speedy close, and the readiness with which that aid had been granted seemed to afford ample assurance of the sincerity with which it had been given. The words, therefore, which had just been delivered, were listened to with surprise and indignation, and it was some time ere any one could be found to reply to it. At length, however, a citizen rose slowly from his seat, and looking sternly towards the person who had last addressed the members of the council, he said,—

"I little thought to have heard such expressions fall from the lips of one who professes to be amongst the foremost of those who love their country. Are we not threatened by a force far superior to any that we can hope to call into the field, and shall it then be said that we ought to reject the assistance of a friendly power, when, by accepting it, we may hope to bring the war to a speedy conclusion, and thus spare the shedding of that blood which has been nobly warmed in our cause ? Has not France hitherto proved a faithful ally ? —and is it for us, I ask, who have received so much benefit from her hands, to turn round and declare that she is actuated by unworthy motives ? Let us then hear no more such language as this, but receive each Frenchman as a brother, and more particularly do I recommend that John Ruthven shall experience all that gratitude from us that his great and important services have so justly merited."

"In my opinion," said a much younger man than any that had yet spoken, " we are wasting time in an argument that will never bring us nearer to the great design that lies before us. We have fought well and nobly ; the enemy has been driven from before our walls ; their ships are sunk in our harbour, and it will be some time before they are able to attack us with any chance of success. Let us then show our joy in scenes of revelry and triumph, for it will do much towards inspiring the hearts of our citizens with renewed confidence and courage, and we must not forget that John Ruthven, the gallant advocate of our cause, is now amongst us, and that it is our duty to prove to him that we are grateful for what he has done, and confident in his future sincerity."

This speech was received with more favour than the last, and after a few minutes another venerable man arose, to whom all listened with deference and profound respect. Turning himself towards the stranger who had arrived amongst them, he said in an impressive tone,—

"Captain Ruthven, through me the people of America beg to return their grateful acknowledgments for the important services you have rendered to their cause. We have now accomplished the object of our meeting, and you have heard opinions expressed both in favour of yourself and against the interposition you have generously bestowed in our behalf. You will, however, have perceived that the general voice is in your favour, and I, as one of your warmest, but humblest friends, beg to tender you the thanks of this assembly for the important services you have done us in our struggle for liberty. You will now, I trust, return with me to my house, where you will remain a brief period, till I can send you with a fitting escort to receive the warmest thanks of those great and good men who have taken the chief place in our affairs, till peace once more rewards us with her smiles, and restores our land to its wonted state of prosperity."

"And when," asked Ruthven, "am I to proceed to the city where your chief men are to be found?"

"With as little delay as possible," answered the old man; "but the road is unsafe to travel in this period of anarchy and confusion, and we must therefore provide guides and an escort to convey you to your place of destination in safety. You will, however, remain with me for the present, and at a fitting time I will send you forth on your journey."

The old man then rose, and taking the arm of Ruthven, quitted the court-house, accompanied by Andrew Forster, who could not help thinking within himself that the man who had spoken most to the purpose was he who had offered them the hospitality of his house.

CHAPTER XXXII.

" What woes unnumbered follow in the train
Of war and bloodshed! Whole plains are strewed
With festering corses, and the very air
Tainted and foul from those corrupted forms
Which fell in battle!" THE TARTAR KHAN.

AT the expiration of three days it was announced to Ruthven and his companion Andrew that they could depart for the place appointed, but circumstances had occurred in the meantime to render it advisable that they should proceed without the escort of soldiers, and it was therefore determined that they should be accompanied only by a couple of guides, who were to meet them at an appointed hour at a certain place just beyond the outskirts of Boston.

Accordingly, a little after sunset, Ruthven took leave of his kind-hearted host, and accompanied by Andrew Forster, proceeded towards the appointed spot, where they stood gazing for a few minutes on the scene of ruin and devastation that had been left by the recent conflict between the English and American armies. Their contemplation was, however, soon disturbed by the sound of advancing horsemen, and ere they had time to inquire from whence the parties were coming, they were accosted by a couple of mounted Americans, who, in a few hurried words, informed them that they were the persons who had been entrusted with the task of conducting them in safety to the place where the chiefs of the army of independence were to be found.

"What assurance have I," demanded Ruthven, "that you are the persons you represent yourselves to be?"

"The watchword," answered the foremost of the men, "is liberty."

"Right; and your names?"

"I am called Stephen," answered the man who had spoken before, "and my companion is known by the name of Robert."

"And whither are you to conduct me?"

"To the army, and then I believe you are to be introduced to Congress."

No further question was asked, and they now proceeded on their way in silence, which was only occasionally broken by Andrew Forster, whose mind was not altogether at ease about the persons under whose guidance they had placed themselves, and who now and then whispered a few words in Ruthven's ear to ascertain whether he had any more confidence in them than he felt himself. Whether Ruthven felt the same sort of fears is uncertain, but at any rate he did not think proper to explain himself, and after the questions had been put to him several times, he said,—

"I would have you take care, Andrew, how you let these men suspect your want of confidence in them, for we are in their power, and strangers as we are in this country, it would not be easy to escape from them were we to give occasion for any explosion of their anger."

At this moment Robert drew his horse's rein till the two Englishmen came up to him, and then, pointing to a valley on the right, he drew their attention to a number of dead bodies that were lying thickly strewn upon the ground, and who, he informed them, were those who had fallen in the deadly fight which had taken place only a few days before. Wolves and other wild animals were scared away from their horrible banquet by the approach of the travellers, and the whole scene was of so repulsive a character, that the man's heart must have been hard indeed who could have looked upon the sight without shuddering.

"There," said Stephen, "are the bodies of some of the choicest veterans that England could send out against us. They came to subjucate our soil, and behold the fate they have met with. And what else could they have expected when they left England to war against men that fought to give freedom to the land of their birth?"

"And do you not expect," asked Ruthven, "that the heart of every English subject will burn with fury when the news arrives of the slaughter that has been committed on their countrymen?"

"Why, I dare say they will not be pleased at it," answered Stephen, "but if the English people have the wisdom the world gives them credit for, they will take a lesson from the past, and give us the liberty we have demanded. They may send forth their thousands to subdue us, but we are not such cowards as to fear their wrath, and as surely as I now speak to you, the time is not far distant when we shall obtain peace on our own terms, and American independence will be acknowledged by the whole world."

"But suppose France should grow tired of spending any more money in your wars," exclaimed Andrew; "how would you then manage to beat these islanders from your shores?"

"France will not grow tired of doing that which is every day rendering the power of her foe less dangerous to herself," replied Stephen. "This, however, is a subject that we had better not speak of any more at present, for we may chance to fall out upon it, and I would rather pursue the remainder of our journey as friends than as enemies."

For some hours after this they proceeded in almost unbroken silence, but at length reaching an open glade that was beautifully illuminated by the rays of a full moon, the American guide paused, and in a subdued tone, said :—

"We are now near that part of our country, which, for the present, is in the hands of the English. In yonder river they have many ships of war, and as they hold the place in subjection, we must proceed cautiously, lest an unfortunate accident should betray us into their hands."

"I have submitted myself to your guidance," replied Ruthven, "and will, therefore, obey you in all things where I know our safety depends upon caution."

"Humph!" exclaimed the guide; "that was spoken with more gentleness than I could have expected from Captain Ruthven. Yet, for all that," he continued, "I believe I could show him, without much difficulty, one whom he would gladly meet, if it was only for the satisfaction of stabbing him to the heart."

"Of whom do you speak?" demanded Ruthven. "I have, indeed, had foes; but America, I believe, contains not one man against whom I owe any ill feeling."

"The sea," answered Stephen, "has been unfaithful, and one has risen from it who I know you have long since numbered among the dead."

"Hah! you mean Captain Starkie!"

"No,—he lies where he did when you saw the waters close over his ocean grave."

"You mean Paton, then?" exclaimed Ruthven; "and yet, how could he rise, when I beheld him breathless ere they cast his body into the foaming billows. He was a traitor, and had he been my dearest relative, I would have slain him, when I saw that he was seeking to dishonour his country by lowering her flag to the enemy."

"And yet," answered Stephen, in a tone of peculiar meaning, "the time may not be far distant when you will have to answer for that man's death to those who have formed better opinions of him than you seem to have done. Lieutenant Paton obtained his preferment because his countrymen had the utmost confidence in his courage and discretion, yet you have shot him like a dog, without waiting to inquire whether he was as guilty as you imagined. You may have been mistaken, and in that case America has lost one of her bravest sons through the intemperate haste you displayed upon the occasion."

"I shall not shrink from meeting this inquiry fairly and honourably," answered Ruthven, with a haughtiness that he could not control. "Lieutenant Paton betrayed unequivocal marks of cowardice; he would have struck our colours to the enemy; and regarding him as a traitor to his country, I shot him, as one that well deserved his fate. The act I deny not, and I am now ready to answer it."

"I have nothing to do with the affair," exclaimed Stephen, "nor do I go so far as to say that any blame attaches itself to you for what has been done. So now, let that matter rest, and tell me if you know a certain Scottish nobleman, whom the world accounts tolerably brave, yet for whom you entertain a mortal antipathy?"

"Your description," answered Ruthven, "assures me that you allude to Lord Dalmeny."

"It does."

"And would you tell me, then," asked Ruthven, "that he comes from his ocean grave to haunt me here?"

"By an accident," answered Stephen, "he was picked up, conveyed ashore, and recovered from the stupor into which he had fallen. He then joined the invading army of England while you were in the French metropolis, and is now perhaps nearer to us than you imagine. Nay, interrupt me not, for I have scarcely yet finished all the marvels I had to relate. You have a sister, Captain Ruthven, and——"

"I have," groaned the other; "she was dearer to me than life itself, but was carried away from home, as I have reason to believe, by villains in the employ of Lord Dalmeny. She is now in America, you tell me, and by Heaven, I will yet rescue her from those who hold her in bondage!"

"Be cautious, or you will defeat your own ends," exclaimed Stephen.

"Many miles of wood and wilderness lie between you and her you seek, and were you even to overcome all difficulties, there are still reasons why you should not see Effie Ruthven at present. She is, however, in honourable custody, surrounded by friends who would perish in her defence; and whatever designs Lord Dalmeny may have formed against her, he cannot approach the place where she is without my previous knowledge. But, hark!—persons approach,—and I would, therefore, have you hang back a little while, till I have ascertained who the persons are that have caused this interruption."

At this moment an officer was seen issuing from the wood, and directing the horse on which he rode, along the banks of the river;—a native savage ran by his side, carrying a rifle in his hand, while a fierce blood hound ran on before, and detecting Ruthven and his companions, he sprang forward, and uttered so loud a growl, that the officer snatched a pistol from his holster, and the savage advancing a step forward, raised the gun to his shoulder, and was about to fire, when Stephen, addressing himself to the English officer, assured him that they were peaceable inhabitants of the country, returning home from a neighbouring town. This seemed to satisfy the other, and he was turning away, when a number of American riflemen crept out from their place of ambush, and were about to fire upon him, when Stephen, by a sign, commanded them to desist, and the order was obeyed with a promptitude that did not fail to create no little surprise in the mind of Ruthven, who saw the English officer escape unharmed and unconscious of the peril in which he had been placed.

"Do you know who yon officer was?" demanded Stephen of his companion.

"I do," answered Ruthven; "when last my eyes beheld him, he had been wounded, and cast overboard into the sea. It is Lord Dalmeny, but how he escaped death either from drowning or his wounds, I am unable to imagine."

"You are right, sir," interposed Andrew Forster;—"it was, indeed, Lord Dalmeny; "but I'm thinking it's much more likely to be his ghost than a living man."

"Are you certain it was him?" asked Ruthven.

"I am certain it was his spirit," answered the other. "There's no doubting that, I believe; for when a man that's covered with wounds gets soused into the sea, there's very little chance of his getting out of it alive."

Ruthven made no reply just then, for his mind was occupied with a thousand wild conjectures, and he became thoughtful and anxious. The journey, however, was continued along the river bank, but nothing was said by any one for at least an hour, when Stephen, riding up by the side of Ruthven, said:—

"I wish, sir, to warn you of dangers that perhaps you little dream of; you are bold and resolute, and though possessing courage equal to any emergency, I much doubt whether you have prudence enough to hear the advice I would give."

"That will depend upon the nature of what you have to say," answered the other.

"Well, then, to be plain," exclaimed Stephen, "can you submit with patience to hear what your own countrymen will say of you for the course you have been lately pursuing. They will call you a traitor; yet, what of that, if your own heart tells you that you have not done amiss. Wronged, and goaded by oppression, you have espoused a good cause, and though some may calumniate, you have only to proceed with resolution, and the time will come when justice will be done, and your name rescued from obloquy. Yet there are present evils which will annoy and perplex you, for having once turned against the country of your birth, there will be people found in this land unwilling to trust you, lest, in a moment of disappointed ambition, you should turn round against them."

"I am aware of all that," answered Ruthven, "and can endure much, because the people of this country will have an opportunity of seeing that I serve them with truth and fidelity. Besides, I am not to be suspected with impunity, and he who utters a word against my honour will yet find that I have an arm quick to resent an injury."

"Bravely said," exclaimed the other; "and if anything was wanting to fix my esteem for you, it was the certainty that you could rise superior to the temporary disadvantages you may be under for a time. Be not depressed, however, by what I have said, for though many may contemn, there are more persons in America who will admire that spirit that induced you to cast off your allegiance to one country in favour of another, that was groaning under oppression. Washington will himself receive you with favour, and that circumstance alone will be more than sufficient to counterbalance the paltry jealousy of other parties."

"And if he wants another friend he will find him in me," exclaimed Andrew Forster. "Aye, Stephen, you may smile, but though I am a humble fellow enough, there may be found more real honesty under my rough coat than you would be able to find under the embroidered jerkins of any half dozen of your frippery lords. But what do I see yonder?" he exclaimed, pointing towards the middle of the river;—"an English ship, and we so near as to be within gun-shot!"

"Be silent, and follow me," whispered the guide; and as he spoke he turned his horse towards a place where they would be safely concealed beneath the dark shades of a clump of trees. Here Stephen gently blew a whistle, which was immediately responded to, and then a large boat was seen gliding towards them, on board of which men and horses were quickly conveyed, and ere Ruthven could well recover from his surprise they were safely landed on the other side, and being once more mounted on horseback they again pursued their way across the country.

No. 28

CHAPTER XXXIII.

" Yet war was still the cry, and men were found
To follow to the field where death so oft
Had thinned our gallant ranks. 'Twas emulation
Urged them on; and yet, alas! how few
E'er saw their homes again."

TIMOLEON.

AFTER proceeding four or five miles across a rough uncultivated country, Ruthven, and those who were with him, began to perceive indications of being in the spot near which the next struggle for victory was to take place. They could plainly hear the sounds of martial music, intermingled with the discharge of small arms, and at some distance off they could perceive smoke rising from the earth, which the guides assured them proceeded from the camp of one or other of the armies. Dead bodies were also occasionally seen lying upon the ground, which was torn and ploughed up as if by cannon balls, and there were other proofs, if any such had been wanted, that a skirmish had recently taken place, though which party had been victorious it was impossible to determine.

At length, upon reaching the summit of a hill, they saw the British army advancing just beneath them, and notwithstanding the disadvantages under which they laboured, there was a coolness and precision in their every movement that called forth the admiration of those who were watching them from above. Even the principal of the two guides, though professedly an enemy, could not restrain the admiration with which he viewed them, and as he pointed them out to his companions, he said,—

"I can never look upon the well disciplined troops of England without feeling that they are superior to any others that are to be found in the world. Yonder men, for instance, in a fair and open field would be more than a match for three times our number. But we know the advantage of fighting in ambush, and as surely as you now see them advancing full of confidence and hope to give us battle, they will fall beneath our destructive fire, and scarcely one half will survive to tell the shame and defeat that has again fallen upon them."

"And yet," exclaimed Andrew Forster, "though they have hitherto met with nothing but disaster, they are still resolute to fight the battle fairly out, and in that respect are something like the bull-dogs that many of your foreigners have compared them to."

"Aye, aye," answered Stephen, "we are willing to give them all praise, for they are noble fellows, and I know not of an American but feels proud of acknowledging that he has sprung from such a stock. But we are colonists, and as they thought proper to treat us as inferiors and slaves, it was high time that we should gird on our swords and assert our claims to equality with them. And now what has their obstinacy cost them? Are they not defeated in almost every battle, and is not America almost wrested from their possession?"

"Does the American army lie near here?" asked Ruthven.

"So near," replied Stephen, "that before the sun rises above yonder hill the battle will have been begun, and I am much mistaken if the British will not have to acknowledge another defeat."

"That is to say," observed Ruthven, "if yonder vessel of war does not do its part fairly in the strife."

"It will be the duty of our people to prevent any mischief from that quarter," replied Stephen; "and that they will do so we can have very little doubt, since we know too well that we are no match for them in naval affairs.

But let us proceed, for we are in some danger of being seen here, and I wish to approach the scene of battle."

They moved on as he spoke through a small wood, where they could pass unobserved, but had not proceeded very far when a rustling was heard among the trees, and in a moment or two afterwards a party of Americans emerged from their hiding-place, leading four horses, which they informed the travellers had been provided for their use, and then, having opened their wallets, they spread upon the grass such refreshments as the travellers stood most in need of. The meal thus suddenly provided was as hastily despatched by those for whom it had been brought. The strangers disappeared; and once more Ruthven and Andrew, preceded by their guides, went on their way.

The glade which they entered immediately after quitting the wood was broad and tolerably clear of timber, and it was easily to be seen that a considerable body of men had marched that way not very long before them. Those who acted as guides quickly detected this circumstance, and mentioned it to their companions, with a strict injunction to remain silent till it was ascertained whether they were following the route of their friends or enemies. In this manner they ascended a lofty eminence, which commanded a wide-spreading view of the country. The report of a musket was soon afterwards heard, and this was succeeded by the rolling of a drum, when the British army was seen advancing; but scarcely had the troops appeared in sight, when the Americans, who were in ambush, poured a destructive fire upon them,—the effect of which was soon apparent, for numbers of the men fell, and the remainder were thrown into such confusion that they knew not whether to advance or retreat from the unseen foe. But at this juncture a well-directed cannonade was commenced from the English vessel that was lying in the river, and encouraged by this the British troops maintained their ground for a few minutes, and then pushed forward in spite of the enemy's riflemen, who continued to harass them with the deadly discharge of their weapons.

Eager to join in the fray, Ruthven leaped from his horse, and hastening towards Stephen, exclaimed,—

"It is now time that I should throw off this inactivity, and join myself with those whom I came to aid. The English are now in a dilemma from which they cannot extricate themselves; and if Washington will place a vessel at my disposal, I will undertake to silence the guns of yonder ship, and thus save the lives of many a gallant hero, whom America cannot afford to lose in the struggle that is yet to take place ere your liberty has been acknowledged."

"We shall not need the aid you speak of," answered Stephen, "for the British have already felt the force of our arms, and long before your assistance could be of avail the victory will have been declared in our favour."

And he spoke prophetically, for the fire of the Americans became more destructive than ever, and the effect upon their adversaries was too apparent to be doubted, for they evidently reeled under the deadly attack they were subjected to, though their valour was not to be damped even by the unfavourable circumstances in which they were placed. Trees in all directions were shivered by the constant fire that was kept up on both sides, and the fatal effects of the flying storm of bullets was painfully apparent in each army, though more particularly so on the side of the British, who were exposed to the attack of an enemy whom they were unable to reach in return.

Ruthven and his companions had paused for a brief period to look upon this scene, but on a sudden they seemed to be roused from the deep meditation into which they had fallen, and then, riding forward, they approached that part of the battle which was occupied by the American troops. Upon reaching the midst of them, the guide, who had thus long passed under the assumed name of Stephen, threw aside the large horseman's cloak in which his form had been wrapped, and raising his hat, he was instantly recognised and hailed as

George Washington, the man who, sacrificing all selfish objects, had placed himself at the head of the army of Independence, either to obtain liberty for his country or perish in the attempt. In a few brief and animating words he addressed the men by whom he was surrounded, assuring them that victory was theirs if they pursued their present advantage, and calling upon them by every tie that they held most sacred, to use every exertion towards bringing the war to a speedy termination. His speech, though short, was received with the utmost enthusiasm by the men who had willingly placed themselves under his command, and even if there had been any waverers in his army before, there was not, at this moment, one among the hosts that surrounded him who was not determined to shed the last drop of his blood, ere he would allow the battle to be won by those who were regarded as men sent to intimidate them into submission. As for Ruthven, he stood for some few minutes wrapped in wonder at the discovery that had been made, but at length, recovering a little from his surprise, he advanced towards the leader of the American army, and bowing with respect, said,—

"Till this moment, sir, I was unconscious that a man so illustrious in the annals of his country had deigned to become the guide of an humble individual like myself; I would now, however, venture to offer a suggestion that I believe may go far to bring this battle to a speedy termination. Yonder vessel, as you see, is begining to pour a destructive fire upon your troops, and if I may be entrusted with the charge of a few boats, I believe I can soon contrive to silence their guns, and thus bring the issue of the day to a speedy termination."

"Captain Ruthven," answered the republican general, "your fame as an experienced and excellent naval commander has already reached me, and I should be glad if it was in your power to accomplish the service you have proposed. I must, however, confess that we have no boats here, and I am afraid your good intentions must fall to the ground. Yet I will go and make inquiries, and if the thing is practicable, you may rely upon it there is no person to whom I would so cheerfully entrust the task as to yourself, as the proved friend of our cause."

Washington rode away as he uttered these words, and almost as he did so Andrew Forster came galloping up with a countenance expressive of satisfaction and delight.

"I have just been down to the river side, captain," he exclaimed, "and there, as good luck would have it, I found four or five of the English boats rowing about scarce an oar's length from the shore. Now, to my thinking it will not be a very difficult task to get possession of these boats, and as there seems to be plenty of arms in them, we may make short work of it, and stop the firing on board the ship before much more harm is done."

"And who," asked Ruthven, "is to assist us in getting possession of these boats?"

"Oh, there's plenty here that will be glad to lend us a helping hand in such an affair as this," replied Andrew, looking round upon about a score of fellows who seemed to be waiting to be called into the more active duties of the battle. Nor was he mistaken in the notion he had formed of them, for scarcely were the words uttered, than every one of the men thrust themselves forward and cheerfully avowed their willingness to give the required aid.

Scarcely had these words passed their lips, when Ruthven darted away in the direction pointed out by his faithful follower, and being closely backed by those who had tendered their services, he soon succeeded in taking possession of the boats, and immediately upon this object being achieved, they rowed towards the ship, and by dint of courage and perseverance, succeeded in boarding her, when the riflemen that accompanied him poured in so destructive a fire upon the crew, that the English were compelled to relinquish their guns in order to repel their unexpected foes, and in a few moments the deck was converted into a battle-field, with every advantage on the side who had made the attack. At length the British captain and one of the men fell almost simultaneously, and the courage of the men failing under these circumstances, they almost immediately yielded themselves to the enemy, and within a quarter of an hour from the time when the Americans made their first attack, Ruthven became the conqueror of the vessel. At the same period, too, the English army, being deprived of the assistance they had received from the guns of the ship, began to yield more and more to the force by which they were opposed, and from that moment it became evident that the English had suffered another defeat, and consequently that the enemy had gained an accession of strength that would render them more formidable than ever. Yet the men seemed resolved not to be conquered without making every effort that was in their power. Again and again they returned to the charge, but it was only to feel the utter hopelessness of their situation, and rank after rank was mowed down in a useless effort to retrieve the honours of the day.

In the meantime a party of the British troops was sent through the wood in order that they might fall upon a portion of the American army, and thus withdraw their attention from the murderous attack they were engaged in. This service was entrusted to an officer upon whom the greatest reliance could be placed, both for his personal courage and the coolness which guided him even in the moments of extremity and peril. At this juncture he appeared to be more than ever sanguine of success, and addressing himself to the men by whom he was to be accompanied, he said in a tone of confidence and encouragement :—

" If there is any one among you that doubts the issue of our present task, I would have him quit the ranks, and leave the duty of conquering the foe to those who feel that it requires only a little exertion to teach these rebellious Americans that they are not invincible. Too often, it must be acknowledged, we have suffered defeat from them, but our disgrace should teach us a lesson of valour, and an opportunity has now been given us to prove that as our cause is a just one, so shall victory in the end be ours. On, then, my brave companions, for a glorious triumph awaits you, and this day shall serve to hand down our names to honour and renown."

But those they had to encounter were prepared for an attack from the quarter from whence it came, and when the opposing parties met, a skirmish ensued so resolute and determined, that for some time the scales of victory hung evenly balanced. At length, however, the English were again doomed to endure the bitterness of defeat, for the rifles of their foes were levelled with unerring precision, and the brave soldiers fell till scarcely twenty of them remained alive. The English officer, however, was still resolute to stand or fall in the duty he had undertaken, and addressing himself to the person nearest to him, he said :—

" This is more than I bargained for, Hugh Lorimer, for the rebels are again victorious, and it will be well if one among us remain alive to tell the story of our defeat. But what brings you here, man, when your duty is in quite a different part of the field ?"

" The truth is I could not help following you, my lord," answered the other, " for I saw you were rushing into the thick of danger, and I thought that if you lost your life in this forlorn hope, I might as well do the same."

Lord Dalmeny hastily shook the hand of his faithful follower, and then galloped off ; but he had not proceeded far when the horse he rode was shot dead beneath him, and before he could sufficiently recover himself to rise, he was attacked by a savage, who rushed upon him from a thicket sword in hand, and there is no doubt he would have fallen a victim to the assassin had not the latter suddenly recognized him, and rushed into the wood. At the same instant Lord Dalmeny beheld the well-known countenance of his assailant, and springing upon his feet, he set forth in rapid pursuit.

CHAPTER XXXIV.

"Born in the desert, I am free as air,
    And own not sovereignty in living man.
    Come with me, then, and taste the joys we feel,
    For I can show thee much thou little dream'st of."
                                            THE MEXICAN.

FAST and steadily Lord Dalmeny pursued the flying Indian, but though fleet of foot, he was not more than a match for the person who had thus unexpectedly appeared before him. Up mountain steeps, and across desert plains, he pursued the object that had thus singularly interested him, but still he seemed neither to gain ground upon the savage nor to lose so much as to give rise to any despair that he would fail in overtaking him. At length the Indian suddenly disappeared behind a bush, and the nobleman, redoubling his former speed, dashed along at a rate that it is almost impossible to conceive. A short time, therefore, served to bring him to the place where the fugitive had disappeared, but scarcely had he reached it, when a huge serpent reared itself in his path, and was in the act of darting upon the Indian, which it would have surely done, had not Lord Dalmeny at the instant drawn his sword and severed the terrific reptile in two. For a moment the savage appeared to be electrified with astonishment, but almost immediately recovering himself, he said in tolerable English :—

"You have saved my life, friend, and I owe you some gratitude for it. Do not, however, remain here any longer, for thoughts of evil are in my brain, and I would spare myself the ingratitude of injuring one who has but just now served me."

"And upon my word I see no reason why we should not be friends," answered Lord Dalmeny. "In fact I have had a hard day's fighting, and nothing to eat, and as you appear to have food in your scrip, the better way to show your gratitude will be to sit down and share it with me."

This was said in so free and careless a tone that the Indian made no objection to it, and throwing himself upon the green sward, he opened his knapsack, and having produced its contents, invited his stranger guest to partake with him. This the other was by no means loath to do, and having made a tolerable meal together, the nobleman said with his characteristic coolness :—

"It is to be hoped, my friend, that we now understand each other better than we did, and since we appear to be on more familiar terms, you will perhaps not hesitate to explain why you fled from me in so mysterious a manner?"

"Before I ask you a question," replied the Indian, "I must in turn ask you one. Are you not from Scotland?"

"I am."

"Then I can respect you, for I have known many of your countrymen, and we have been sworn friends together. You are welcome, therefore, to our deserts, and shall dwell with us till there is peace between your country and America."

"Aye, aye, I'll dwell with you cheerfully enough," answered Lord Dalmeny; "but perhaps you'll tell me where your habitation is?"

"We need no other habitation than such as at present contains us," returned the Indian. "The world is my dwelling place, and from place to place I rove according as my humour or destiny chance to lead me."

"Humph!" ejaculated his lordship; "there is everything in having a contented mind, certainly, though for my own part I think a fixed home is far preferable to a wandering life. However, we will not argue that point just now, and as we have no better subject to talk about, you will perhaps tell me which side you take in this war, the American or the English?"

"Neither," answered the other. "I hate them both alike, for both would overrun our country, and bring the free-born sons of the soil to slavery. I have followed the armies, and with my rifle shot down the men, without heeding whether they were Americans or English."

"Very impartial, upon my word," exclaimed Lord Dalmeny; "and now, since you have been pleased to answer so many questions, may I make so bold as to inquire your name?"

"I am called Ulabar."

"Well then, friend Ulabar," resumed his lordship, "for the uncommon courtesy you have been pleased to exhibit, you shall henceforth have the honour of serving me as a domestic."

"I am no slave," exclaimed the other, fiercely; "and even if I were, my inclination would not prompt me to accept service from your hands."

"Well, well, as you please about that," replied the nobleman; "but since you have been so explanatory to me, I will be equally so by informing you that the person you are speaking to now is Lord Dalmeny, whose native place is that very Scotland of which you spoke a short time since with so much rapture. Nay, more, there is, as I have been told, a colony of my countrymen somewhere in these deserts, and if you will take me to it, your service shall be amply rewarded."

"I know the place you speak of," answered Ulabar; "but it is many hours journey to it."

"I care not for the distance," exclaimed Dalmeny; "so lead me to it, and I will not be worse than my word."

"You shall be obeyed, Lord Dalmeny."

"And pray what is the name of the chief of this community?"

"They call her the Bounding Elk."

"Her!—are they governed by a women, then?"

"They are," replied Ulabar, "and by such a one, too, as you have been rarely accustomed to see. She must be approached with respect, for should I detect treachery in your actions, you will make a foe whom nothing but your death can appease."

"I will promise anything you please," answered Lord Dalmeny; "but it must be on condition that you conduct me to the place immediately, for I must acknowledge your description of this superlative woman has excited my curiosity."

"Will you go on horseback or on foot?"

"On foot, I suppose," replied his lordship; "for I see little chance of getting horses in this wild place."

Ulabar made no reply to this, but taking a small whistle from his pouch, he blew a sharp note upon it, and presently afterwards a youth came forth from the thicket, leading a couple of horses that appeared never to have been broken or trained. The Indian uttered a few words to the youth, that seemed to be expressive of his approbation, and as the latter once more returned to the place from whence he came, Ulabar resumed the conversation that had been broken off.

"I have provided horses for us, as you see, my lord, but they have no saddles, and perhaps you are not able to ride as we sons of the desert are obliged to do."

"Oh, that will be no obstacle in my way," answered his lordship, "for in Scotland we are oftentimes obliged to put up with greater hardships than riding without a saddle."

The savage made no reply to this, but with a bound sprang upon the back of the impatient steed, an example that was quickly followed by Lord Dalmeny, who had too much spirit to be outdone in activity, even by the hardy and more accustomed native of the soil. Scarcely were they seated, when their horses were put in rapid motion, and for some time they seemed to fly over the wild track they had to cross.

At length the sun began to sink behind the western hills, and as the air became more cool and refreshing, Lord Dalmeny could better endure the fatigue which had at first appeared almost overpowering. He spoke to his companion, in hopes of cheering the solitude of the night ride, but Ulabar made no reply, for his thoughts were intent upon other subjects ; he heard not the words that were addressed to him. Lord Dalmeny, therefore, contented himself with continuing the journey, for he also had thoughts to indulge in ; and then came visions of home and earlier times, that were far, very far from proving consolatory under the circumstances in which he was then placed. The image of May Grayson rose before him, and he saw her as he had made her through the indulgence of his own intemperate passions. As a maniac she seemed to flit and glide before him, till conscience could endure the thought no longer, and as his fevered tongue clove to his mouth, he entreated Ulabar to stay their rapid flight till he had supplied him with water to quench the burning thirst with which he was consumed.

"I have none left," answered the Indian, slightly reining in his steed, "for it was useless to encumber ourselves with water, when I knew that we were approaching a place where our thirst might be slaked without trouble."

"Is it far from hence ?" asked Lord Dalmeny.

"Scarcely half a league," answered the other. "We shall presently reach the banks of an immense river, where both ourselves and our horses may be refreshed till we complete the remainder of the journey we are going on."

"Thirst like this I cannot endure," exclaimed Lord Dalmeny, scarcely able to articulate the words. "Hunger I could bear without complaining, and fatigue should never wrest a murmur from my lips, but to endure this parching drought is more than I can do."

"Then you were mad to undertake a journey across this wild desert tract," answered Ulabar. "Endurance is a virtue that all men can boast, but few are able to practise except those who, like myself, have kept far from your crowded cities, where effeminacy prostrates the powers of those who yield to indulgence. Yet they look upon us uncultivated sons of nature with scorn, and few are there, I believe, among them who would trust themselves with me as you have done."

"Then you at least give me credit for being, in some respects, superior to the prejudices you speak of ?"

"I do," answered Ulabar, "but in other things you fall far below the standard of excellence."

"How !" exclaimed his lordship, with surprise ; "what do you know of my faults, who have never seen me before ?"

"I know more than you imagine," replied the other, "and, were I urged upon the subject, it is posssble I might speak of things that you little dream of being known in the wilds of America."

"Your words are full of mystery, Ulabar," exclaimed Dalmeny ; "and yet I suppose they are spoken only to create my wonder, and to give me an idea that you are possessed of a faculty that enables you to read the destinies of men "

"It would not be very difficult to read yours, my lord," replied the Indian, with a look of meaning.

"Indeed! and pray what may my destiny be?"

"Upon that subject I shall be silent, at present," answered Ulabar, "because it is better for a man to be in a little uncertainty than to know too much. I can, however, tell you, that among the females of your land you have made many conquests, and that there is not one among them, but bitterly regrets the hour when first chance threw her in the way of Lord Dalmeny."

"Nay, that can scarcely be called a crime," exclaimed the other, "since love is a passion that we cannot govern, and it must be owned, I am rather susceptible when beauty happens to cross my path."

"But you have been inconstant," replied the Indian; "and where is the woman that can endure coldness and neglect from him upon whom she has bestowed her love and confidence. You have caused many a broken heart, Lord Dalmeny, and there is one poor creature you have left behind, whose mind is a wreck, but who still wanders upon the sea shore, and anxiously looks across the waters for your return."

"You mean, May Grayson?"

"I know not the name of the girl," answered Ulabar, "but your own conscience will acknowledge that I have not overdrawn the picture. The girl is now a maniac, and you have the bitter reflection of knowing that your own conduct has made her so."

"And from whence do you derive the knowledge of this secret?"

"That remains to be proved hereafter," replied the Indian; "that I do know it, I suppose, by this time you are convinced, and the source from whence my information comes, is such as I can rely upon, and you cannot dispute."

No. 29

"Enough of this," exclaimed Lord Dalmeny, impatiently. "You said, some little time since, that we should soon arrive at the banks of a river where we might quench our burning thirst. Are we now far from the place?"

"It is close at hand," answered the native, and emerging, as he spoke, from the wood, they beheld before them one of those immense rivers which are found only on the vast continent of America. Lord Dalmeny gazed upon it with surprise, and could not forbear an expression of astonishment at the magnificent scene he beheld. His parching thirst, however, overcome all other feelings, and throwing himself from his horse, he darted towards the edge of the water, and with his hands supplied himself with the welcome liquid for which he had so ardently longed. Ulabar was more moderate in partaking of the cooling draught, and bidding his companion remount his horse, they galloped along the side of the noble river till they reached a part where its channel was considerably contracted, and where Ulabar, urging his horse forward, boldly plunged in, and motioned for the other to follow him. This Lord Dalmeny hesitated to do, but perceiving that the Indian was crossing the river in safety, he plunged in; and after buffetting about for some time, they both landed on the opposite shore.

CHAPTER XXXV.

"In the midst was seen
A lady of a more majestic mien,
By stature and by beauty mark'd their sovereign Queen.
*   *   *   *   *
And as in beauty she surpassed the choir;
So nobler than the rest was her attire.
A crown of ruddy gold enclosed her brow;
Plain without pomp, and rich without a show;
A branch of Agnus Castus in her hand,
She bore aloft her symbol of command."

THE FLOWER AND THE LEAF.

Two days were passed in this long dreary journey, and when the second night was just closing in, Ulabar suddenly reined in his horse, and leaping upon the ground, called upon his companion to do the same. This, however, Lord Dalmeny hesitated to do, alleging that he had an object for visiting the settlement towards which he was making his way, and that it was his wish to accomplish his design as quickly as possible, in order that he might return to head quarters, and once more join the forces of his country against the foe.

"And that you can soon do," answered the Indian, "for yonder, where the lights are shining, is the settlement formed by your countrymen, and over whom a female governs supreme, with a degree of firmness and wisdom that has gained for her the admiration of all who have submitted themselves to her rule."

"Then since we are so near to the place," exclaimed his lordship, "why should we not proceed at once without wasting time which I can but little afford to bestow?"

"You can do as you please, my lord," replied the other; "but I have vowed never to pass a night in any human settlement, and therefore I choose to remain till morning."

"Humph! then there is no objection to my going on condition that I proceed to the place alone?"

"None at all," answered Ulabar. "Here I shall take my rest for the night, and in case you should want my services any more, you know where I am to be found."

"But we may chance to miss each other," said the nobleman, and taking out a small purse of gold from his pocket, he placed it in the hand of his guide. "This will repay the service you have done me," he continued, "and should we meet again, I will not forget to increase the reward in just proportion to any further assistance I may require from you."

"Before you go," exclaimed Ulabar, "you will perhaps tell me whether the female ruler of yonder community is the object of your journey across this desert?"

"It is," answered Lord Dalmeny, "and if she is half so excellent as your description would lead me to suppose, I should not hesitate to traverse three times the distance for the honour of obtaining an introduction to her. But it is likely my enthusiasm is thrown away, for you, perhaps, do not love the gentle portion of creation as I do?"

"I have loved once and fondly," replied Ulabar, in tremulous accents; "but she was slain in a sudden attack that was made upon us by our enemies, and from that time I have never looked upon woman with pleasure."

"But you revenged her death, of course?"

"I did," answered the Indian, "and dreadful was the anger with which I retaliated the wrongs I had suffered. Our people gathered about me, and we pursued the foe whom we vanquished, and not one of them escaped to triumph in the cruel deed that robbed me of all I most fondly loved. But spare me, Lord Dalmeny, the remembrance of this dreadful subject;— your way lies yonder, and should you need my services further, I am to be found here till sunrise."

Lord Dalmeny obeyed the hint which had thus been thrown out, and having bid farewell to the companion of his journey, he set forward to reach the village, towards which he was guided by the light that shone from almost every hut. On entering the village, he was struck with the quietness which everywhere surrounded him, but at length approaching a building, which was considerably larger than any of the rest he had passed, he was struck by hearing sounds within; and impelled by curiosity, he entered, and found the whole community occupied in prayer. Fearful of disturbing their devotion, he would instantly have retired; but, as he was turning to do so, he was startled by a female figure that was seated near him; and as he gazed once more towards the fair object who had thus rivetted his attention, he was amazed at discovering that it was no other than Effie Ruthven, whom his myrmidons had forced away from her home some little time before he had left England. The sight appeared to rivet him to the spot, and though he strove to advance towards the place, his feet refused their office; and whilst he was thus spell bound, the congregation arose, and began slowly to depart from the scene of their devotions. In an instant Effie was lost to his sight, and whilst he was yet pondering what to do, a hand was laid upon his shoulder, and an old man whispered in his ear to follow him.

Almost mechanically Lord Dalmeny obeyed, and accompanying the stranger, he was quickly led across the street into a long chamber, at one end of which, Effie was elevated on a seat higher than the rest, whilst on each side of her were gathered the elders of the community to whom she could apply for advice or assistance whenever it might be needed. Dalmeny could not fail to observe that there was a paleness on her countenance that he had never observed there when she was a joyful and a happy girl in the cottage of her mother;—but she allowed him little time for reflection, for almost immediately upon his entrance, she glanced coldly towards him, and said, in a voice that betrayed not half the agitation she felt :—

"Lord Dalmeny, as a stranger among us, you are welcome to the hospitality you may need. This meeting may have been as unexpected on your part as it was on mine; but whatever may have brought you here, I trust you will see the necessity of leaving our village so soon as you are refreshed from the fatigue of your journey."

"My visit here was premeditated," he replied, "for I had obtained a clue by which to find you, and I am now come to ask forgiveness of the past, and to prevail on you to quit this solitude for the scenes of busier life you have quitted."

"Lord Dalmeny may be assured that I entertain no thoughts againsts him," she exclaimed, "for it was through him I came to this place; and so well content am I with it, that no persuasion shall ever induce me to quit the wilds of America. You, however, have different duties to fulfil, my lord, for your country demands your service, and the word coward would be branded on your name, were you to remain inactive whilst rebellion stalks triumphantly abroad and defeat follows each action that you fight."

"Nay then," he replied, "if I must go, you must return with me, and my future life shall manifest the deep contrition with which I look back upon former events. Come with me, Effie, and henceforth you shall know me for another man. You shall be my wife, and the world shall at last own that I have made all the reparation in my power."

"But the world is not so charitable as you would represent it," answered Effie, "for there are people who would look upon you with scorn, were you to wed one so much beneath you as the daughter of your tenant, Dame Ruthven."

The nobleman fixed his eyes upon her as she spoke, for her voice trembled with emotion, and the tears which fell from her eyes betrayed the grief with which she looked back upon the happy days that she had spent ere the persecutions of the man before her had forced her from the land of her birth. Hardened as he had ever been, he could not look upon her sorrow without a deep feeling of remorse, and with some agitation he said :—

"I know, Effie, you still reproach me, but be assured my repentance is sincere, and that I will sacrifice even the world's opinion to make reparation for having violently compelled you to quit your home. Say, then, you will be mine, and ere another week passes away, you shall be Lady Dalmeny."

"It is in vain that you ask me," she replied, "for here I have found a happy home, and never will I again quit it. All in this community have voluntarily placed themselves beneath my sovereignty, and there is not a man or a youth who owns my sway that would not willingly lay down his life were it necessary to do so for my safety."

"She speaks truly," exclaimed a youthful warrior, brandishing his spear as he spoke. "We are all devoted to her cause, and woe be unto those who dare come hither to molest her."

At that moment a loud noise of strife, intermingled with the clashing of swords was heard near the entrance, and ere any could go forth to see what was the cause of it, the door was suddenly thrown open, and John Ruthven, excited to the utmost fury, rushed into the room, followed by a number of men who were about to seize upon him, when he recognised the form of his beloved sister, and springing forward, he caught her eagerly in his arms.

"Effie—dearest Effie !" he exclaimed, "by what wondrous chance do I thus find you an inhabitant of this dreary desert? Speak to me, sister, for I see Lord Dalmeny is also at hand, and should it prove that this has been his work, I will never sheath my sword till full and ample vengeance has been accomplished."

"Lord Dalmeny, my dear brother, is not to blame in this matter," she replied, "for my residence here has been the result of my own choice, and it is by a mere accident that he had found out the place of my retreat. And, oh! my brother, how much it joys me to see you once more, when I had thought that distance would for ever separate me from those I love. And, my mother!—tell me of her, dear John; say that she is happy, and I shall not have another care left in the world."

"That is a question that I can scarcely answer," replied Ruthven, "for this war has kept me long from our native land, and I know not that I shall ever return to it, since the cause I have adopted has rendered me an alien."

"Alas!" sighed Effie, "then you have proved a traitor to the land of your birth!"

"I am fighting for liberty," answered Ruthven, "and therefore my cause is a just and sacred one."

"And your object here?"

"I have been sent by General Washington," answered Ruthven, "on a message to your people to know—since they have hitherto taken no part in the contest that is going on—which side they mean to take in future. This he considers necessary, as, whilst they are undecided, he will not be able to protect them as friends, should the war approach any nearer to your frontiers."

"General Washington," answered Effie, "should have known ere now that our people never enter into war unless forced to do so by the aggressions of their neighbours. We cultivate peace, and whilst the war is thus far from us we are content that the strongest should gain the victory, whether he is in the right or the wrong."

"And this," exclaimed Ruthven, "is the answer you undertake to give in the name of the people you govern?"

"It is," replied Effie; "and I am the more induced to do so because I know the confidence they repose in me. There are, however, older persons than myself present, and if any of them have any reason to offer why we should mix ourselves in this contention, I am ready to hear them, and act according to the majority of their numbers."

"There is no occasion for any further opinions to be offered," exclaimed a grey-headed old man, who rose in the midst of the assembly. "We are satisfied with the wisdom of your resolution, and I believe there is not one among us that thinks it expedient to go to war when we are in no way interested in it."

"But you, my sister," cried Ruthven, "will, I trust, see the necessity of taking part with the Americans in a war that is founded upon justice. Besides, the victory is sure to be theirs, and when the enemy has been driven forth, it is not unlikely that the people of this country will turn their arms against all those nations and tribes who have stood coldly by, whilst the freedom of the land was being contested for."

"You have my answer, brother," exclaimed Effie;—"return to General Washington, and say, that those who desire to cultivate peace and good will are never to be induced to join him in a war in which they feel no interest."

"And if you are the brother of this maiden," interposed one of the elders, "you will not only bear the message she has charged you with, but you will also reflect deeply upon the part you have taken against the country of your birth. Aye, you may frown upon me in anger, but in such a case as this the truth may be freely spoken; and I say unto you, John Ruthven, that future generations will scorn the man who could basely sell his services against his own country, because he chanced to have a private pique with a few persons. You and Lord Dalmeny will know what I mean; yet much as you effect to despise the friend of your youth, he has chosen a more honourable path than yourself, and has already done much towards wiping away the stain which early depravity has left upon his name. Reflect, therefore, upon my words. John Ruthven, for it is not yet too late to retrieve your error, and when once you have renounced the cause you have madly adopted, you will soon feel that no aggravation can ever prove an excuse for becoming a traitor to one's country."

"You have heard me reviled, sister, by your people," said Ruthven, endeavouring to smother his indignation, "and I now ask, for the last time, whether you will renounce these people, and go where glory and honours await your brother?"

"Never!" she replied, firmly. "Here I have found home and friends, when I believed the world contained none such for me, and with those who have fostered me will I live and die. You have heard my decision, John, and it may be with sorrow and indignation, but I can endure that even from you, rather than prove ungrateful to those I have every reason to regard. Go, therefore, from our presence; food shall be provided to refresh you, and, when your hasty meal is over, depart from our land, and let us never see each other again unless you can come and tell me that you have seen the sin and folly of your ways, and that you are no longer a traitor to the land of your birth."

"And is it thus we part, sister," exclaimed Ruthven, bitterly, "after the long absence we have endured, and the love that bound us ere you were torn away from home by the hands of a villain and his equally infamous associates?"

"We part not in anger," she replied, "but you have heard my reason for wishing that a separation should take place. Farewell, brother, and may Heaven open your eyes to the evil you have done in taking up the sword against your own country."

Ruthven uttered not another word, but rushed from the hut, and mounting his horse rode off towards Andrew Forster, who was waiting at no great distance from the place, and they immediately commenced their return. Almost at the same time, Lord Dalmeny left the community with many expressions of kindly feeling, and proceeding with rapid footsteps he took his way towards the spot where he had not long since left Ulabar.

CHAPTER XXXVI.

"Away! our journey lies through dell and dingle,
Where the blithe fawn trips by its timid mother,—
Where the broad oak, with intercepting boughs,
Chequers the sunbeams in the greenwood alley.
Up and away!—for lovely paths are these
To tread, when the glad sun is on his throne;
Less pleasant, and less safe, when Cynthia's lamp
With doubtful glimmer lights the dreary forest."

ANON.

THE Indian was fast buried in sleep when Lord Dalmeny arrived at the place, but his quick ears instantly caught the sound of footsteps, and bounding upon his feet he hurriedly enquired whether it was the will of his lordship to proceed on their journey back. To this an answer was given in the affirmative, and the two horses having been secured they once more set forward. For two days they continued their journey with little intermission, and at length reaching a spacious bay, in which an English vessel was riding at anchor, Lord Dalmeny gave a signal to those on board, and directly afterwards a boat was lowered into the water, and quickly rowed towards that part of the shore on which he and the Indian were standing.

"Ulabar," exclaimed Lord Dalmeny, "I have been going to ask you several times whether you feel inclined still to follow me. I am going to leave this country for ever, and may perhaps wander over many others ere I return to my native land. Say then, will you go with me and be the same faithful guide and attendant that I have hitherto found you?"

"You ask much, Lord Dalmeny," answered the other, "of one who from childhood has been used to the freedom that can alone be found in such desert wilds as those we have passed through. Liberty is dearer to me than life itself, and much as I should have liked to follow one that I have begun to respect, I must refuse your offer, that I may die in the land that gave me birth."

"I expected as much, my good fellow," exclaimed the nobleman, "and therefore will not urge you to do that which you may afterwards repent. Take this purse, however,—'tis well filled with gold, and sometimes think of him who for the last few days has been your companion across these pathless deserts."

Ulabar would have refused the offered reward, but at that moment the boat was heard grating upon the shore, and Lord Dalmeny instantly leaping into it was quickly borne away towards the ship. As the Indian gazed upon his retiring form he could not restrain a tear that stole to his eye, and instantly leaping from his horse he sprung into the sea, and by dint of extraordinary strength soon succeeded in overtaking the boat, which he quickly scrambled into, and assured Lord Dalmeny that he was willing to sacrifice home, kindred and friends, to follow one for whom he had formed a lasting friendship. Lord Dalmeny was well pleased to hear this determination, and no sooner had he and his faithful attendant got on board the ship, than the sails were spread to the winds, and in less than a couple of hours the long line of American coast was for ever lost to their view.

But we must now return to Ruthven and his companion, Andrew Forster, who also had to cross the same trackless desert on their return to the camp where Washington was anxiously awaiting the return of his envoy, to learn the success of the mission upon which he had been sent. The two travellers passed on their way nearly in silence, for Ruthven's mind was filled with the singular meeting he had had with his sister, and Andrew felt too much respect for his master to interrupt him when his thoughts were thus seriously employed.

Having passed the night in journeying onwards, they looked out anxiously in the morning to find some place where they might rest themselves for awhile, and obtain that food of which they began to stand so much in need. For some time, however, their search was unavailing, but at length the report of a gun startled them, and making their way in the direction from whence the sound had come, they reached a spot where they saw a man busily engaged with the deer he had just shot, and which he had already begun to divest of its skin. At their approach he looked up, and perceiving a couple of strangers, exclaimed,—

"Holloa friends, what brings you to this wild part of the country, eh? I guess you've travelled a pretty considerable distance, or you wouldn't have found me out here."

"We are travellers, and need refreshment," answered Ruthven, "and if you can supply us with it I have the means about me to reward your hospitality."

"Oh, if you can pay for it, I'll give you the best I've got," replied the settler; "but you must accept such fare as happens to fall to your lot, for there's nothing to eat but a steak of venison off this deer that I've just shot, and so if that will content you I'll have a fire in no time, and the thing shall be done as nicely as if you went and ordered it at one of the first taverns in Boston or New York."

"Oh, we are content to take things just as we find them," answered Ruthven; "so set about your task, man, with what quickness you can, for we have keen appetites, and can scarcely wait for any ceremony save the bare time it will take to cook the meal we have been so lucky as to fall in with."

The man made no reply to this, but collecting together a quantity of dry wood he set fire to it by means of a flint and steel with which he was provided, and having accomplished this necessary part of his labours, he next cut off the steaks and laid them across the glowing embers, watching them as a cook would do, and expatiating upon his own abilities in that particular branch of art, to the great amusement of Andrew Forster, who could scarcely forbear cracking a joke now and then at the expense of the man who was thus diligently occupied in their service. At length the delicacy was placed before them, together with a liberal supply of a blackish looking bread, which, however, gave great satisfaction to the travellers, who did ample justice to the meal that had been placed before them. When the meal was over, Ruthven paid the man liberally for the trouble he had been put to, and with a friendly "good morning," he and Andrew Forster once more set forward on their journey towards the camp.

But it is unnecessary to follow them through the remainder of their tedious travels, and it will therefore be sufficient to say that after passing three more days and nights they reached the immediate neighbourhood of Washington's encampment, when a couple of the American soldiers sprung from a thicket close by, and after seizing them by the arms, demanded whither they were going and what they had to do in that part of the country.

"We are friends of liberty," answered Ruthven, "and are on our way to see General Washington, for whom we have news that he is most anxious to hear."

"And how am I to know that you are telling me the truth?" demanded one of the sentinels.

"Why, because the gentleman you are speaking to happens never to tell a lie," answered Andrew, indignantly.

"I know him not," exclaimed the soldier, "and therefore have only your word for it."

"Then you shall know his name," replied Andrew, "and now tremble when you hear that the person you have laid such irreverent hands upon is no other than Captain John Ruthven, who has done so much towards gaining the independence of your country."

"Aye," interposed Ruthven, "we are friends to the good cause. But tell me, soldier, where Washington and his soldiers have assembled, for I would see them instantly on an affair of importance."

"They are hard by," answered the sentinel, pointing towards the rude encampment that was seen before them. They've got what they call a council of war, but as I don't know for certain yet whether you are a friend or an enemy, I can't let you pass till you have convinced me that you are indeed Captain Ruthven."

"Nonsense, man; I can answer for it there's no mistake about its being John Ruthven," exclaimed the other sentinel. "I saw him with the general just before he was sent sowewhere up the country, so let him pass on, or we shall find ourselves in the wrong when it comes to be told that we refused to let a friend of the cause pass."

"Well then you can proceed, sir," said the other, "and if you make

your way towards yonder clump of locust trees, you'll find General Washington and his officers in consultation about what's to be done next."

Ruthven, closely followed by Andrew Forster, adhered to the directions that had been given him, and after proceeding somewhat less than half a mile, he beheld a number of officers assembled together, and having heard his name repeated two or three times, he motioned for his attendant to remain still and silent, and placing himself behind the trunk of a tree, could hear all that was going forward without being seen by those he was watching. It was soon evident to him that Washington was not present, and this circumstance, perhaps, afforded an opportunity for the others to open their minds more freely.

"The general," said a veteran officer, "seems to place too much reliance upon foreign assistance, and too little upon the courage of those who are fighting for their homes and liberties. For my own part, I would have sent these French troops back from whence they came, and, when left to their own resourees, our American forces would fight with greater confidence, since all the honours of victory would then be theirs."

"And why should we dictate to Washington, who has so often proved his wisdom by the results that have followed his every action?" demanded another of the officers. "We have so far willingly obeyed him, and our enemies have been made to feel the wisdom that has inspired his every movement, and it is my opinion that if we wish to see a speedy termination of the war, we must go on in the same steps we have already taken."

"But there is a foreigner he must dismiss from his service," said a greyheaded old man, "for he slew my son, who was an officer under him, and I am now childless and alone in the world."

"I know who you mean, Silas Paton," exclaimed another of the officers.
' You are speaking of Captain Ruthven, who slew your son in the moment
' No. 30

of victory, because he had good reason to believe that he was about to prove a traitor to his country. The act was a necessary one, and, therefore, none should blame Ruthven for committing it."

"A necessary one!" cried Silas Paton, with surprise; "and do you not call it murder to shoot one of your own people, when a court-martial might have decided the affair in a much more satisfactory way. But I will not argue this point any further, for it is my intention to impeach Captain John Ruthven immediately after his return upon the mission he has been out upon."

"Old man," exclaimed Ruthven, stepping among them from his place of concealment, "I am here to answer any charge you may have to make." And as he said this several of the younger officers advanced to arrest him as their prisoner, but ere they could accomplish this intention, Washington himself appeared among them, and with some severity commanded them to desist.

"Captain Ruthven," he continued, addressing himelf to the party he had named, "you are welcome back again, though I could have wished your reception was more cordial than it seems to be."

"I am accused," exclaimed Ruthven, "of having unnecessarily caused the death of Lieutenant Paton, but if time and opportunity is given me, I shall be able to prove that the act which deprived him of life was provoked by his treachery, and that he was seen in the act of striking our colours to the enemy in the moment of our hard earned victory."

"And the witness is here that can prove it," exclaimed Andrew Forster, approaching the party as he spoke; "for my captain has spoken nothing but the truth, and here am I to stick to it to the very last, be the consequences what they may."

"And who are you, sirrah?" demanded Silas Paton.

"An honest man, whose word is never doubted by those who know him," answered the plain-spoken sailor. "The battle we fought with the English was an obstinate one, and lasted many hours, so that numbers fell on both sides, and for a long time no one knew which party would gain the victory. At last, however, we got the best of it, and you've heard, I dare say, what a pretty dressing we gave the enemy."

"We have heard of the victory," said one of the officers; "but at present you have given no reason why Lieutenant Paton should have fallen by the hand of his captain."

"Well, then, you must know," continued Andrew, "that Lieutenant Paton proved himself to be an errant coward throughout the battle, and just as the action was finishing in our favour, he began to lower our colours as a token of defeat   Upon this both Captain Ruthven and I drew a pistol, and aimed at the villain, and as both of them were discharged at the same moment, it is impossible to say by whose hand he fell. I am, however, inclined to believe that I slew him, and right well it served him, for he would have basely sold the honour of his country to the enemy when the victory was already our own."

The explanation thus offered served materially to alter the complexion of the affair as far as regarded Ruthven, and whilst the officers were engaged in discussing the affair among themselves, Washington took the arm of the captain, and led him towards his own tent, in order that he might learn what news he had brought from the community to which he had been sent on a commission.

CHAPTER XXXVII.

" Ascend the watch tower yonder, valiant soldier,
Look on the field, and say how goes the battle ?"
                                                MAID OF ORLEANS.

WE must now pass over the American war to its conclusion, at which period Ruthven began to find that even the influence of General Washington had little effect towards removing the jealousy that had been engendered against him, and scorning to stoop to men whom he had learnt to despise, he quitted the new world, and betook himself to Russia, where a hot war was at the period raging against the Turks, who were just then the objects of the Empress Catherine's most furious hatred.   Of course the assistance of a man like Captain Ruthven was readily accepted, the dignity of admiral was bestowed upon him, and a captain's commission given to Andrew Forster, who thus found to his great joy that he was not to be separated from the man he had so long and faithfully served, but that he was to sail in the same vessel, and still fight under the orders of his old commander. Nor was it long before their services were called into requisition, for a seaport town belonging to the Turks had long been besieged by one of the ablest of the Russian generals, and as there seemed to be little chance of the garrison surrendering, it was proposed that Admiral Ruthven and his squadron should immediately sail and aid the land force by making an attack upon the sea, or at least prevent any supplies being sent in for the succour of the besieged.   This was a service which Ruthven readily undertook, for he was soon weary of an inactive life, and within three days of the orders being given he put to sea, and made towards the place which was to be the scene of his future operations.

A short time served to bring them before the besieged town, and Ruthven, whose thoughts were occupied in the business he was about to be engaged in, was gazing upon the fortified walls of the city before him, when a well-known voice addressed him, and Andrew Forster stepping up said :—

" My life for it, now, admiral, you are planning some project by which we may have the honour of getting possession of yonder town.   And yet they say it has been besieged for some months by a gallant general, who is just now as far from taking the place as he was when first he sat down before it with his army."

" That," replied Ruthven, " is no fault of his, for the town is strongly fortified, and by some oversight of the Russian government, they have permitted stores and reinforcements to be brought into it, by which means the siege has been protracted, and thousands of lives sacrificed.   Now, however, we will put an end to the state of things, and before many days have passed away, I hope to see the town in our possession."

" That is," exclaimed Andrew, " if this Prince Berenzoff can be got into the humour to second you in it.   But I see the name of that person is not very palatable to you, and little is it to be wondered at, since he knows nothing of his profession, and yet the Empress has thought proper to place him over your head.   And look you, admiral, they are making signals from his ship for us to go on board, so, as I suppose you don't want to break discipline, I shall give orders for the boat to be lowered."

Ruthven made no reply to this, for his thoughts were at the time too much occupied with other subjects.   When the boat was ready, however, he stepped into it with Andrew, and they were immediately rowed to Prince Berenzoff's ship, where they were received with distant courtesy, in which coldness and jealousy were easily to be detected. The business on which they had been summoned was, however, quickly introduced, and it was suggested that the two admirals, accompanied by some of their officers, should immediately proceed ashore, and seek an interview with the general commanding the land forces, in order that they might hear from him in what way their co-operation would be most beneficial towards bringing this long protracted siege to an end. This was of course agreed to, but as they approached the shore, their progress was rendered dangerous by the continued discharge of cannon and smaller arms with which they were assailed by the besieged. At length, however, they landed in safety, and were speedily introduced to General Kermsdorf, who received them with a soldier's rough welcome, and in a few words pointed out the aid he was most in need of, and the means by which they could best forward the views he had in contemplation. Towards the Prince Berenzoff he seemed, even in this short conversation, to have conceived the utmost contempt, for he evinced shallowness of intellect, and an obstinacy of disposition that argued but indifferently for the success of the service upon which he had been sent. His conduct, however, was far different towards Admiral Ruthven, who he at once perceived to be a man after his own heart, since he was prompt in the execution of his plans, and had sufficient firmness of purpose to forbid any alterations when he saw that they tended towards the advantage of the service in which he was engaged.

But Kermsdorf had his motives for not just then wishing to offend the prince, who was in high favour at court, and having invited his visitors to partake of such soldier's fare as happened to be within his reach, he proposed that they should walk with him round the walls in order that they might offer any suggestions that struck them for the more speedy termination of the siege. In this excursion the prince, as usual, betrayed his ignorance of all the arts of warfare, and thereby added to the contempt he had already earned for himself. But on the other hand, Ruthven made so many excellent suggestions, and altogether exhibited so profound a knowledge upon the subject submitted to him, the old general grew quite enraptured with him, and could not forbear, on several occasions, expressing the admiration with which he had listened to him.

"You have convinced me, Admiral Ruthven," he said, " that the Empress of Russia has sent me an ally upon whom I can depend, in the most difficult situation in which a man can be placed. Your advice, I am sure, will at all times be worth taking, and with this confidence, I ask what you think of planting a battery at the skirt of yonder wood, by which we shall command a most important portion of the city ?"

" Since you ask my opinion," replied Ruthven ; " I must make free to say, that a few armed ships in yonder bay, will be of more service than anything you can do on land. We shall then divert the attention of the besieged, and whilst the greater part of the garrison is engaged in the new quarter of attack, you can take advantage of the confusion, and by storming the walls, I have no doubt you will soon obtain admittance to the town which has so long held out."

"By Jove you have just hit it, and the city shall be mine !" exclaimed the enthusiastic veteran. Then addressing himself to Prince Berenzoff, he requested him to give Admiral Ruthven full power to carry his design into execution. But the prince was already jealous of the superiority the admiral was likely to obtain over him, and he replied resolutely,—

"The command of this fleet, general, has been committed to me, and if any adverse circumstances should arise, I alone shall be answerable for them to her imperial majesty. Admiral Ruthven, therefore, must be content to remain under my orders, and he may depend on it I shall lose no opportunity that may add to the glory or safety of the nation I am proud to serve."

"As you please, prince," exclaimed General Kermsdorf, in a tone of pique. "You will, of course, be watchful of our country's honour; but at the same time I must tell you, that the Sultan has deposed the late governor of yonder fortified city, and that he has sent his favourite vizier, who is reported to be a man of firmness and courage, and consequently one who we must not expect to conquer without some trouble. And now, since you have heard my opinion freely expressed I shall return to my duty, and let me hope your highness will not be forgetful of yours when the moment for active service arrives."

With a significant look towards Ruthven, the old general turned away, and the other immediately returned to the prince's vessel, where a consultation was held as to the course that should next be pursued. Ruthven proposed that they should, without loss of time, commence an attack upon the Turkish fleet, since, without dispersing that, they could hope to do nothing towards the fall of the city. But Berenzoff would not hear of it, and at last Ruthven, unable to contain his fury any longer, expressed his determination to commence the battle without orders, and instantly quitted the ship to return to his own, for the purpose of putting his project into execution without delay.

And the result of the naval action that ensued proved the correctness of Ruthven's views, for he was shortly able to destroy and sink several of the Turkish vessels by means of the squadron he commanded, and the rest of the enemy taking alarm at the fury with which they had been attacked, quickly drew off their ships, and thus left the Russian fleet free to attack the city from the bay.

This feat performed, the next orders issued by Admiral Ruthven were to storm the walls from the side they were on, and thus divert the attention of the besieged from that part of the city which was the chief object of General Kermsdorf's attack; and so well was this managed, that the vizier was so sorely pressed as to be driven to the last extremity, and in his despair he ordered the gates to be thrown open, in order that he and the greater part of the garrison might rush out and meet the enemy in a fair and open fight. But this determination of the Turkish leader had nearly cost him dear, for the attack made upon him was so impetuous, that he fell in the first rush, and would have been slain by one of the soldiers had not General Kermsdorf rode up at the instant, and commanded that the vizier's life should be spared, and that he should be conveyed to his tent as a prisoner till after the issue of the battle was known. This was accordingly done, and within an hour from that time, General Kermsdorf again presented himself before his captive.

"Vizier," he exclaimed, "the victory is ours, and your city now belongs to the Empress Catherine, my mistress. I, however, do not mean to triumph in the downfall of a foe, but as my prisoner, I am come to say that any indulgence you may require, shall be freely at your command."

"I require no indulgence," answered the vizier; "at least none for myself; but I have a friend who I fear has been badly wounded in this day's strife, and as I believe he is also a captive, I wish to have him conveyed hither in order that I may watch over and attend upon him."

"Why, that is both an honourable and humane wish, and it shall not be long before it is gratified," exclaimed the general, and whispering to one of the men in attendance, he desired him to bring the prisoner to him, and also to inform Admiral Ruthven that he wished to speak to him as soon as it was convenient. The soldier instantly disappeared and shortly returned with the captive, who it seemed was not wounded so seriously as had been imagined ; the greeting between him and the vizier was warm and kindly, but the conversation that ensued was at last suddenly broken off by the general's exclamation of,—

"Vizier, if your compliments are over, I have the happiness of introducing you to a particular friend of mine and a gallant man. Permit me to make you acquainted with Admiral Ruthven, who—— but what in the name of wonder does all this mean ? Why, as I live, you have known each other before !"

"John Ruthven !" gasped the vizier, in a tone that betrayed the wonder that almost overwhelmed him, and at the same moment Ruthven, with equal astonishment, articulated the name of Lord Dalmeny ; nor did the wonder end here, for in the wounded friend of the nobleman was recognized the faithful Ulabar, who had thus followed the fortunes of his master in his travels from America to Turkey. General Kermsdorf gazed upon this scene with wonder, and could not suppress an exclamation of surprise to which it gave birth ; he however did not seek any further explanation at that moment, but leaving them to do this at their leisure, he made an excuse that he had business to attend to elsewhere, and hurried from the tent.

"John Ruthven !" exclaimed his lordship ; "our meeting thus is scarcely more singular than almost every other event of our lives. My folly, or wickedness, if you please to term it so, drove you from the land of your birth to seek a home somewhere else, and fortune, who smiles not on everybody, seems to have taken pleasure in heaping her favours upon you. Thus my mad career of thoughtlessness and crime raised you to eminence, when perhaps you would otherwise have been a humble cottager upon the lands which your father tilled before you. You are now in the zenith of glory, and may I hope that the years which have passed away, have softened your heart towards one who cannot deny that he has wronged and injured you ?"

"I bear no enmity, my lord," answered Ruthven ; "else should I long ere this have sought you out to avenge the violence offered to those I loved. But time softens the rancour of our feelings, and as reflection steals upon us, we become wiser and better men. May I hope, my lord, that you have profitted in the same school of experience, and that you are not now the same as when we were young men together in Scotland. And yet the habit that you now wear, assures me that even in religion you cannot be firm or consistent."

"Fate has made me what I am," exclaimed Lord Dalmeny ; "and who, let me ask, can resist his destiny ? I left America scarcely knowing whither I was going to, or caring what was to become of me. It happened, however, that we were taken by a Turkish vessel, and I was carried in captivity to the country house of the person who had made me his prisoner. We soon grew upon good terms with each other, and liberty was offered me on two conditions,—the first of which was, that I would embrace the Mahommedan faith, and the second, that I assisted to repel the Russians, who at that time were threatening the dominions of the Sultan. I accepted the offer, and in the first battle we had with the enemy, I acquitted myself so satisfactorily that I was promoted to rank, and in the end was appointed governor of yonder tower, which I have every reason to believe I should have held out till relief had been sent, if you had not battered the walls from the bay. But this is only a trifling change in my fortune, and as I cannot return to the Sultan with safety to my head, I shall either enter some other service, or return to Dalmeny Castle,—marry my pretty cousin, Lady Agnes Drummond, and thus settle down into one of those steady, comfortable men, that your good wives delight so much to talk about to their gossips."

At this moment General Kermsdorf entered the tent, and the conversation terminated for the present. It, however, shortly afterwards took another turn, and the veteran officer became so well pleased with the cheerfulness of his prisoner, that when he found he had no intention of returning to the Sultan, he offered to obtain his liberty for him as soon as he could communicate with the heads of the government. This, however, seemed to be a matter of very little consideration with Lord Dalmeny, for he would make himself happy under any circumstances, and he perhaps felt as comfortable where he was, as if he had been at liberty in his own country.

CHAPTER XXXVIII.

"And yet he thinks
I am the tool and servant of his will.
Well, let it be ; through all the maze of trouble
His plots and base oppression must create,
I'll shape myself away to higher things,
And who will say 'tis wrong?"———— OLD PLAY.

A SUDDEN uproar and the sound of many voices caused the party in the tent to start to their feet, and hastening to the outside, they beheld a blaze of light in the direction of the sea, the cause of which appeared to be immediately comprehended by General Kermsdorf, who said to Ruthven,—

"This light has been raised by the Prince Berenzoff to suit his own particular purpose, and I suppose you, my friend, are at no loss to understand it."

"I can see it all," exclaimed Ruthven, bitterly ; "yonder light proceeds from the burning ships that I this day took in the bay, and the prince takes this means to lend a light in honour of your victory, though it must be acknowledged he has done it at my expense. But I see he is jealous of what I have done, and wishes to deprive me of the honour I have fairly earned."

"These words are safe when spoken to me," whispered the general, "but I would have you be cautious that they come not to the ears of the prince, for he is an especial favourite of Katherine's, and many as good a man as yourself has been sent to Siberia for uttering less offensive words against those she regards."

"It shall be risked at any rate," exclaimed Ruthven, impetuously ; "and as good luck will have it, here comes the prince to hear what I have to say upon the subject."

At this moment the prince approached them, and Kermsdorf addressing himself to him, said,—

"Your highness, we have to congratulate each other upon having obtained a glorious victory both on sea and land for our royal mistress. I, however, was overtaken by darkness, and I have to thank you for lending me so good a light to see how complete the defeat of the enemy has been."

"The truth is," replied Berenzoff, "I found that the half dozen vessels we had captured were so much injured as to be useless, and so I set fire to them to save all further trouble on their account. They burnt well, as you saw, and at any rate we have deprived the enemy of the use of them."

"We !" exclaimed the general, with surprise. "Upon my word I thought all the merit of capturing the Turkish vessels belonged to our friend here, Admiral Ruthven."

"You may give the honour to who you please," answered Berenzoff ; "but in my despatches to the empress, I shall not fail to represent the affair in its true light."

"And so shall I in mine, your highness," returned Kermsdorf, firmly; "both will be placed in the hands of the royal Katherine, and we shall then see to whose version of the story she gives most credit,—to the old soldier's or the young courtier's."

"You can do as you please," answered the other, haughtily; "but I am not to be intimidated from doing my duty either by the threats of a blustering old man, or the presumptuous arrogance of a foreign adventurer, who having drawn his sword against the people of his own country, has no other alternative but to seek a home in some other."

"Prince!" exclaimed Ruthven, "neither your high rank, nor the interest you have at court, shall save you from the wrath of the man you have thus injuriously spoken of. You have destroyed ships which were mine by conquest, and not satisfied with that, you have insulted me upon a subject that you had no right even to allude to. As a freeman I am your equal, and the world will acknowledge me to be something more than that, if you are too great a coward to resent the words I now address to you."

"Nay, put up your sword, sir," returned the prince, with an affectation of composure; "for notwithstanding your opinion upon the subject, I must still think there is a vast difference between your rank and mine. So farewell, Admiral, and remember you are to remain on shore as I have business of importance for you to undertake; in fact, sir, you will convey my account of this naval victory to the empress, who, no doubt, upon my recommendation, will give you a very warm reception."

He turned haughtily away as he spoke, and the general observing the anger that had kindled in Ruthven's eye, said,—

"Admiral Ruthven, you will also be the bearer of despatches from me to the empress, and I can at least say, that in mine she will learn the truth as to whom the honour is chiefly due."

"I had rather the duty of bearing these despatches had been entrusted to anybody else," exclaimed Ruthven; "for I am not much acquainted with court manners and customs, and, I fear, shall make but a rough messenger to royalty. However, there is no help for it I suppose, and, therefore, do I undertake the task."

"Why, that is well said," returned Kermsdorf; "for depend upon it the misrepresentations of this prince will not go so far with the empress as my own straightforward despatches. She knows the value of ardent spirits like your own, and having the good of her country at heart, will, no doubt, reap honours on you. But, remember, your conduct must be watchful and wary, for there will be many Russians jealous of your advancement, and plots will soon be arranged for your overthrow. Prudence, however, will thwart all these, and rely upon it, my dear general, you will have one trusty and honest friend in the man who now tenders you this advice. So now prepare yourself for your journey, for my despatches being brief will soon be written, and Berenzoff, I dare say, will not be long before he returns with his."

The general now turned away, and Ruthven having made the few arrangements necessary for his journey, was once more summoned to the tent of his friend, where he found Lord Dalmeny, Andrew Forster, and Ulabar, already waiting for him. The horses which were to contain them were soon in readiness, and having received the despatches, he threw himself in the saddle and rode off, accompanied by Dalmeny and the others.

It will be unnecessary to follow them on their dreary journey through an almost trackless country, and it will therefore be sufficient to say, that on the third day they penetrated a fast forest of pines, through which they passed with difficulty, but having at length reached its furthest extremity, they were about to dismount and refresh themselves, when the notes of a

bugle were heard not far off, which were succeeded by the report of fire-arms; then came the cry of hounds, and ere they could move from the spot, a female equestrian came in sight, but scarcely had she done so, when an infuriated boar, of immense size, sprung fiercely towards her, and threatened her with instant destruction. Ruthven saw her danger, and was hastening to her assistance, but it was scarcely necessary, for in an instant she thrust her hunting spear into the side of the infuriated animal, which thereupon turned from the object of his wrath, and disappeared amongst the thick entanglements of the woods. At this period several other hunters rode up in terror, but she quickly allayed their alarm, by assuring them she had received no injury from the attack of her savage assailant.

"But to you, sir,". she continued, addressing herself to Ruthven, "I owe a debt of gratitude for the gallantry with which you came to my assistance. You will, therefore, accept my thanks, and be assured, should we ever meet again, I will not fail to reward your services in a more substantial manner."

"I have no claim even to your thanks, lady," answered Ruthven, "for you had yourself compelled the boar to retreat ere I could hasten to your aid."

"Well, that is a compliment to my courage that I did not expect," cried the female, "and the modesty which prompted it raises you in the opinion of her you would have preserved from what appeared to be almost certain death. And now I am about to ask a question that may appear a bold one, and yet I cannot restrain my curiosity to know the name of the person to whom I am so much indebted."

"The truth is, madam," answered Lord Dalmeny, "my friend here is so shy that I can but take it upon myself to reply for him:—This is no other than Admiral Ruthven, who has just gained a naval battle against the

Turks, though I believe there is a painted butterfly of a prince who would take the honour from him for the purpose of placing it upon his own shoulders."

"A victory has been gained over the Turks, then?" said the lady, in a tone of joyful satisfaction. "This is indeed good news, and the empress will be much pleased when she hears it, which, I believe, will be to-morrow, for word has been sent that she will visit her country palace in this neighbourhood at the time I have mentioned. So follow me, gentlemen, and I promise you rest and refreshment; and you shall also see her majesty, who, I am sure, will be glad to hear from your lips that a victory over the Turks has at length been obtained."

"But," exclaimed Ruthven, "may I be sure of seeing the empress if I remain here a short time? Nay, think not that I doubt your words, but I am the bearer of important despatches, and it would argue a want of zeal in her service were I to play the laggard when such business demands my every exertion."

"There is no need to doubt my word," replied the lady; "but if it will afford you any satisfaction, this signet ring which I wear upon my finger, will prove that I am in the habit of receiving communications from the Empress Katherine."

Lord Dalmeny advanced to look upon the signet ring, and so charmed was he with the fair and beautiful hand which wore it, that, carried away by his momentary enthusiasm, he seized it in his grasp, and rapturously kissed it. He then stepped back a pace, crossed his hands upon his bosom, and hanging down his head, remained like one that was waiting to hear his sentence pronounced.

"Slave!" exclaimed the lady, passionately, "how dare you presume to be thus bold towards one who has given no encouragement for such presumption? By Heaven! sirrah, you know not the fate you have tempted, for one word of mine would give you to death for even a less offence than you have committed."

"Lady," returned Lord Dalmeny, with an affectation of the deepest humility, "I know I have grievously offended, and yet who could resist such a temptation when offered him?"

"Your excuse, sir, is a bad one," answered the lady, "and does not in the least mitigate the anger it has given rise to. At present I will not say what your punishment shall be, but rest assured I shall not forget the presumption which prompted you to this act of folly and boldness."

"Madam, there is no penance that I will not endure rather than suffer your anger any longer. That I have given deep cause of offence, I am free to admit, but the provocation was great, and I should have been something more than man could I have abstained from pressing so fair a hand to my lips. Why, even the imperial Katherine herself could not refuse me such an honour, and surely, if that is the case, I may be pardoned by you."

"You are pardoned, sir," answered the lady, "but it is on condition that you repeat not the offence, for should you do so, the consequences of your presumption will prove fatal."

"In that case," answered Lord Dalmeny, "I must e'en promise to be on my best behaviour, for much as I may like to kiss a pretty woman, I am not yet so tired of my existence that I can afford to throw it away for so temporary a gratification. You will, therefore, find me all submission to your will, and should I offend in the same way again, I will submit to any punishment you may think proper to inflict."

"My friend is thoughtless," interposed Ruthven, "and perhaps his words, no less than his actions, have given offence to you. I, however, must be his mediator in this instance, and if it pleases you to pardon him, I will take care that he no more enters your presence."

"There is no necessity to take such a precaution as that," answered the lady, "because I have plainly explained to him what will be the consequence of his presumption. I have given him fair warning, and I doubt not he will be wise enough to accept it."

"You may depend upon it I shall not forget the narrow escape I have had," replied Lord Dalmeny, "and now that I know that death is the price of a kiss, I shall take care how I pay so dearly for it. But methinks this Russia is a strange place, for in other countries I could salute the girls without any fuss being made about it."

"You have been warned, sir," he exclaimed, "and I therefore trust you will not lose the advantage of it, for in this country there are punishments for even less offences than that, and I would advise you not to subject yourself to them."

As she uttered these words she urged her horse onwards, and followed by her retinue and the travellers, she quickly made her way homewards.

CHAPTER XXXIX.

" But I have griefs of other kind,
    Troubles and sorrow more severe;
  Give me to ease my tortured mind,
    Lend to my woes a patient ear;
  And let me, if I may not find
    A friend to help—find one to hear."

                                                    CRABBE.

OUR fair huntress did not proceed very far before she diverged a little from the path she had been pursuing, which led towards a mansion which possessed no peculiar features in the exterior except that the royal standard floated above, denoting it to be one of the residences of royalty. Upon entering it, she almost immediately retired with an assurance that she would see the strangers again with as little delay as possible, and inform them when they might see the sovereign, for whom they had brought the despatches. Nor where they suffered to remain long in suspense, for shortly afterwards an officer approached with an intimation that they were to follow him, and having passed through a suite of three or four chambers, they entered the hall of audience, where they beheld the Empress Katherine seated upon her throne, and in whom, to their surprise and consternation, they beheld the huntress with whom they had been on such familiar terms in the forest. She, however, observed their confusion, and with a smile of encouragement, bade them advance, exclaiming :—

"There is no need, gentlemen, to look back upon the past, for though you were somewhat bold, considering in whose presence you were, the fault was my own for not having discovered myself sooner. And now let us to business ;—you bear despatches, I believe, from Prince Berenzoff, announcing an important victory that has been gained over the infidel Turks."

"We do, your majesty," answered Ruthven ;—"the Turks have been defeated both on land and sea, and judging from the complete overthrow the enemy has sustained, I believe it will require but little more exertion to procure a peace honourable to Russia."

The empress glanced eagerly through the despatches, and from the exclamations that occasionally escaped her, it was evident that her admiration was chiefly called forth in favour of Prince Berenzoff, who had in reality done so little towards securing the honour of the victory. Ruthven listened to these words with astonishment, and as the empress concluded, he boldly, yet in respectful words, demanded whether the prince had mentioned no other person as having fairly earned her praise.

"He has not," she replied ; "but your name and former deeds are well known to me, and I can therefore well conceive that you have had a little share in procuring the glory that has brought so much gladness to my heart. Indeed General Kermsdorf has in his despatch spoken of you in the highest terms, and it therefore becomes my pleasing task to confer upon you an honour that is granted only to those who have well and faithfully discharged their duty to my empire. Kneel down, Admiral Ruthven, and receive from my hand the decoration of the highest order of merit."

Ruthven knelt as he had been commanded, and having been invested with the insignia, retired a few paces, whilst the empress addressed a few words to Lord Dalmeny.

"Vizier," she said, smilingly, "the fortune of war has made you my prisoner, but believe me you will not find your chains too heavy for endurance. Say, then, will you remain as a freeman in the court of the Empress of Russia, or return to Constantinople, where in all probability the bowstring is prepared to punish the result of a battle which it was impossible for you to foresee."

"Truly, my royal lady," answered the nobleman, gaily, "the advantages are so much on one side that I cannot hesitate to make this court my future home. I hope, however, your majesty is not resentful, and the little familiarity I was guilty of in the forest will not be remembered, or —"

"Enough has been said," interposed the empress, with an evident wish that no further explanation should take place upon the subject he had alluded to. "I can pardon an act of gallantry," she continued, "and it must be your care never again to mention an occurrence that it would be better to forget. Henceforth you will become a subject of mine, and should you be deserving of my bounty, the time may not be far distant when you will have to congratulate yourself upon having taken the oath of allegiance to the Empress Katherine of Russia. And you, Admiral Ruthven," she said, turning towards the person she addressed, "shall not find that you serve a mistress who is unmindful of your great talents and bravery. But yours I know is a fiery spirit, that will not bear to be placed under the command or control of another, and I shall therefore imediately consult with my council as to the service upon which you shall next be employed. Be assured, moreover, that it shall be an honourable one, and such as will give you an opportunity of displaying the energy and talent for which even your enemies give you credit."

The empress rose as she spoke, and quitted the audience-chamber to take her seat at the council table, where matters of deep import were to be immediately discussed. At this period Ruthven lost sight of Lord Dalmeny, and followed only by his ever-faithful friend, Andrew Forster, he strolled from the royal lodge to meditate upon the circumstances that had taken place since he had accepted service under the Russian government, and to shape out the course by which he might best secure his own future interests. That he would soon become an object of jealousy amongst all those who were looking for preferment for themselves he could not doubt, for he knew that, as a foreigner, every mark of distinction that might be bestowed upon him would be certain to give offence, and aware also of the tyranny exercised in the court, he saw every reason to apprehend that the favour of the empress might be snatched away as suddenly as it had been bestowed, and that consequently he might in a moment fall into disgrace, and thus become a sacrifice to those who regarded his advancement with envy or ill-nature. This was a thought which a man like Ruthven could not endure, and with the same hastiness of resolution which distinguished his almost every action, he determined upon quitting Russia without delay; but whither he went, or to what nation he next offered his services, was a subject which he cared not then to discuss. Andrew Forster heard his sudden resolution with surprise, but he too well knew the ardent disposition of Ruthven to throw any objection in the way, and when he found that their departure was to take place without the loss of even a moment's time, he expressed his readiness to follow, and even praised the resolution which he had just heard expressed.

He, therefore, accompanied Ruthven back to the palace, where an audience was quickly obtained with the empress, in which the reason for their departure was fairly and candidly set forth, but which Katherine for some time attempted to combat. At length, however, when she found that Ruthven was not to be prevailed upon to remain longer in her dominions, she bestowed upon him a magnificent diamond ring, as a token of her esteem, and assured him that should he ever desire to enter the Russian navy, his return would be welcomed with joy, and he might be assured of meeting with a reception equal to his most ambitious hopes.

The next day saw Ruthven and Andrew Forster on board a vessel that was bound for one of the Scottish ports, at no great distance from the Castle of Dalmeny, and consequently near the scenes in which the former had passed the younger and happier portions of his life. As day after day rolled by, and they approached nearer to the land of their birth, the effect upon these two persons was widely different, for whilst one felt a melancholy satisfaction in re-visiting a place connected with so many varying associations, the other thought only of once more seeing old familiar faces, and being greeted by those who, whatever might be their opinions about his fighting under the colours of an enemy, would forget their anger when they saw that by his bravery he had raised himself to the rank of captain. At length, after a favourable voyage, they cast anchor in the port to which they were bound, and Ruthven, accompanied by Andrew Forster, and both of them attired in the Russian uniform, immediately hastened on shore. The latter, however, remained at an inn just beyond the town, and Ruthven, full of the melancholy thoughts which these scenes recalled to his mind, proceeded towards Dalmeny Castle, which rose towering above him at no great distance off.

Twilight was just setting in as he entered the avenue of venerable oaks where he had so often strayed in his youth, and he was slowly making his way towards the castle, when a deep sigh arrested his attention, and looking on one side he beheld Lady Agnes Drummond sitting listlessly at the foot of one of the trees, and evidently occupied in deep and serious thought. She, however, started up at his approach,—recognized him, and would have fled had he not gently taken her hand, and entreated her to give him a few moments' audience. She seemed reluctant to stay, and regarding him with a look of sorrow, exclaimed :—

"Ruthven, your presence here was unlooked for and unwished. As a traitor to your country, I cannot but despise you, though I must fain hope you are not so lost to all shame but that you feel some for the baseness of which you have been guilty. Leave me, sir, and let me caution you to beware that all here about are your enemies, and that should you chance to be seen, the law will not fail to avenge itself upon the man who has drawn his sword against the country of his birth."

"Nay," he said, "do not reproach me thus, Lady Agnes, for I know my faults, and am here to visit dear and well remembered scenes for the last time."

"It would have been well," she replied, "had you never ventured here again; all good men loathe and execrate the crime of which you have been guilty, for you have aided an enemy when you ought rather to have drawn your sword against them, and to you alone must be attributed at least one victory that has been gained by the rebellious Americans over the country from which they sprung and had their being."

"It cannot be denied, Lady Agnes," he answered, "that I have been led away by a violence of temper over which I had no control. But who, let me ask you, has been the cause of it? To you I need scarcely mention his name, for you know the injuries I received from him, and hating all that belonged to my country, I offered my services where I knew they would be gladly accepted. From that moment I have been praised and pampered by those whose notice is best worth having, but I have also been a man of sorrows, and when balls and bullets flew about me, I should have rejoiced had one of them ended a life which has grown wearisome and oppressive."

"You repent, then, having done that which must hand down your name with dishonour to posterity?"

"I repent nothing," answered Ruthven, proudly; "but existence was never very highly prized by me, and perhaps it is less so now than ever it was. Your good opinion, Lady Agnes, was ever valuable, and I would have made any sacrifice to preserve it, but I have forfeited all, and must now be content to pass the remainder of my days as a wretched outcast."

"And upon leaving this place," asked Lady Agnes, "where do you intend to go next?"

"It matters little where I go," he repleld, "for I believe my actions are condemned as much in one country as another. I had, however, some thoughts of going to France, for I hear there is likely to be warm work in that country, and if so I shall find employment that may occupy my mind, and chase away the remembrance of things that I would gladly forget. Perhaps I may then meet my death, and if so, a period to my wretchedness will have arrived."

"Go, then," she exclaimed, "for here you are in danger of meeting an ignominious death; and much as I despise the crime you have been guilty of, I should grieve to know that you came to a shameful death. Leave me, therefore, John Ruthven, and let this, I charge you, be the last interview that ever takes place between us."

She turned away as she spoke, and hurried from the spot ere he could prevent her flight. For a moment only he paused to consider in which direction he should next bend his footsteps, and then perceiving the green hill beneath which stood the humble cottage of his mother, he moved forward in that direction, scarcely conscious of the thick heavy gloom which night had brought with it. At length, however, a grey shadowy form seemed to rise before him, which to his fancy assumed the shape of a human being, and instantly drawing his sword, he advanced to attack what he believed to be an enemy. But the figure still remained at the same distance from him till he reached a spot on which were the remains of an ancient stone cross, when it instantly disappeared in a manner that was utterly unaccountable. Ruthven, however, continued on his way, marvelling upon the strange adventure he had met with, and at length stood upon the threshold of his mother's cottage. In another moment his well-remembered voice drew her towards him, and no sooner did she see that it was indeed her son that stood before her, than she uttered an exclamation of joyful surprise, and sank fainting in his arms. She, however, soon revived, and then, collecting her scattered thoughts, welcomed him with a fondness that he had never expected to experience again.

It would be useless to detail the conversation that ensued, for the nature of it may be well imagined; but when Ruthven spoke of the mysterious form that had just appeared before him, a marked alteration took place in her manner, and as he described the figure more accurately, she with a shudder declared that it was the apparition of the late Lord of Dalmeny, his father, and instantly sank upon the ground, overcome by the intensity of the feelings which had been thus conjured up.

CHAPTER XL.

Flower of warriors,
How is it with Titus Lartius?
Marcius. As with a man busied about decrees,
Condemning some to death and some to exile,
Ransoming him or pitying, threatening the other.
CORIOLANUS.

AT the sound of rapidly approaching footsteps, Ruthven cast a fond but last look upon his unconscious parent, and hurrying out by another door, soon found himself wandering in the village churchyard, where there were many tombstones, which he quickly recognized as those he had gazed upon before, and which he knew had been placed there in memory of persons he well remembered to have seen in his younger and happier days. But there was one among them that seemed to have been erected more recently than any of the others, and as the moon just then shone out brightly, he stepped towards the spot, and perceived that it had been erected to the memory of May Grayson, whose sad history was there detailed in a few brief lines, which had been sculptured as a warning to others of her sex to avoid the artful blandishments of men, as the only means of leaving behind a name which no calumny could blacken. Ruthven could not forbear a sigh to the memory of one whose career he could trace from the period when they were children together, and at length quitting the dreary receptacle of the dead, he returned to the place where he had left Andrew Forster, and without waiting to rest or refresh himself, he instantly set forth with his attached follower, resolving to quit his native land with as little delay as possible, and by seeking naval service in some other country, to court that death which could alone release him from a load of bitter care and anguish that had of late grown intolerable.

It was in vain that Andrew endeavoured to prevail on him to remain a few days longer, in order that he might fully decide upon what course he was going to pursue, for he had resolved upon quitting Scotland without delay, and as the revolution had already broken out in France, it was his intention to offer his services and advice to the unhappy king, who already began to feel the tyranny of the people, who had risen in arms to destroy not only that which was bad, but that also which was really excellent in itself. Thus determined, Ruthven and his companion soon found a vessel to convey them to the land of discord, which they had no sooner reached than they saw reason to wish that they had chosen any other direction than that which led them to France.

In the town where they landed discord reigned triumphant, and the blood of thousands had already been shed as a sacrifice to the demon of anarchy. Ruthven, used as he was to scenes of violence and death, could not forbear shuddering as he looked round upon the traces of destruction which blind fury had left on every hand. Churches and noble edifices had been levelled with the ground, whilst blackened masses of ruin showed where fire had been brought to aid the horrors which had been conjured up by the mad wretches who had allowed themselves to become the victims of their own unbridled passions. Ruthven gazed upon the scene before him with a sickening sensation of horror, and thoughtless of the consequences, he gave utterance to the feelings which naturally took possession of his soul.　But this indiscretion had nearly cost him his life, for he happened to be over-heard by a number of the ruffians who were passing at the time, and in an instant they would have sacrificed him to their fury, had it not been for the interposition of Andrew Forster, who, throwing himself before the mob, declared that the person they were about to slay was no other than John Ruthven.　This had the momentary effect of saving his life, but immediately afterwards one of the ruffians advancing himself before the rest, said in an authoritative tone,—

"You may be John Ruthven or anybody else for aught I care, but we are the sovereign people, and you must either declare yourself to be friendly to our cause, or perish as an enemy, as thousands of others have done before you."

"I am a friend of liberty," answered Ruthven; "but certainly not to the anarchy I behold in this distracted country.　As a people you may have been oppressed, but surely those who fight with liberty upon their lips, should not be the first to set an example of despotism such as I have this day beheld."

"He is an enemy, and must die the death of a traitor!" exclaimed three or four voices, and at the moment a rush would have been made upon him had he not been prepared with his pistols in his hand, and threatened to shoot the first man that approached to offer him violence.

"I am myself a lover of violence, as you know," he exclaimed; "but if kings are to be prevented from acting as tyrants, I see no reason why the sovereign people, as ye call yourselves, should not be restrained in a similar manner.　In America, where I have fought and bled for the good cause, we have ever battled with our foes fairly and honourably; cruelty has never marked our path to victory, for we knew that the eyes of the world were directed towards us, and had we ever disgraced ourselves as you have done during this brief reign of anarchy and confusion, we should have been looked upon with abhorrence, instead of being regarded, as we now are, in the light of honourable men, who had no other motive for drawing the sword of warfare than to redress the wrongs we had endured, and to raise ourselves to a rank with the other nations of the world."

"You speak somewhat boldly, sirrah," exclaimed the leader of the mob; "but we may not think any the worse of you for that, on condition that you and your companion join our ranks to procure the downfall of royalty."

"I'm obliged to you all the same," answered Andrew; "but for my own part I have very particular reasons for declining the honour you have pro-posed.　In truth, sirs, France seems to be no place for us, and so, with your kind permission, we'll make our way out of it as fast as we can."

"Are you both cowards?" demanded another of the ruffians.

"My previous actions," answered Ruthven, "will best tell you whether I am a coward or not; but if valour consists in butchering the helpless, then will I be content that you set me down for the veriest cur that ever lived."

"He is a slave, and deserves death," exclaimed a voice almost at his ear, and at the instant a fellow rushed towards Ruthven with a knife in his hand, which he would have buried in the heart of his intended victim, had not Andrew struck up the weapon with his sword, and sent it flying over the heads of the multitude.　This act only served to exasperate the more violent portion of the multitude, and the two friends would doubtless have been torn to pieces had it not been for one of the assailants, who seemed to possess a little more humanity than the rest.

"Nay, brothers," he exclaimed, addressing himself to his companions,

IN
MEMORY
OF
MAY GRAYSON

"these men are strangers in our land, and we can therefore owe them no grudge. They have not, like ourselves, felt the grinding oppressions of the government we have overturned, and as they have entered our country in confidence, let them now depart from it in peace."

Then, whispering to Ruthven, he added,—

"You are among men who are drunk with the blood they have already sacrificed, and another word of reproach to them will surely cost your lives. Be silent, then, and I will find means to get you safely out of this country."

"Come, come," exclaimed a rough voice, "we must have no whispering, Pierre, between you and these strangers. It seems to me that they take part against us, and if I was only certain of it I would have their heart's blood before they are a minute older."

"The best way is to let them go about their business quietly," answered Pierre. "They don't want to stop here, I'll be bound, now that they have found out what's going forward; and even if they meant us any mischief, there's only two of them, and what's that against the millions that France can bring on the other side? So now," he continued, addressing himself to Ruthven, "just satisfy these people that you and your companion mean to leave France without delay."

"And why should I submit to satisfy them at all upon the point?" demanded Ruthven. "I have ere now been received in this country with honour and distinction by your king, and I will not now submit to have my actions questioned by the blood-thirsty villains who have converted their country into shambles for human sacrifices."

"Down with him!" vociferated a dozen voices; "kill him, and shew the enemies of the people that we have power to punish those that dare oppose our sovereign will."

"Aye," replied Ruthven, bitterly, "the truth is ever unpalatable to those

No. 32

who, like yourselves, are engaged in acts disgraceful and unjust. I see my words offend you, but I have spoken with as much honesty of purpose to greater men than yourselves, and have yet contrived to escape the consequences which my rashness may have tempted. And now, demons of discord, look upon us once more: we are two men opposed to at least two hundred, yet we shrink not from speaking the truth plainly, even though death may be the penalty."

"This insolence can no longer be borne," exclaimed a ruffian, whose blood-stained garb betrayed how active a part he had performed in the butchery that had just taken place. "We have already put up with too much from these enemies of freedom, and since no other hand can be found to do the deed, I will myself punish the man that dares remonstrate against the acts we have committed for the liberation of France."

Whilst speaking he flourished a naked dagger above his head, and as he concluded his brief address he struck the weapon into the breast of Ruthven with such rapidity that Andrew Forster's attempt to avert the blow was made in vain. The unhappy man sank to the ground with the force of the blow, and a dozen more weapons were raised to complete the deed which the other had done; but Pierre, throwing himself between the people and the object of their fury, exclaimed,—

"Those who strike another blow at his heart must first reach it through mine! You have already wounded him mortally, and therefore, I pray you, my friends, let vengeance be satisfied, without proving that you are beneath your fellow men in humanity."

"We want no lectures, Pierre," muttered the assassin, "and perhaps if you say another word I may serve you as I have him."

"Let there be no bloodshed on my account," said Ruthven, in a low and subdued tone. "I have met my death blow, and though each of you may triumph in my fall, there is not one among you to whom my death gives more joy than it does to myself."

"Nay, speak not so," exclaimed Andrew, leaning sorrowfully over the body of his friend. "The wound may not be mortal, and if you do but recover from this, we'll leave the cursed country we are in, and go to some place where men are not quite so handy with their daggers against the lives of other people."

"All hope of surviving this wound is in vain, Andrew," answered Ruthven, with increasing feebleness. "And in truth I am not sorry that death approaches, even though it has been produced by the hand of an assassin, for I had begun to grow weary of existence, since the world no longer regards me with kindliness, and even my best friends do not forget to remind me of the one act which has forfeited their esteem. They call me a traitor to my country, and, to confess the truth, I believe, if my time were to come over again, I should perish rather than draw my sword against the land of my nativity. But it is too late to think of these things now, Andrew, for my moments are fast drawing to a close, and when death has snatched me from this world it will matter little what my enemies may please to say of me. But of this I feel assured, my friend: the time will yet arrive when men's passions will cool into sober reflection, and when that is the case they will learn to forget the worst passages of my life, and to remember only those which have raised me from the condition of an humble cottager to become the friend and confidant of princes."

"And if it had not been for yonder ruffian's dagger," cried Andrew, "you would yet have reaped the glory you have been at so much pains to earn."

"Hush! my friend," exclaimed Ruthven, "and do not by your own rashness tempt them to consign you to the same fate that they have dealt out to me. You may yet live to enjoy many years of happiness, and by the friendship that has subsisted between us for the last few years, I conjure you to say nothing that may irritate these fierce men against you. You will perhaps remain in France long enough to see me laid in the narrow grave, where peace awaits me, after the turmoil I have endured through life, and when that is done I would recommend you to return to America, where, for my sake, I trust they will reward you according to the service you have done that country. Honour there lies before you; and my last wish is that you may sometimes think of your friend, John Ruthven, with kindness, and that you will endeavour to rescue his name from the disgrace which at present clings to it."

"Let us hope matters are not quite so bad with you, my friend, as you seem to think," interposed Pierre, who seemed to be really concerned at the fate which had befallen the Englishman. "I have seen many a man fall with as bad a wound as yours, and yet live to serve his country afterwards."

"I have no reason to wish for life," answered Ruthven, faintly. "All whom I have ever loved on earth have perished before me, and all that I now wish for is to find peace and quiet in that grave to which the rancour of my foes cannot hunt me."

"But you forget that there is yet honour to be gained in the field," exclaimed the faithful Andrew. "America still offers you a home; and, though peace has now been proclaimed between her and the mother country, there will be war in other quarters to find employment for your sword."

"And who shall stay the hand of death when it is once laid upon you?" asked Ruthven. "Have I not fallen beneath the weapon of an assassin? and feeling, as I do, the life blood ebbing from me, shall I now look forward to length of days, and that honour which you would fain present before me?"

"And yet," said Andrew, "could you but have returned once more to America, there is one who would have hailed your presence with joy, and by her kindness made some amends for the ingratitude you have elsewhere met with."

"You speak of my sister Effie?"

"I do."

"It would indeed have been some consolation to see her again," replied Ruthven, "for her gentle nature might have softened reflections which have long pressed heavily upon me, and thus have rendered me more fitted to join with the world, which I have for some time learned to regard with loathing and abhorrence. But it is in vain to think of that now, for the shaft of death has been hurled at me with an unerring aim, and no earthly power can save from a fate that I do not deplore."

"Will you suffer your friend and me to bear you to my house?" asked Pierre. "My wife will attend to you with all the kindness and care of a mother; and who knows but we may yet be able to restore you, in spite of your own opinions to the contrary."

"My own feelings assure me that all your kindness would but be thrown away," replied Ruthven. "Each moment I grow weaker, and ere another hour has passed away, I shall no longer be an inhabitant of this world."

"Nay, man, never give way to despair," exclaimed Pierre, "for you may take my word for it that it's nothing but loss of blood that makes you feel low and despirited."

"Aye, sir," interposed Andrew, "accept the offer that has been made, and let us take you to the house of this worthy citizen, where you will receive the care and assistance you so much require. He says it's not far off, and if you are too weak to bear removal by our hands, we'll soon find a conveyance that shall carry you there without much trouble."

"Hear me, Andrew," exclaimed Ruthven, "and do not any longer press me upon a subject upon which I have already told you my determination. For the well meant kindness of yourself and this stranger, I am most grateful, but upon this spot I have received my death wounds from the hands of my cowardly assailants, and here will I yield up my last sigh. Perhaps I might have wished for an end more honourable, since my days have been passed in war and bloodshed, but my destiny was not to be averted, and I am content to be released of the weary burden of life upon any terms. I have ever been a wayward child of fate, and having fought against my country, it is fitting that I should perish in a foreign land."

"Have you any directions that you wish to leave?" asked Andrew, who saw that the end of Ruthven was fast approaching. "If you have anything to charge me with, I will obey your last injunction, even though I should have to wander over the whole world to fulfil my errand."

"I have nothing to say beyond what you have already heard," replied the other, "unless, indeed, chance should ever throw you in the way of my sister, and in that case I would charge you to assure her that my end caused me no regret, and that her name was the last in my thoughts, and that I died pronouncing it."

The rapidly encreasing weakness of Ruthven now became apparent, and from that time he spoke not another word. Pierre, however, procured a litter to convey the wounded man to his own house, but on reaching the place it was discovered that the once bold and dauntless John Ruthven had ceased to exist. The grief of Andrew at the loss of his friend was excessive, but as the disturbed state of the country at that period rendered his stay in France extremely hazardous, he was compelled to commit the body to the earth on the following day, and having thus performed the last sad offices of friendship, he embarked on board an American vessel that was on the point of sailing, and within a month from that time he was once more an inhabitant of the new world.

His history from this period contains little that would interest the reader, but it may be satisfactory to know that his gallantry was justly appreciated by those he served, and having spent a long life of honour and renown, he closed his days in peace, though not before he had heard the conduct of John Ruthven lauded by the very men who had at one time ranked themselves amongst the bitterest of his denouncers.

THE END.

www.ingramcontent.com/pod-product-compliance
Lightning Source LLC
Chambersburg PA
CBHW080720290626
47170CB00017B/2801